THRILL GIRL

a novel by Jack Curran

THRILL GIRL

Digital Edition, published by *La Verita* Publishing 2018

Copyright June, 2018 by Jack Curran

ISBN: **978-1-7321997-2-9**

Acknowledgements

Cover design by Milan Jovanovic and 99Designs

Copy editing by Angela Polidoro

Formatting by Merry Banerji of Anessa Books

Thank you each for your creative and professional support.

For Dick Gamble, one of the good guys.

CHAPTER ONE

June 1951

Los Angeles

Susan Baldwin stared down at her legs. Tiny red dots speckled her white pumps and nylon stockings and wrapped around her left ankle like a macabre tattoo.

To her left two men lay on the sidewalk, blood flowing from their bodies in twin trails, pooling into a puddle that was bright in the center, darker at the edges. Despite the warm night air, she trembled and pressed her wounded hand to her chest. She fought to reconstruct what had just happened. But she could not remember, could not think clearly. All she knew was that she needed to get home and help…

Help who?

A siren blasted at the end of the street, and for the second time that night she saw men with weapons drawn rushing toward her. She turned to run but tripped and fell, banging her knees violently against the asphalt. With a groan she rolled onto her side, pulling at her dress to try and cover herself, to hide the blood, to hide herself.

Two policemen loomed above her.

"Don't move," the first cop ordered.

"What happened? What's your name?" the other shouted.

I don't know, Susan thought. And then she passed out.

# # #

The ringing telephone woke Jack Curran from an unplanned nap. He grabbed at the receiver, knocking the base of it off his desk and onto the scarred floor of the newsroom. Was Goldblum finally calling back, he wondered?

"*Eyes of LA*. Jack Curran." He set the phone on his desk and reached for his cigarettes.

"Jesus, don't you ever go home?"

"Hey, what's up, Georgie?" Georgie Miller was a night duty dispatcher at the 07, Wilshire precinct. He only called when he had a hot tip. "You got something good for me?"

"I do indeed. Word over the squawk is your girl's made another appearance."

"Again?" Jack slicked back his hair with his free hand and glanced at his wristwatch. It was 9:44 p.m. She was early tonight, he thought.

"Yep. And true to form, she took a powder and was nowhere to be found when the patrols rolled up. But she left her handiwork bleeding out, all over Dewitt Street."

"How many dead?" The reporter dropped the match on the floor and stepped on it.

"Two. Bumped off one with a bang-bang, one with a blade. This dame is a dangerous bit of skirt, Jack. You better be careful chasing her. She might catch you."

"Nothing I'd like better. Who did she save tonight?"

The first person she rescued was a Korean grocer. The second, an old lady bum, was still recovering in the county hospital. On her third appearance a week ago, she came to the aid of teenage brothers.

"A shop girl walking home from work," Georgie replied. "Patrols said she was roughed up, but she's okay."

Jack slipped his cigarettes into his coat pocket and stood up. He glanced again at his watch, estimating that the crime scene was five minutes away. "What time did this go down?"

"Male called it in at 9:12 p.m."

"Anonymous? Same as the others?"

"Yep. People don't give their name when dead bodies are involved."

"Who caught the call, Georgie?"

"The lieutenant sent Glass and Martin. Since the victim told the patrols the dead guys were wasted by a gorgeous dame, it's Thrill Girl's M.O. Those two are stuck with her until it wraps."

"Great info, Georgie. Okay, I'm out of here. I'll see you at the Pantry tomorrow to thank you in person." The dispatcher had breakfast every morning at the LA joint known for never closing its doors.

"Swell, as long as your thanks have Andrew Jackson's picture on it. And remember, you never talked to me about this."

"Roger that." Jack hung up and grabbed his fedora, but turned and stared at the phone for a moment. He should call Quentin Deville, *The Eyes* publisher, and tell him Thrill Girl had struck again. He looked again at his watch.

A team of reporters from the LA Times was also filing stories on the vigilante murderess mesmerizing the City of Angels, three to every one of his. It would only be minutes before they got a tip. Probably from Georgie.

Jack headed for the door. The story was gold for circulation, and Deville would understand he had to get to the crime scene ahead of the competition. As his source said, Thrill Girl was his girl.

The sooner he found her and introduced himself, the better.

#

The man in the rear seat of the Cadillac settled back against the plush leather. He undid the buttons of the glove covering his left hand and slipped the uniquely tailored garment off. He inhaled sharply at the slam of pain, patient as it cooled and receded.

He peered out into the night. Dewitt Court, up one block from Wilshire, was barricaded by police vehicles. A uniformed cop kept the growing crowd of civilians on the other side of the street, away from the warehouse that had served as a backdrop for the murders.

The man glanced up at the roofline where an hour earlier he had crouched near the rusting fire escape and watched the unexpected scene unfold. His mind replayed the events like a newsreel. Shocking, violent, and confusing.

He was going to have to stay closer to his targets. While the gun and knife had been removed from the street, along with all traces of the killer, anything could happen now. Because tonight, unlike the previous three nights of mayhem he had observed play out, he was not the only hidden witness to murder.

An older man with greasy hair, a vagrant, had watched from the opposite side of the street, concealed in bushes at the edge of the building.

Where is he now? Is he with that group of homeless at the corner?

The man in the Cadillac had exceptional vision in the dark, but he did not spot the derelict anywhere in the milling crowd.

Without a sound, he lowered the window a few inches and sniffed the summer air. It smelled of eucalyptus and car exhaust. And something else.

Fresh blood.

He frowned. With his right hand, he reached into his jacket and withdrew the flashlight he had picked up off the sidewalk after the murders, left behind by mistake. He contemplated it, raising and lowering it to compute the weight of the German Army artifact.

It was a model ERT 2700.

He clicked it on. Then off.

The light was very bright. He returned the item to his pocket and hit the button to lower the partition separating him from the front seat.

"Yes, sir?" Janus, his driver, asked.

"In twenty minutes, drive to Griffith Park. The police will be done interviewing the woman by then. Park the same place as before."

"Yes, sir."

The man hit the button, and the glass hissed upward.

In the quiet, he massaged his left fist. He was hungry, but

there was no food in the car, and no time to stop. He reached into the satchel at his feet and took out a small bag. It contained linen cloths, moistened with soap and water. He methodically cleaned his face and hands and deposited the soiled cloth back into his satchel.

Running his tongue over his lips, he touched his right index finger to his mouth and stroked his eyebrows to slick them down. Every hair in place. The voice of the doctor who had raised him echoed inside his head.

A gentleman keeps up his standards, no matter the situation.

The man closed his eyes. Rage suddenly took control of his emotions, filling his mouth with a bitter taste. It was becoming more difficult to be patient, to wait for the justice he had sought for most of his remembered life.

He balled his hands into fists and pain exploded up his left arm, radiating through his shoulder and neck. After a moment he swallowed. Once again, he ran his right index finger over each eyebrow.

A breeze flowed gently over his face, the air smelling less of death and more of summer. The muscles sheathing his spine twitched as he settled once again into the seat. As a trilling vibration crawled up his throat, his eyelids closed to slits and, in a moment he was asleep.

# # #

Jack kept his head down and eased between the two LAPD vehicles parked at the curb. He didn't want the cops to stop him before he got a look at the crime scene.

It was ten-thirty, but the illumination of the moon and streetlights was bright enough to see the pool of blood congealing next to the two corpses. The woman who had been attacked was standing near a patrol car. Her dress was ripped and her hair disheveled. Standing next to her was Detective Jimmy Glass.

Glass was one of homicide's sharpest and most tight-lipped detectives. His partner, Stu Martin, was a Neanderthal. As a citizen, Jack was glad Glass was on the case. As a reporter, not as much.

He pulled his hat lower over his forehead and walked around

the sawhorses the cops had set-up. Lucas O'Connor, a bucket-faced uniform from Wilshire division, seemed to be in charge of the crowd control. Jack had poured cheap scotch into him more than once to get information.

Maybe his investment would pay off tonight.

"Stay the fuck back, Curran!" O'Connor ordered. "No press, not even war heroes."

Jack frowned. He had been dealing with this war hero crap for a month, ever since The LA Times included a profile on him in a series on local veterans, and what they were doing six long years after VE Day.

The public had eaten the story up, but not the cops, the majority of who had been categorized as essential public servants during the war and never got the chance to fight. Jack understood why they would take umbrage when he was called a hero, while their daily brushes with death went unnoticed.

But their attitude was still a pain in the ass.

"Like everyone else in the army, I only did my job." Jack squinted at the scene across the street. "What's going on?"

"None of your beeswax." O'Connor tapped his nightstick against his thigh. "Take off."

"I'm free, white, and more than twenty-one, Officer. I'm sure that gives me the right to stand and watch LA's finest in action."

"As long as you watch from behind the line."

Jack took an uneven step closer. His left leg was held together with three steel pins and was a half inch shorter than it had been before the war. He hated the limp for a lot of reasons, but mostly because it made him stand out in a crowd.

"What are you hearing, O'Connor? Those two dead bastards, they local men? Gang bangers?" The reporter pointed at the bodies, which were being moved onto gurneys.

"Why ask me? I'm not one of your snitches."

Jack offered a piece of gum to the cop, who curled his lip in rejection. Jack put it in his own mouth. "*The Eyes* doesn't pay cops. Someone's pulling your leg if they told you that."

"Yeah, right." O'Connor laughed. "Like your ma pulls your daddy's fat dick."

Jack thought of his mother, who had been dead for almost ten years, and his Dad, who was gone for twenty. He wondered if O'Connor shot off his gun as blindly as he did his mouth.

Across the street, Jimmy Glass was leading the victim to a patrol car. Jack squinted. She was a pretty brunette, dressed for work. Probably from one of the stores on Wilshire. Her right hand was bandaged.

She's young. And shell-shocked.

His gut twisted. He had seen plenty of women with that look of vulnerability and despair, but that was during a war that had torn Europe apart at the seams. This is Hollywood in peacetime, for Christ's sake.

"The Vic is only a kid. Pretty," Jack said as Glass closed her into the police cruiser.

O'Connor grunted.

"All of twenty maybe, and she gets attacked on a central street at this time of night? What the hell's happening to our city?"

O'Connor spat, landing his wad a foot away from where Jack stood.

"You ask me, we need more cops if a girl like that can't walk down a street in Los Angeles after dinner," Jack continued. "Or maybe we need better ones?"

"Fuck you, Curran."

The reporter grinned. O'Connor was about to say something he should not, which Jack could quote in the column he was writing in his head. "I hear the Mayor's been told this is connected to the other unsolved murders. You hear that?"

"I ain't heard nothing." The cop spat again; the white glob hit the toe of Jack's wing tip.

Jack did not move. The patrol car was starting to roll. "Come on. Did they get clocked by Thrill Girl? Maybe we ought to put the dame on regular patrol when you catch her. She could pinch the rats and clean up LA once and for all."

O'Connor lurched toward him, exactly as Jack had hoped, giving the reporter a clear view of the number painted on the rear of the patrol car as it turned onto Wilshire Blvd.

Number 1-2-4.

O'Connor breathed into his face from six inches away. Jack smiled and flipped his gum wrapper into the gutter. "Pick that up for me, will you Lucas?"

He turned away from the cops' fresh stream of cussing, wincing as he stepped off the curb. He glanced at his watch. Ten-fifty. In an hour he had a date to meet the waitress he had been seeing at the Coconut Grove, the swank nightclub at the Ambassador Hotel, a couple of blocks up Wilshire.

But first, he had to make a few calls.

Jack hustled to the telephone booth across the boulevard, jingling the change in his pocket to find a nickel. He would have time to buy Carol a beer after her shift, but instead of going home to her ratty rental now he would have to go back to the office and write up his notes.

He would swing back here later when the cops were gone, and the crime scene less crowded. He looked up and down the length of Dewitt. It was a good choice for a mugging, dark and deserted, narrow and hard to see from Wilshire. A group of uniforms was talking to some bums at the opposite corner.

Jack glanced in the other direction. A black Cadillac with curtained windows was parked at the curb a block down. As he watched, it pulled out and rolled away, the headlamps off. It was too far away to read the plates. Jack knew from experience that everybody wanted a look at murder.

Even rich guys.

He filed the image of the caddy away and crossed the street. If he could confirm Thrill Girl had bumped off these mooks, *The Eyes* would put out a Special Edition on Saturday. Deville had already green-lighted the extra expense for the print shop if she struck again.

He stepped into the phone booth. His first call was to Deville, but he was at a dinner party, according to the maid. She said she would let his boss know he had rung.

Jack dropped in the second nickel and waited for the service to pick up. "Hey, Minnie, Jack Curran. I got any calls?"

The operator was her usual friendly self. "Hi, Mr. Curran. Yes, you have three messages."

Two were citizens with leads on the identity of Thrill Girl. He had a slew of those already. Most of them looking to get an enemy in trouble.

The third message was from Sydney Goldblum.

"Mr. Goldblum said you were to call him at home tomorrow morning, early." She giggled. "Is that the Sydney Goldblum, Hollywood producer?"

Like half the young girls in LA, Minnie was an actress wannabe.

"It is. And if I hook up with him, I'll be sure and let you know, doll. What's the number?"

Jack wrote it in his notebook and thanked Minnie. He stood quietly for a moment, getting his thoughts in order. He had waited a long time for this conversation. He pulled out his cigarettes and got rid of the gum, a smile playing at the corners of his mouth.

CHAPTER TWO

At 8 a.m. the next morning, Quentin Deville sat across from Jack's desk in the editorial offices of *The Eyes of LA*. "You need a quote. A direct, attributed quote confirming it was a woman who killed the two men attacking Susan Baldwin."

"It's the same M.O. All the way."

The publisher removed the ivory cigarette holder from his mouth and glanced at his wristwatch. "The cops have not confirmed it, and we can't link the attack on Susan Baldwin to the other three Thrill Girl cases without it."

"The link is obvious."

"To whom?"

"To us and to all my sources on the police force. The dispatcher at Wilshire said he heard several guys talking about it being Thrill Girl. The cops have no doubt, which means there are elements connecting it to the other three crimes. Links we haven't heard about yet."

"Did your police snitch give you the names of those 'guys'? You know you have to quote a witness with firsthand knowledge, even if we keep it as an anonymous source. Why don't you call Detective Glass and ask him to go on record?"

"I called Glass before he went off shift this morning and he told me to pound sand. The LAPD doesn't want the public to know these crimes are linked. They think people will panic."

"They will." Quentin took a drag. "Mayor Bowron is squeezing the chief every morning for an arrest. This woman is making the police department look foolish, and the mayor by proxy. You need to convince Glass to talk to you."

"They'll come around. Eventually." Jack lit another cigarette before he noticed the one shouldering in the ashtray. He had only slept three hours before coming in to report the details of last night's double murder. He stubbed out the fresh cigarette and set it on the edge of his desk.

"What's your plan?" Quentin arched his brows. "No quote, no Special Edition."

"Thrill Girl is four for four. We can say, 'Police sources say the vigilante was the same woman involved in the previous cases.' That's true. *The Times* implied as much in this morning's edition."

"Implied? We don't have the money, the legal team, or the clout of the Los Angeles Times and the Chandler family. I might publish sensational tabloid trash, but it is factual sensational tabloid trash. When in the five years you've worked for me have I published anything other than soundly sourced reports in a breaking news story?"

"Never. Okay, I'll get a quote." Jack looked around the quiet newsroom. Neither his rookie reporter, Eddie Wentz, nor the other feature writer, Lucy Cherry, had come in yet.

"From who?"

"A witness." Jack put out his cigarette and re-lit the one in waiting. He tossed the match into his empty paper cup, which promptly rolled off his desk onto the floor.

The Eyes of LA operated out of a two-story building fronting Western Avenue. It was narrow, two rooms up, two rooms down, and the print shop was in a building across the parking lot. The walls were institutional green and had not seen a paintbrush since Hoover was president.

"We need to get this place painted." Jack tossed his coffee cup into the trash can.

"Why?" Quentin glanced around at the worn desks and naked bulbs. "I like it. It looks like the set of His Girl Friday. You know I love anything to do with Cary Grant."

"It would help morale."

"Whose?"

"Mine." Jack stretched his stiff leg out and rested it on the trash can.

"Is your leg hurting you?"

"No."

"Why is your morale bad?"

"We've got a huge story on our hands, but we don't have enough help to track down all the leads."

"You need to utilize Eddie more."

"He's got talent, but he's an inexperienced kid, Quentin. Maybe you need to hire more seasoned help." Most of the writing staff they used for the stories that didn't make the front page were stringers, freelancers paid by the word.

"Is this your way of telling me you're quitting?"

"For Christ's sake. No." Jack thought about his call with Sydney Goldblum. He was going to make it as soon as he found a phone booth outside the office.

"Good." Quentin brushed ashes off his sleeve. "Who are you getting a confirming quote from?"

The men's glances met.

"I'll go see the victim," Jack said. "Susan Baldwin can confirm the blonde was on the scene, plus give us new facts to juice the story."

"Juice the story?"

"You know, describe Thrill Girl. The color of her eyes. What she smelled like." Jack grinned. "LA has fallen hard for this dame. But we need to keep them interested."

"The cops surely told Miss Baldwin not to talk to newspaper hounds like you. You know they've kept a tight rein on all the witnesses." Deville got up. "You're charming, Jack. But not so charming a woman would risk a contempt rap."

"I need to try. The worst thing about the coverage is that no one has been able to get face to face with the citizens Thrill Girl has saved. The fact that I got to talk to Mr. Kim the morning after he was mugged was a fluke."

Georgie Miller, bless his soul, had given him the Oriental's home address. Jack had arrived at the old man's door no more than five minutes after the cops had dropped him off. Mr. Kim had told Jack everything about the attack, including the fact that the blonde had said, "I was thrilled to help you…"

Jack gave her the nickname 'Thrill Girl' in his first story, and it stuck. The cops were pissed about that more than the fact he had talked to a witness, although they pressured the old Korean to go to San Francisco to stay with a sister.

"What about the other victims? Maybe you should try them again before you charge over to see Miss Baldwin." Quentin slowly paced in front of Jack's desk.

"Joan Becklund is under guard in the hospital. I can't find out where the Taylor kids are holed up, and they're minors anyway. I say we move fast and get the facts straight from the latest source."

His publisher raised his thin eyebrows. "The cops threatened to put you in jail if you went near Mr. Kim again. What do you think they're going to say if you show up at Susan Baldwin's?"

"They aren't going to say anything because I won't tell her I'm a journalist."

"I'm not sure I approve of that."

"I'll tell her the truth before we run the piece. Concealing my profession at first is a forgivable white lie if we get an interview. Get the truth out there."

"Ah, yes, the truth." Quentin continued to pace. "You need to have her on the record to be quoted."

"I know that. Once I break the ice, I'll appeal to her civic instincts to keep the public informed. I'm also going to stop by and talk to the coroner. See what she'll give up about the cause of death." Jack had seen Millie Hatchett, aptly named for her job, at the crime scene last night.

Efficient and formidable in her bottle-thick glasses, Millie had earned her male colleagues' respect as the first female to hold the position. And it didn't hurt that the doc was built like a Hollywood sex bomb.

"I like Millie." Quentin sniffed. "Although she is rather aggressively female."

"She's stacked, but she's fair." Jack wondered, not for the first time if Quentin appreciated women in the same way he did. "I'm also going over to the hospital later to check on Joan Becklund's release. The cops can't keep her away from the press forever."

"You have an ambitious day planned."

Quentin's expression tempered Jack's enthusiasm. He leaned back in his chair. "Do you doubt that I can, or should, get to the witnesses?"

"No. But I'm not sure either of us is prepared for what this case may turn into." Quentin stopped and folded his arms across his chest. "I have a feeling about the way this story is developing. The first mugging incident seemed spontaneous, but now that it's happened a fourth time…"

"I'm not following you, boss." Jack squinted. "You smell something fishy?"

"Maybe I'm too cautious as I get older." Quentin sniffed. "Cautious is a bad thing when you're chasing a hot story."

"Which is exactly why I need to get going." Jack stood and grabbed his hat off the desk.

"Remember, we have to finalize the special by eight Friday to get it out Saturday morning."

"I'll be in with a quote this afternoon. Keep the print shop on standby."

"Don't we always? I'm thinking of changing our masthead motto from Truth without Fear to No deadline goes unmissed."

"That's colorful, boss. Maybe you should retire and be a comedian. You could do nightclubs."

Quentin stared at Jack's hat as if he wanted to comment on its disreputable state. "I may need to. When we have to close this place down because we didn't get a sourced quote about your blonde."

"I'll get a goddamn source."

"Famous last words," Quentin said.

Jack scowled and hurried out of the office, knowing Quentin's eyes followed him. His boss stared openly at everyone. As though he could read a person's mind if he concentrated hard enough.

Quentin struck a lot of people as a dilettante. As far as Jack could tell, the publisher's convictions weren't those of a spoiled rich guy, even if his family was rolling in it. They ran bone deep.

Out in the parking lot, he climbed into his car, a 1951 Packard 250, cream with a soft white top. Though he had owned it for months, Jack grinned every time he saw it. It was the first new car he had ever owned. He breathed in its smell and rolled down the windows, then pulled out onto Western Avenue.

Two gals on the sidewalk smiled as he drove past, and he tipped his hat. The Packard was a hit with women. Carol Johnson had squealed like a kid at Christmas the first time she had seen it. Jack glanced at the time. If he pushed, he should be able to stop at the Ambassador for lunch. Carol might give him a free meal, or offer him a quickie in an unoccupied room upstairs.

He pulled out his cigarettes and pushed in the car lighter. But first, he had a phone call to make.

# # #

Alana Maxwell tapped her fingernail against the desk as she waited, the telephone receiver pressed to her ear. It was 9:00 a.m.

I need a manicure. She stared at the two broken nails on her free hand and flexed her left pinky. It was tender, and the knuckle was lightly bruised, though it did not look swollen.

"Miss? Sorry I took so long." Through the phone line, the flower store clerk sounded flustered. "Your order is out for delivery now. Two dozen long-stemmed white roses. I tied the red satin ribbon around them personally."

"And you included my card?"

"Yes, ma'am."

"Thank you. I appreciate your help."

"It was a pleasure. And if you don't mind me saying, that was a gorgeous outfit you had on when you came in yesterday. All white except for that tiny red hat! You looked like a movie star."

"Thank you."

"Anytime, ma'am."

Alana hung up and looked again at her hands. She could not remember how she broke her nails. *Did I fall out of bed again?* She couldn't remember anything about last night, but that was not unusual. *It's the drugs.* She sighed and picked up the newspaper and scanned the headlines for the second time that morning.

The news was the same.

"Another Murder by Mystery Blonde? Cops Baffled."

A young woman, identified as Susan Baldwin of Mariposa Street, had been attacked by two strangers on her way home from work. The thugs who had accosted her were now dead at the hands of an unknown citizen. The article closed by reporting the police would not confirm whether these killings were related to three recent vigilante attacks by a blonde woman.

The blonde woman. Thrill Girl, one of the other newspapers called her, Alana remembered. She chewed her bottom lip and read the article a second time, tears brimming in her eyes. How terrified the young woman must have been, and how thankful that a fellow human being had come to her rescue.

Alana folded the paper and pushed it away. Everyone had the responsibility to help their fellow man, especially now, as the world struggled to rebuild after the war, she thought. Alana's spiritual guide at Nepenthe Center, Swami Dhani, extolled sacrifice for others as the only path to personal salvation.

I need to do more, she thought.

"Hey, beautiful. Did you order breakfast?"

Alana turned toward the male voice. Gino Venice, known as Gino Handsome to a million women who loved his movies and albums, stood a few feet away, naked and glistening wet from his shower.

He opened his arms wide. "Or would you rather have another helping of me?"

Gino had arrived uninvited, ravenous after a night of carousing and club-hopping, at 6 a.m. this morning. A few minutes ago, Alana had left him in her bed, sated and sound asleep.

Her eyes swept over his body. It was obvious he was ready for another round.

Her mouth curved into a smile. "You need to dry off. I'm meeting my brother for breakfast in a few minutes, so there's no more room on my dance card this morning, Mr. Venice. Sorry. But do ask again, won't you?"

Gino ran his fingers through his hair, the muscles in his abdomen tensing as he stretched. He flashed his white teeth, like a shark. "Maybe you should check your card again. And tell your brother to get breakfast on his own."

"I don't stand Tommy up. Besides, I'm very hungry." She touched a bruised finger to her cheek. "As you can see, I've already done my makeup. Unlike you, I tend to get quite a bit accomplished before noon. A person can do that if they go to bed at a decent hour."

"I play at night." He rested a hand on his hip bone.

She kept her eyes on his face, although she could see his lower body. Heat washed over her. I want him. Again. Right now.

Alana moved toward Gino, but suddenly her eyesight dimmed, and tiny, star-shaped lights sparkled and swirled in the air between them. Her eyes followed them, transfixed, as they shifted to the wall across from her. The surface shimmered silver as if liquid dripped down the creamy plaster. At the top corner, near the ceiling, the stars danced closer together, assuming a different shape.

Alana squinted and reached out a tentative hand, and the flickering image solidified. A triangular head, green eyes against black skin, tilted toward her and hissed a wisp of red tongue.

There is a snake on my wall.

A scream convulsed in her throat and she grabbed the table to steady herself.

"What's wrong?" Gino rushed to her and pulled her into an embrace.

She blinked, and the lights and serpent disappeared. The room once again held only the gentle California morning light. Leaning her weight against Gino, she ran her hand through her hair. "It's, I saw, you know. Lights..."

"Lights? What kind of lights? Like the other night?"

It had happened before, she remembered, the last time she was with Gino. "Yes."

"You need to tell the doctor about this shit," Gino said. "Those goddamned pills you're taking are making you crazy."

"I will. I will. They must be affecting my sight."

"What kind of medicine makes you see things that aren't there, anyway? And why won't you tell me what you're taking?"

I've already told Gino too much, she thought.

Alana rubbed her face hard against his, the stubble on his chin prickling her cheek. Her insides warmed as she remembered the sensation of those same whiskers against her inner thighs. Alana wrapped her arms tightly around him. "Hold me."

Gino kissed her neck and ground his naked hips against her, his questions forgotten. Alana knew well enough that Gino didn't care that much about her problems with the drugs she was taking. He cared only about sex.

Alana shivered and licked the hollow at the bottom of his neck.

He slid his hand inside her silk wrap, stroking her left nipple to hardness. "You want more now? I think you're the only woman I've been with who is insatiable."

"I'm satiable."

"Not that I've seen. But I don't mind working on it," Gino said.

She smiled and let him rub her with his finger as her head lolled back. She was satiable. But only for a while. These last few months her appetite had spiraled out of control.

Even when her body was raw and trembling from hours of coupling, even when her muscles told her she had reached her limit, she craved more. She had developed a hunger for pleasure that was never quite satisfied, one which overwhelmed good sense and free will.

She loved that it helped her forget her worries. For a few minutes. But she hated how it was affecting her memory. Alana pushed her hand against Gino's chest. "Stop now. We can pick this up again later."

"When?" he demanded.

"I'm coming to the club for your midnight show. After you perform for your fans, you can perform for me." Gino was booked for the next month at the Coconut Grove nightclub, downstairs in the Ambassador Hotel, where Alana lived.

"Perform? What am I, a trained animal, living to please you?"

Alana moved her hair off her face. "You needed no training to please me. None at all."

He pulled her closer and nipped her shoulder, resting his mouth on her ear. "I'm going to screw you tonight until you can't get out of bed. You won't be able to stand for a week."

She moved out of his embrace and leaned against the desk, her legs trembling. Out of the corner of her eye, she saw tiny green sparkles in the air, gathering into a group against the window. She resisted them and stared at Gino's face. "One of us won't be able to stand for a week. We'll see who. Now get dressed."

"Kiss me first. One kiss. Then I promise I'll get dressed." He rubbed his hand against his belly. And then rubbed lower. "Come on, baby, one kiss for the road."

After a moment, Alana moved her eyes down the long, muscled length of him. "Okay." She dropped to her knees and wet her lips. "But just one."

CHAPTER THREE

Jack dropped his last nickel in the phone at the booth on Sixth and Western. He shut the glass door and dialed the number he had been given last night from memory.

"Jack Curran for Mr. Goldblum. He asked me to call," he said to the woman who answered the phone. He lit a cigarette and let himself daydream. The producer had his screenplay for months. If he bought it, Jack would have a ticket out of tabloid newspaper journalism. He could finally take a year off and write the book that haunted his dreams. A novel about the war.

After five years of living with the memories of what he had seen and done in Italy, he was ready to try and make sense of it. *I'll rent a place by the ocean, or out in the hills of Laurel Canyon. One with a pool. A swim before breakfast would be good therapy for a bum leg that wasn't going to get better.*

"Sydney Goldblum." The voice cut through Jack's thoughts; an implied get on with it in the delivery.

"Good morning, Mr. Goldblum. This is Jack Curran. I sent you my script and ..."

"I know who you are," the producer interrupted. "Let me cut to the chase. I'm taking a pass on your screenplay. It's written well, but too old-fashioned for 1951."

Jack froze. *He doesn't want it.* Two years of work in the crapper, months of hoping he had interested a producer, dead. "Old-fashioned? How do you mean, if you don't mind my asking?"

"It's sentimental. Chock full of good intentions. Bottom line is, nothing is the same as it was ten years ago, Curran. I don't know if it's the bomb, or the dames working in the factories thinking they could replace the men, or the sick evil in Germany gassing babies and old ladies. But whatever it was, people don't want brave, goody-goody Mrs. Miniver stories anymore. Viewers want whacked-out, sex-starved dames on the screen. Like the ones in All About Eve and Sunset Boulevard. The mother in Home Fires has the virtue of a nun, for Christ's sake."

Home Fires was about his mother, an Irish immigrant who came to America when she was thirteen. She had worked her whole life — three jobs after Jack's old man left town – and died at forty-two, while her only living child was off fighting fascists in Europe.

"I see. Well, thank you for your time, Mr. Goldblum." Jack kept his voice steady.

"Hang on a minute. I didn't take this call to tell you I was passing on your script. A secretary could have done that. There's another piece of business I want to discuss with you."

"What's that?" Jack slid his notebook into his coat pocket; his mind empty.

"You know how to do a treatment?"

"Treatment? You mean write another screenplay?"

"No. A treatment. An outline. Five pages."

"No. I've never done one of those."

"Where'd you learn how to do a screenplay, mail order school?" Goldblum's tone was brutal.

"UCLA. At night." Jack had learned the basics from three years of classes. But his desire to write had come from watching movies every chance he got when he was a kid, working as an usher until one a.m. He had loved sitting in the dark, getting away from the harsh light of day.

"Westwood, huh? With all those rich kids? You a rich kid, Jack?"

"G.I. Bill."

"Hey, you're the fucking war hero I read about in the Times, aren't you? Killed a dozen Krauts or something when you were in Italy?"

"That was a long time ago."

"You're right there." Goldblum cleared his throat. "Look, no one wants to think about that war, especially now that we got ourselves a shiny new one in Korea. What I want now is five pages on Thrill Girl. I saw your stuff in *The Eyes*. It's sharp. People like stories ripped from the headlines. Murder and mayhem, a gorgeous bitch that is crazy as a loon, hopped-up on dope like half the actresses I know. That story has huge box office potential. I'll meet you for lunch next week, at the Derby, and look at pages. Call my office tomorrow, and my secretary will schedule the time."

"I can't do that, Mr. Goldblum." The words escaped from Jack's mouth before his brain could edit them. "I can't write about Thrill Girl for anyone except my newspaper."

"Why the hell not?"

"Thrill Girl is a live story. I have no idea who she is, let alone why she's doing what she's doing. No one does. Until the police catch her, I will treat it for what it is – news. And my reporting is exclusive to my newspaper."

"*The Eyes* is a two-bit weekly. Don't be a sap, Curran. I'm offering you more than knee-jerk loyalty."

"I appreciate your offer, Mr. Goldblum." He inhaled. "But aside from the conflict of interest, it would be crazy for anyone to write a screenplay about her now. No one knows how this story is going to end."

"A screenplay can end however the fucking writer wants it to."

Jack cracked open the telephone booth and flicked his cigarette into the street. "That only works with fiction. Not the news. Not the facts."

"Whose facts?" Goldblum's challenged. "You've been

badgering my secretary for weeks now, but when I give you a chance at the gold ring, you punk out? You telling me you can't take advantage of this opportunity?"

"I would jump at the chance to do a treatment on Thrill Girl, once she's caught. But to do it before, it would just be fantasy."

"Hell, son, you're in Hollywood," Goldblum said with contempt. "If you don't understand fantasy is what people prefer to real life, you got no business being here."

Jack knew the call was going from bad to worse, but there was nothing else he could do. "Thank you for the offer, but I have to pass."

There was a long moment's pause.

"I should kick you to the curb," the producer said. "But since you're a big-deal war hero, I'll meet you for lunch anyway. This story is going to make a killer movie. One I plan to make, with or without you. You understand what I'm saying?"

"I do." He did. If he didn't play ball, Goldblum would hire someone else to write a screenplay. About his girl.

"Be smart and bring pages with you. Hollywood isn't war, Curran. It's not right and wrong, or black and white. It's about finding an advantage, and grabbing the gold ring if you're lucky enough to get a shot."

The line disconnected.

Jack stared at the receiver before he replaced it. He stepped out of the glass booth, his mind humming. War was black and white, a time when men killed and died fighting for what they cherished most and believed in. He didn't plan to live his life off the battlefield any different, even if the chance of a gold ring was offered.

He hurried toward his car, the conversation with Goldblum playing on a loop in his mind. He wondered if turning down the producer's offer to do a treatment would kneecap his hopes of ever working for a studio.

It would kill his credibility as a journalist if anyone in the press caught wind of it. Jack shook his head. He still had a paying job. The smart choice was to follow the facts and report on the vigilante murder story until the public had all the truth fit to print.

After that?

Jack pursed his lips. The Thrill Girl story suddenly felt a lot more complicated.

# # #

An hour after Gino left her apartment, Alana walked out of the Ambassador Hotel lobby into the blazing sunshine, tugging on her gloves. She smiled at the man waiting for her on the sidewalk.

"Good morning, Miss Maxwell." Her chauffeur, Edgar Robinson, opened the door of the Rolls.

"Good morning." She slid into the seat as her stomach grumbled. Her mouth watered and she reached into her bag for her handkerchief.

Robinson leaned into the car. "Do you want me to go upstairs and get Mr. Tomas?"

"No. I called him and he said to give him five more minutes." She looked up. "Did he get up late this morning?"

"No, ma'am. He was already out of the bath and drinking his coffee when I arrived."

"How was he feeling?"

Robinson shaded his eyes and glanced at the traffic out on Wilshire Boulevard. "Fine, Miss Maxwell. I think he slept well."

"How did he look?" Alana stared at the Army veteran who was her brother's nurse, valet, and driver for the past three years.

"Good. Good." Robinson grinned. "Man needs a haircut though. He's got the barber coming up this afternoon."

Robinson was kind. Usually Alana liked that about him, but today it irritated her. "Tommy looked horrible yesterday. Pale. I think he's lost more weight."

"Do you?" He paused. "He's been swimming a lot. I've been taking him down to the pool most days, ma'am. That's a lot of exercise."

"It's good for him. But whenever I have a meal with him, he never seems to eat."

"Oh, he eats, Miss Maxwell. I brought him a dish of tapioca

pudding before I left last night. And those cookies you get from Jewel Tea. He has those most evenings."

"Thank you for doing that." Her face softened, and she glanced at her wristwatch, the diamonds glittering in the sunlight. "It's eleven. Why don't you go on up now and get him? I'll wait with the car."

Robinson nodded okay and walked back to the hotel.

Alana pulled off her gloves and reached for her cigarettes. Her mind swam back to Gino, and she rubbed her swollen top lip.

When she saw Dr. Preminger this afternoon, she was going to ask him about her out-of-control hunger. For food. For sex. For excitement. And about the bizarre hallucinations. They frightened her.

Alana leaned against the plush seat. She would have to be careful with Preminger. She did not want him to panic and overreact to her symptoms. She would not let anything interfere with his medical research. Not when Tomas was getting weaker.

She was her brother's only hope.

Tears welled in Alana's eyes, but she blinked them away. Her own temporary physical discomfort was not important. All that mattered was for Dr. Preminger to make a breakthrough in his research and find a cure for Tomas.

Before it was too late.

Ten minutes later, Robinson helped Tomas Maxwell out of his wheelchair and into the Rolls, where his sister sat waiting.

Alana barely controlled a gasp. Her brother looked worse than he had last night. In fact, he looked worse than she had ever seen him.

The bags under his eyes were purplish and puffy, and his skin had a yellow tint.

"Alana! Oh my god, you're not smoking inside the car, are you?" Tomas batted at the air and gave his sister a disapproving frown. "Maybe we should leave the doors open until the oxygen levels return to normal."

Alana stubbed out her cigarette. "Don't be dramatic." She waved away a trace of haze. "Come get settled, and we'll get breakfast. I'm starving."

Robinson shut them into the plush space and slipped into the front seat. "Stella's?" he asked.

"Yes," Alana said. "I'm having bacon and eggs and pancakes. I've been thinking about pancakes for hours."

"We'll be there in fifteen, Miss Maxwell." Robinson hit the switch, and with a soft purr, the window between the front and rear compartment closed the siblings into a private space.

"You look devastating in that color blue," Alana said, nodding at his tie.

"I look like bleached driftwood, sister dear, but your lie is appreciated." Tomas kissed her cheek. "Why are you always starving lately? And by the way, that's quite a hat."

"Thank you." She patted it. "I love hats."

"I know you do." He frowned at the enormous feather. "Did you kill that bird yourself?"

"You know I couldn't hurt a fly."

"I know no such thing."

Alana raised her eyebrows. "Stop teasing me. How are you feeling?"

"Wonderful."

"Truly?"

"No. I feel like a piece of gum squashed onto the bottom of a shoe."

Nervously she pulled off her gloves. "Are you taking your medicine? Doing your exercises? You know how important the exercises are, Tommy."

He turned away. "Yes, I know. Robinson drags me to the pool once a day. I think I'm growing gills."

She put her hand on his left leg, though he could not feel her touch. "Sorry."

Tomas covered her fingers with his fully functioning right hand. "I'm sorry too. You should criticize me. I know I've not been much help to you lately with your fundraising. How's it going?"

"You're always a help. And it's going fine." The research foundation she headed, seeking a cure for paralysis, was thriving, thanks to her hard work and her step-brother's connections. Alana took off her hat and fluffed her hair. "Maybe we should both stop drinking before dinner. I think it interferes with a good night's sleep. I'm going to cut down. Keep to orange juice, hold the vodka."

"I'll hold it for you." He smiled, and a shadow of the carefree young man he should be flashed across his features.

Alana touched his face. His skin was warm. Too warm. "I mean it. We need to take care of one another, for one another."

"Okay. Less drinking. More swimming."

"It's a deal." She dropped her hand into her lap, squeezing it into a fist. "But first, breakfast."

"Pancakes." Tomas frowned. "Do you remember the time when I was four and bit our dog because she stole my waffle off the table? Mother was horrified."

"I do." Alana didn't want to think about their mother. She was dead, and it did not help to think about the dead.

"Look, you can still see the scar where he nipped me in retaliation." Tomas held his hand out in front of her face.

"I believe I told you then it was foolish to bite a creature that could bite you back. Much smarter to stick with the food on your plate."

"What's the sport in that?"

"Not everything in life is about the sport, you know."

"Isn't it?"

"No. Most people's lives are spent doing a series of tasks, over and over again. It's called work. And duty."

"Have you switched from Buddhism to Thoreau? The mass of men live lives of quiet desperation. I quite agree with that line." Tomas grinned.

"I don't. And you should read more of the Theravada Buddhism I've given you. It's inspirational and calming. I think you'd like it more than gloomy old Thoreau."

"Are you suggesting Mr. Thoreau should have studied what, the five precepts?"

"Don't be condescending, Tommy. Millions of people live by those precepts."

"I'm not making fun. I've memorized them actually, thanks to your constant supply of reading material. Refrain from taking life. Refrain from taking that which is not given. Refrain from sensual misconduct, and lying, and intoxicants, which lead to loss of mindfulness. Did I get them right?"

"Yes. Bravo." She clapped lightly. "Another reason to cut down on our drinking."

"I'm going to be twenty-one in ten days. If you're hoping I should do more than memorize those precepts, let me overrule you right now. I cannot live by them as you do. Okay?"

"I don't live by them. I try and fail. Every day." She flushed. "The key to progress in life is to keep trying."

"Try, try, again. Blah, blah, blah. I do wonder if it's worth the effort. Life."

"Don't be bleak." She plastered a smile on her face. "I want to talk about clothes. You need clothes for the foundation benefit on the ninth. I want to get you a new tuxedo. And a gorgeous new cummerbund. Something shocking. Maybe paisley satin?"

"I don't need a new tuxedo." Tomas cringed as Robinson took a corner and merged into heavy traffic.

"Oh, come on. My treat."

"No." Tomas stared out the window. "Are you coming to Lynton's on Saturday night?"

"No. I checked my diary, and I have other plans."

"Lynton is expecting you."

"Poor him."

"It's my birthday dinner."

"What?" She pursed her lips. "I'm taking you out by myself on your birthday. You enjoy the night with him. Bring a few of your lovely friends, and you won't have to talk to him."

Tomas turned to her. "Come anyway; it will be fun to watch

him try to please you while you ignore him."

"No."

"If you were nicer to our step-brother, your journey toward nirvana might go quicker."

"Don't tease me about my religion, Tomas. Besides, I never have fun at Lynton's." She looked down her nose. "Neither do you. He's always got an odd general or two hanging around. I don't want to go there."

"Don't you think it's time you overcame this attitude?"

"What attitude?"

"Your attitude. You were allowed to be rude to Lynton from your crib because Mother hated him. But don't you think it's time to call a truce?"

"You're being unfair" She fussed with the netting at the edge of her hat.

"Are you saying you don't hate him?"

"No, I do hate him."

"And how does that fit in with you trying to be a better person? It's time for you to set your hatred aside. It's affecting my relationship with him."

She stopped fidgeting. "How?"

"I can't be civil to people you hate. We're alike in that way. Loyal to a fault." His voice rose. "But I don't want to be bogged down in pettiness. There's not enough time…"

Alana swallowed. "You're angry with me. What's wrong?"

"Everything." Tomas clenched his jaw. "I find that lately, I'm angry about everything."

"Did you have a bad night?"

"I had the same night I always have."

She wanted to ask more, but there was nothing to be gained by it. For the past year, all her brother's nights had been terrible. Pain in his legs, pain in his spine. Itching and burning nerve endings that would drive most people mad.

And nightmares. Tomas had suffered from night terrors since he was a tiny baby.

"After we have breakfast and go shopping, I have an appointment with Dr. Preminger. Maybe you should come with me and let him check you out?"

"No thanks. I have my regular appointment with him next week." He turned to her. "I don't want you discussing me with him."

"I'm not seeing him about you. I need to talk to him about the medicine he prescribed for my headaches. I've been experiencing side effects."

"The memory problems? Good, tell him you're having conversations with me that you don't remember the next day."

She narrowed her eyes. Tomas didn't know the half of it. "That only happened a couple of times."

"Which is a couple of times too many for a woman who is twenty-four." Tomas grasped her hand with his bony fingers. "Don't snoop about me with Preminger, okay? It makes me feel like a baby. If you want to know anything about my health, ask me."

"Fine."

"And don't ask that red-haired cow of a nurse, either."

Alana chuckled. Preminger's nurse did have an unfortunately bovine habit of staring at people with her huge bloodshot eyes. "Don't be unkind about Deidre."

"Calling her a cow is kind. She's a drunk and doesn't care enough to cover up her gin breath when she's giving me injections. I don't know what she's got on Preminger to convince him to keep her around."

"They're married."

"Really? Then she must have something really big on him."

"I've never smelled gin on her breath, Tommy."

"Breathe deeper."

They both chuckled. Alana glanced out the window as the big car snaked slowly down Santa Monica Boulevard.

"Alana, please say you'll go to Lynton's with me on Saturday. We don't have to stay long. I need you there." His voice dropped.

"Why?"

"I'm going to ask Lynton to give me control over my trust fund."

"What? Why?"

"I want to move out of the hotel."

"Out?" She sat back, stunned. "Where?"

"Europe possibly. Or Italy, near Lake Como. Our family still owns the estate there."

Her heart jolted. "It's too far. And none of us have lived in Europe since you were a child! Besides, you can't leave now, not in the middle of your treatments with Dr. Preminger!"

"Yes, I can."

"But why? His treatments have led to the first signs of improvement in your condition! You've said as much yourself."

"There are plenty of doctors in the world."

"Tomas, listen to me. You are a tremendous help with the foundation's fundraising. Everyone loves meeting with you, and they all talk about the inspiration you provide. You can't run off. Besides, isn't it fun, living at the Ambassador?" A frantic edge had crept into her voice.

"Fun is a difficult word for me."

"Oh please!" Her frustration bubbled over. "You need to change your outlook, Tomas. Your life won't be any different in a new place if you don't think differently."

"I'm trying! I'm almost twenty-one, for god's sake! Not too long ago, millions of lads my age fought and died in war while I sat and watched. All I'm asking for is the independence to buy my own place. A house. If not in Europe, then here."

"But how would you manage, Tommy, even with Robinson?"

"How would I manage? Honestly, you're the one who's always telling me not to let my disabilities limit my life. I have the wonderful electric wheelchair that you bought me, and I'll hire a cook. Robinson can live with me full-time. I think I would manage nicely."

They both stared at the back of Robinson's head. Alana turned to Tomas. "Have you asked Robinson if he wants to move into a private house with you?"

"Not yet."

"He does have a home of his own, you know."

"Which he can keep. I'm not selfish. But I want to do this, and as long as Lynton gives me control of my own money, I can."

She heard the yearning, excitement, and stubbornness in her brother's voice, but turned away to stare out at the traffic. She hated to ask Lynton for anything. Every favor he bestowed came at a cost. "I'll need to think about it."

"Why?"

"Because I'm hungry, and when I'm hungry, that's the only thing I can think about."

"If you don't stop eating all the time, you're going to be the size of a city bus. A beautiful city bus, but still…"

A huge bus pulled up beside them at that exact instant, its tailpipe belching smoke as its brakes drowned out conversation.

Tomas began to giggle. "Although you could put billboards on your fanny and advertise the fundraising gala." His laughter grew, and he threw his head back against the seat.

For a moment Alana felt like choking him. But the impulse melted away at the joyful sound rumbling from Tomas. She leaned against him, and both of them chortled like kids. When she finally pulled away and wiped the tears from her eyes, she realized she could not imagine her life without him.

"You are a horrible, horrible brother." She kissed the shoulder of his sports coat, feeling the bone beneath.

"And you're a wonderful and supportive sister," he replied. "We can get a list of properties together for Lynton to look at after we have dinner. He'll be pleased I'm prepared."

"All right. I'll come. On one condition. You have to promise not to move to Europe, and to continue your treatments with Dr. Preminger at least for one year. He is getting results."

"Is he?"

"You must never give up hope, Tommy."

"I'm not." He cleared his throat. "A couple of weeks ago Dr. Preminger began incorporating what sounds like your Eastern mumbo jumbo about positive thoughts into my treatment. And he's added hypnosis sessions. I don't know if I told you that."

He had not. "How does hypnosis help?" Alana asked.

"According to Preminger, the mind controls the body in ways we don't fully understand, and our thoughts may be able to heal us physically. He's added an hour session to both of my physical therapy appointments. He feels he can implant positive images inside my brain."

His words made her feel uneasy. They had tried many different cures and procedures and doctors over the years. But it wasn't that. Wasn't hypnosis a scam? "I don't know anything about hypnotism. How does it work? Does he wave a wand at you and then you go to sleep? Like that magician we saw at the Warner?"

"No, it's nothing like that. No dangling watches and bosomy assistants. I concentrate on an image, a 'trigger' he calls it, which he introduces at the beginning of our session. He has tape recordings of things like the sound of rushing water. I listen to the recordings while I focus on the image, and evidently, that's all it takes. I've found these sessions release inhibitions."

"What kind of inhibitions?"

"Fear of doing things mostly. Like swimming. I told him about my fear, and he addressed it in one of our sessions. Alana, it worked. I don't worry I'm going to drown whenever I go in the pool." Tomas smiled. "Did you know that hypnosis can't make a person do anything they are morally against?"

"How does anyone prove that? Did he ask you to do something you think is wrong?" Alana gripped her hands together, as the tension knotted in her stomach.

"Of course not. He only mentioned it to illustrate the usefulness of hypnosis. It helps a person do the things they are only resisting out of fear. He thinks I might be afraid to be well."

Robinson pulled the car into the restaurant parking lot and stopped.

"That sounds ridiculous. Why would you be afraid of that?" Alana asked.

"Because I've never been well. I don't know what it is to be healthy and pain-free."

"You will soon." She clutched his hand. "Don't give up."

He looked at her, his face pinched. "I am afraid, often."

"Nonsense. You've never been afraid of anything."

Tomas blinked and watched as Robinson walked around the car to get the wheelchair. "Thanks for coming with me." The tension between them lifted. Tomas bent to kiss her hand but stopped. "What on earth happened to your nails? Have you taken up bowling?"

"I can't remember how I broke them." Alana pulled on her gloves. "It's nothing. Snagged them on the blanket while I was sleeping, or smacked them on the bedside table. You know how clumsy I am."

"You're bruised, Alana. It's not nothing."

"It is. Now come on."

She smiled at Robinson when he opened the door. "It's time for pancakes."

CHAPTER FOUR

Jack parked the Packard a block away from his destination. He was in the mid-Wilshire district, an aging neighborhood of clapboard and stucco houses. Most were in need of paint or new shutters or both. He lit a cigarette and looked around.

As he walked to the address he had copied out of the cop log book last night, a black-and-white came roaring up the street. But the driver was speeding up, not stopping – he hit the lights and siren as he jumped out onto Sixth Avenue.

Be thankful for small favors, Jack thought.

The police lot mechanic he had tipped for a quick look-see at patrol car 1-2-4's logbook would keep his mouth shut. The kid was smart enough to know he would lose his job if anyone found out he had given a reporter information.

Jack sucked down a lungful of smoke when he reached the house and tossed the butt into the street.

The house at 706 Mariposa was a typical 1920s bungalow with a raised stoop and sloping roof. Light green with white shutters and a sagging screen door. There were two sets of louvered windows on the front, both closed tight even though it was nearly ninety degrees outside and it wasn't yet noon.

Jack loosened his tie and climbed the cement steps up to the front door. He heard a dog bark inside, the kind of yappy dog he hated, followed by the sound of a person dragging a heavy object across a wood floor.

Then silence.

He tried to peer through the glass inserts but didn't see anything.

He knocked.

The dog barked and whined as if it had been smacked.

Jack knocked again.

More silence.

He turned to walk to the rear of the house but stopped at the sound of someone fumbling with the chain lock. The door creaked open seconds later.

"Yes?" The woman was middle-aged. Though her eyes were bleary, she wore a classy blue dress and makeup. Good looking but fading fast, Jack thought.

She held a tiny white dog. It growled low in its throat as if it smelled a threat.

"Mrs. Baldwin?"

"Who?" The woman hiccupped.

Unless she was pouring gin into the dog's dish, Jack would bet the woman already had several drinks today.

"Are you Mrs. Baldwin?" Jack kept his voice low, and the woman had to lean closer to the screen door to hear him. "Susan Baldwin's mother?"

"Yes, I'm Ellen Baldwin. Who are you?"

Jack smiled. "I'm from the Mayor's Office. Jack Curran, Mrs. Baldwin. Mayor Bowron asked that I swing by to see how Susan's holding up. After that horrible attack last night, his honor wanted to personally let her know the City of Angels is here to support her. And if there's anything we can do to help your family, we'd be glad to help."

He stuck out his hand, but the screen remained closed.

The dog yipped. Ellen knocked it on the head with her knuckle. "Shhh, Snowball. No barking!"

"Cute dog." Jack dropped his hand. "Is your daughter home? I'd like to deliver Mayor Bowron's regards to her in person. If she's up to the company, I mean."

Ellen stared at him. "Susan's not here."

Damn. Jack reached into his shirt pocket for his cigs. He offered one to her, but she shook her head. His silver lighter glittered in the sunshine. He lit up and took a puff. "That's good news. Is she feeling well enough to go out? The mayor will be delighted to hear it."

"Do you have any identification? Proving you're who you say you are?"

"Well, of course. But I don't understand, Mrs. Baldwin. Why would I pretend to be someone I'm not? Has this happened before?"

"No. But I can't let just anyone in my house. Women have to be careful. Look what happened to Susan." Ellen clutched the dog closer to her chest.

"Yes, of course, you're right." He patted his jacket pocket. "I think I do have business cards in my wallet. How about I leave one with you, and Susan can call me later?"

"We don't have a phone."

"I could come back." Jack pulled out his wallet and acted as if he were looking for a card.

"Oh, you might as well come in." Ellen pushed the screen open. "Never mind about the card. Susan should be home any minute. She went to the market for milk and aspirin. I was going to go, but I need to leave for an appointment as soon as my ride shows up."

"Thank you." Jack slipped his wallet back into his jacket. He did have business cards, but none of them said he worked for the Mayor.

Jack followed Ellen into the house. She led him into a living room where a metal fan hummed on a side table, blowing a ball of air around the space as if it were invisible tumbleweed.

It was stifling.

"Sit down anywhere." Ellen dumped the dog on the sofa. It

immediately began scratching its neck with its rear leg, warranting another knuckle whomp.

Jack took the chair across from the fan. Perspiration ran from his armpits down to his ribcage, but he didn't want to spook Mrs. Baldwin by taking off his suit jacket. He took a casual look around.

The place was tidy. There was a brick fireplace, its walnut mantle decorated with a group of photographs. He spotted one of Susan Baldwin in tennis clothes, holding a trophy aloft.

It stood next to a clock whose time read 3:18.

A broken clock is right twice a day, his Mom used to say.

The smell of booze from Ellen Baldwin dissipated, leaving a heavy sweetness in its wake. It wasn't the rotting scent of old food, Jack thought, but it was overpowering nonetheless.

Ellen sat silent, staring at him.

He waved his hand around the room. "Lovely place you got here."

She continued to stare.

He looked away. Through the archway on his right was a dining room with seats for six. An enormous vase of white roses stood on the table, at least two dozen of them, which explained the smell.

"Can I get you a drink, Mr. Curran? Water? Coffee?" Ellen pushed herself to the edge of the sofa. "You want a beer?"

"No, no, I'm fine."

"You're a veteran, aren't you?" Ellen stared at his bum leg. "Hurt in the war?"

Though Korea was America's current war, Jack knew the war she referred to was WWII. For people her age, it was the only war.

"Yes. I got off pretty easy, though." He patted his knee. "Grenade took out part of my kneecap, but I got to keep the rest."

"What outfit were you with?"

"I was infantry. Army. In Italy."

"My husband was a Navy man. Gerald Baldwin. He was killed Dec 7, 1941, in Hawaii. On the Arizona."

The Arizona went down in Pearl Harbor with twelve hundred

men on board. Jack swallowed. It had to be hell to lose a husband in the war, even harder if you didn't get a body to bury.

No wonder she starts the day with a drink or three.

"Dirty Japs." Ellen kept her voice low. "We should have kicked them all out of this country. Instead, we fed them and kept them and their slanty-eyed kids in camps on our dime. What chumps we are."

The hatred in Ellen's voice was raw despite the fact WWII had been over for more than five years.

"I'm sorry to hear about your husband, Mrs. Baldwin. December 7th was a terrible day. I remember President Roosevelt telling us what happened on the radio." He had been a young man at the time. With a brand new wife and a job in the journalism department of Ohio State University.

"I heard FDR's speech on the radio. It was horrible."

"It was a day of infamy like the President said." Jack clapped his hands together. "It changed the world. And every person in it."

"Not for the better."

"We got rid of Hitler," he said gently. "We saved millions of people from an unimaginable monster."

"And I lost my husband."

"He was a brave man."

"He was unlucky. Marrying him made me unlucky." Ellen gestured angrily as if she could swat away the past like a fly. "I don't want to talk about this." She stood. "I'm going to fix myself a drink. My ride is late, and it's hot as Hades in here. You sure you don't want one?"

"I'm good."

"Suit yourself." She disappeared into the kitchen.

Eying Snowball, Jack slowly rose to his feet. The dog growled at him, but then rested its rat head on its paws. Beyond the dining room was a narrow hallway with two doors ajar. He could see the edges of beds. He got up and took a cautious step. The hardwood floor creaked.

He craned his neck to see further. At one end there was a third door, closed. It had a printed notice taped to it.

Danger. Oxygen. No smoking!!!

Jack glanced at the flowers. They were lush and sweet. A white envelope lay beside them. He leaned forward and took note of the name engraved in the corner.

Lily's Lilies. On Wilshire Blvd.

Ellen slammed a drawer in the kitchen, and Jack hurried back to his chair.

Snowball bared its fangs as Ellen reappeared with a juice glass full of pale orange liquid in her hand. She sat next to the dog, told it to shut up, and downed her drink in three swallows.

The smell of alcohol overpowered the whiff of roses. He cleared his throat. "I hope Susan was given a few days off work. To get over the shock of what happened."

Ellen seemed lost in thought.

He tried again. "She works at Bullocks Wilshire, right?" According to the police report he had glanced at, she worked in ladies' wear.

"Yes." Ellen began to tap her foot.

"Did you get your dress there? It's a lovely color on you if you don't mind me saying."

Ellen shrugged. "Susan brings stuff home. Gets a big discount when things are end-of-season. Or when they get returned because a button popped off or a rich lady spilled her soup." She motioned toward the dining room. "Will you look at those flowers? I can't believe how many of them there are. A deliveryman brought them to Susan this morning. Two dozen white roses. What's that cost? Ten, twelve bucks at least? Geez."

"They're beautiful. Are they from a friend of hers?"

Ellen snorted. "No. My daughter keeps plenty of secrets from me, but she said a crazy person sent them and didn't sign the card. Imagine spending all that loot on someone you never met."

"I don't understand," Jack said.

"Neither do I. But I haven't understood this world for years." Her voice was fuzzy. "Let's not talk about the flowers anymore.

That kind of waste makes me sick." Ellen turned her reddened eyes to him. "What were you asking me about?"

"Ah, I was wondering if Bullocks gave her a few days off to recuperate."

"Not enough. Cheap. Susie talked to her boss this morning. Called him from our neighbor's house next door. He told her she could stay home today and tomorrow if necessary, but they're not going to pay her."

"That doesn't seem fair."

"It isn't. We need the money. I can't work. Not that there's that much work for a woman anymore, now that the men are home and the war is over. I have a Navy pension, but that don't help any with the boy."

"The boy?"

Ellen blinked. She sat up and glanced at the front door as if she had heard something. "I think Susan's going in for a half shift later. At four. They're having a sale you know. Wednesday's a big sale day for ladies' things."

"I see." Jack continued wondering about the boy. *Who is this kid, Susan's brother? Where is he?* It was late June, and school was out for the summer.

He cleared his throat to ask another question, but Ellen set the empty glass on the table with a sharp rap.

"I'll take one of your cigarettes now, Mr. Curran."

Jack thought of the danger sign on the door of that back room and wondered if it was okay to smoke in the house. His mind raced as he pulled out the pack and walked over to Ellen. She took his cigarette, but the front door opened before he could light it.

"Mom? You still here?" a woman called out.

Snowball levitated off the couch and made a beeline for the front door, yapping all the way.

Jack turned and found Susan Baldwin, the dark-haired assault victim, staring at him.

She was taller and prettier than he had made out in the dark last night. Today she was dressed like a college girl in a checkered blouse and denim pedal pushers. Her hand was bandaged and covered with a compression wrap.

Susan dropped her purse and a paper sack on a chair and picked up the hysterical dog. "Mom? What's going on?"

The cigarette dangled from Ellen's lips. "Say hello to Mr. Curran, Susan. He's from Mayor Boring's office."

"*Bowron.* Fletcher *Bowron.*" Jack took a couple of steps toward Susan. He held out his hand and then dropped it. "Sorry. I'm Jack Curran, Miss Baldwin. Nice to meet you."

"He came to tell you how sorry they are at City Hall that you got yourself stabbed last night." Ellen began to laugh. "Not good for tourists to read about, I guess."

"I don't understand." Susan stared at Jack. "The Mayor of Los Angeles sent you here? To see me?"

"We wanted to let you know how sorry we were to hear about your encounter." He took a step. "We thought we might be able to help you. I'm surprised you're already up and about. The mayor will be happy to hear you're doing well."

"Why did you let him in, Mother?" Susan's expression was wary. "The police said we weren't to talk to anyone about last night."

"I didn't talk about nothing you said this morning when you started remembering. Not those weird lights at the end of the street, or what Thrill Girl said, or…"

"Mother!" Susan turned to Jack. "Please don't tell anyone my mother said that."

"Oh, I won't. Of course. But do you think it was Thrill Girl who came to your rescue?" Jack's adrenaline was pumping. "What was she like?"

"Susie said she's a real looker. A blonde," Ellen cut in. "But don't tell anyone."

"Mother. *Shut up.*"

"Don't talk to me like that, Susan Yvonne." Ellen waved her left hand in the air. "I know to keep quiet about things, don't I? All I told Mr. Curran was that you got flowers today. Which he surely knew anyway since you can smell the goddamn things all the way down the block."

"Mother, please don't swear." Susan met Jack's eyes. "The police don't want anything getting out about *anything* while they're investigating. If you work for the mayor, you should know how this works. I'm sure the detectives would not be happy to hear a man who works at city hall is running his mouth about me."

"Whoa, all I'm going to say is you're doing okay. And look fantastic." His brain hummed. Ellen's comment about weird lights felt important, but he wouldn't risk adding fuel to the fire blazing between those two by asking her more about it now.

"I hear you're going to work today," he said.

Susan blinked. "What else did my mother tell you?"

"Nothing," he replied.

The room fell silent except for the ticking of a clock. Jack glanced at the one on the mantle, but it still said three eighteen.

"Mr. Curran, I think you should leave now." Susan put the dog down and pointed to the front door.

"Okay." He had his quote. *More than one.*

Ellen Baldwin had confirmed a blonde woman had come to Susan's rescue, and as a bonus, she had told him Susan had referred to her rescuer as Thrill Girl. His article would be even more powerful if he could get a quote directly from her.

"He doesn't have to go! Don't be rude, Susan." Ellen hiccupped again.

"Mom, you're in no shape for company."

"Don't tell me what kind of shape I'm in." Ellen threw her cigarette onto the floor and stomped on it. "Where the hell is Mary? Check outside. Maybe that dingbat is parked at the curb, listening to all this nonsense. I've got to get going."

Ellen staggered to her feet and tripped, banging her left knee against the coffee table before falling onto the floor with a moan.

"Mother!" Susan rushed to Ellen's side.

Jack leaned down to help, but Susan waved him off. "Please go! I can handle this better if you leave."

"Of course." Jack glanced at the roses, eyeing the card. "But are you sure there's nothing I can do for you?"

"Yes. I'm sure." Susan wrapped her arm around Ellen's shoulder. "Sit still a minute, Mama. Catch your breath."

Snowball growled at Jack's shoes. He managed to repress his instinct to lift the creature with his foot and toss him out of his way.

"Thank you both for your time. Take care." Jack closed the front door firmly behind him. He made his way down the steps and took out his cigarettes and lit one.

Ellen had said Susan was working later today. He would walk over to Bullocks Wilshire tonight and wait for her. Offer to walk her home.

Buy her dinner, even. Then he would explain his affiliation with *The Eyes* and tell her he wanted to use what her mother said in his article. If she balked, he would ask her for an interview about Thrill Girl and promise to leave her mother out of it.

The public deserved to know the facts. If Susan Baldwin gave him an eyewitness account of what the woman looked like, what she had said, and how gruesome it was to watch her kill two men, it would be dynamite.

Hell, there'll be enough for two or three Special Editions if I pull this off. A smile played over Jack's face as he hurried back to the car.

CHAPTER FIVE

Jack walked into *The Eyes* and stalked over to the desk where Eddie Wentz sat typing. "Eddie, I need you."

The young man lurched to his feet. In his haste, he knocked his elbow against an open drawer. "Sure, Mr. Curran." The phone started to ring on the kid's desk. "Should I let that ring?"

"Answer the phone, Eddie."

"Okay, I'll get this." He turned and banged his elbow a second time. "*Eyes of LA*. News desk. Eddie Wentz speaking." He rubbed his arm with his free hand.

Fresh out of LA City College, the kid was scared of his own shadow. Everyone ribbed Eddie about being clumsy and bookish, but Jack knew the kid always listened and knew more than most about what was going on around him. Both in the newsroom and in the community at large.

Eddie read all three daily papers cover to cover, listened to radio programs at night, and his family had invested in their first television set in order that he could watch the Edward R. Murrow broadcasts. He was always prepared for discussions about current events. The kid was green, but Jack would bet money that he would go far.

The newsman threw his hat on his desk, which was five feet from Eddie's, and sat down. When Eddie hung up the phone, Jack asked, "What's going on around here?"

"Uh, you have three telephone messages, and Mr. Deville was looking for you a few minutes ago." Eddie pushed his black glasses firmly against his round face.

"Yeah. What's he want? Did he tell the print shop to give us more time for the special?"

"He didn't say that, Mr. Curran. All he told me was that he wants to see you."

"*Who, what, where, when, and why.* You've got to remember to get the five W's, Eddie. You might have good instincts for a story, but those can't compete with facts." Jack rested his bum leg on top of his desk and lit a cigarette.

"Yes, sir."

"Okay. Now, who are my messages from?"

Eddie read them. The first two calls he could ignore, but the third gave Jack a jolt. It was from Jimmy Glass.

"Detective Glass left a number and said for you to call him immediately, if not sooner. Those were his exact words."

"Did he give us any clue about what he wanted?" Jack took a deep drag off the cigarette. *Could the cop have found out about his visit to Susan Baldwin already?*

"No, sir."

"And you didn't ask him?"

The kid's voice went a notch squeakier. "No, sir. But I will if he calls again."

"Where's Quentin now?" Jack glanced at his publisher's empty office.

"Ah, I don't know. Mr. Deville was behind closed doors all morning. I'm not sure where he went."

"Who was with him?"

"Miss Cherry."

Lucy Cherry reported on Hollywood gossip and society marriages for *The Eyes,* two of Quentin's favorite front page topics.

"What's up? I've never known Lucy and Quentin to meet behind closed doors."

Eddie's voice dropped to a whisper. "I don't know, sir."

"Lucy's been cultivating a cop source, and she was likely giving him an update," Jack said, answering the question for both of them. "Okay, look, when you see Mr. Deville, tell him I've got his quote. And ask him to make sure our print shop is ready for a special on Saturday."

"Will do."

Jack stood. "I'm going out to the county hospital. I'll be back by six. Can you stick around? I'm going to need research, and maybe a sidebar or two."

"Yes, sir." Eddie blinked. "Anything you want me to get started on?"

"I need background on the latest victim, Susan Baldwin, and her mother, Ellen. And Ellen's husband, Gerald Baldwin. Killed on the Arizona in 1941. See if we have anything on any of them. Oh, and check if Susan has a brother." Susan's family history wasn't all that unusual, but the 'Danger' sign had given him pause.

Something serious was going on in that house.

Eddie wrote furiously. "Are you going to call Detective Glass before you leave?"

"I'll do it when I get back. If you hear from him again, ask him specifically what he needs to speak to me about."

"Yes, sir." Eddie cleared his throat. "But I won't tell him you were in, right?"

"Right. No gratuitous information to anyone. Especially cops." Eddie's willingness to stonewall a cop kicked up the kid's chances of being a professional journalist another notch in Jack's mind. He grinned at the kid and sauntered out the door.

# # #

"Do you mind if I call you by your first name, Miss Maxwell?"

"Call me whatever you like, Doctor Preminger." Alana leaned back in the chair and exhaled. The sound of the silver wind chimes tinkling in the breeze behind her seeped into her brain, and she fought the urge to sleep.

She was at the doctor's clinic in the Los Feliz hills, above Hollywood. His office was on the ground floor of his home, and the rustic setting usually made it easy to relax. The neighborhood was secluded and heavily wooded, and the window directly across from her looked out over a hillside of crimson poppies in bloom.

Usually, she relaxed as soon as they drove onto the property, but a strange thing had happened today. Alana saw a large animal furtively slinking through the underbrush beside the doctor's iron fence. It had appeared hurt.

Robinson had not seen anything. But she was sure the creature hadn't sprung from her imagination. This wasn't like the star-shaped particles or even the occasional fantasy creature she conjured up when she was sleepy. No, she was sure of what she had seen.

"Do you have dogs, Doctor?"

"Dogs? No. Why do you ask?"

"I saw an animal that looked like a large dog in your yard when we drove through the gates today."

The doctor frowned. "Often we have a deer manage to jump the fence, and once in a while a mountain lion gets in, but I've never known a dog to intrude." Preminger removed the needle from her arm and pressed a square of gauze to her skin. "Are you sure you saw something?"

"Yes."

"I'll have Josef check, all right? Now hold that for a moment."

Alana applied pressure and watched as a bubble of blood stained the cotton crimson.

The doctor applied a bandage. "You can take this off in a few minutes."

Studying Dr. Preminger, she slowly rolled down the sleeve of her blouse. The doctor was tall, round of body and always antiseptically neat, with a curt and professional demeanor, but he made her uneasy. She often felt him furtively peering at her.

Preminger sat behind his desk and carefully marked the labels on the vials of blood he had drawn. He put the last in its slot in a metal tray and looked up.

"Are you feeling well? Not dizzy after such a big donation? Drink that juice I left there. It's freshly squeezed from a tree in my garden." He waved at the glass of orange juice on the table.

"I'm fine." She folded her hands in her lap. She hated his juice. It had a metallic aftertaste.

"Excellent. Well now, do you have anything to report? We're at the twelve-week mark of our testing. Any change in your overall health? Any symptoms, or side effects, from the drugs you're taking?"

Alana thought about her symptoms and side effects. The tiny lights exploding in the air that only she could see. The lost memories. The dead sleep with no dreaming. She closed her fist. The inexplicable injuries to her hands.

And the increased appetite for food, sex, and drink. Pressing her lips together, she reached into her purse for her cigarettes.

She lit a cigarette and took a puff. "I'm feeling oddly energetic. And hungry all the time. For food, drink, what have you." She waved the cigarette in the air. "I'm experiencing a few hallucinatory episodes you warned me about."

"Stars? Colors? Things floating in the air?"

"Yes." She was shocked he knew this. Shocked and relieved.

"Anything else?"

Alana was hesitant to admit she also saw creatures. A tiny mouse. That snake this morning with Gino. She didn't want the doctor to stop the experimental drugs regimen out of an excess of caution. "No. By the way, has my weight changed?"

Preminger pulled her chart out of the folder next to the blood vials. "You have gained two pounds. Which is nothing at all to worry about, my dear. Water weight. I could give you salt pills, but I'd rather not. It's within the expected fluctuations of a woman's monthly cycle to gain weight."

"I see." Alana stiffened.

Dr. Preminger stared at her. "You told me you had not had normal menstrual cycles since the surgery when you were fifteen. After the car accident. Is that still the case?"

"Yes." She blinked. She did not want to think about the accident that had killed her mother.

"Well, the surgery didn't change your hormonal activity, although the drugs we are testing may." He leaned back. "Anything else to report?"

"I crave sweets." She thought of Gino Venice and a bottle of chocolate liqueur he had brought to her last week. "Especially at night."

"Have you considered using hypnosis for the cravings? I have a theory that it might be able to help. We could design a session or two for you if you're worried about controlling your weight."

Her face warmed at his tone, which was suddenly quite intimate. "I'm not worried about that." She stared at him. "Tomas told me you were using hypnosis as part of his treatment."

"He did? Yes, I use it to help relax him during his transfusions."

"He told me you said hypnosis only works by putting a person in touch with their natural inclinations. A reason for you not to use hypnosis on me as my appetites aren't normal lately. It might actually make me eat more."

"I doubt that. But you are the best judge of what you need. And in my opinion, you are normal in all ways."

She blew smoke in his direction. It rose and circled his bald head. "Didn't you say last week that I have abnormal genetic traits? Have you changed your mind after studying me these last couple of months?"

"No. But I would not call you abnormal in any other way, my dear." Preminger folded his hands in front of him like a jolly troll in a Grimm's fairy tale. "Your genetics are rare. And complex. My research indicates you inherited very unusual characteristics in your genes from your father. Not as complicated as your brother's, but they're still quite interesting."

"Dear daddy." Her pulse quickened. She didn't want to discuss her father.

"When your father was aggressively treated for his blood cancers in the 1920s, the drugs he was given caused him to pass on certain mutations to you and Tomas. Unfortunately, your father's doctors did not know about the possible side effects at the time they treated him."

Which is one more reason to hate doctors, Alana thought. "Maybe I should sue my father's doctors for malpractice," she said heatedly.

The doctor adjusted his glasses nervously. "If your parents had not had Tomas, would you be happier?"

"Of course not."

"Medicine is advancing all the time, Alana. Your father's physicians did the best they could at the time. Let's hope we can correct what their ignorance started." He stepped away and folded his arms over his massive chest. "Do you have any other questions for me today?"

"You said my part in the drug testing would continue for the next nine months. Is that still your plan?"

"Approximately. We need at least that much time to know how you tolerate these compounds. It's helping us enormously in our engineering of the variant vaccine we're using on your brother."

"I have a question about that. Don't Tomas and I have the same genetics? We have the same parents. I still don't understand why he's...damaged, while I have no trace of the birth defects he suffers."

Preminger's voice gentled. "Tomas was more severely impacted in the womb because of the cumulative effects of your father's use of amethopterin. The drug degraded his sperm more and more over time. Tomas, as the youngest child, suffered the most." He paused. "I can't scientifically prove this yet, but I also believe the animal bites your mother endured while she was pregnant with Tomas further compromised his physical development."

Alana twitched at the mention of the attack. She had told Preminger about it in their interview about the family's medical history.

The memory of her mother's screams echoed inside her head.

When she was five years old, her pregnant mother had been attacked in the garden by a feral cat. The ill and dehydrated creature, guarding two half-dead kittens, had attacked and bitten her mother. The wounds had become infected, and her mother had nearly died from septic shock.

It had happened in her third month of pregnancy.

Alana focused on Preminger. "The baby in the womb shares the same blood as the mother, yes?"

"Yes. Which is the reason I believe your mother's infection affected Tomas."

"I see." Mother had bad karma, she thought. Which she passed to Tomas. Alana stood up. "Are the initial doses of the experimental vaccine helping Tomas?"

Preminger pursed his lips. "Not as aggressively as I'd hoped, I'm sorry to say. I see decreased bone density in his paralyzed leg and his spine, but there is strengthening in the muscles of his left arm."

She froze. "But there is still a chance the vaccine will reverse his disease? That he might be able to walk someday?" Alana's voice wavered. "That's the whole point of this treatment, isn't it?"

"That's what we're working toward. We may have to get more aggressive over the next couple of weeks, but I don't want to endanger your health in any way, my dear."

"You said I'm strong." She took a step toward the doctor. "You know I'll do whatever it takes to help Tomas."

"I understand that. Sisters will do anything to help their brothers, won't they? We may need more visits a week for blood donations. I may increase your sleeping pill prescription to make sure you're rested and producing replacement blood cells. As long as you're not suffering too many ill effects..."

"Don't worry about side effects. I can handle them." And she could.

"Very well." Preminger crossed his arms. "Your brother is very fortunate he has your support. Because of your help, it is much more likely we'll have a breakthrough in curing his paralysis."

"Well, that's worth any risk, isn't it?"

"I agree."

Alana tucked her handbag into her side. "I hope you will continue taking precautions to prevent Tomas from finding out that I'm actively involved in his treatment."

Preminger nodded. "He knows nothing of my research. Your brother thinks you see me only because you have migraine headaches."

"Good."

"Are you seeing any change in his moods, by the way? I would expect him to be more tired than usual due to the drug therapy."

"His energy level seems unchanged. Which reminds me. Tomas told me earlier he's planning to move out of the Ambassador Hotel. He's determined to live in his own home."

"Not alone!" Preminger blinked. "How can he handle his injections, his baths, and the rest of his daily care regimen? As his physician, I must strongly argue against his plan."

"I agree, but he's determined. He'll have Robinson full-time, and I'll be by. But if you think I should arrange for a nurse to come in twice a day, I will."

"I could arrange for a nurse," Preminger said.

She suppressed a grin at the thought of Tomas being sent the drunken Deidre. "I'll handle that. I want you to concentrate on one goal, Dr. Preminger, finding a cure for Tomas."

"Certainly." He inclined his head.

"I have instructed the bank to transfer funds from my trust to your clinic. It's the figure we agreed upon for the next six months of treatment. After that, we can discuss how much more you need to complete your research."

"But I thought we agreed you would fund my work for another full year?"

"I will. Six months at a time."

"However you wish to arrange it, Miss Maxwell." Preminger's round cheeks pinked.

Alana walked toward the door. "I'll be off then."

"I'll see you next Tuesday. Four o'clock?"

"That's fine." Alana headed out into the clinic's foyer. Deidre, her face as heavily made up as a stage actress's, was two-finger typing at the desk. She did not look up.

Dr. Preminger followed Alana out of the examination room and all the way to the front door.

Robinson was waiting outside. "Shall I bring the car around, Miss Maxwell?"

"Yes, please do. And put the windows down. It's hot."

"Yes, ma'am." He strode off.

Alana turned to Preminger. A question had been clawing at her throughout the appointment. "Doctor, there is one other thing. Tomas told me that a few nights ago he came into my suite and found me sitting on the couch in the dark. He thought I seemed like I was in a trance. He claims I didn't recognize him for a time."

"No?" The doctor cocked his head. "Did you?"

"I don't remember the incident he's talking about. At all."

Preminger blinked rapidly. "Do you mean you blacked out?"

"No, I mean I don't remember it at all."

"How are you sleeping?"

"Like the dead. But I'm not dreaming."

"That's because you're sleeping deeply. Has anyone else reported odd behavior from you?"

"No."

"Are you forgetting appointments, names, or incidents that happened recently?"

"Not that I remember." Her lips curved. "But then, maybe I wouldn't."

"Ha, yes, very good, Alana." Preminger opened the door as Robinson drove up. "An isolated incident isn't any reason for worry. You were overtired, sleeping even when Tomas came in. The drugs you are taking are powerful, as I've warned you. I wouldn't mix alcohol with them."

"But if I spoke to Tomas that night, why don't I remember it? Was I sleepwalking?"

"I doubt it. You don't remember the incident because you went to sleep as soon as Tomas left. The mind only recalls details it deems significant. This incident was not important to you, and it was deleted from your memory. I will note it in your chart, but I wouldn't fret over it."

"Well then, I won't. Thank you for your opinion. I'll see you next week." Alana walked to her car.

She climbed inside and took out her pack of cigarettes and lit up. As Robinson drove down the drive, she scanned the brush at the fence. There was no sign of the animal now. Had she imagined it after all? She shook her head and took another drag from the cigarette. Soon she lost herself in daydreams of the future, imagining Tomas dancing, laughing, and flirting with all the girls in the room.

Alana smiled.

She would stay positive. Hadn't she scolded Tomas to never give up hope? She needed to set a good example.

Or die trying.

Alana inhaled as the smile faded from her lips.

CHAPTER SIX

L A County Hospital covered six square blocks on Olympic Blvd in what most Angelinos referred to as East LA, as if it were a separate municipality from Los Angeles proper. It was separate only in that poor folk, immigrants, and blue-collar families lived there exclusively, Jack thought as he headed for the double glass doors.

East LA did not have an abundance of rich enclaves like Pasadena in the north, Los Feliz in the west, or Hancock Park in the south. In this mosaic city of forty-eight square miles, East LA was one neighborhood full of people barely scraping by.

Jack stopped at the nursing supervisor's desk at central patient information. He had visited twice before without success. But there was a different woman sitting at the desk now. Maybe this would be his lucky day.

The pretty, petite woman looked up and recognition beamed from her dark eyes. "Is that you, Jack Curran? How great to see you."

"Lydia Lopez." Jack leaned in and wrapped her in an embrace. He had not recognized her in her nurse's uniform. Lydia was married to a buddy of his from his Army days. The last time he had seen them was at a party at their house three years ago. "How are you? How are Joey and the kids?"

"Everyone's great. Joey and his brother Richard opened a car repair shop in Whittier. You'll have to come over and see them."

"I will. I will." He smiled. "Gosh, you look great. How long you been here at County?"

"A few months. Got my nursing degree in January." She giggled. "You look spiffy too, Mr. War Hero. What a great article about you in the *Times*." Her smile faded for a moment. "Joey always said you're the only reason he made it home."

"Joey was a great soldier, Lydia. Don't let him kid you."

She brightened again. "He's a great everything. What about you?" She glanced at his left hand. "No wedding ring?"

"Nah, I've been waiting for a sweetheart like you. Got a sister?"

"No. Are you still working at that newspaper?"

"Yeah. Yeah, *The Eyes of LA*. Actually, Lydia, that's why I'm here today. To see Joan Becklund. I've been doing stories on the crazy broad who killed the men who attacked Joan, but I'd love a moment to talk to her."

"Thrill Girl, right? Gee, Jack. The police said Miss Becklund can't have visitors." The R.N. folded her arms, suddenly not quite so friendly.

"Yeah, that's what I've heard. How's the old gal doing, by the way? Is she ready to go home?"

"If you mean is she ready to return to living on park benches, then yes, she has been medically cleared to return to her previous life. But we're trying to hold onto her until we can find a relative to take her in."

"I see." Jack had no ready line of bull for this sad situation. Down and out people from all over the country were migrating to LA. They figured that if they had to sleep outside, at least they would stay warm in LA.

"Has she fully recovered from her injuries?" Jack asked.

"No. But she's close."

"Well, if she's homeless, maybe I can help. I know of a

privately funded program that helps women living on the street. If I can talk to her about it, make sure she understands this program has no booze on the menu, maybe I can get her a place." Quentin's spinster sister was a major donor to the group, and Jack had done a piece for *The Eyes* on it.

"Gosh, that would be great." She smiled, once again a friend. "Have a seat over there." Lydia motioned to a row of chairs across from her station. "I'm going to ask Miss Becklund herself if she wants to talk to you about the program." Lydia grinned. "If anyone asks, I'll tell them I didn't know you were a journalist. Only a war hero."

"No hero here." Jack smiled to cut the edge off his words. "I'm going to get a cup of coffee. Can I get you one?"

"No, thanks. Get your coffee. I won't be long."

"Okay. Thanks, Lydia." Ten minutes later he was in the chair, slugging down coffee and reading a day old sports page lying on the table.

Both the Giants and the Yanks were stumbling, but it was a long time until September.

Lydia reappeared and tapped her finger on her watch. "Miss Becklund is in room 313. She's agreed to see you if you want to go in now."

"Great." He got up.

"I said you were a man who might be able to help her. You have fifteen minutes. Don't tire her out, okay?"

"Are you releasing her today?"

"No. Our attending signed an order for a twenty-four-hour blood work evaluation this morning. She'll have a bed for another couple of nights."

"Good work. That will give me more time to get her a place to stay." Jack tipped his hat. "Which means I'll come back tomorrow. Maybe you'll let me buy you that coffee then?"

"Sure."

Jack grabbed two carnations out of the vase of flowers on the counter and headed down the hall. A minute later he sat down at Joan Becklund's bedside.

The old gal had only a few teeth left and a face lined from decades of hard living. Her forehead was bruised where she had been bashed in the attack a few days ago, but her color was normal, and her eyes were clear.

Her left arm was fractured in the attack, and it hung in a sling across her slight body.

Jack introduced himself and hoped she wouldn't remember his name to the cops if they showed up again.

He presented her with the carnations. She smiled and asked him to put them in the empty vase by the window.

"You like flowers, Miss Becklund?"

"They're okay. They die pretty quick, though. I like them better outside and alive. And call me Joan, okay?"

"Okay. I bet you've received a lot of flowers while you were here."

Joan Becklund blinked. "Not a lot. But I got roses a couple of days ago. White ones. Seemed like a hundred of them, all tied up with a red ribbon. They smelled nice. But too strong. They made me sneeze."

"Oh yeah? White roses, huh. Who sent them?" Jack kept his voice neutral.

Joan shrugged. "No one I know has money for that. Don't think there was a name anyway. Gave them away to the nurses because I'm leaving soon, and I wouldn't be able to bring them with me."

Bells went off in his head so loud he worried she might hear them. "I'd like to talk to you about where you're planning to go after you're discharged, Miss Becklund." Jack launched into a pitch describing Quentin's sister's charity. He stressed he could help her get into the housing program as long as she agreed to a few ground rules.

"Sounds nice, but I don't know. I'm no church person, and I don't like living with a bunch of women. I was one of seven sisters, and it gets to be a catfight, all those girls."

"I understand how hard it is to try something new. But it would be safer than living on the streets, wouldn't it?"

"Maybe. Maybe not." She wiped her mouth with her sleeve. "During the war, I worked at an airplane factory in Long Beach. Assembling B52s. We worked twelve, fourteen hour days. Until I hurt my foot in an accident." She slid her leg out from under the covers. Her right foot was scarred, and she was missing part of the outer two toes. "I lost my job after that and moved back to Los Angeles. But for my money, that damned plant was more dangerous than living on the street."

"They didn't give you another job at the plant? That stinks."

"They said they would find me a job in the office or the warehouse. But I can't hardly read or write. Nothing came of it." There was no embarrassment in her voice.

"Is there a family member who could help for a while? One of those sisters?"

"We all scattered during the Depression. I hear from a couple of them, but none that would take me in. It's okay." She looked at her sling. "This is the first time I been attacked. You might not believe it, but I've got friends outside. We look after each other."

"Where were your friends the night you got mugged?" Jack was sure the cops had checked out if there were any witnesses to her assault, but it was worth asking.

"They were around." Her lip quivered. For all of Joan Becklund's bravado, she was still shaken. "I don't remember anything about that night, you know? One of my friends might be hurt too. I hope not."

"The police didn't find anyone else injured at the scene. Except for the mugger, I mean." He gentled his voice. "Do you remember the person who came to your aid?"

"The cops said I told them that it was a woman, but I don't remember nothing about it. Must have been the drink talking. I had a snoot full that night." Joan looked down.

"You can't remember now if it was a woman who helped you?"

"No."

"The cops are sure that's what you said that night. About your rescuer being a woman."

She peered up at him. "It would be strange if it was a woman, wouldn't it? A cold-blooded killer? Never heard of a girl doing such a thing."

"Well, there was Ma Barker." Jack ran through his list of infamous women. "And Lizzie Borden."

"Gave her ma and pa both forty whacks, right?" Joan grinned.

"That's what I hear. I also hear a female has helped protect three more people since you were attacked. It could be the same woman. Have the cops told you about the other attacks, Joan? Or asked you to come in to identify anyone?"

"Nope. Haven't seen the cops for a few days now."

"I see. Well, I'm sorry to bring up bad memories, but would you mind telling me what you do remember? I promised the mayor I'd get a first-hand account."

She studied his face for a few seconds and laced her fingers together. "I was walking around, waiting. It was hot. I saw a guy coming toward me, then I heard a yell, and a bright light shined into my eyes."

"A light?"

"Like a headlight. Then a guy smashed my noggin with a pipe, and I blacked out. Woke up here." She seemed uneasy. "There's too much sunshine in the afternoon. Hurts these old eyes. Could you pull the blind down behind you?"

"Sure." Out on the street he saw a dark Cadillac parked at the curb, a curtain across the back window.

Jack frowned and closed the blinds.

He returned to the chair next to the old woman. "You sure you don't remember what the person you heard yell looked like? Or what they said?" He pulled out his cigarettes and offered one to Joan.

She took two and secreted them under her blanket. "Don't light up in here. Them nurses don't like folks smoking in the rooms. They say it hurts the lungs or some such nonsense."

"Okay." He took the cigarette out of his mouth and stuck it in his shirt pocket. Casually he tossed the full pack onto the hospital bed. "Why don't you keep those? For when you get out."

Joan took the pack and stuck it under the blanket. "Thanks. I'd be thrilled to keep them."

"Thrilled?" Jack narrowed his eyes at the familiar word.

"What?"

"You said thrilled. Where did you pick up that word, Joan?"

Joan put her hand over her mouth. It was trembling. She leaned toward him and said through her fingers. "Are you a cop? I noticed you got a limp. Did you get that on the job?"

"I'm not a cop. I got the limp in the Army."

"What are you, then?" She dropped her hand. "You from the social security? Are you trying to scam me?"

"No." Jack took a breath. "I'm none of those things."

"You ain't? Then why are you lying to me? You don't work at no City Hall, a boy like you. Those men down there are hard. You're kind of soft. Kind, even. What do you really do?"

They stared at each other for a long moment.

"You're right, Joan. I lied. I'm not from the mayor's office. I work for a newspaper. It's called *The Eyes* of LA."

"Newspaper?" She waved her hand in disgust. "I told you I don't read. I don't have no use for them, do I?"

"Many people do. I'm writing a story about the woman who helped you the other night. But I don't know much about her besides she's in trouble with the cops. Can you tell me anything that might help me find her?"

"She might not want anyone to find her."

"She might not. But she's playing a dangerous game. You wouldn't want anything to happen to her, would you?"

The old lady's eyes dulled. She wiped at them, then cocked her head and gestured toward the door leading out to the hallway. "Who's out there listening to us?"

He glanced out at the empty hall. "I don't see anyone."

"Check. I heard something. Close the door, too."

"Okay." Jack got up. He had half a notion to see if the Cadillac was still at the curb, but he didn't. The door to the room next to Joan's room was closed, but there was no one in the hallway.

He shut the door except for a crack and sat back down. "No one is there. We can talk. Is there anything more you can tell me about the night you were attacked?"

Joan squirmed to get comfortable. In the gray light, Jack saw she wasn't much older than his own mother had been when she died. Though his mother had fought to have a respectable life, both had led hard lives amidst the American dream.

"What's your real name?" Joan demanded.

"It's Curran. Jack Curran. I didn't lie about that."

"What?" She scowled and closed her eyes. She didn't say anything for a long time, and Jack wondered if she was sleeping.

It would serve him right. He had not handled this visit well at all. He should have been straight from the get-go with her. His desire to get information on Thrill Girl was making him take shortcuts he never had before. He rubbed his knee, which was throbbing. "Joan, are you awake?"

"Did you lie about the free house thing?" She opened her eyes.

"Excuse me?"

"The home for old lady drunks like me. Were you making that up? Not that I'm saying I'd go, but I'd like to know if it's real or not."

"No, ma'am. That's a real place. It's called Phoenix House." He explained he would reach out on her behalf, and that he knew the woman who ran the program. "There's one on Figueroa Street. About five blocks from here."

"I'll think about it." Joan closed her eyes again.

Jack waited.

"I lied too, Mr. Curran." She opened her eyes and sat forward, lacing her bony fingers together in her lap. "I remember everything about that woman. I could never forget her. Swanky blonde. Looked like a million bucks. Dressed in a pink dress with tiny black dots. I didn't want to talk about her because I didn't want her to get in trouble for killing that man."

"She did it to defend you, right?"

Joan inhaled. "Right. She told me to turn my head, and that's when she killed him. I couldn't believe how loud her gun was. Like a firecracker went off in my ear. She hugged me when it was over, and said she would wait until she heard the cops coming. She knew they would show up because of the gunshots. She did, too. She held my hand." Joan looked into the distance. "She smelled like cinnamon. And her skin was as soft as silk."

"What else did she say, Joan?" Jack tensed. He knew the answer, but he had to hear her say it.

"When I thanked her, she said, *I'm thrilled to help you, dear. Thrilled.* Her voice was amazing." Joan's eyes sparkled. "Like a movie star, low and sweet. Almost sounded like the purr of a cat."

Goosebumps raised on his arms. "Thanks for sharing this, Joan."

What kind of freak is this dame, Jack wondered? One who gets thrills killing people? He was the one who had given her the nickname, but up until now, it had simply been an artful turn of phrase. He hadn't considered how fitting it might be.

"No one called me that before, Mr. Curran. Dear. I think she meant it, too. About being thrilled. She's the kind who don't put up with people getting pushed around. I could see that. Spunky she is. She wants to help folks. Even me, who's nothing to her. Nothing to anybody."

"You're not nothing." Jack squeezed Joan's arm.

She grinned, showing her gums. "It's the most amazing thing that happened to me in my whole life. That's why I blurted out the whole story to that bald copper the night I got whacked. I was only pretending to forget when he asked me about it again. Boy was I lucky, you know?"

"Lucky?"

"That she came along to that corner. She came, but the man I was there to meet never did show up. Lucky me."

"I don't understand," Jack said. "What man didn't show up?"

"That man I was waiting for. I met him on the street in front of the courthouse, after my arrest. When the coppers pulled me in for being drunk, even though I wasn't. Anyway, a fussy piece-of-work with nice clothes stopped me on the sidewalk and said he had work for me and my friend." She shrugged again, her words slurring with fatigue. "I don't know. I don't remember much about him. Maybe it didn't even happen. I need to rest now, Mr. Curran."

Joan arranged her sling carefully and burrowed into the bed. She closed her eyes.

"Before you go to sleep," Jack said, "may I ask one more thing? May I have your permission to print what the woman said to you in my newspaper?"

"The fuzz won't like that. They'll be mad I told them I didn't remember nothing."

"I'll handle the cops, don't worry about that. But it's up to you."

Joan squinted at him from the hospital sheets. "Go ahead. It's the truth, ain't it? That beautiful lady should get a medal."

Jack took out a business card and wrote his home phone number on the back. "This is how you can reach me at work." He tapped the number on the front. "The number on the back is for my apartment. Ask Nurse Lopez to call me before you're discharged from the hospital. I'll drive you over to Phoenix House, and introduce you to the people who can help you. If you want help."

The woman nodded. "I'm going to take a nap now. This is the softest, cleanest bed I've ever had beneath me, and I need to enjoy it while I can. Slip your card in that pack of smokes. And when your news story comes in the paper, I'll have someone read it to me."

"I'll bring you a copy and read it to you myself," he said.

Her eyes were droopy. "Suit yourself."

Jack slipped his card into the cigarette pack and tucked the pack back under the blanket near her hand. "One last thing, Joan."

"Uhuh," she whispered. "Go ahead."

"Was there a note with the white roses?"

"I think so. Look in the drawer in the table there."

He opened the drawer. There was a bible. He picked it up and found a white envelope under it. Joan's name was scrawled on the front, but the envelope was empty. The florist's name was embossed on the outside.

Lily's Lilies. On Wilshire Blvd.

"Do you know what happened to the note, Joan?"

"Nope."

"Have any idea what it said?"

"Can't read, remember?" She squeezed her eyes closed. "Goodbye, Mr. Curran."

"Goodbye until later. And thank you."

He didn't see Lydia at the desk and hurried outside. It was blazing hot. He slid into the Packard and glanced at his wristwatch. Twenty to three. Even Quentin Deville's cool demeanor would heat-up when he heard what Joan Becklund had to say, and about the roses both women received.

If an employee at Lily's Lilies could tell him who sent them to Thrill Girl's rescued citizens, he could blow the lid off the whole story.

CHAPTER SEVEN

Even though Jack knew Mr. Kim was out of town, he had stopped at his shop on the way back to the office. He was glad he had, for he had discovered an exciting piece of news from the man's nephew, who was running the place for his uncle.

When he walked through the nearly vacant newsroom, he ignored Eddie, who stood up like a pop-goes-the-weasel toy.

He rapped on Quentin's office door. "I'll see you in a minute," he said to the kid. It was after five p.m. Quentin was waiting for him.

"Well, Mr. Curran. I understand from Eddie that we have a quote for the Thrill Girl special?" He leaned back languidly in his desk chair.

"Yes. Several in fact." Jack threw his hat on the side table, sat and lit a cigarette. "Susan Baldwin's mother, Ellen, confirmed it was a blonde woman who saved Susan when I went to see her this morning. She also said Susan had referred to the woman as *Thrill Girl*." He grinned.

"Very good. You informed Mrs. Baldwin you were going to use her quote in your story and expose her to the wrath of the LAPD?"

"I haven't told either of them anything yet. My plan is to see Susan later, tell her what I'm working on, and why we need her help. I think I can persuade her to give us an exclusive."

"An exclusive? You do have confidence in your charm, Mr. Curran." Deville's eyebrows, which looked like they were drawn on with a charcoal pencil, arched higher. "Of course, after you admit you've been lying to her, she may call Detective Glass and have you arrested. Then I'll have to hire a new reporter since you'll rot in jail for the next ten years. I do believe it's a felony to pose as a public servant."

"No jury of my peers would convict me. I'm just trying to keep the public informed."

Deville picked nonexistent fuzz off his lapel. "Tell me about Susan Baldwin. Do you really think she'll open up?"

"I don't know." He thought about his interview earlier. "She's worried about the police. I think she might be hiding something." He was bursting to tell Quentin about his conversation with Joan Becklund, but Quentin liked a calm delivery of facts. In chronological order.

"Hiding what? A criminal background? You said she was a solid, working-class woman?"

"She is. She's a kid, only nineteen, but she seems older. Susan's mom is a widow with a drinking problem, and there's a younger boy in the household. Could be her brother, or maybe her own child. Eddie's checking on that for me. But one of the bedrooms is rigged up like a hospital room, and I think he's sickly, which has got to be expensive."

"She's got a lot on her plate."

"I think she does, but she seems up to handling it."

"You sound smitten."

Jack lit a cigarette and blew a series of smoke rings above his head. "I admire her grit. She didn't let the memory of two bastards lying gutted in the street keep her from going to work the day after they attacked her."

"What a colorful phrase, 'gutted in the street.' You should be a writer, Jack."

"I'm trying."

Quentin pointed at him. "Try harder. Even if we get Ellen Baldwin's quote, it's not enough to warrant a Special Edition. Even though it is attack number four, it could wait until our regular edition on Tuesday."

"Before you decide that, you need to hear the rest. There's more. A lot more." Excitement colored his voice. "I got in to see Joan Becklund today at the hospital." Jack stretched out his leg as he carefully repeated most of his conversation, ending with a verbatim replay of Joan Becklund's words. "So the blonde tells her, *'I'm thrilled I could help you.'*"

Quentin seldom looked impressed, but there was no mistaking his expression now. "Well, that's quite a story. Same as what Thrill Girl said to Mr. Kim?"

"Word for word."

"And Miss Becklund said she told the cops all of this the night she was mugged?"

"Joan said she told the 'bald copper' all about it. She had to mean Jimmy Glass."

"Well, well." Quentin tapped his cigarette holder on Jack's desk. "The good detective has done a stellar job of keeping that particular quote out of the news reports. I thought perhaps Mr. Kim's telling you about the 'I'm thrilled' thing was just a one-of. But if the blonde said it more than once, it seems to prove it's the same woman."

"Thrill Girl was certainly the right nickname to hang on her, wasn't it?" Jack grinned.

"Proud of that, are you?"

"Everyone's calling her that now. So yeah, I guess I am."

"The nickname is lurid as a whore's mouth, but it's a winner, all right." Quentin pulled his appointment diary closer and drew a circle around Saturday. "We'll go with a Special Edition. I need that final copy, Jack. Sooner rather than late."

"You'll have it." Jack stood. "By the way, there's another angle I'm pursuing that could necessitate a special next week, too."

Skepticism regained control of Quentin's features. "Don't get greedy, Jack. What else do you have?"

"Joan Becklund got white roses from a stranger in the hospital. Expensive ones all tied up with a red ribbon and delivered to her hospital room. From a place on Wilshire. I'm going to go out there before they close tonight to try and find out who sent them." Jack pulled the tiny, folded envelope out and tossed it onto the desk. "If there was a card in there, Joan doesn't have it anymore."

"Why are we interested in this?"

"Because Susan Baldwin also got two dozen white roses this morning. *From the same florist*."

Deville was quiet for a moment. "Two dozen?" He whistled. "Sounds like you're not the only one who likes Susan Baldwin."

"Her mom said Susan didn't know the person who sent them."

Quentin sniffed and leaned away from the envelope. "What do Susan Baldwin's two dozen unappreciated flowers have to do with Joan Becklund's? Even if the same florist sent both women flowers, what's the connection?"

Jack paced as he talked. "When I left Joan's, I stopped over at Mr. Kim's market because I remembered that when I was in there a couple of days after he was mugged, I noticed several bunches of dried herbs and flowers hanging on the wall. They were upside down. I guess that's how you dry them. Anyway, they were *white roses*. A lot of them."

"Like Susan's? And Joan's?"

"Exactly."

Quentin fell silent, but Jack could almost hear the man's thoughts clanging against one another.

"My god, this could be important. Roses?"

"Strange but true." Jack shrugged. "I asked Kim's nephew about the ones I saw in his store. He said he didn't know where they came from, but confirmed his uncle got them after he was saved by our girl. Mr. Kim told the nephew to dry them, and they could use them to make tea."

"Rosehip." Quentin blinked.

"Excuse me?"

"You make tea from rose hips, the berry pouches on the stems. They're full of seeds. You dry and boil them. The government put out handbooks during the war telling maids and housewives to go to their gardens, and use rose hips because they were very high in vitamin C. More than oranges, even, and of course cheaper."

Jack stubbed out his cigarette. A phone rang out on the floor, his phone, and he saw Eddie grab it. "Do you know everything, Quentin? "

"I try to." Deville clenched his ivory holder in his perfect white teeth. "This is certainly a lot to digest."

"I think so too."

"Of course, even if all the victims got roses, it could be completely innocent. Their names were printed in all the newspapers. Any random person could have found out their address and sent the roses to cheer them up."

"That's true." Jack grabbed his hat. "But you don't believe that any more than I do. Which is why I'm heading over to the florist." Jack glanced at his watch. "I'll be back here to write it up by ten tonight. You'll have it on your desk when you come in tomorrow."

"Good luck."

Jack hurried out the door, waving off Eddie's "Mr. Curran, you have another message!"

"I'll call you later, Eddie." He had a lot to do and not enough time to do it.

# # #

Jack walked into Lily's Lilies on Wilshire and glanced around. It was a posh joint in a high rent district. The woman behind the counter, Mary Ann Little, her name tag read, looked like she would be worth what it would cost to take her to dinner. She was pretty in a fleeting way, with a direct gaze that said she knew how to please a man, and was ready to.

"Can I help you?" she asked.

"I bet you can." Jack lit a cigarette and offered it to her.

She took it and gave it a serious suck, then handed it back to him.

Jack put his mouth on the moist end and inhaled before introducing himself. "Do you read *The Eyes of LA*, Mary Ann?"

"I've seen it."

"You like the pictures?"

"Yeah." She smiled. "But I *can* read, though. If that's what you mean."

"I knew you were smart the minute I walked in the door." He leaned on the counter. "I'm doing research for a story, and I need to find out who sent flowers to a residence on Mariposa Avenue yesterday. Can you look at your receipts and give me the information? Two dozen white roses." He casually pressed two crisp dollar bills onto the counter. "I don't need to tell anyone where I got the information."

Mary Ann put her finger on the money and dragged it toward her. She slid it inside her blouse, her eyes on Jack's face. "I do remember the woman who ordered those. She's been in before."

"A woman sent the flowers?" Jack's brain buzzed. *A woman?* He had not let himself expect this.

Mary Ann walked to a file drawer and pulled out a yellow ordering form. She brought it over to him. "Here it is."

Jack saw Susan Baldwin's name and address in the 'deliver to' section. The 'from' information was blank. "You got a name for the dame who bought the roses?"

"No. And she wasn't a dame. She was a lady, classy if you know what I mean. Rich. Even has a chauffeur. A Negro." Mary Ann's eyes widened. "He waited outside."

"How did she pay?"

"Cash. She doesn't have an account with us. I asked her if she wanted to open one, but she didn't." Mary Ann leaned on her arms, giving him a view of his money tucked into her cleavage. "She's a worry wart. Called the morning after she ordered them to check if the flowers were delivered. Said she wanted to be sure we included her card."

"You don't happen to know what she wrote on that card, do you?"

"Nope. She sealed it herself."

Jack cursed silently. "What's this lady look like?"

"Why on earth would you need to know that for your story?" Mary Ann pursed her lips together.

"I like to paint a picture for my readers," Jack replied smoothly. "It helps if I have a good sense of the people who were involved."

"Spiffy dresser. Rich. Blonde. About twenty-five, I'd say."

Jack dropped his cigarette in the ashtray on the counter. He kept his eyes down because he did not want the flower clerk to see the excitement in them.

Once he had himself under control, he looked up. "The rich lady came in and ordered flowers. Then called the next day to make sure you'd sent them. That woman takes her gift giving seriously."

"No kidding. The other times she ordered, she also called to check that the flowers had gone out."

"Other times? How many other times has she bought flowers here?"

"A lot. Half a dozen, maybe."

Thrill Girl had saved people on four occasions, as far as he knew. *Could there have been other attacks the cops were hushing up?* "But you're sure you don't know her name or address?"

"Nope. But I think she lives around here."

"Why?"

"She bought flowers for herself once. Irises and daffodils. She wouldn't let me vase them or wrap them up fussy like most of the society ladies ask me to do. Said she didn't have far to go before she could put them in water, so I put cellophane around them."

"I see."

Mary Ann poked Jack in the arm. "You said you were doing a story, Mr. Curran. But you seem pretty interested in this woman. If you don't mind me saying, this blonde looks out of your league."

Jack looked pointedly at Mary Ann's dark hair. "Yeah? That's okay; blondes aren't my type." He leaned closer. "The dame has a driver, huh?"

"Uh huh." She rubbed her arms up and down. "He's big, too. Scary. I wouldn't want to be alone in a car with a man like that."

Jack tightened his jaw. He tapped Mary Ann's freckled nose. "What else did you notice about this woman? What kind of car is the big man driving her around in?"

"It's a huge one with lots of chrome."

Jack bet if he hit the restaurants and gas stations in the area he would find anyone else who had seen a well-dressed white woman with a black chauffeur. Someone who actually knew her name.

"Do you know when she first bought flowers here?"

"It's been a couple of months. My boss is due at any minute, but I could go back through the receipts before I go home. The bouquets she sent out were all the same – two dozen white roses." The clerk leaned on her elbows. "I can call you later. How's that sound?"

"Sounds great." Jack slid a business card across the counter to her. "There's another couple of bucks in it for you if you check the receipts for the last six months. And I need the addresses and names of the recipients."

"Okay." Mary Ann tapped his business card against her bottom lip. "How about if I bring the information over to your office instead of calling? Then you could buy me a drink."

Jack winked. "That might work. See you later, doll."

He beat it out of the store before Mary Ann leaped over the counter at him. She was a tad too willing for his tastes. And her sentiments about Negroes, though common enough, rankled. He had fought side by side with men of color in the war. He had admired their skills and knew first-hand they bled red when they died for America, like any man.

# # #

Jack scanned the façade of Bullocks Department Store from the bus bench across the street. The gleaming, twelve-foot-high windows, cleaned each morning, were intimidating enough to keep the riff-raff at bay, and the store's dazzling art deco tower beckoned the way for the upper crust. The building sprawled along an entire block of Wilshire Boulevard.

He had been inside a couple of times, he had even written an article about the place after Bette Davis held a luncheon there, but the store gave him the willies. Inside, he felt as if the clerks were expecting him to trip on the glossy marble floors. Not because of his gimp leg, but because they sensed he was a tire maker's son from Akron, who had no business buying underwear in the same store where Gary Cooper shopped.

The war hadn't changed how important having money was to getting respect in America, he thought. Even from poor shop clerks. With a sigh, Jack shifted his weight and kept an eye on the employee's exit, moving his thoughts to the latest twists in the Thrill Girl story.

An hour ago, he cruised by last night's crime scene and talked to the derelicts on the street. No one he had spoken to knew anything, but according to the locals, one guy, Trixie, who was passed out dead drunk, had been mouthing off earlier. His buddy, who would not give a name, said Trixie had mentioned seeing strange things the night before, "bright lights" the bum had insisted.

"But Trixie sees lots of weird shit," his buddy had added. "One time he said he saw a flying saucer crash into a herd of cows on Third Street."

Jack had given the guy his card and told him to have Trixie call him once he sobered up. He needed to ask Susan about lights.

Ellen and Joan had both mentioned them too.

Just then, Susan walked down the stairs to the sidewalk. She wore a navy suit and a string of white beads. The dressing on her hand was wrapped over in a scarf as if to disguise her injury.

"Hey, Susan!" Jack waved.

She returned a tentative acknowledgment and crossed the street to him. "What are you doing here, Mr. Curran? The Mayor sent you again?"

Her words dinged Jack's conscience. "I was thinking you might be nervous walking home tonight, and I came over to walk a different route with you. Or, even better, take you out to dinner."

Susan frowned. "You want to take me to dinner? Did the

Mayor ask you to do that, too?"

"No." He smiled and flicked his cigarette into the gutter. "That's all my idea. How about a steak?"

"I can't go to dinner with you."

"Why not?"

"The police don't want me talking about what happened last night. *To anyone.* I told you that this morning."

Jack shrugged. "And that's fine with me. We can talk about other stuff."

"Like what?"

"The weather. Or President Truman. Or how the Giants are going to beat the Yankees in the series this year."

"I don't know anything about baseball."

"That's okay. There are plenty of things I don't know anything about. The weather, for one. For example, why is it freakishly warm all the time in Los Angeles? I'm from Ohio, and we have a big change of seasons. How do you people live here without a break from all this sunshine?"

The shadow of a smile played on her pretty mouth. "We have seasons. It gets cold. For a month or two. In the morning, anyway." She tucked her purse closer under her arm. "Look, I need to get home. But thank you for the invitation."

Jack fell into step with her as she headed toward Mariposa Street, four blocks east. "Okay. But I'd still like to talk about the President. He used to sell hats, did you know that?"

The smile bloomed. "Yeah. I read that story in *Life* magazine, too. But I don't think I should be talking to you about anything."

"I'm harmless."

She gave him a sideways look. "I don't want to risk getting the cops mad at me. I don't need them coming out to my house and upsetting my mother."

"I won't do anything to cause you any problems with the cops."

"You will if I talk to you."

"Okay, no talking. But may I walk you home?"

She looked around quickly. "Suit yourself."

They walked a block. As the silence lengthened, Jack rubbed his face and wished he had shaved again. His five o'clock shadow brought new meaning to the word shadow.

A black-and-white cruiser stopped at the curb in front of them.

"Oh my god," Susan whispered.

"It's okay." Jack took her gently by the elbow. He did not recognize the cop in the passenger seat. The car pulled a U-turn and on came the sirens and lights as it screeched off in the opposite direction.

"See? They aren't watching you." Jack dropped his hand from her arm. "You sure you can't grab a bite?"

"How do you know I don't already have a date?" Susan asked.

The question caught Jack off guard. "I'd never be surprised to hear you had a date, Susan. Do you?"

She laughed, a surprisingly mature sound from a girl this young. "I don't have a date tonight. I never do. As I said, I have other responsibilities."

"Responsibilities?" He thought of the oxygen sign posted in her house. He called and checked, but Eddie hadn't yet turned up anything on a boy in the house. "We all have those. But are yours so big they don't give you a night off?"

She stopped walking. "It's not only my mom I have to think of. My brother, Paul, is sick and lives in a hospital. But he comes home weekends. I don't want the police coming around when he's there. He gets agitated around strangers, and besides, he needs rest and quiet. Not visitors."

That explains that, Jack thought. A knot of guilt formed in his gut. "That's a tough break. I'm sorry to hear he's ill, Susan."

"Are you? Then you should stop asking questions."

He took a step back. "I..."

"I work forty-six hours a week. I need that money to help take care of my brother, and I can't let what happened last night jeopardize my income. If the cops decide to haul me into jail for talking to you and I miss work, I could lose my job. It would ruin everything. Can you understand that, Mr. Curran?"

"I can. Yes, of course." The knot in his gut tightened. *Now*, he thought. *Tell her now who you are.*

Before he could begin, Susan interrupted his thoughts.

"The biggest reason I can't go out tonight is that Paul is coming home from the hospital in the morning for a long weekend." She started walking again. "I'm making cookies. Oatmeal with raisins. And I got a pot roast. Paul loves pot roast."

"Sounds like a feast." Jack tried to fit Ellen Baldwin into the happy scene Susan was painting. "Does your mom cook, too?"

"No, only me."

"Paul's lucky to have you."

"I'm lucky to have him."

They stopped in front of her house on Mariposa. A breeze picked up out of nowhere, blowing Susan's hair into her face. She reached up and pushed it away, looking once again like the nineteen-year-old she was.

"Thank you," she said. "I've never had a man walk me home from work before. I hope it's not because the Mayor told you to."

Jack put his hand under Susan's left elbow and squeezed. She smelled like lilac. "I'm nice to you because I like you, Susan."

"I like you, too. Maybe you should ask me to dinner again in a few weeks. If it's okay with the Mayor." She turned her face up.

Jack dropped his hand. "I don't work for the mayor, Susan. I'm a reporter for *The Eyes of LA*. I lied to you this morning."

Susan drew her arms up to her chest and moaned deep in her throat.

"I'm sorry I did that. But I need to ask you a couple of questions about the woman who attacked those men. You told your mother you thought she was Thrill Girl. Can you describe the woman for me?"

"I can't believe this. You lied to me." Tears filled her brown eyes. "You can't write about anything my mother said. It will get me into trouble. How could you…"

The sound of Susan's mother screaming from the front stoop

stopped all conversation. "Susan Yvonne! You better come inside. I knew you would get yourself into trouble. The police were here looking for you earlier. And they're coming back."

"Oh no." Susan took off running toward the door.

Ellen gripped the railing, the front door wide open, and Snowball darted past her, aiming straight for Jack. The dog was yipping and yapping and barking its fool head off, fangs bared as if it wanted to kill him.

At that moment a dark sedan with a revolving red police light on the roof sped up the street. Before Jack could register what was happening, the dog latched onto the calf of his right leg and bit down for all it was worth. He shook it off reflexively, sending the mutt rolling into the path of the car.

Susan screamed.

Ellen screamed.

The sedan skidded to a stop with a squeal of tires, its rear end fishtailing into the curb beside Jack. He scrambled out of the way, but there was no mistaking the dull thud and pained yelp that followed.

Both women screamed again in horror.

"Jack Curran!" Jimmy Glass yelled as he jumped out of the car, his pistol drawn. "You're under arrest. Put your hands up now!"

Susan rushed to the car. "You killed my dog!" Oblivious to the gun, she slapped at Glass's arm with her open hand several times, crying hysterically, and fell to her knees.

Jack moved to intercede, but the detective pointed his gun at his forehead. "Stay right where you are, Curran."

Glass looked down at Susan. "Calm down, Miss Baldwin."

She cried louder as she gathered the broken body of her pet in her arms.

"You sons of bitches coppers! Don't hurt her!" Ellen lurched off the last step of the porch and fell into a heap on the front lawn.

"You better get an ambulance," Jack shouted to the detective.

Glass stepped around Susan and slapped cuffs on Jack's

wrists. "Shut up, Curran." He shook his head. "The mutt should have been on a leash."

Behind him, Glass's partner Stu Martin shoved Jack against the side of the car. "Spread 'em, asshole," he said.

Jack sprawled, falling head down against the hood. The metal was hot, near to burning against his cheek, but he stayed put.

Neighbors poured out onto the sidewalk on both sides of the street. Jack heard the police dispatcher asking for information, followed by the crackle of the police radio as Glass called for more units for crowd control. Another patrol car slid to a stop at the far end of Mariposa, blocking the west end of the street.

There were sirens in the distance, but all Jack heard was Susan crying. He lifted his head to tell her he was sorry, only to have it slammed down a second time.

"If you fucking move again, I'll break your arms." Detective Martin jerked the handcuffs hard.

Jack's bum knee banged against the bumper and pain radiated through his thigh. "You acting like the SS because I talked to one of your crime victims?" Jack shouted at Martin. "What the hell? Ever heard of freedom of the press?"

"Shut up."

Jack tasted blood on his lip. "I'm going to make sure to spell your name right in the front page article I'm writing about police abuse."

"You're not under arrest for that, shit head."

"Put Curran in the car, Stu," Glass yelled.

Martin pulled Jack by the neck as another uniform came over to help. It was Lucas O'Connor.

"Hey, it's the war hero." O'Connor put his huge hand on top of Jack's head, helping Martin push him into the backseat of the cruiser.

"Don't go anywhere, Curran. I wouldn't want to have to waste a bullet on you." O'Connor smirked and yelled at the crowd. "Attention, everyone step away! This is a crime scene!"

Jack licked the blood off his lip. His heart was beating hard enough to blow an artery. He took four deep breaths to clear his head.

When he peered out the window, Jimmy Glass was conferring with the uniforms. A patrolman was helping a clearly confused Ellen Baldwin up off the grass and into the house, and Stu Martin led Susan, still clutching Snowball, up the stairs.

Jimmy Glass leaned inside the car. "You should have returned my call, Curran. If you'd come into the station, this whole ugly scene could have been avoided."

"Why the show of force, Detective?"

"We heard you were spotted hanging around the police garage this morning. I called you to tell you to butt out. But you didn't warrant my personal attention until tonight when you became a suspect."

"A suspect in what?" Jack looked behind him at his handcuffed arms. "And what's with the cuffs? Afraid I might write down your badge number?"

"If you don't have a lawyer, I suggest you get one pronto. You're under arrest for murder."

"For murder?" Jack felt a sudden flash of fear. It was the same feeling he had experienced in Italy every time the first shot rang out in a battle. "Who am I supposed to have murdered?"

"Joan Becklund. She was found thirty minutes after you left her this afternoon at county hospital. Suffocated with a pillow." Glass frowned as if he were personally disappointed in Jack's crime skills. "We found your business card tucked nice and tight into the old drunk's pack of Lucky Strikes. Those smokes weren't as *lucky* for you, Curran."

"I didn't kill Joan Becklund. She was alive when I left the hospital." Jack sounded like the defendant in every crime story he had ever read.

Or written.

The ambulance siren drowned out Glass's reply.

But Jack knew the detective wasn't saying anything that would fix the disaster this night had spiraled into.

CHAPTER EIGHT

Hank Rhodes was a drunk.

He lived on the streets below the Griffith Park Observatory at night. During the day he sat outside the Los Angeles Zoo with a handful of pencils and a beggar's cup until the cops hauled him off.

He ate once or twice a week in jail, and once or twice a week from the trash cans at the zoo. The rest of the time he ate at the Mission kitchen down on Figueroa.

But he had not been to the Mission this week. Too many do-gooders and holy rollers hung around there now, trying to get him into an alcohol abuse program for vets.

At three a.m., Hank woke up in the high grass near the service road of the Observatory parking lot. A sound had roused him from his stupor, but he was too groggy to tell what it was.

A coyote or a dog?

He rolled over and reached for more whiskey, but the bottle was empty. Cussing to himself, he pulled the greasy sleeping bag up to his neck. He started kicking his legs to get the blood flowing but stopped when he heard a rustling in the tree line.

Whatever creature had made the sound was coming nearer, moving through the high grass, thrashing, and panting. The sounds chilled him and made him flashback to being a teenager in WWI France.

In the trenches.

There was a loud snarl, and then a growl and the hair on Hank's arms rose up. He saw eyes. Glowing gold eyes looking at him where he lay.

Hank curled up tight and held his breath, hoping the thing would not come any nearer.

For a moment nothing happened.

Hank stared at the creature. Maybe after thirty years of drinking, he was starting to full-on lose it. He squinted at the bulky shape in the weeds.

No, he had never had a hallucination like this one. The thing even had a fetid animal smell. *It's real.* And it was watching him.

After a moment of studying it in the dark, Hank let out a ragged exhale.

His senses had deceived him. It was only a boy.

Skinny and pale, the kid looked no more than twelve or fourteen. He was lying on his side and moaning. One of the kid's hands was stretched out toward Hank like he was begging.

What the hell is wrong with him?

Hank sat up and spat, rubbing his eyes to get a clearer look. Was the kid hurt? Had someone dumped him here?

His arms and legs trembled as he stumbled to his feet, and for a moment, Hank wondered again if he was awake.

The boy let out a scream more horrible than any sound Hank had ever heard a human make.

The sound split his head like an ax.

Hank put his hands over his ears, but he could not block it out.

As he made that ungodly sound, the boy lurched up onto his knees and crawled closer. What happened next, Hank could hardly believe, especially since the whiskey had long since worn off.

The boy, who from a distance looked normal but sickly a moment before, was, in reality, a mass of twitching, convulsing, writhing flesh. The clothes covering his body were torn to shreds, revealing patches of hair like a wolf's. His face was covered with the stuff, even on his nose and forehead, and he had claws, curved and yellow and deadly, on his misshapen hands. As Hank stared at the thing, its ears, with perked-up points at the top, twitched.

Hank whimpered and moved slowly backward on the slick grass. He kept his eyes on the creature, petrified by the sharp whiskers that seemed to have sprouted from its nose. Its eyes were bright as they bored into Hank's.

The boy threw his head back and howled like a nightmare come to life, and Hank screamed. He raised his fists to defend himself as a second figure emerged from the tree line and galloped toward him.

"Help!" Hank called out.

But there was no helping him now.

The attack was merciless, more terrifying even than that night in the trenches at the Battle of the Somme when rats had swarmed over his unit, biting, growling, and ripping men apart while he lay there with his empty gun, impotent against attack.

Hank Rhodes knew he was going to die. There was no bargaining for his life, no postponing the fall into nothingness. No chance to have one last conversation, one last kiss, or one last gulp of liquor.

He had a second to feel regret for his wasted life, but only a second.

# # #

The jailer let Jack use a telephone at three o'clock on Thursday afternoon. He knew he should call Quentin, but he needed to talk to Eddie first.

"*The Eyes of LA*, this is Eddie Wentz."

"Eddie, it's Jack."

"Mr. Curran! Are you really in jail?"

"Yes. Now shut up and listen. I need you to grab a taxi to Bullocks Department Store and get my notebook out of the Packard. It's in the back lot. My column on Joan Becklund is in there. Give it to Quentin. As soon as I get cleared of suspicion of having anything to do with her death, he'll want it ready."

"But-"

"Don't talk. Listen and write. After you get the column to Deville, you need to canvas the gas stations and restaurants a couple of blocks on either side of Wilshire Blvd." Jack gave him the address of Lily's Lilies, as well as the shop girl's description of the car. He added the fact that the dame had a black driver.

"*Why* am I doing this?"

"You're trying to find a woman connected to the Thrill Girl case. Take some petty cash from my drawer and spread it around. Someone in the neighborhood must have noticed this woman, a big foreign car and a chauffeur. If you find the vehicle before I get out, call our contact at the Department of Motor Vehicles. Say you're calling for me and she'll get you the information on who owns the thing. You got all that?"

"Yes, sir. But Mr. Curran, I have to tell you something before you hang up."

"Shoot. I don't have much time."

Eddie took a nervous breath. "Mr. Deville knocked Thrill Girl off the front page of the Special, and he's moved it to tomorrow instead. And he's hired a lawyer for you."

"Two minutes, Curran!" The custody officer kicked Jack's chair.

"Take it easy!" Jack glared at the cop. Could he have heard Eddie correctly? What he was saying made no sense.

"Say again, Eddie. What are you talking about? Why would he knock Thrill Girl off the front page of the Special? She's the reason we're doing the goddamned thing!"

"There's a bigger story. Last night a homeless guy was killed by some kind of monster up at Griffith Park. It ripped the bum's head off. Lucy got a source at the 06 who is feeding her information. It's a huge story, Mr. Curran!" His voice rose higher with every word.

"Where the hell is Quentin? Put him on!" Jack stomped his heel against the floor, sending a flash of pain up his leg.

"Time's up, war hero." The cop jerked the phone receiver out of Jack's hand and slammed it down. He pointed his club to the left. "Lock up. That way. Now."

Jack's arm tensed to throw a punch and knock the son of a bitch cop on his ass, but the reality of what would follow cut through his fog of anger.

He clenched both fists. "I get another telephone call tomorrow, right?"

"If you ain't shipped out."

Jack unclenched his hands. "Okay. Hey, you got a cigarette?"

"No smoking in here. Get going, and you'll get dinner and a smoke before they do final lock up." The cop gestured toward the hallway.

"Thanks." Jack limped down the hall.

A fucking monster? Jesus H. Christ. What's going to happen next? Martians land in the Coliseum?

# # #

Friday at ten a.m., Quentin Deville and Jasper Meeks, a Los Angeles criminal attorney Jack knew from his reputation for the aggressive defense of the rich and powerful, met him in the discharge area of the Los Angeles County Jail.

Jack had a black eye and a headache to go with his swollen lip. He had picked up the shiner in his jail cell last night after a punk named Fat Rodney decided to cold-cock him and steal his jacket.

The brush-up had cost Jack his telephone privileges and dinner last night. There were a hundred questions he wanted to ask his boss, but the most important one came out first.

"Am I really getting out?"

"Yes." The attorney extended his hand. "Jasper Meeks. You look like a welterweight who was downed in the sixth round, Mr. Curran." Meeks handed Jack a brown envelope with his wallet and personal effects inside. "It's nice to meet you."

"Thank you for your help, Mr. Meeks. And for the record, I feel ten times worse than I look." Jack tucked the envelope under his arm and turned to his boss.

"Hello, Quentin. How bad did I screw up your night?"

"Bad. But as I don't have children, I have the luxury of putting an employee's arrest ahead of my dinner plans. When you telephoned Eddie, who is apoplectic with worry, by the way, I had already made a strategic call to Jasper. Lucky for us, he was available."

Jack chewed his lip. Meeks wore a bespoke three-piece grey suit and a black bowler hat. An antique pocket watch on a gold chain, worth more than Jack's Packard, hung from his vest pocket.

The man reeked power and connections.

Jack felt like kissing him. "They said they weren't going to let me post bail until I was arraigned on Monday."

"Change of plans. I'll let Quentin explain the details."

Quentin guided Jack by the elbow as the three men headed for the exit under the hostile gaze of several uniformed policemen. "Jasper called the DA last night and raised several varieties of hell about your arrest. When he arrived at the jail this morning, he found out they've dropped the murder charge against you."

Jack stopped. "What? That's great. But what changed?"

"Millie Hatchett is insistent that Joan Becklund was murdered with an overdose of drugs, not a pillow," Meeks replied. "I pointed out to the DA that since you have neither a prior record nor any known access to or expertise with drugs, it was going to be a hard sell to keep you in custody. The DA quashed the warrant. For now."

They stepped into the elevator and began the slow trip down.

"I can't believe Joan Becklund is dead," Jack said, running a hand through his hair. "Who would want to kill her?"

And why.

"It may have been a mistake. I doubt she was even smothered. Most likely a nurse gave her the wrong dose of medicine, and she died in her sleep." Meeks shrugged. "Indigent patients die at a higher rate than the rest of us. But it's the hospital's problem now." The attorney straightened his silk tie. "You need to know the police are talking about filing charges against you for witness tampering via the Baldwins and for withholding information about an active criminal investigation given to you by Miss Becklund.

They also know you've called the Taylor boys' mother several times and visited Mr. Kim's store again. They're upset with you. In my opinion, they're posturing because they know they overreached in arresting you. They're worried you'll sue."

"Would I get anywhere if I did?"

"No. But we could stretch out the bad publicity, and my fees, if that's what you want."

"We don't want that," Quentin said quickly.

"Then be sure you keep to the speed limit, Jack." Jasper's voice was stern. "Don't give the police any reason at all to bring you in."

"The coppers are after us now." Quentin sounded happy about this situation. "Your arrest was about more than Joan Becklund, in my opinion. And despite Jasper's advice that we should back off this story, we are of course going to stay on it. Hard. Our coverage is going to be even bigger now that one of the rescued victims has turned up murdered."

"Speaking of murdered, that monster in the park story was a horrific thing to wake up to, Quentin." The lawyer narrowed his eyes. "Do the police know what kind of animal killed that man?"

"The police speculation is that it's a big cat of some kind. Mountain lion maybe."

"The special made it out onto the stands this morning?" Jack asked. "On a Friday?" His feelings were raw, and he knew it showed.

"It did," Quentin said. "I had to pay the print shop men overtime to work a double shift, but I wanted it out on the streets today. The other papers will be all over it this afternoon. Our subscribers had theirs delivered first thing. And we've got five thousand on newsstands and racks."

Jasper shook his head. "I worry about the state of our society that a picture of a man without his head attached could be published at all." He pointed his finger at Quentin. "Next time I'm going to get a call to get you out of jail."

"Counselor, you give me too much credit. It was a drawing, after all. Grotesque and violent, but that's what people like with their Wheaties." Deville bit down on his cigarette holder. "Sales will be amazing."

Jack cracked his knuckles as the elevator chugged to street level. He wanted another cigarette but was too tired to dig out his pack and lighter.

"I'm hoping my car is still parked in the lot behind Bullocks. Can you drop me there?" Jack squinted at Quentin as they came out into the sunshine.

"Yes, of course." The publisher shook hands with Jasper. "Thank you, sir. For your promptness and your discretion. Will I see you Sunday at the Monroe's' party?"

"Sadly, yes. My wife has insisted."

The two men shared polite chitchat about mutual friends, and then Meeks turned to face Jack. "I'll be in touch, Mr. Curran. Did the cops rough up more than your mouth? You seem to be limping. I would suggest you have a doctor look you over."

"I don't need to see a doctor. I'm fine." Jack smiled around his swollen lip.

"He always limps. War wound. I told you about all that, Jasper. Remember?" Quentin raised his brows. "Italy. The Battle of Naples in '44? This man is a genuine war hero."

"Well, in that case, let me add my thanks for your efforts in the war, Jack. And bid you goodbye. I urge you to have an uneventful weekend."

He walked to a chauffeured Lincoln waiting in the no-parking zone in front of the jail. Meeks glanced at the cop standing beside it, and the cop saluted.

"No reason to trot out the war, Quentin," Jack grumbled. "That hero bullshit is getting old."

"You're too modest by half. And sharing your exploits helps open doors, especially for a man like Jasper, who has deep connections in the military. He'll work harder for us now. With a lawyer that successful, a client needs to throw a little extra into the pot to keep him interested." Quentin dropped his voice. "He loves helping veterans. The dead guy the monster ate for breakfast was a vet, too. Though I imagine Jasper saw immediately there were no billable hours to be had there."

Jack shook his head as Quentin chuckled.

"I know Eddie only told you the bare bones of the monster story. Let me fill you in on Miss Cherry's amazingly sourced reporting." Deville summed up the details as they walked the long block to where Quentin was parked.

"That's crazy," Jack said. "Surely the cops know it's only an animal attack. Not a monster."

"Of course, but the public loves to be entertained. It's most likely a rabid cougar, but it is fun for now." He pointed to his ancient Bentley on the other side of the boulevard. "My car is on the side of the street without police protection. Would you like to stop and get breakfast? I assume jail food is inedible."

"No, thanks. I'll go home and shower. That way I can get to the office by noon. I want to rough out a new Thrill Girl column as soon as I can. Do you know if Eddie got anything for me on the Rolls?"

"I'm not sure. I'll let him fill you in. He called early this morning to say he would be in around lunchtime because he's doing field work."

"Good." He hoped Eddie would have a name for the woman who owned the fancy car and had a predilection for sending flowers.

Deville pulled a cigarette from his case and offered one to Jack, who gladly took it. "Eddie said your arrest made *The Times*, by the way. Along with Miss Baldwin's dead dog. Although the article merely stated that you were detained by police at a private residence. They kept Susan Baldwin's name out of it for now. Evidently, they don't want you to be publicly linked to any more of Thrill Girl's crime victims."

"Bastards."

"I think they're worried you're on to something, and it makes them look bad. Between Thrill Girl, your arrest, and our monster exclusive, it's going to be a busy few weeks at *The Eyes*."

"An embarrassment of riches."

"How eloquent. Isn't it lucky you write for a living?" Quentin pulled his keys out of his pocket. "By the way, I took a message from a young woman in Mr. Sydney Goldblum's office for you. Seems you have a lunch appointment? I guess I should think about hiring more staff."

Jack blew out a lungful of air. He was in all ways exhausted and did not want to explain his conversation with Sydney Goldblum. "That doesn't have anything to do with work."

"No? They called you at the office."

"It's nothing, Quentin."

"Good." Quentin smiled, but only with his mouth.

They crossed the street to the car. The sun was hot and bright, but Jack was cold inside as he walked around to the passenger side and got in.

He slammed the door. He had to call and tell Goldblum's secretary he didn't have time for lunch. There were other things more pressing, like trying to talk to Susan. He had to apologize for lying, and for the poor dead mutt's demise.

As Quentin eased the Bentley onto Wilshire Blvd, Jack realized that if he did get Susan to answer her door, she might blacken his other eye.

His mouth twitched.

It might make them both feel better.

# # #

No one answered when Jack knocked at the Baldwins' door Friday afternoon, and no dog barked a warning that danger lurked on the porch. He put his ear to the screen but heard nothing from inside.

He limped down the stairs and got into his car and drove home.

Jack rented a one-bedroom apartment in an eight-unit stucco apartment building at the corner of Vine and St. Anne. It was at the right side of the top floor, with a picture window looking out into two date palms that had seen better days.

The inside of his apartment felt like a pizza oven.

Jack opened all the windows and switched on the table fan. He grabbed a beer and chugged it, then shook out two pain pills and three aspirin and grabbed another beer to down the lot.

His head buzzed as he picked up the mail from under the slot in his front door and threw it away without looking at it too closely.

Mail had meant bad news to him since a letter from his wife, Polly, caught up to him in the bombed out town of *Pieta d'ligne* in Northern Sicily in 1944. She had written to say she was sorry, but she was in love with another man and wanted a divorce.

Jack had been gone from home for two years at that point. His eyes burned from the memory of that letter, though he realized he could no longer remember her face. She was slim and dark haired. Long neck.

Did she look like Susan Baldwin?

Maybe.

"Enough." Jack crushed the beer can and stripped off his stale clothes.

After a shower that felt like redemption, he put on his best chalk-striped suit and a black, skinny-brimmed porkpie that he knew was rakish, but what the hell. It felt good not to be in jail.

# # #

Jack parked in the lot at *The Eyes* at two fifteen. His stomach grumbled, but he could walk without feeling like razor blades were twisting under his knee.

After he found out what Eddie had dug up on the flower-sending blonde, he would dispatch the kid out for food.

But when he walked into the newsroom, there was no sign of Eddie or Quentin. Lucy Cherry was the only one there, and her perpetually smug smile melted the moment she saw him.

"Jesus, Jack, what's the other guy look like?" She sat in front of her desk, legs crossed, lipstick fresh, looking like she was waiting for a man to take her to dinner.

"Hey, monster girl. Where did you get that story? Hanging out with the boys in blue in the 06 finally paid off."

Lucy crossed her arms over her chest and gave him a once over. Her desk was directly opposite the door; a location Quentin had chosen strategically. Her face was the first thing visitors saw when they walked into the office.

Or, depending on how she was sitting, her black lace garter belt.

"I got sources. Don't be jealous. I'll make *The Eyes* lots of money on this story, and it'll give you and Eddie more time to chase after that crazy blonde who's killing all those big bad muggers."

"That's the spirit. All for one."

"And each man for himself. At least as far as you're concerned, Curran."

He grinned and sniffed the air. "You don't smell half bad. Got a date?"

"Yeah. My cop friend is taking me to the Brown Derby to celebrate my first Special Edition headliner. But I could work you in later if you're asking."

"Thanks, but I'm not a fan of seconds."

She threw a pencil at him.

Jack went to his desk and sat down slowly. He noted a lump on his calf while he was showering, which was further interfering with his ability to walk. That bastard Stu Martin had done a number on him. He was going to have to go to the VA hospital and get his leg checked out. It would make Meeks happy if nothing else.

Maybe I will sue the fucking cops, he thought.

"I was sorry to hear the old lady Thrill Girl saved is dead. What happened with that, anyway?"

"I am too. She died after I paid her a visit. The cops put one and one together and got five. But the rap went away."

"After you spent a day and a half in the cooler! Jeez, you should sue."

"Comes with the territory."

"Not my territory. You need to be careful. You're always pissing the cops off, Jack. None of them can wait to take a shot at the war hero. You've got a reputation."

"Don't we all?"

"Is that a crack?"

"Nothing gets by you, does it, Lucy?"

"Screw you."

He chuckled. "A man can hope."

Lucy called him a word he had never heard a woman use before and stomped back to her desk. Jack turned away from the nice view of her ass and regarded his empty desk. "Did you take any calls for me while I was gone?"

"What do I look like, your secretary?" She smoothed her fingers through her wavy hair, her green eyes flashing. "That stack of messages on Eddie's desk is yours. He was in here earlier."

"Yeah? Where did he go?"

"Mr. Deville sent him on an errand."

"What kind of errand?"

Lucy shrugged. "I have no idea."

"And you call yourself a reporter."

"You are such an arrogant son of a bitch. Just because you went to college doesn't mean you're better than me."

"I never said I was better." He sighed and gave her a sincere smile. "You should go to college. You're a smart woman."

"If I'm so smart, how come you're always reminding me *who, what, where, why and how"?* I know how to write a column without going to college."

"When."

"What?"

"When not how. Although how is important if you know how." Jack laughed and realized the pills and booze he had consumed on an empty stomach were taking over his brain. He had to eat. And soon.

"Just quit making fun of me all the time, Jack. You do it and then that little ferret Eddie thinks he can laugh at me too."

Eddie did kind of look like a ferret. A chubby one. Jack grinned. "He doesn't laugh at you. He's got the hots for you."

"Yeah, like that's going to happen. You better watch that kid. He's always sneaking around. If I didn't know better, I'd think he and Mr. Deville were running a book out of this place."

"No, only a newspaper that evidently believes in monsters."

"Screw you."

Jack shook his head but let her have the last word. He took off his hat and lit a cigarette, and snagged the stack of messages off Eddie's desk. There was one from Mary Ann from the flower shop. He set that one aside. He saw the message from Goldblum written in Quentin's exacting script.

He blinked and threw it away.

At the sound of a car horn outside, Lucy stood and grabbed her pocketbook. "There's my date. I'll be in on Monday, Jack. Put a steak on that eye, and you might get a date for next weekend."

He looked up, wishing she hadn't mentioned steak. His stomach grumbled in anticipation for a meal it wasn't going to get. "Lucy. Congratulations on your story. It was well done. The art was gory as hell, but you had all the facts. And it was scary."

Scary sold newspapers, they both knew that.

"Thanks." Lucy looked surprised at the compliment. "See you later." She slammed the door behind her.

Evidently, her cop boyfriend didn't make a habit of coming into the office to pick her up, Jack thought. "Married," he said to the empty room.

CHAPTER NINE

Jack rolled a sheet of blank paper into the Olympia. Before he could type a word, the front door opened and Eddie hurried into the room. He carried bulging paper bags of food and a tray of coffee cups.

"Whoa! Mind reader. Tell me all of that is for me, Eddie boy."

"Welcome back, Mr. Curran! Yes. I got lunch!" He stopped in the middle of the room, his eyes wide behind his heavy glasses. "My gosh, what happened to your face? You look terrible."

Jack touched his lip. "Jimmy Glass's partner was feeling like King Kong when he cuffed me; then I ran into a psycho who tried to steal my clothes in lockup. I'm two for two as a punching bag."

"A prisoner hit you?" Eddie went white.

"Forget it. Do I smell roast beef?"

"What? Oh, yeah, you do. Good nose, sir. Roast beef, rare, on an onion roll with horseradish. And I also got you pastrami on rye with sauerkraut." He sat one of the bags in front of Jack.

Jack pulled out a five and handed it to Eddie. "Keep the change, kid."

"I don't need money, sir. Mr. Deville told me this morning to bring food in. He said you would be ravenous after your, eh, incarceration. He bought lunch for everyone."

"Quentin is a great man."

Eddie glanced at Lucy's desk. "Where's Miss Cherry?"

"Date. Gone until Monday." Jack whacked Eddie on the arm. "That's okay. I'll eat hers too unless you want it."

Eddie blushed, and Jack pointed to the food. "Lunch first. Then be prepared to update me on everything you found out about the blonde, her car, and the chauffeur."

The office door opened at exactly that moment.

"A blonde, her car, and the chauffeur. Now there's a headline." Quentin threw out the comment without missing a beat. He had changed from the dark suit he had worn to the jail and was now dressed in a seersucker jacket and straw bowler. He looked like he was going on a riverboat ride.

"Eddie. Did you get my egg salad?"

"Yes, Mr. Deville. On white toast." Eddie yanked on one of the paper cups and held it out to his boss. "And tea. Milk, no sugar."

"Excellent. Hello, Jack, glad you made it in. I want to see what you have on Thrill Girl before you leave today."

Jack wiped the corner of his mouth. "You'll have it as soon as I find out what Eddie dug up for me while I was in the slam."

Quentin picked up the bag with his egg salad sandwich and sniffed at the bag. He grinned widely.

Jack had never noticed how sharp Quentin's eye teeth were. Like a cat's. *Maybe he killed the bum at Griffith Park.* The thought made him chuckle.

"Take your time, gentlemen. You've got two hours." Quentin took his cup of tea and disappeared into his office.

# # #

Jack pulled into the Ambassador Hotel parking lot. He left *The Eyes* without giving Quentin his columns because he did not want to commit until he checked out the information Eddie had uncovered.

A gas jockey at the Shell station across from the Ambassador Hotel had recognized the kid's description of the woman in the Rolls and her black chauffeur. The car, he had told Eddie, was a dark grey with a light grey top. He had seen it at the hotel lot several times.

"It's one sweet ride," the guy had said. "And the woman riding in it was prime grade A. Too rich for my blood, but a real looker."

Jack was glad Eddie had not followed up at the hotel desk. He didn't want the blonde to hear anyone was asking about her.

He wheeled the Packard slowly up and down the rows of cars, but while there were plenty of Caddies, Buicks, and Lincolns – half of them with out-of-state plates – there was no sign of a Rolls. Jack allowed himself a moment to appreciate two Jaguars with California tags, their bodies as sleek as the snarling jungle cat hood ornaments. The beautiful beasts were parked next to each other in spaces marked reserved.

There was another lot around back where the valets lined up the patrons' cars for the Coconut Grove nightclub, but Jack doubted a chauffeur would allow a valet to park his vehicle.

Especially that chauffeur.

Jack let the Packard idle outside the empty nightclub. The sign above for the Coconut Grove heralded the current act, Gino Venice. The neon still glowed from last night.

That guy was a sap in Jack's opinion. Not as good a singer as Sinatra, and not much of an actor judging from the one thing he had seen him in.

Jack parked and walked toward the hotel. He hoped to find a witness to give some details on the blonde in the car, beyond that she was gorgeous. A young couple with a toddler was trying to get her into a stroller. "Look, Mommy, a castle," the kid said.

The hotel did kind of look like a castle, Jack thought. Similar to Bullocks Wilshire, the Ambassador was a landmark that reeked of L.A. glamour which sprawled over several acres of prime real estate. Its seven-story Art Deco tower and gracious gardens were known around the world. The Coconut Grove nightclub, famous for hosting Academy Award ceremonies and the best singing talent in Hollywood, was on the ground floor.

Inside, Jack stopped a moment to revel in the icy air blowing over his head. Then he smoothed his hair and pushed through the glass doors into the café.

He spotted Carol Johnson, her red hair gleaming under the perky white cap, and headed to a table. She was at his side five seconds later with a tall glass of ice water.

"Hey, gorgeous," she greeted him. "Looking for a bite?"

He grabbed her arm and pulled her toward him for a quick kiss. "I always have an appetite when I see you, sweetheart."

"The sight of you makes a girl hungry, too, Mr. Curran." She leaned closer and gasped. Gently she pulled off his hat. "At least it usually does. Your mouth! And your eye! What happened to you?"

"Nothing bad. I had a misunderstanding with the coppers, but we're best friends now."

"What kind of misunderstanding?"

"Nothing much." Carol obviously had not read about his arrest in *The Times*. "Can I get a coffee?"

"Is that all you want?" She touched his cheek. "How about an early dinner like soup or something for that poor mouth of yours."

"Sounds great, but I had a late lunch. Can you sit a minute?"

She narrowed her eyes. "I can, but I'm still mad that you broke our date last Tuesday."

"I was working. If I could have made it, believe me, I would have. It was a hell of a night."

Carol frowned. "That blonde crazy again, right? Okay, I believe you. Let me go get a nice piece of pie. There's always room for dessert."

He smiled and drained the ice water. When she returned with a slice of apple pie, he asked if she needed a lift home after work.

"No. I've got the old putt-putt." She drove a 1941 Dodge coupe that made rude exhaust noises.

"Where do the employees park their cars? In the lot out front?"

"Yeah. But we're not allowed to take the first twenty spots in a row. Those are for hotel guests."

"Have you noticed a Rolls Royce out there? Two-tone grey

job? A colored man would be driving it." Jack sniffed. "A big guy."

"A Negro? I don't think they're allowed to stay at the hotel, Jack. Or go to the nightclub, unless they're with the band."

"I'm not asking if you've seen him *inside* the hotel, honey. Have you seen him in the parking lot?"

"Are you taking a tone with me?" She crossed her arms over her ample chest.

"No. Sorry, I'm not clear. Forgive me, okay?" He touched her arm. "It's my mouth. It hurts."

A smile touched her lips. "What's a Rolls Royce, anyway?"

Jack took a bite of pie. "It's a British car. This is delicious. Did you make it yourself?"

"Don't be silly. I don't cook." Carol leaned close to Jack's ear. "Come to the club tomorrow night, and I'll get you a table. Lola will comp your drinks. I have to work in the bar until around one, but then you can follow me home."

"What time does the Grove open?"

"You need to be here by twelve-thirty at the latest. Gino Venice is strict about closing the doors before he goes on. Doesn't like people wandering around when he's singing."

"Okay, see you tomorrow night. I'm looking forward to it."

Carol folded his check in half and stuck it in her apron. She moved on to another table.

Jack finished his pie and slipped a buck for Carol under his plate. He checked his wristwatch. It was four thirty. He sauntered out of the café and over to the front desk.

No one had seen a Rolls Royce, although Jack felt the clerk was lying to be discreet.

On the way to the exit, Jack spotted a tall colored man pushing a wheelchair into the lobby. The man gave Jack a solemn nod. He wore a dark suit and immaculate white shirt. Built more like a bodyguard than a nurse, the guy had spots of grey in his close-cropped hair.

The young man in the wheelchair was slight and pale. Dressed immaculately. It was clear he was partially paralyzed and looked about seventeen. The kid hadn't been injured in the war.

"Good afternoon," Jack said.

"Thank you. You too," the young man replied.

The valet said nothing.

Jack hurried outside into the sunshine, considering if he should go back and ask the black guy if he knew the Rolls' chauffeur, but stopped in his tracks. He whistled low under his breath. Next to the black Jaguar he had seen earlier was parked a massive, two-toned grey Rolls Royce.

Jack pulled out the notebook he always carried and jotted down the license plate number before slipping into the Packard.

The guy wheeling the handicapped kid into the hotel was most likely the same black man Mary Ann had seen driving the blonde. Jack looked back at the luxury hotel and framed a direct question in his head. He could go back inside and ask the guy who he worked for. But then he realized that if he asked about the blonde woman, he could be tipping his hand.

Jack lit a cigarette and put the Packard in gear. He would head back to the office and run the plates. With any luck, he would have information tomorrow that would let him ask for his blonde by name at the front desk.

Jack wondered how the man in the wheelchair fit into her life.

Husband? Brother?

He gunned the car, his fatigue and aching leg forgotten. He had what reporters lived for, an important break in a very hot case.

# # #

Jack hung up the phone and checked the office wall clock. It was after six, but his source at the DMV had come through with info on the Rolls.

"Eddie, the blonde's car is registered to a Lynton Maxwell." Jack read out the address in San Marino, an old California money community south of Pasadena. "I want you to get me everything available on this guy."

"Okay, Mr. Curran." Eddie got up but pointed to a new stack of messages. "You should look at those. Mary Ann Little called again and said she needed to see you *today*. And Mr. Sydney Goldblum's secretary called back. She wants to set up a lunch appointment next Friday at the Brown Derby." Eddie's eyes were bright behind his heavy glasses. "Is that the big Hollywood movie producer?"

Jack grunted. He wadded up the message from Goldblum and dropped it in the trash. "Where's Quentin?"

"Ah, Mr. Deville's in the press shop. He told me to ask you to go see him before you leave again." The kid grinned. "He personally fielded thirteen telephone calls today. Several from the police chief, two from city councilmen, and one from the mayor's office — all screaming about Lucy's monster story."

Jack yanked on his necktie. He stared at the mock-up of the front page of today's Special Edition, which Quentin had taped to the wall.

"Quentin loves poking the cops in the eye, but he damn well knows this monster thing is bullshit."

"What do you think killed that man?" Eddie blinked.

"An animal, for Christ's sake!"

"You're angry…"

"Damn right I'm angry. It chaps my ass that the whole city has stopped worrying about Thrill Girl. When the LAPD figures out the homeless man was dismembered by a mangy mountain lion, Quentin is going to regret sidetracking our readers."

"But *The Eyes* had to go with it. Any paper handed that scoop would have done the same."

Eddie's glasses bounced Jack's reflection back at him. "Are you saying you think what Quentin did was right?"

"What do you mean, sir?"

"You know what I mean." Jack knocked an empty paper cup off his desk. "He let Lucy and her fake monster story steal Thrill Girl's Special Edition! We should have focused on Joan Becklund's murder in the special, not an imaginary B-movie creature."

"Thrill Girl *was* mentioned on page two, and—"

"Page two! Who the hell reads page two? Jeez, Eddie, I thought you had good instincts for what's newsworthy." Jack glared at the young man. "Would you have dropped Thrill Girl for this garbage?"

Eddie stepped uneasily from one foot to the other. "I think any story that can carry monster in the headline is a must do. And by waiting until Tuesday for another front page Thrill Girl story, Mr. Deville gave you time to find and interview the woman who sent the roses. Besides, you were in jail, sir. And Mr. Deville won't let anyone else write copy on Thrill Girl."

Eddie was trying to console him.

Jack crossed his arms and used his good leg to kick his desk chair, which hit the wall with a thud. "Get hustling, Eddie. I'm going to go see Maxwell this weekend, and I want to know as much as possible about him before I head out. Especially about his family. Wife. Sisters. Girlfriends. If the Rolls is his car, it figures one of the women connected to him is riding around in it. Call your source at *The Times*, too. They have access to a lot of international stories we don't keep in our archive."

"Yes, sir." Eddie picked up his notebook and took a step toward the room dubbed the 'morgue,' where years of news clippings and microfilm from *The Eyes* resided.

"I need to see a picture of Lynton Maxwell," Jack yelled over his shoulder. "And any blonde he's been photographed with."

"Photos of Lynton Maxwell with blondes, coming right up." Eddie was reaching for the door when it opened from the other side, nearly knocking him down.

"Lynton Maxwell?" Quentin walked through the door and into the room. "Glad you're still here, Jack. Eddie, what did you say about Lynton Maxwell?"

"The car connected to the lady who sent the roses is registered to him," Eddie said.

"Is that true?" Quentin went still.

"Eddie's going to do research before I head out to talk to Maxwell." Jack narrowed his eyes. "Unless you've got a problem with that."

"Stay right there for a minute, Eddie." Quentin sat next to Jack's desk. "Are you saying Lynton Maxwell might be involved with the Thrill Girl murders?"

"No. I'm saying his car has something to do with the blonde who sent flowers to all the citizens Thrill Girl saved." Jack reached for his lighter and smokes. The pack was empty.

Quentin offered Jack his cigarette case, a heavy gold job with his initials engraved on the front. "I want that back, Curran. For your information, I know Lynton Maxwell. At least I've met him. He's got a lot of clout, both with government and industry. Owns an armaments plant, along with several DOD related manufacturing concerns. We have to tread carefully with him."

A bell went off in Jack's brain. He handed the case back to Quentin and lit up. He remembered seeing a mention of the man in the *Times* business section. "Is Maxwell a politician?" He inhaled the smoke deep into his lungs.

"God, no. He's got too much money to bother with that. He prefers running corporations. Although I seem to remember he helped the Army in some capacity during the war. He's Austrian, distantly related to the Hapsburgs."

"Great. So he's a *royal* pain in the ass."

"Know your European history, do you?" Quentin blew a trio of smoke rings above his head. "Please give me a heads-up if you're going to bring his wrath down on *The Eyes*."

Jack pointed at the door. "I'm not bringing wrath down on anyone. Except for Eddie, if he doesn't get going on his research."

"Yes, sir." Eddie ran from the room.

"Keep me apprised," Quentin said. "I mean it, Jack. And may I suggest you call and request an appointment before you show up at Maxwell's. I can't imagine he's the type of fellow who appreciates unannounced guests."

Jack chewed his lip, realizing that for the second time in as many days Quentin Deville seemed reluctant to rattle anyone's cage. "Will do." He sat up and grimaced.

"And get that leg looked at. I need you functioning at least until Thrill Girl is wrapped up. Then you can rest on your laurels."

"I'll go as soon as I get a chance." He reached for the telephone, ignoring the look Quentin gave him.

Jack caught Mary Ann at work. He told her he would come by in an hour to pick up the receipts. He also left a message for Jimmy Glass with a prickly sounding Sergeant at the 07. He hung up and rubbed his eyes as a wave of fatigue washed over him. He had not slept a wink in jail.

As he set down the receiver, he rested his aching left leg on the trash can. He needed to visit the VA hospital or risk being seriously laid up.

The phone jangled.

"*Eyes of LA*. Curran."

There was the sound of car traffic. Someone calling from a telephone booth with the doors opened. A man's shaky voice came over the line. "Hello? I need to speak to the reporter writing the coverage on Thrill Girl."

"That's me. Who is this?"

"That don't matter. Hey, mister. Can you meet me? I need to give you a bit of information about that story."

"What kind of information? And I don't meet anyone who won't give me a name."

The old man started coughing, a chronic sound that spoke of bad health and heavy drinking. "My name's Trixie. I have information about those men who got killed the other night on Dewitt Street."

Trixie. The bum who saw the lights.

"You should call the police. You got information about the murder; you need to tell them about it. Not me." Jack reached for his empty cigarette pack and crumpled it. He could talk to the guy, but he wasn't about to keep evidence from investigators.

"I ain't calling no coppers. Look, man, you don't want to hear what I got to say? I thought you were a big war hero."

Great. Derelicts were taunting him now. "What's me being a veteran have to do with you or anything else?"

"I'm a vet too," the guy said. "I fought the Kaiser before you were in diapers. I thought a fellow GI would understand what I've been going through since the war. Maybe buy me a meal and listen to what I saw the other night."

Jack frowned. He was being played for a free meal, but there was something in the guy's voice that got his attention.

Fear.

"Okay." He glanced at his wristwatch. "Where are you going to be at around ten o'clock tonight?"

"Wherever you want me to be. I mean, I spent my last nickel on this call, so I can't take the bus. But I can hitch if you want to meet up downtown."

"You know the Pantry Cafe? On sixth?"

"Hell, yeah. But they won't let me in there. Bastards want to see cash money before they let you through the doors."

"They'll let you in with me," Jack said. "See you at ten, Trixie. Wait for me if I run late."

"Yes, sir. Ah, what's your name again?"

"Curran. Jack Curran."

"See you then, Mr. Curran."

The severed connection clicked in his ear. Jack wondered what Trixie had seen that he was too scared to tell the cops about.

CHAPTER TEN

At nine p.m., Eddie reappeared with a pile of yellowed news clippings and a tablet page of notes. He had used the microfilm reader to browse through years of stored articles from *The Eyes, the Los Angeles Times* and *the New York Times,* as well as from *The Paris Herald Tribune.*

Eddie had recently talked Quentin into buying microfilm from the European news bureau. The kid had made good use of that resource checking out Lynton up to 1940. The bureau had suspended coverage after that because of the war in Europe.

Jack propped both legs up on his desk and read avidly for several minutes.

Lynton Maxwell was the son of Victoria Williams-Smythe and her first husband, Jonathan Smythe of London. Smythe died in 1919 from wounds suffered in World War I. Victoria married into the wealthy Maxwell family of Innsbruck, Austria the next year, bringing her six-year-old son into the marriage. Karl Arnold Maxwell adopted Lynton and gave him the family name. Three years after the marriage, Victoria Maxwell died of influenza.

Lynton was sent away from the resort town near the Alps that he grew up in to attend private school in the US, followed by Yale University, where he rowed crew and graduated with honors in

1935. There were six additional articles about Maxwell's business contracts and his meetings with all the movers and shakers in American and European manufacturing and steel business. There was also a snap of Maxwell standing with General Eisenhower, taken at a black-tie event honoring veterans last May.

Jack frowned. Eddie had also unearthed a biographical society piece on Lynton's father from the Paris papers in 1924. The elder Maxwell had married again three years after the death of Lynton's mother. She was a Welsh woman, Margaret Burton, and together they had two children, Alana and Tomas.

Tomas Maxwell was mentioned in an article in 1940 from *The Los Angeles Times*. The Maxwell family had settled in LA in 1935, and Karl had died a year later of a "blood illness." Before his death, he had created an endowment in Tomas's name to establish a foundation for research into paralysis and genetics.

Current articles in *The Times* reported that Tomas's sister, Alana Maxwell, had assumed the directorship of the foundation in 1945. There were no pictures of Tomas, whom he imagined was in a bed or wheelchair, but there were a couple of her.

She was willowy, blonde, and always dressed to the nines.

Jack squinted at the images. Was she the woman in the Rolls? Slim and elegant, she looked like money. Her face was turned away from the camera in both pictures.

He kept reading the research material while Eddie, knowing how Jack liked to digest things before asking any questions, sat quietly proofing pages for next week's edition.

The only public mentions of a woman in Lynton's life were of his step-sister.

The last article Jack read was from *The Paris Herald*, dated December 27, 1939. It covered a car accident that had killed Lynton Maxwell's step-mother, while the family was vacationing at the Ritz.

Jack stopped for a moment and remembered a day, during the war on his way to Italy, they had been in Paris. He and a buddy had stood out on the *Place Vendome* and gawked at the gorgeous hotel, its windows polished like gems. They had considered going in to see if anyone would buy two Yanks a drink but decided against it.

Jack turned back to the clippings, banishing the memory, which now felt as if it had happened to another person. The article reported that Alana Maxwell had been with her mother in the car, which had run off the road and down a ravine.

The reporter quoted Lynton Maxwell's claim that Margaret had been the one driving the car, but it was clear there was speculation that Alana Maxwell might have been behind the wheel.

Jack looked up at Eddie. "Nothing else on who was driving the car when Lynton Maxwell's step-mother was killed?"

"I didn't find anything. I called Abe at *The Times* and left a message to see if he can find any follow-up from their Paris bureau. We only have the U.S. articles on our microfilm."

"Humph." Jack put the clips down. "What have we got? Run it down for me, kid."

"Me?" Eddie cleared his throat in response to Jack's nod. "Lynton Maxwell is rich and well-born, but he lost both his parents before he was ten. He was adopted by his step-mother Margaret and her husband, after which he was shipped off to the States to go to school. He works hard and has his picture taken with very important people. He has a crippled step-brother and a step-sister who might have been involved in her mother's death in a car accident. She runs a foundation that's seeking a cure for paralysis."

Jack squinted down at the articles. "And the step-sister doesn't like to get her picture taken."

"You're right, sir. I did notice that. She never looks into the camera." Eddie pushed his glasses up on his nose. "Do you think Alana Maxwell is the blonde woman who was seen in Lynton's Rolls Royce?"

As usual, Eddie's mind was ahead of most. Jack pointed his finger at the young reporter. "Don't speculate. It screws you up when you do that. You start rooting for a story to turn out a certain way, which makes you no kind of journalist at all. You got to wait and see where the facts lead you."

"Yes, sir."

"Good job on the research. Why don't you head home for the

weekend? I'll see you early Monday morning, okay? We'll have a whole front page to do on Thrill Girl." Jack picked up his hat.

"Yes, sir. But call me if you need me to come in tomorrow. Or Sunday."

"I will." Jack stared down at Eddie's research again. "No negative stories on Maxwell, are there? No bad business deals, traffic accidents, scandals with women, nothing like that?"

"Nothing, sir. He looks squeaky clean. And loyal to his family."

"We all know looks can deceive, right, Eddie?"

"Right, sir."

"Okay, see you later."

# # #

There was no sign of anyone fitting Trixie's description on the street in front of The Pantry. Jack glanced at his watch. It was five after ten. He walked into the twenty-four-hour diner at 9th and Figueroa, famous for having been open twenty-four hours a day since 1924. The joint smelled heavily of fried steak, fried onions, fried hamburger, and fried grease.

He told his favorite waiter, Milton, he needed a table for two and went to wash up. When he emerged from the restroom, he spotted a shabbily dressed man through the front window.

Before the manager could chase him off, Jack went to the door and said, "Trixie?"

"Mr. Curran? Yes, sir. It's me, Trixie."

Jack shook hands with the old guy, who didn't smell as bad as he looked. "He's with me," he said, escorting Trixie inside.

Trixie was allowed to walk in unmolested, and Jack led his guest to the corner table.

Under Milton's frowning gaze, they ordered steak and eggs and toast and potatoes and coffee. Trixie tried to order a beer, but the Pantry did not do liquor.

It was the spot people went to in order to relieve a hangover, not induce one.

Jack lit a cigarette and offered the pack to Trixie.

"I don't smoke, Mr. Curran. They're bad for the throat."

"Yeah? Why do you care about that? You a singer?"

"Nah, but I like to take care of myself as best I can." He grinned, showing his five remaining teeth.

Hopefully, he can handle that sirloin I'm going to pay good money for, Jack thought. He refrained from asking how living on the streets in a drunken stupor counted as taking care of oneself. "What do you have for me?" he asked instead. "Did you see anything the other night?"

Trixie shook his head vigorously. A few bits of debris fell off his matted hair like fairy dust, but they stayed on his side of the table. "Yes, sir. It was exciting. These two mooks, a spic and a chink, were waiting for this girl. There was other guys hiding around the corner, and they shined a light…"

"Whoa!" Jack leaned across the table. "You telling me there were other people there besides the guys who got whacked? Hiding around the corner?"

"Yeah. Two more. White guys. One had on a suit and a bowl hat…at least I think you call 'em bowl hats." He made a round shape with his trembling hands.

"Bowler? Bowler hats."

"I guess. The man in the bowl, eh, bowler hat, and the skinny guy with him had equipment in a box. And lights. Flashlights, maybe. Anyway, I think they were trying to blind the girl so the other guys could get her." He shrugged. "That's my guess anyway."

Jack took a pull from his cigarette. He wondered if this whole story might be the product of an alcohol-soaked imagination. "What did the white guys do when the other two men grabbed the girl?"

"They watched, I think."

"You think?"

"I don't exactly know, 'cause I was trying not to get seen. The girl was hollering awful. I was worried one of the men might notice me, and I ducked behind the phone booth. That's where I was hanging out before this all went down."

Which meant he had been relieving himself. LA phone booths usually reeked of urine.

"Here you go." Milton walked up with two huge platters of dinner, which he placed on the table. "Need more coffee, Mr. Curran?"

"I'm good. Thanks." Jack glanced at Trixie, who was staring in stunned disbelief at the amount of food. "You need more coffee, Trixie?"

"No." The bum looked at Milton. "Do I get to take what I can't eat right now?"

"Yeah, I can put it in a sack for you. Eggs aren't all that good cold, though."

"Oh, cold eggs are plenty good when you're hungry." Trixie picked up a knife and fork and dug in.

Jack did the same as he mulled over what Trixie had told him. He remembered Joan Becklund's claim that a man had told her to meet him on the street where she got mugged.

What the hell is going on? The Thrill Girl story had seemed straightforward in its way, but maybe there were layers of meaning he was missing. He had considered, several times, what weird luck it was that Thrill Girl had stumbled upon the muggers and their would-be victims.

But maybe it wasn't luck at all? Maybe someone had set up the attacks?

Jack put his knife and fork down and wiped his mouth with the heavy cloth napkin. "Trixie, did you get a good look at the woman who beat the hell out of the two muggers before she killed them?"

Trixie nodded and said through a mouthful, "Yeah. Tough cookie, that one."

"Did you see how she did it? Shoot one first, then use the knife?"

Trixie swallowed. He wiped his face on his filthy coat sleeve, leaving an egg yolk stain.

"Well, maybe I didn't see much. I mostly heard it. Like I said, I was across the street behind that booth. But I heard the shot.

Covered my head then, and didn't look up again. Not even when a guy called the cops from the phone booth."

"You heard a man call the cops? Who was it?"

"I didn't see him. I was wedged under the jade plant outside the booth. Didn't dare move. Could have been the guy in the bowling hat. Could have been anyone."

"And you never actually saw the blonde?"

"What blonde?" Trixie picked up his unused napkin and slid the remainder of his food onto it.

"The blonde we've been talking about. The blonde who killed the guys and came to the shop girl's rescue."

"I don't remember a blonde. I like blondes, too, so I would. The only one I recall is the dark-haired girl."

Jack stared at the bum, disappointed his story was falling apart. "You heard of Thrill Girl, Trixie? Seen the papers lately?"

"Nope." The old man folded the napkin around the half of steak he had not managed to eat and stuck the bundle inside his coat. "Can you get dessert here?"

"You going to stick an apple pie down your pants too?"

"I would." Trixie grinned. "Do they have apple pie?"

"Yeah. We'll get it in a minute, but we'll let them wrap up the leftovers next time, okay?"

"Okay."

Jack leaned back. "I need you to focus a minute here, Trixie. You're saying you never saw the blonde woman come to the rescue of that girl?"

"Nope. I heard screaming. And a gunshot. But that's when I put my head down. I kept it there, man. I learned that in France during the big one. My friend Billy Sixx got his brains blown out when he peeked over the side of our trench. He was looking at a rat chewing on a Kraut's head when a sniper got him."

Jack finished his coffee. He stood as Milton approached. "Thanks. Great food, as usual." He handed the waiter a bill, more than twice the total. "You bring my friend here a double slice of apple pie, and a hamburger wrapped to go, okay? The rest you keep for a tip."

"Sure thing, Mr. Curran." Milton picked up the plates and glared at Trixie. "You stay put. I'll be right back."

"Thanks, Mr. Curran," Trixie said.

"No problem." He handed the old man two singles, folded together. They disappeared into Trixie's shirt.

"Call me again if you hear anything on the street about the other night. Ask around. See if your friends saw the guys with the flashlights or the blonde."

Trixie grinned. "Will do. Will do."

Jack walked out into the sultry LA night. He glanced at his watch. It was ten fifty-five. He needed to get to the office and write all of this down, leave a message for Jimmy Glass and see if he knew what Trixie was saying.

Most of it is bull, he thought, but the twitch at the back of his neck told him some of it wasn't.

He had to figure out what was what.

# # #

Jack tipped the chair off the floor and frowned at the mess of notes on his desk. The clock on the wall outside Quentin's office showed it was after midnight.

He had written up his notes about Trixie and then started in on Tuesday's lead on Thrill Girl, but he was having a tough time trying to decide how to approach it. After Susan Baldwin was mugged, the facts of the story had seemed clear-cut. He looked down at the outline he had made.

Who: Four attacks, six men dead.

More Who: Five civilians rescued by an unknown Samaritan. They represented a wide swath of the population – an old lady, a middle-aged immigrant, two teenagers, and a single girl.

Biggest Who: Their savior was a beautiful blonde woman.

What: Vigilante murder.

Where: The dark, mean streets of Los Angeles

Why: The big unknown.

Jack tapped his pen against the sheet of paper and thought

about the lights and Trixie's claim that he had seen two other men watching the mugging of Susan Baldwin.

He could trust Trixie's memories about as much as he could the trash can currently serving as his leg rest. Except for one thing. The man was telling the truth. Trixie might be a bum and a drunk, but he wasn't a liar. At least not an intentional one.

The phone rang. Jack picked it up. "Eyes of LA. Curran."

"Jimmy Glass. I got your message."

He refocused quickly. "Thanks for calling back, Detective. Can we meet for a cup of coffee?"

"Why?"

Jack reached for his cigarettes. "Well, since we're cutting to the chase, I'd like to discuss a couple of things about the Thrill Girl case."

Two beats of silence passed. "When?"

"Anytime, Detective."

"I got nothing to discuss with you. What do you want from me, Curran? You know I won't give you any details about a police investigation."

Jack took a drag on his cigarette. "I have information I want to share with you." He repeated what Joan Becklund had told him about how she had arranged to meet a guy in the exact place where she was mugged. "She said she told you the story the night it happened, Detective. You make any progress on checking it out?"

"I got no comment. Except to say you shouldn't have talked to my witness. You're interfering with police business again."

"That's your take. My take is I'm reporting the news."

"Yeah? Well if that's all you got, I'm hanging up."

"Wait. There's one more thing," Jack said. "A street bum who goes by the name of Trixie called me. He hangs around by the soup kitchen behind Dewitt Street." He relayed Trixie's story about the men who had watched from the shadows as the attack on Susan Baldwin went down.

His words were met with several moments of silence.

"Trixie is a drunk who doesn't know what day it is. I wouldn't use him in a news article if I were you," Glass finally said.

"He may be a drunk, but he mentioned seeing lights, same as Joan Becklund did. And according to Susan Baldwin's mother, Susan saw lights too. That's three witnesses with a similar story, Detective. Seems significant."

"Maybe. But nothing you can use. Don't print it, or you'll be sorry."

"You asking me for a favor, Detective?"

"No."

"Can I ask you for one?"

"No. But I'll be sure Martin goes easier on your leg the next time we arrest you."

Jack laughed. "I'd appreciate that."

"How is it? The leg?"

"It's fine." Jack stubbed out the cigarette. "Is there any chance you'll comment on the record that the strange lights are part of the investigation?"

"I don't provide information for newspaper stories, Curran."

"I'm not asking for information. I'm asking for confirmation. Cops can do that, right?"

"Good night."

Jack sighed. Jimmy Glass was totally by-the-book and impossibly decent for a cop. He had never heard him swear, even when he was aiming a gun at him.

"Good night, Detective."

The line went dead.

Jack put the receiver down. He would bet his last dollar the cops were already looking into the lights.

CHAPTER ELEVEN

Despite Quentin's suggestion that he call first, Jack decided to simply show up at Lynton Maxwell's home Saturday evening. He didn't want to give the rich man time to wonder why a reporter wanted to know who was driving his Rolls.

But first, he was going to stop at Lily's Lilies and see Mary Ann. He needed to confirm the flower receipts showed the blonde had sent white roses to all the attack victims, and then find a way to thank the salesgirl that they both could live with. He parked the Packard at the curb just before six p.m. and hopped out.

Mary Ann was waiting for him by the door. "My god, what happened to your face?" she asked.

Jack's skin from cheek to eyebrow had turned shades of green and purple and black from his run-in with the cops. He touched his lip, which had almost returned to its normal size. "Be kind. I walked into a door, and I look like hell."

He gave her a peck on the cheek.

Mary Ann smirked. "You sure it wasn't a fist you walked into? I saw in the news you got arrested on Wednesday night. It didn't say for what. Should I worry about my safety, Mr. Curran?"

"You are as safe as you want to be with me, honey. The arrest was a mistake. The cops and I kissed and made up." He touched her nose with his finger. "You want to get a drink? I got time before an appointment tonight. How about the Brown Derby?"

"I love the Derby. Or we could go to the Ambassador. It's right down the street, and they have a great bar. Nice and dark and cool."

They also had a red-haired waitress who would make a scene if he walked in with Mary Ann. "I'd prefer the Derby. Better booze."

"Okay." Mary Ann locked the store and walked toward his car with him. "The newspaper also said a dog got killed. How did that happen?"

"A cop ran it over."

"Oh no. How sad. The cops drive too fast."

"They've seen too many Cagney movies."

"Whose dog was it?"

"A gal who lived in the neighborhood where they picked me up." Jack opened the passenger door. "What are you doing the rest of the weekend?"

Mary Ann blinked. "I'm pretty open. If you want to come over later, after your appointment, I'm available." She slid into the front seat, flashing a lot of skin.

He walked around the car and got in. "It's going to be too late tonight to come your way. But there's always Sunday. What do you do on Sundays, Mary Ann? Go to church?"

"No. No, I'm not much of a church person." She put her hand on his right thigh. "I usually stay in bed most of the day on Sunday. How about you, Jack? You go to church much?"

"Sure. Every Sunday."

"I knew you were a good boy."

Jack opened a fresh pack of Lucky Strikes. He lit one and offered it to Mary Ann, then took a hard drag off it when she shook her head. "Did you bring those receipts for me?"

"Right here." She strummed her fingers on her pocketbook. "The woman I told you about bought white roses five times."

Five? Who else had received flowers from his mystery

woman? He only knew about four victims. Jack kept his voice casual. "Great. I appreciate you going to all this trouble for me."

"And I appreciate the drinks you're springing for. We're almost even."

He braked to let a yellow cab cut in front of him. Her hand remained on his pant leg, and he felt the heat from her naked palm. "Almost?"

"Almost." Mary Ann's voice was husky. "Why don't you take the next right? We can go to my place for that drink. It's only a couple of blocks from here, and I've got a brand new bottle."

Jack blew out a lungful of smoke. He didn't want her to hold a grudge against him. *Turn down a woman's offer of a drink, and she'll call another reporter.*

Mary Ann drove a hard bargain.

He glanced at his watch. He had enough time to return the favor.

# # #

Lynton Maxwell's estate was in San Marino, an exclusive enclave at the western edge of Pasadena. Jack had read that it was named for the colony on the Italian Riviera that was the world's oldest constitutional republic. The California version was populated by old money natives with names like Stanford and Huntington.

General Patton was born there.

Jack headed up the private drive and stopped at the black wrought-iron gates. He wondered idly why the beauty of the surroundings had not tempered that old bastard's approach to life.

It was after seven-thirty, and Maxwell was surely in the middle of cocktail hour.

"Jack Curran," he said into a speaker. A beefy kid who would look at home on the UCLA football field stood inside a flimsy structure on the other side of the gate. "I'm here to see Mr. Lynton Maxwell."

"Your business, sir?"

"I'm from *The Eyes of LA.*"

"Wow! I saw that about the monster story in your newspaper this morning."

"Great. Buzz me in."

"Yes, sir."

The guard pressed a button. The gate slid open, but the kid stepped in front of the car and held out a hand for Jack to stop.

Leaning down, the kid addressed him through the open window. "Did it actually rip the guy's head off?"

"That's what I hear."

"Have the cops found it yet?"

"The head? Yeah, I think it was a few feet from his body."

"No, not the head. *The monster*. Did they catch it?"

"Not that I've heard." Jack rolled his gaze around the grounds. "Don't be a hero if you hear something funny out there in the bushes. Lock yourself in and call the real cops."

The guard frowned. "Has that thing been spotted *in* San Marino? I thought the bum was killed near Griffith Park?"

"He was. But no one knows what killed him, let alone how many of those things are out there." Jack shrugged. "All I'm saying is be careful."

The guard scanned the hillside. "I will. Ah, is Mr. Maxwell expecting you?"

"No."

"I'll have to call up to the house and get you cleared first. Please stay in your car."

"Okay. Tell Mr. Maxwell I'm doing a story about his Rolls Royce."

The guard waved him by. Two minutes later he waved him up the driveway.

Jack drove up the quarter-mile-long road, hoping the kid wouldn't shoot himself, or a neighbor's cat if he heard a rattle in the bushes. Thanks to Lucy's article, the city was no doubt full of people who were afraid to go out and enjoy their summer evening. He grinned despite his chafed feelings about losing page one of the Special Edition.

At the end of the drive, Jack braked and put the car in park. He stepped out and sucked in a breath.

The house was impressive. The main *hacienda* stood two stories tall, timbered with oak and built of white adobe; the roof was made of Mexican *terracotta* tiles. A covered porch wrapped around the lower level while metalwork enclosed balconies off every upper floor window. Everywhere he looked was gleaming paint and shining glass. The yard was as groomed as a racehorse. Jack felt as if he had driven onto a film set, and it wouldn't have surprised him if Zorro dropped off the roof and carved a 'Z' onto his chest.

Lynton Maxwell was a very, very rich man.

A servant in a white coat hurried across the drive and asked for his keys. Jack watched as he drove the Packard off toward a building where several other vehicles were parked. There was no sign of the Rolls, but it was likely garaged if it was on the property.

An old man in formal dress waited at the main entrance.

"Good evening, *señor*. Mr. Maxwell and his guests are in the patio garden. There are people inside who will direct you."

"Thanks."

The interior of the home was as elaborate as the outside. Huge wooden candelabra with candles ablaze were suspended from chains above his head, spilling shadows down the walls and across the imported tile floor.

It feels like a church, Jack thought. *Quiet and safe.*

Fleetingly he thought of the lie he had told Mary Ann earlier. In reality, he had not been inside a church, except the bombed-out ones in Italy, since the Sunday before he shipped out to Europe. War had proved to him that religious faith would not save a person's life. Not while man ruled the earth, anyway.

Jack straightened his tie.

It was ten degrees cooler inside. He met a second servant at the end of a sweeping staircase and was directed into a comfortable room with four open doors leading out to a patio.

The place smelled like gardenias and cigars. Music from a piano drifted in on the breeze, punctuated by the gentle tumble of water in a nearby fountain and the sound of voices.

He peered out the open doors. Lynton Maxwell stood in the

middle of the patio a few yards away. Two middle-aged men and an extravagantly dressed woman surrounded him, their body language making it clear he was the center of their collective attention. One of the men, balding and bespectacled, appeared to be trying to convince Lynton of a point.

There were a dozen or more people out on the lawn, walking in pairs or sitting at wrought-iron tables.

Off to the other side of the patio, a pianist in a tuxedo was in the middle of a gentle rendition of "You're Nobody Till Somebody Loves You." Everyone was smiling, but Jack got the feeling none of them were having much fun.

They're all working, he realized. *Same as me.*

Rather than interrupt Lynton's conversation, Jack shifted his attention to the room around him. There were two couches and a group of leather chairs, along with a game table set for chess. The room boasted two bookcases full of leather-bound volumes shoved into untidy rows that suggested they weren't there for appearances.

He was about to light a cigarette when he noticed the enormous oil painting hanging above the fireplace. It was a study of three people gathered in a candlelit room. After a moment, he realized the figures in the painting had posed for their portrait in front of the same fireplace the painting now hung above.

Maxwell's family.

A pale boy sat at the center of the gathering. He wore a blue sweater and held a book on his lap. He looked familiar, but Jack couldn't place him until he noted the blanket over his legs. It was a younger version of the blond man he had seen in the wheelchair in the lobby of the hotel.

Tomas Maxwell.

To the left of him, arms folded, stood an older man. He was tall and athletically built, with a big head of wavy blond hair cropped to military precision on the sides.

Lynton Maxwell. The man in the painting looked to be around thirty, at least a decade younger than the one who was standing outside.

His gaze settled on the third figure.

A girl on the cusp of womanhood stood to the right of the boy, her hand on his shoulder. She was aggressively beautiful, with a chiseled nose, full lips, and eyes that tipped up at the outer edges. Tall and lithe, her blonde hair hung like a curtain around her shoulders.

Despite her physical perfection, tension emanated from her. She looked as if she was daring the painter to show her feelings.

It had to be Lynton's step-sister, Alana Maxwell. The dame with the flowers.

Jack turned away and lit a cigarette, peering outside again. Maxwell was standing with one other man, both of them gazing off into the valley below. Taking a deep drag, Jack smashed the cigarette into the ashtray by the door and stepped out onto the patio.

# # #

Jack extended his hand. "Hello, Mr. Maxwell. Jack Curran of *Eyes of LA*." He was surprised at the welcoming expression on the businessman's face, especially considering he had arrived unannounced in the midst of a cocktail party.

"Mr. Curran. Nice to meet you." Maxwell stared at Jack's black eye but did not ask about it. He put his right hand on the shoulder of the gentleman standing next to him. "This is General Conrad. Norman, this fellow is a reporter for a local newspaper, come to do an article on my car collection."

Jack did not correct him.

"Curran, nice to meet you." The general in civilian clothes clapped Jack on the back. "You've arrived at an opportune moment. I've been bending our host's ear about the threat of communism, but I think Lynton would rather talk about other things on such a lovely evening."

Jack looked up at the sky, a riot of red and purple streaks eating away at the blue. "It is a lovely night, General."

"Your newspaper is the one that published the story about that monster up at Griffith Park, isn't it?" Maxwell asked.

"Yes, that's us."

"What the hell kind of animal do you news guys think killed

that man?" the general barked.

"The cops and coroner are working on the answer to that, sir. A big cat of some kind, I'd guess." Jack's hand twitched. He wanted another cigarette. And a pain pill. After the workout with Mary Ann, his leg was trembling.

"What, like a lion?"

"Maybe. Mountain lions are common in California."

"They need to call in the Army," the general replied. "Your idiot police chief is in over his head. Get enlisted men up there. They'll beat the bushes and find the thing."

"I doubt the police are willing to give up their turf to the army," Lynton said. "But if I lived near the observatory, I'd have my rifle by my bed."

"Are you a good shot, Mr. Maxwell?" Jack asked.

"Excellent. How about you?" Maxwell squinted. "Didn't I read an article recently that mentioned your name? You were quite the hero in the war, according to *The Los Angeles Times*."

"I never read *The Times*, Mr. Maxwell. I've spent the last few years writing instead of shooting." He reached for his cigarettes.

"Different prey in your sights these days." General Conrad slapped him on the back a second time. "Well, nice to meet you, Mr. Curran. Lynton, I'll see you in Washington next week."

"Thank you, General." Lynton nodded to Jack. "The guard said you had questions about my Rolls?"

"I do have a few."

Maxwell glanced at his watch, a Cartier on a brown crocodile band. "I can give you ten minutes. My family will be arriving for dinner soon, and I need to have this bunch cleared out before then." He said it with a smile, but it was obvious he meant it.

"Certainly. Thank you for making time for me." The piano player launched into "Some Enchanted Evening," and Jack offered Maxwell a cigarette.

"No, thanks. I'm trying to stop. My sister doesn't like the way it smells on my clothes."

"Sisters," Jack echoed. He felt a stab of pain at the word but stayed focused on Maxwell's.

Lynton motioned to the room Jack had exited. "Shall we go in?"

"Thank you. If you don't mind me asking, do you agree with the general's assessment of the situation with Russia?"

Lynton Maxwell laughed. "Well, off the record, no, I don't agree with the general, or his ilk, like that jackass Senator McCarthy. I doubt the Soviet Union is planting spies in our midst, or that there are communists under every bed in America. There are threats to democracy in the world, but I don't count communism as the biggest one."

"What do you see as a larger threat?"

"That's easy. War. Serial wars are a threat to any civilization. Here we are, not a decade away from the two wars that slaughtered tens of millions, and we're opening up a new front against the Chinese." He looked surprisingly emotional. "It doesn't make sense, and it's unsustainable."

"Washington sees Chinese communism as a threat to our way of life. If one country falls, they'll all go. Domino effect, they're calling it." Arrows of hot pain shot up Jack's leg as he took a step up to the patio.

"That's bullshit. The guys in Washington are saber rattling against communism because of one thing. Money. War means money to them and their friends. They're not worried about our democratic way of life; I can assure you of that."

It was a provocative statement from a man who ran a multi-million-dollar conglomerate which included munitions, steel, and half the automobile parts companies in the country. A conglomerate that had hundreds of millions of dollars' worth of contracts with the Department of Defense.

Jack peered at Maxwell. "Is that also off the record, sir?"

"Absolutely. Now, what can I get you to drink? Scotch?" Maxwell walked through the open French doors.

"Thank you, yes."

Lynton waved Jack over to the sofa. "Where did you see service, Jack? The Pacific?"

"Army infantry. Italy."

Lynton handed him a tumbler that sparkled in the fading light. "I was with the Air Force briefly. Flew eight sorties over Japan."

The hair on Jack's arm tingled. Eddie's research had not mentioned that. "Hiroshima?"

"God, no. I was saved that tragedy."

"You don't believe we had to drop the bomb?" Jack kept his voice steady.

"Of course we did. But it is a tragedy nonetheless. One I am sure we'll pay an enormous price for eventually." Lynton settled into the chair across from Jack. "The chickens always come home to roost, don't they?"

"I'm not sure what you mean, Mr. Maxwell."

"We killed hundreds of thousands of Japanese innocents to win a war. Which we did. It was an honorable victory. After all, the sons of bitches killed our guys at Pearl, Iwo, and a hundred other miserable rat-hole islands. They deserved what they brought on themselves. But now we have to live in a world with a whole race of people who will hate us for eternity because we incinerated their family members. I can't imagine that millions of them don't go to bed every night thinking of a way to avenge their dead."

Jack was itching to reach for his notebook, but the man had said this was off the record. His story on Thrill Girl felt a million miles away. "Why fear retribution? The Japanese have no military at all now."

"Fear?" Lynton's face darkened. "I do fear that. I think revenge is nearly impossible to divert once the raw need bites into a man's heart. And there is no defense against a person whose intent on it."

Jack sipped his drink. "President Truman said we had no choice but to use the bomb. The Japanese were never going to surrender, and we were going to lose a hundred thousand men if we tried to invade their mainland."

"And you respect Truman, I take it?"

"He's the commander-in-chief." Jack blinked.

"Once a military man, always one, yes?" Lynton didn't wait

for Jack's reply. "Well, in this case, he was right. But we killed three hundred thousand men, women, and children in five days." Maxwell shook his head. "Was that really self-defense?"

"What would you call it?"

"Vengeance. Greatest motivator of human beings in history."

The air was still, and the melody of the piano music drifted around them. Inside his head, Jack heard the sickening whistle of a bomb dropping, followed by the agonized screams of a dozen friends dying around him.

He knew about vengeance. And survival. "Don't misunderstand me, Mr. Maxwell. I'm not arguing the atomic bomb was a good thing. But nations make impossible decisions when there are no good options available."

"I agree. And frankly, once we built the bomb, it was inevitable we'd use it. Einstein warned us. He said victory is always temporary, claimed only by those blind to the reversal of fortune that is sure to come."

Jack moved his head awkwardly as if to shake off a cramp. "I am sure the atomic bomb frightened Americans as much as it did the rest of the world. But hopefully, we'll never use it again."

"Man will never give up war. Our best hope is that science develops a way for it to be less costly, in terms of human suffering, in the future."

"How do you mean?"

Lynton studied his drink for a moment. "I was recently given a preliminary proposal for a new way to train our soldiers. Many of my military friends think its science fiction. But the officer who gave it to me is serious about pursuing new methods, including the use of certain drugs that can cut down on battlefield losses by making warriors tougher. He's got the ear of a few guys at the Pentagon."

"Really? Who is this scientist?"

Lynton glanced around his backyard. "If I told you, I'd have to kill you."

The men laughed.

"I asked because I am interested," Jack said casually. "I was stationed in DC at the end of the war, and I heard rumors the Nazis had a program along those lines that went horribly wrong. If the US was going anywhere down that path, it would make an interesting story."

"In your paper?" Maxwell's face closed down as if it suddenly occurred to him this was a conversation he shouldn't have with a reporter. "You do realize everything I said is off the record."

"Of course, but why? It's certainly thought-provoking."

"Because my personal interests and thoughts don't always mesh with what I do to earn a living. I have a board of directors, and it wouldn't please them to see me painted as a crazed pacifist in your newspaper. It would make a lot of people nervous."

"I would never quote you without your agreement, Mr. Maxwell."

Lynton's eyes narrowed. "Of course you wouldn't. Now, let's stop yammering and talk about more enjoyable topics. You're here about my cars. Are you going to do a feature on them?"

Jack set his glass down. If it was another time or place, he would have enjoyed continuing the discussion with Lynton. "Actually, sir. I'm not doing a feature on your collection."

"I don't understand." Maxwell's body stilled.

"The guard gave you slightly inaccurate information. The reason I came to see you tonight was because of one car registered to you. A 1939 Rolls Royce." Jack rattled off the license plate from memory. "Is that your vehicle, Mr. Maxwell?"

"Why are you asking?"

Jack kept his gaze level. "I'm trying to determine the identity of a woman seen riding in it. Blonde. Quite the stunner. She has a Negro driver. Can you tell me who she is?"

Maxwell's eyes flickered toward the oil painting. "Let me ask again, Mr. Curran. Why are you interested in the car? And the woman?"

"I'm working on a story, and I need to verify the facts. If you don't give them to me, I'll go to the police with information I've developed. Then they'll be the ones asking about the car. And the woman."

Maxwell took a sip of his Scotch before answering. "A story about a crime?"

"Yes, sir."

"I see." Lynton looked directly into Jack's face. "It is my car. A 1939 Phantom III. World War II ended their production. There were only about 700 made, and half of those were lost in the war. First Rolls with a 12-cylinder. It's registered to me, but it belongs to my step-brother, Tomas. He's a cripple and can't drive, but he loves that damn thing. It belonged to his mother before she died."

Jack wondered if it was the car she had died in. It would be impossible to ask that question without revealing how much he had already investigated Maxwell's family. "And the woman?"

"Who owns *The Eyes of LA*?" Lynton set his empty tumbler down.

"Quentin Deville."

"Ah, yes, I've heard of him." Maxwell stood. "I'm going to say goodnight now, Mr. Curran. I'll see you to the door."

Jack stood. "Is the woman your step-sister? Alana Maxwell?"

Maxwell narrowed his eyes.

"Hello? Who is bandying my name around?" The female voice came from behind Jack, rich as brandy.

"Alana. You're early." Maxwell scowled and moved as if he hoped to block Jack's view of her.

"I hate tardiness. You know that." The woman who had spoken walked into Jack's line of sight.

He felt for a moment as if he had too much to drink. The image in the painting was gorgeous, but in the flesh, Lynton's step-sister was too gorgeous to believe. She sparkled with intensity as if she couldn't wait to experience every second of life.

The blonde let Lynton kiss her cheek while her gaze stayed pinned on Jack.

Jack held out his hand. "Hello. Jack Curran. I'm a reporter with *The Eyes of LA*."

A smile curved her mouth. She ignored his outstretched hand and touched her fingers to his face, directly against his bruised cheek. "What happened to you, Mr. Curran? Don't journalists usually stay away from rough stuff?"

He didn't move. "I ran into a door."

"Lucky door." She dropped her hand. "I'm Alana Maxwell. What exactly were you asking Lynton about me?"

She had a hint of an accent. "I wanted to know if you ride around town in the Rolls Royce he owns." Jack relaxed his arm at his side. "Do you?"

"That's enough, Curran." Lynton's voice was brusque.

"Lynton! Where are your manners?" Alana seemed amused. "Yes. I do ride around town in the Rolls Royce. I even drive the beast but don't tell Lynton. He doesn't have any faith in my driving skills. The car belongs to my brother, Tomas. Is there a problem?"

"No. Of course not." Jack knew he should take this opportunity to press her about the roses – whether it ended with him being pummeled by Lynton Maxwell or not – but all he could do was stare.

Alana's white silk gown skimmed the floor. She was slim but curvy in all the right spots. Her blue eyes were as warm as the summer sky, and her silky mass of blonde hair danced around her shoulders.

"Well, if there's no problem with the car, why were you asking about me, Mr. Curran?" Alana motioned for him to give her a cigarette.

"There are a couple of reasons."

She took the cigarette, let him light it, and a moment later blew smoke toward him. "Let's hear them."

She seemed to be enjoying herself. Before Jack could answer, Lynton stepped between them.

"Don't banter with this man. He's not a friend of our family. He's a reporter, for Christ's sake. And he's leaving." Maxwell gestured to the door. "After you, Mr. Curran."

Jack inclined his head to the side. "Nice to meet you, Miss Maxwell."

"Let's do it again real soon," she replied.

"This way," Maxwell ordered.

Jack followed the tycoon down the long hall, but not before turning once to see if Alana Maxwell was watching him. She was.

He continued walking behind Maxwell.

"What are you driving, Mr. Curran?"

"1951 Packard."

Maxwell barked the information to a servant and turned at Jack. "Don't come here again under false pretenses. In fact, don't come here for any reason at all." The mogul stalked back into the house and slammed the door behind him.

Jack lit himself a cigarette. He had hit a nerve. Lynton Maxwell was not only protective of his family. He was possessive. *Especially of Alana Maxwell.*

Her image filled Jack's mind. If a photo of that woman was published in connection with the Thrill Girl story, it would be a sensation.

Up until now, his reports had contained plenty to engage the public – murder, mystery, and a blonde responsible for both. If he hinted Thrill Girl might be a socialite knockout with two brothers, one a millionaire industrialist and the other a cripple, the print shop would have to work around the clock, every day of the week.

And if he had the chance to do it, a screenplay about her would write itself.

Jack shook his head at that unwanted thought. He took the keys from Maxwell's servant and slipped into the Packard. He wondered what the industrialist's reaction would be if a movie was made based on his step-sister.

Not good.

Not good at all.

Jack grinned as he drove down the hill.

CHAPTER TWELVE

Alana eyed her step-brother from across the room. She was curled up under the family portrait she hated, smoking the last of the cigarette the reporter had given her.

Lynton had dispatched the last of the guests and was making her a cocktail. He handed the crystal tumbler to her, his voice hard. "You shouldn't smoke."

"You shouldn't tell me what to do." She took the whiskey.

"We shouldn't argue." He crossed his arms.

She took a last drag from the cigarette and snuffed it out. "Maybe we shouldn't talk at all. We never get anywhere."

"Why is that?"

"Why do you think?" Alana raised her eyebrows, feeling tears in her throat she would never let out in front of Lynton.

"Because you don't trust me." He paused. "It's been over a year since you've visited. I've missed you."

"You're right. I don't trust you." She took a drink.

A sigh rattled out of Lynton. He sat on the sofa across from her. "I'm not your enemy, Alana. I never have been."

"Why is this Jack Curran asking about me? He's quite good-looking, by the way, despite the black eye."

"I don't know." Lynton glanced out at the patio, where Tomas sat in his wheelchair, chatting with Shagg Waters, the piano player. "He said he's working on an investigative piece for his newspaper. He wanted me to identify a blonde woman seen in my car." He turned back to her. "Did you or Robinson run over someone and not stop?"

"That's a nasty thing to say, even for you." Her voice rose. "Is that a cheap crack about my mother? Are you that cruel?" It was. And he was.

"Don't be ridiculous. I wasn't referring to Margaret's accident."

"You were. Stop lying."

"I don't lie to you."

She snickered.

"Alana, please."

She held up her hand. "You know I don't ever want to discuss my mother with you. Let's concentrate on Curran, shall we? Are you going to find out what he's writing about?"

"Of course."

"Maybe he's doing a piece on Gino. The press is always trying to tie him to the Mafia. Perhaps he's interested in me because we're dating."

"Is that what you're doing with Gino Venice? *Dating?*"

Alana swallowed. If not for Tommy, she would leave now and never see this man again. "If I didn't know better, I'd say you were jealous."

"Of what? I'm your brother, not one of your suitors."

"*Step-brother*. But I'm glad you understand the limits of our relationship."

They stared at each other. Alana let the silence lengthen as Lynton's face reddened.

"*Is* Gino Venice connected to criminals?" he asked.

"I have no idea."

"Maybe you should ask him."

"We don't talk much. Too busy *dating*." She took a deep breath, enjoying Lynton's discomfort. "Are you worried about him? Curran?"

"Not in the least. And don't you worry, okay?"

"For your information, I never worry about anything. What will be, will be."

"Now who is lying? You worry about everything." Lynton paced to the bar and poured himself another Scotch. "Especially Tomas. How is the treatment going with Preminger?"

"Tomas thinks it's going well."

"What do you think?" He stared at her.

"I think my brother is making remarkable progress." Alana tilted her chin upwards, ready for the fight to come.

"How can you say that? He looks worse than ever. Maybe it's time to take him back to UCLA, or to the clinic I mentioned in Switzerland."

"Tomas chooses his doctors now, Lynton. He's of age." She twisted a strand of hair around her finger. "You were right to recommend Dr. Preminger. He's got some interesting research going. Tomas is going to give him a while longer."

"And you're fine with that?"

"I'm fine with anything that will help Tomas."

"We all know that. Which is why I'm sure if you told him you wanted him to be evaluated in Europe…"

"No. We're not shipping him off again. And he doesn't need to be evaluated by another doctor. He's been to ten in the last twenty-one years. None have come up with a course of treatment that has helped the atrophying of his limbs or the paralysis. The research Dr. Preminger is doing is the first Tommy has been excited about. It's actually offered him hope."

"I pray it's not false hope."

"You pray? Since when?"

Lynton scowled. "I have prayed for that boy a million times since the day he was born. Despite what you think, his condition has broken my heart too."

Alana pressed her hand against her face and closed her eyes. It always came back to this. Ancient history neither of them could forget. Or forgive. She should never have come to his house tonight. "I'm sick of you bringing up the past. You do it hoping I'll forgive you for what you did. I'm never going to do that."

"I don't want your forgiveness; I want your respect. I saved this family."

"You killed it," she replied softly.

"I did what our father told me to do."

"My father. You did what my father told you to do, despite what that turned you into."

"What did it turn me into, Alana?" He walked closer. "The kind of man who helped you the day your mother was killed? The kind of man who handled the police and the reporters, and made sure you got the medical care, and protection you needed?"

"The kind of man who only wants control." Alana kicked at the coffee table, sending the candlesticks skidding across the waxed surface. "You proved my point. You hold the past over my head like blackmail every chance you get."

"That's absurd."

Alana stood. "I'm leaving."

He blocked her way. "You tear me down, take umbrage at innocent remarks, and accuse me of being interfering every time we have a serious discussion." He grabbed her shoulders. "What do I have to do to get you to end this vendetta against me?"

"Tomas and I don't need you." She pulled out of his grip. "Stop trying to act like a brother to us; stop pretending we're any kind of a family at all."

"How can you say that?"

"I can say it because it's true. You're not our brother, you're our banker. You control our money and try to control our lives. But you don't care about Tomas. All you want to do is get him out of the way."

"Out of the way of what?"

"Your fantasies of what might happen between us if Tomas weren't around. And those are very sick fantasies, Lynton. Which will never come true."

"Don't flatter yourself," he shot back. "You act like a slut with that two-bit movie star, and now you're thinking like one."

Alana threw her highball glass at the fireplace, and the crystal exploded.

"Alana! Lynton! What's going on?" Tomas, his face drawn and fatigued, rumbled across the threshold in his wheelchair.

"Nothing." Alana rushed toward him. "Lynton and I are jousting about the affairs of the world. He's an imperialist, like always. And we were enjoying a drink."

"It didn't sound like you were enjoying anything." Tomas rolled closer. "Lynton, did you break a glass?"

"No. I did." Alana gestured toward the bar. "Clumsy as usual. Lynton, fix me another, won't you? Whiskey. No ice."

Lynton took a breath. "What can I get you to drink, Tomas?"

"Nothing. Thank you." He continued to stare at his sister.

Alana collapsed on the sofa. "Tommy, it's time we shared our ulterior motives for coming here tonight, I think."

"Is it?"

"No time like the present. Or I'm leaving."

Both men tensed. "Okay." Tomas turned the wheelchair toward his step-brother. "I need to ask you for help."

"Ask away." Lynton handed Alana a fresh drink and sat across from the young siblings, but kept his eyes fixed on Tomas. "What is this about?"

"Money. I want control of my trust fund. I'd like to buy a house of my own and live in it. By myself."

Lynton reached for his empty glass. He dropped his hand, and the silence hardened into a wall around the three of them.

"You would continue to supervise all the Maxwell family accounts on our behalf," Tomas continued. "But I want sole control of my individual trust. Alana has control of hers."

"All right," Lynton finally said after several moments. "I'll call the attorney tomorrow. Where are you thinking of buying? In Los Angeles?"

Tomas blinked. "Yes. I'm hoping Hancock Park. She talked

me out of Europe." He looked at Alana. "What did you do to convince him to agree to this?"

"You give me too much credit. Lynton always does what he wants," she said. "This is exciting, Tommy. May I go with you next week to look at properties?"

"Yes, of course." Tomas turned to Lynton. "Thank you. I must tell you, I thought you would put up more of a fight."

"Why? It's your money. I'm not trying to control your life."

Alana grinned. "Well, now that that's settled, can we have dinner? I'm starving, and I have a date with Gino later." Without waiting for Lynton to reply, she got up and pushed Tomas toward the dining room.

#

Jack's stomach grumbled. He looked up at the clock, which showed it was already after eleven. He should have stopped for dinner after he left Maxwell's, but he had a lot of work to do before he met up with Carol at the Coconut Grove later.

Before he could get up to raid the office refrigerator for leftovers that wouldn't give him ptomaine poisoning, the telephone rang. "*The Eyes of LA*. Curran."

"Good evening, Jack." Quentin Deville did not sound happy.

"Hey, boss. What's going on?"

"You're working?"

"Yes, sir. Saturday night is good for that. No one else is here."

"How industrious. I wish I spent my evening in an equally productive manner. Instead, I was forced to endure a half-hour hide-whipping from one Mitchell Brown Harrington, ESQ., and Mr. Lynton Maxwell's attorney. What did you say to Mr. Maxwell to engender legal threats this quickly?"

Jack tapped his pencil on the desk. "Nothing. I asked him about the blonde woman driving his car. Turns out it's his step-sister, Alana Maxell."

"He said that?"

"No. *She* did. Walked in right before I got thrown out of the place. Maxwell went into full-on protection mode when she appeared."

"Why did he feel he had to protect his step-sister from you? Did you accuse her of anything?"

"No. Maybe I should have as I'm sure she's the one who sent flowers to Thrill Girl's victims."

"And what would you have accused her of, exactly?"

"Of being connected to the victims. And I can prove it was her. All I need to do is show the shop girl a picture of her."

"If that's true, you could certainly prove Alana Maxwell sends flowers. And?"

"Well, it connects her to the Thrill Girl case."

"Not in any significant way, and you know that, Jack. And there certainly isn't a shred of evidence that she *is* Thrill Girl, isn't that also true?"

"I never said she was."

"But that's what you're thinking, isn't it?"

He was. But he wasn't going to admit that to Quentin. "What if I gave the cops a tip about Alana Maxwell and the roses? They would go see her, and since she matches the description of Thrill Girl, they might stick her in a lineup in front of Mr. Kim, the Taylor boys, and Susan Baldwin. That tip could crack the biggest case since the Lindberg baby kidnapping."

Jack pictured Alana standing in a lineup with five or six other blondes, holding a placard with a number stenciled on it. The only problem was the cops would be hard-pressed to find a group of women as gorgeous as her. Even in LA.

"Jack, listen carefully." Quentin's voice was tight. "As your employer, I am giving you a direct order not to do that. Although I doubt the police would be stupid enough to make the logical leap that the blonde woman sending flowers must be the same blonde woman who is killing muggers, much less pull said woman into a lineup, they would not be given the go-ahead by either the chief or the mayor. Not if she's as connected, wealthy, and powerful as Alana Maxwell. They understand what you apparently have failed to, which is that Lynton Maxwell would sue us all. Hell, he might have us all killed if we get his sister pulled into a lineup."

"Killed? That's dramatic. After all, she's only his step-sister."

"Don't be obtuse. She's family, and the family reputation means everything to a man like that."

Jack frowned. "Okay, okay. I won't tip the cops off. But I'm going to keep digging until I have solid proof. When I do, we should run it in 12-point type."

"Thank you. Now try to stay out of trouble for the next couple of days. I want to talk to you first thing on Monday. I'll be in the office early."

"Sure thing. See you then."

The receiver clicked loudly in his ear. Quentin did not say goodbye.

Jack massaged his throbbing knee. His boss had been right to chew him out. He was taking shortcuts and relying on hunches. He had absolutely no hard evidence attesting that Alana Maxwell was, or even could be, Thrill Girl.

His stomach grumbled again, and Jack pushed away from his desk. He limped to the refrigerator in the corner of the office and looked inside. A box of Moo Shoo Pork was dripping oil onto the shelf below. A torn brown bag with two moldy oranges in it sat next to half a liverwurst sandwich he had seen Eddie stick inside at lunch.

Jack grabbed it, poured himself a cup of hours-old cold coffee to wash it down, and went to his desk. After finishing Eddie's sandwich, he closed his eyes.

Is there a connection between the muggers themselves? They were all young, poor guys with records. He sat forward and scribbled a note, *check arrest backgrounds of dead guys,* and slapped it onto Eddie's desk.

If a guy was setting up the muggings to give Thrill Girl the chance to play rescuer, well, it was weird and lacked any logical motivation. But the blonde had killed those six men for a reason.

Maybe Thrill Girl is a superhero.

"Shit," he said aloud.

Jack put his jacket on and slammed his way out of the office. He headed for the Packard, eager suddenly to go to the Ambassador for the late date he had set-up as a lustful thought about Carol bloomed in his brain.

Except Carol didn't look like her red-headed self. She looked like a silky blonde who he had no good reason to be thinking about. At the edge of the parking lot, he spotted a familiar black Cadillac. The lights were off.

Jack squinted at the plate, but could not read it. When he took two steps toward it, the steel monster growled to life and backed out, leaving skid marks on Western Avenue.

What the hell? Is it the same car I saw at the Susan Baldwin crime scene? Is someone following me?

He beat down anxiety and got into the Packard, fired it up and rolled out onto Western Avenue. There was no sign of the caddy. But an LAPD patrol car was parked across the street from the front door of his office. It had been there on and off since his release from jail. Jack made out two uniforms huddled inside.

Stifling the impulse to give them the finger, Jack gunned the Packard's engine. He lit a cigarette and drove past the cops, waving politely.

They gave him the finger.

He frowned and headed downtown for the Coconut Grove, hoping booze and sex would clear his clouded mind.

# # #

The Coconut Grove nightclub was a hot spot for Hollywood elites and movie stars. Six nights a week it offered top-rated live entertainment, mediocre food, dancing, and a grand showing by the press that nourished the film industry.

Jack talked his way in at twelve forty-five and was finishing his third whiskey as he checked-out the Moroccan-styled room. Two hundred tables were arranged around enormous pots containing live palm trees. Thousands of sparkling lights and girls dressed in bellman's coats – and little else – set the glamour quotient high and the noise level higher.

Tonight he got a look at Dinah Shore, Linda Darnell, and a new actor with a ducktail haircut named Tony Curtis. He also sucked down a chicken cordon bleu dinner the waitress had snuck out from the kitchen.

But if he did not spot Carol in the next five minutes, he was going to take a powder and go home.

He scanned the room one last time and motioned for the cigarette girl, Lola, to come to the table. "Hey doll, can you do me a favor? Tell Carol I'll call her tomorrow, okay? I need to get back to the newspaper."

"Oh no! The monster didn't strike again, did it?"

She was the fifth person who had asked him about that in the past hour. "Nah, nothing like that. But will you tell her that my boss had me paged, and I've got to go?"

Lola smiled and took the bill he was holding out to her. "Sure thing, Jack. By the way, what happened to your eye?"

"Bee sting," he said with a wink. He was halfway to the rear entrance when the lights went down, and the next show started.

"Ladies and Gentlemen, welcome America's latest singing sensation, Gino Venice." Women squealed, and folks applauded. Jack made apologies as he limped his way out.

Venice launched into an imitation of Vaughan Monroe's "Red Roses for a Blue Lady." Jack pushed his way through the service door. He would rather scrub pans with the Mexican dishwashers than listen to that idiot mangle a song.

But instead of the kitchen he was expecting, there was a quiet, shadowy corridor on the other side of the door. Three rolling carts full of dirty dishes waited a few feet away, outside another door. Jack pushed this second door open and was surprised to feel a rush of cool air.

He was outside in a secluded private area at the back of the hotel. There was a fountain and several empty concrete benches, surrounded by abundant bougainvillea and rose bushes.

Beyond the fountain was a gazebo built in the shape of a birdcage. It was white lattice, freshly painted. As the breeze picked up, Jack walked toward it hoping to sit for a moment and smoke a cigarette before finding the Packard.

Jack stopped in shock, nearly inhaling the cigarette he had just put in his mouth. A woman lay face down on the bench inside the structure, her head nestled into her left arm

The blonde was poured into a slinky white dress cut high on her thighs, exposing the lacy garter belt holding up her silk stockings. Despite his shock, he enjoyed the sight of those legs, shapely and long as a summer night.

A gold evening bag and high-heeled shoes lay on the grass beneath the bench.

She was completely still.

Asleep, or passed out? He took a step closer.

Or dead?

He felt for a pulse as his own heart rate sped up. With a start, Jack realized he knew her.

The blonde moaned and opened her eyes. They were the color of blue diamonds and just as cold.

They stared at one another for a moment. Alana Maxwell sat up and pushed her hair off her face. "You got another one of those?" She pointed at his cigarette.

Jack pulled out his pack and shook one out.

Alana took it from him with cold fingers, and he lit her cigarette and then his own.

She took a hit and stared at Jack. "Do I know you?"

"We met earlier, at your brother's house. I'm Jack Curran, from *The Eyes of LA.*"

"Step-brother," she whispered.

Her voice was fuzzy with drink. Jack smiled. "Sorry. We met at your *step-brother's* house."

"I remember. You were asking him about me. Did you follow me here, Mr. Curran?" Her eyes traveled up his body from his knees to his forehead. She cleared her throat. "What the hell happened to your face?"

"You asked me that earlier. I hit my head on a cupboard door."

"A cupboard door?"

"Yeah. In my kitchen. I left it open when I was cooking breakfast."

"You were cooking breakfast?"

"Yeah. You know, eggs, bacon. The food you eat in the morning."

"I know what breakfast is." She winked at him.

"Great. Would you like some, Miss Maxwell? The Pantry Café is a few blocks over." He grinned at the thought of the look he would get from Milton if he walked in for the second time tonight with this dame on his arm. "Best food in town. Twenty-four hours a day. You know they've never closed their doors since 1924."

"It must get *wet* inside when it rains." She stressed *wet*.

"Maybe. What do you say?"

"I love steak and eggs." She licked her lips. "And toast and orange juice."

"Well, great. Me too." He looked around, wondering if a date, or her brother, or that gigantic chauffeur might show up and put up a fuss. Maybe even her brother's fancy lawyer. "Are you out here alone, Miss Maxwell?"

"Yes. I'm alone. Aren't we all?" She tried to laugh, but the sound contained no humor.

"I guess we are." Jack gestured to her feet. "Do you want to put your shoes on, and I'll drive us over to get that breakfast?"

She stared down for a long moment, then looked up and met his eyes. "Or we could go to my room."

"Excuse me?"

She motioned to the hotel. "I live here. I have an apartment on the top floor. I could call the kitchen and have them send up breakfast. If that's what you want to do now, Mr. Curran. *Eat breakfast.*"

The skin on Jack's abdomen contracted. Alana Maxwell's voice was as smooth as good scotch, and he wanted nothing more than to throw her down on the grass and push himself into that warm, wet space between her legs.

"It's your call," he said. "I'm in. Whatever you want to do."

She stared at him as if he was a plate of steak and eggs and she had not eaten in a long, long time. "Whatever I want?"

"Sure."

"I want you to make me happy. Can you do that, Jack? Can you come up to my room and make me happy?" She took a step toward him and smiled, revealing sharp white teeth and the shiny red tip of her tongue.

Jack thought his bad leg might buckle. "Let's get you upstairs, Miss Maxwell. Then we'll see what happens next." No way would he take advantage of her, especially not in this condition, but he wanted to see the inside of her room. He doubted there would be anything as incriminating as a knife or a gun lying around, but still...

He grasped her elbow to guide her. But she didn't seem to know he was there.

In the dim moonlight, Jack saw Alana's eyes were fully dilated, the blue of her irises were now tiny rings around her black velvet pupils. And she was paler than she had been a moment ago. The only color in her face was on her lips, and even her lipstick hinted at a night of wear and tear.

Alana took another draw from the cigarette and dropped her hand to her side. The cigarette fell from her fingers and rolled onto the hem of her dress.

It smoldered for a moment before Jack leaned down and batted it away. "Hey, watch out, we don't want you going up in flames."

She fell against him, wrapping her arms around his neck. Her mouth was hungry when it found his.

He did not return the kiss, but he held her to his chest. Intimacy with a woman he might write a story about was not good journalism.

But he couldn't pull away.

Alana snuggled into him, breathing hard. She put two fingers of her right hand into his mouth and stroked his bottom lip. "Do you think I have magic powers, Mr. Curran?"

His body was tense everywhere. He made himself think of the war, of the long nights he and the other men had spent waiting for the next battle to break out. He moved her hand from his mouth. "I don't know what you mean, Miss Maxwell."

"I don't know what I mean, either. But I know what I want. I want you to come upstairs with me. And take your clothes off."

"I agree about the upstairs part. But I think you better call it a night. I don't think you're feeling quite yourself."

She put her lips on his left ear, licked it, and said in a husky whisper, "I want you. I'll give you quite a *thrill*."

"A thrill, huh?" Jack held her gently and walked her toward the hotel. "You like that word, Alana? Use it often?"

She fluttered her eyelids as if she was about to pass out. "Is that an ambulance? Do you hear the siren? Has something happened to Tomas?" she whispered, then nestled her face into his chest.

He heard no siren, only the faint notes from the orchestra inside the nightclub. "Tomas, that's your brother, right? No. He's fine. I mean, I think everything's fine with him." Jack kept her walking, baby steps now. "Are you ill, Alana? You want to sit down?"

"I'm taking a lot of drugs. I have to. They make me act strange, but the doctor said it will help Tomas."

He stopped. "How is you taking drugs going to help your brother?"

She looked up at him with eyes that were huge empty pools of darkness. "Who are you?"

"Miss Maxwell? You okay?" A gruff male voice spoke from three feet behind Jack. Alana bolted out of his grasp, and when Jack turned, he found himself face-to-face with the chauffeur.

He had not heard him approach, which was unsettling. Since the war, Jack was aware of the people around him. But Alana's employee had crept up behind him without him noticing.

He was six-foot-five and a good two hundred pounds. Jack always felt plenty big enough, but next to this man he felt like a ten-year-old girl. Now that he had a close look at him, he was sure the man was ex-military.

The man's hands were balled into fists, and the whites of his eyes glowed against his skin.

"Hello." Jack stuck his hand out. "Jack Curran. Reporter for *The Eyes of LA*. Miss Maxwell and I were thinking of getting breakfast. But I'm not sure she's feeling well enough right now. Can you help me get her up to her room?"

"She doesn't need your help to find her room," the man replied.

"Oh. Well, will you be sure she gets back okay? I don't think she's too steady." Jack turned toward Alana.

But the blonde was not there. To his surprise, she was already twenty yards away, hurrying barefoot toward the rear entrance of the hotel's bar.

Jack smiled at the chauffeur. "I guess you were right about her finding her room okay."

"Is there anything else, sir?"

"Uh, no. Except she left her things." Jack walked to the gazebo and picked up Alana's shoes and bag. He handed them to the man and pulled out one of his business cards.

"Would you please ask Miss Maxwell to give me a call when she's ready for that breakfast? Tell her I honor rain checks."

The chauffeur took Jack's card and Alana's things, giving Jack a look that he could not fathom. Then he turned without another word and took off after her.

Jack sat on the bench and lit another cigarette. *What the hell just happened with Alana Maxwell?*

The moon above him was a watery half circle against dense darkness. He took a deep hit from his cigarette. Music from the Coconut Grove orchestra wafted toward him, but he could not identify the melody. He looked around the deserted garden and finally regained his sense of direction.

The parking lot was behind him.

He headed for the Packard as his pulse slowed to near normal. But it spiked again when he heard a clattering sound, like two or three metal trash cans falling over in the alley.

A cat howled in anger, then screeched again, as if it had been grabbed by the tail.

The Thrill Girl story was making him jumpy. Jack took the last drag of his cigarette and flicked it away. But the only thing he tasted in his mouth was Alana Maxwell.

CHAPTER THIRTEEN

J ack set his second cup of coffee of the morning on his desk. He had a slight hangover from drinking too much over the weekend, and from taking too many pain pills. "Five of the six dead men had multiple offenses?"

"Yes, sir." Eddie blinked rapidly.

He stared down at the list Eddie had drawn up. It was the research Jack had requested he do about the muggers and their arrest history.

"The sixth, Lu Chen, had recently been arrested, but his charges were dropped. And as you suspected, all six of them did time in the downtown county jail within the last ninety days."

"Together?"

"Chen and Alvarez, the pair who tried to take Susan Baldwin's purse, were in at the same time."

"All burglary or robbery?" Jack narrowed his eyes.

"Yes. And one public drunkenness."

"Weapons?"

"Alvarez was busted with a gun, but the others didn't commit armed robbery."

"Which means they weren't armed when they tried to mug our

good citizens?" Jack gave Eddie a hard look.

"I doubt it, though of course, we can't rule it out." Eddie pushed on his glasses. "Thrill Girl must have brought the gun and knife to each crime scene, and then took them with her. I got confirmation from a source in the morgue, no guns or knives were recovered by the cops at any of the four crime scenes."

Jack blinked. "You have a source at the morgue?"

"Ah, yes sir."

"Who?"

Eddie hesitated. "You told me to keep sources confidential."

"Not from me. *Jesus*, Eddie, wait until you're working your own story."

"Yes, sir. Sorry. My source is Millie Hatchett."

"The coroner? Your source is the fucking coroner?"

Eddie blushed crimson. "I, eh. My Uncle Teddy is a friend of hers."

"How good of a friend?"

"Very good. He brought her to dinner last week at my mother's house."

Lucky Uncle Teddy, Jack thought. "Well, you be nice to Miss Hatchett. That's a golden source, kid."

"Yes, sir. There's another issue I want to talk to you about." He reached into his desk.

At that moment, Quentin Deville walked into the office. "Jack, my office. You too, Eddie. I want an update on all things Thrill Girl."

Ten minutes later, Jack had finished delivering his update, leaving out his run-in with Alana Maxwell on Saturday night for no good reason except he didn't want to. He included the facts Eddie had dug up about the dead muggers. Jack waited for Quentin to digest the information while he leaned against the bookcase, eye level with Quentin's prized trio of goldfish. He tapped the bowl, and they frantically sucked at the water.

"Don't harass the fish, Jack."

"Sorry." He lit up a cigarette. "There's more going on here

than what meets the eye, Quentin."

Quentin settled back in his creaky chair. "Walk me through your thinking on how we're going to report this. Slowly."

"First, we do a page one piece on Thrill Girl. Lead with Joan Becklund's death and my bogus arrest," Jack said.

"I agree we need to set the record straight that you had nothing to do with Joan's murder, but Jasper told you explicitly not to provoke the cops."

"If they are provoked by reports of their ineptitude, it's got nothing to do with me. After that, I think we should introduce the roses' angle. Carefully note that Joan, Mr. Kim, and Susan all received them. While I've got a receipt showing flowers delivered to the Taylor kids' house, I can't get anyone there to talk to me. I'll leave that out for now."

Quentin sat forward. "You're not mentioning the Maxwells."

It wasn't a question.

"No. Only the roses. Then I'll do a sidebar on the fact that all the dead muggers were in the same jail in the same general time frame and speculate as to where there's a tie-in."

"Speculate? In a news article?"

"I'm going to call the Police Chief and speculate to him in the form of a question. We'll print his answer."

Quentin sighed. "Well, that's certainly not provocative, insinuating the muggers were running a criminal organization inside the Los Angeles County jail. I'm sure the chief will be delighted with your question."

Jack grinned. "I'd like to use our courthouse stringer to look into that." The guy was a retired cop from New York. "He can hang out in the hearing rooms, walk the hallways, pick-up on anything else that ties the dead guys together."

"Okay." Quentin looked down at his hands for a moment. "In the five years you've worked for me, you have never asked for a stringer to help with a story. I feel like you're not telling me everything you're thinking, Mr. Curran."

"What do you mean?"

He crossed his arms, careful not to smash the red poppy stuck in the boutonniere hole of his white summer jacket. "Are you still thinking Thrill Girl is Alana Maxwell?"

Jack swallowed. He glanced at Eddie, who had paled in response to Quentin's question.

"I follow the story where it leads. There are indications Alana Maxwell is complicit, but the facts aren't clear. I don't know if she's Thrill Girl. I haven't prejudged her. But I won't shut my eyes to where the information is taking me, even if it's to the door of a man who is rich, powerful, or both."

Deville's eyebrows raised a fraction. "Let me be sure I understand you. Alana Maxwell, step-sister of Lynton Maxwell, one of Los Angeles's leading citizens, is actually on your list of possibilities for the murderous blonde Samaritan?"

"I don't have a list. But if I did, she would be on it. At the top." Jack put his hands on his hips.

Several moments of silence passed. "Refresh my memory," Quentin asked. "Did Thrill Girl leave any fingerprints on the weapons?"

"As far as I can tell, no weapons were left at any of the scenes." He glanced at Eddie. "And we haven't heard about any fingerprint evidence."

"That's correct. I mean, that's what I've been told by my sources," Eddie interjected.

Quentin looked surprised Eddie was still in the room. "Sources?" He frowned at Jack. "Okay, we'll go with the columns you've outlined for tomorrow's edition. Then what?"

"I've got another angle to check out."

"Oh? Please share."

"One thing that eats at me is that Thrill Girl stumbled on four different muggings in six weeks." Jack's knee was shooting pain all the way up to his hip, and he leaned against the bookcase, nearly knocking off the goldfish bowl. He set it on Quentin's desk. "Sorry. Anyway, I can't figure out how she knows what's going to go down."

"Twenty people a night are mugged in LA. It's a busy city.

She's been walking around dicey places."

"I don't buy it. Susan was attacked off Wilshire, Mr. Kim was in Korea town, and the Taylor kids were behind a movie theatre on Vine. All of them are pretty safe areas. Only Joan was at a location where a person might expect to get mugged, near the bridge by the homeless mission."

"Which means?"

He filled him in on Trixie's comments about the guys who had watched Susan Baldwin get mugged, and reminded him what Joan said about meeting a man. "I told Jimmy Glass about them, and about the lights that keep getting mentioned. He didn't deny it. I'm beginning to think Thrill Girl is working with someone."

"Someone like whom? A tour guide of ambush locations?" Quentin sounded skeptical.

In the corner, Eddie laughed nervously, and quickly covered his mouth.

"I don't know." Jack sat down.

"The police are publicly saying these are crimes of opportunity. This would be new, uncorroborated information if we printed it." He stared hard at Eddie. "Have you heard anything about that from your *sources*?"

"Ah, no. No, sir."

"I know it sounds farfetched, Quentin," Jack said. "But there's got to be an explanation other than chance. The woman hasn't dropped out of the sky into four crime scenes in six weeks. She's not fucking Superman."

"No, that would be Lois Lane," Quentin replied.

Eddie nearly choked on his laugh this time.

"Do I need to send you out of the room, Mr. Wentz?"

"No, Mr. Deville. Sorry."

Quentin rose to his feet to pace the length of his office. "I trust your instincts, Jack, but I'm skeptical about that line of investigation coming to fruition for next week's edition. What else do you have?"

"A couple of weeks ago, Alana Maxwell sent white roses to a

fifth person, a woman named Wanda Keppler."

"Wanda Keppler?" Quentin blinked. "Who is she?"

"I don't know. She's not a crime victim, in fact, Eddie can't find any print references to her. I thought I'd ride over to Monterey Park today to ask Mrs. Keppler about the roses."

Quentin stood in front of Jack. "Or you could go see Alana Maxwell and ask her directly why she sent flowers to Mrs. Keppler."

"You're not worried about her attorney anymore?"

"Of course I am. Damn this." Quentin stomped his foot in a rare show of temper. "We're pussyfooting around this story because the Maxwells have more money than I do. I hate when that happens." He glared at Eddie. "Get to work on the monster follow-up, Mr. Wentz. And make damn sure you spell Commissioner Crotche's name correctly this time. He's still furious about the last article. Said he's being called 'Mr. Crotch' by every cop in town."

"Uh, yes, sir. I'll get on that right now. Except before I do that, I need to update Mr. Curran on my research." He cleared his throat. "I came into the office for a couple of hours last night to read all the weekly locals."

Jack and Quentin stared at Eddie.

"Well?" the publisher demanded.

"I found an article that did mention a Wanda Keppler. In *The Valley Tribune*. Five weeks ago a man named Randall Keppler of Monterey Park was killed in a car accident up near Griffith Park. He was mangled pretty badly. Took the cops a few days to ID him. Hit and run." Eddie pulled out an obituary from the notebook he was clutching and handed it to Jack. "It mentions his wife is Wanda Keppler. No children."

Jack glanced at the obituary and handed it to Quentin. "Mangled pretty bad? You mean like the bum at Griffith Park?"

"No. The injuries were 'entirely consistent with being involved in a car accident,' according to the coroner's report."

Jack frowned. "Keppler's obit doesn't mention that. Where did you get your info?"

"I, uh, called the 06 to inquire. Talked to a detective named

Howard Morrell." Eddie turned a page in his notebook. "Randall Keppler, aged 58, was found on May 1, 1951. Identified through fingerprints and clothing on May 8, 1951. Massive internal injuries and skeletal and torso trauma. Found approximately one hundred yards from the south parking lot at the Griffith Park Observatory. Dead approximately twelve hours when found at 11:33 a.m., according to the time of death from the coroner."

He nailed who, what, where, and when, Jack thought. "Why was Keppler in that area? He lived in Monterey Park, fifteen miles from where he was killed."

"Why? I got that." Eddie pushed his glasses up his nose and flipped to the next page. "Keppler was an assistant at a veterinary practice in Los Feliz, a mile from the scene where he was found. According to his employer, he left their location at approximately ten p.m. in his 1949 Ford sedan. It was found with a flat tire out on the road leading to the observatory. Police conclude Keppler was attempting to change the tire on the roadway when he was struck and thrown approximately twelve feet into the brush. Skid marks on the road near Mr. Keppler's damaged car confirm a collision."

His voice got more strained as he read, and he finished in a whisper. "There are no known witnesses."

No one said anything for ten seconds.

"Is that all?" Quentin asked in an unreadable tone.

"Well, ah, yes. No, I mean. I also got the address of the veterinary clinic from Detective Morrell." He turned toward Jack. "If you'd like, I can check out the facts while you go see Mrs. Keppler." Flushing a deep red, Eddie closed his notebook. "As soon as I finish the article about Commissioner Crotche, I mean. If that's okay."

Quentin drew his head back like a king cobra. "Well, well. *Well.*"

"Great job, Eddie." Jack patted his shoulder. "But I've got a better idea. Why don't you come with me? We'll give the widow Keppler a call and set it up. Then we'll swing by the vet's office and verify what the cops are reporting." He took out his keys and tossed them to the rookie. "You can drive, can't you?"

The ability to talk seemed to momentarily leave the young

man. "But...but you don't let anyone drive your car."

"I don't. My friends know I'll kill them if they get a scratch on it, and no one is willing to risk it. Until you. Ready?" Jack grinned as he limped over to the door of Quentin's office.

Eddie blinked rapidly.

"Go!" Quentin waved them out. "I'll have Lucy finish the Griffith Park follow-up if she deigns to grace us with her presence this morning. And Jack, take one of the cameras. Have Eddie get shots of Mrs. Keppler. And of the veterinary clinic."

"Good idea, boss." Jack took another step and nearly fell. He grabbed the doorframe of Quentin's office for a moment, waiting for his leg muscles to hold his weight.

"Are you planning to go to the doctor before your leg falls off, or after?" Deville asked.

"Soon. I'll have Eddie drop me as soon as I can get an appointment." He had spent hours soaking it last night, but if anything, it was worse today.

"Excellent." Quentin wagged his finger. "I need final copy at eight tonight, gentlemen. I'll keep two inches open for Keppler. And do an inch on Susan Baldwin's dog, Eddie. We didn't have that in the special, and people love to cry over a dead dog story."

He shut his door as soon as they walked out.

Jack called Mrs. Keppler from his desk. It was surprisingly easy to get her to agree to see them. She wanted people to know about her husband's hit and run.

He put on his jacket. When Eddie returned with the camera and two sleeves of flashbulbs, he chattered away about the upcoming interview and what they could ask Mrs. Keppler. Jack listened and limped out the front door behind him.

He lit up a cigarette and crawled into the passenger seat of the Packard. The Thrill Girl story was growing tentacles like an octopus.

And though he was the one who had hung the nickname on her, he was starting to think he should have dubbed her pain-in-the-ass girl, because that's what she was turning out to be.

# # #

Eddie drove Jack's Packard slowly around the cul-de-sac and squinted out the windshield. "I don't see a house number."

They were on Cliff Circle, the third cul-de-sac in a development in the rolling terrain of Monterey Park, a bedroom community ten miles east of downtown.

Jack looked out the side window. "There it is. 301. The second one on the left."

Eddie stopped the car and put on the parking brake.

Set back a hundred feet from the street, the house was newly built. Low and sleek, it had large windows with no sills or shutters, a flat roof, and wide double doors painted bright red.

"Modern." Eddie sniffed and rubbed his nose. "Looks like a big box to me."

Jack squinted. "Everything changes, kid. In fifty years this style will probably be admired even more than it is now for what it says about our time."

"What does it say?"

"Traditional design is dead? There are no more rules about anything? Everything was blown away by Hitler and the bomb?" He shrugged, sounding more serious than he had meant to be. "Who knows."

Eddie pushed his glasses back and stared at the house. "Wow."

"Let's get going. Don't bring the camera in with you. We'll talk to Mrs. Keppler first. And remember our story. We ask her about whether she's satisfied with the cops' investigation of her husband's death but not mention the white roses until later. Got it?"

"Got it."

They made their way down the paved drive. The plantings were sparse and hugged the foundation line, except for a patch of Bird of Paradise plants near the front door. The gaudy orange, green, and blue flowers hung like ripe, avian-shaped fruit at the ends of succulent stems. The clump of flowers was almost four feet tall and ten feet across.

A fat black cat jumped out from the plant's center and ran,

belly close to the ground, around to the back of the house.

Eddie sneezed. "Is that bad luck? It didn't cross our path."

"You superstitious?" Jack grinned. "Those shrubs should be the official flower of LA. Gorgeous, but so gorgeous they look fake. Quentin told me they're poisonous."

"They do look fake. They also don't smell. I thought all flowers smelled." Eddie shrugged and looked around the yard. "Looks like Mrs. Keppler has a lot of money."

"You afraid of rich people, Eddie?"

"No." He pulled on his jacket lapels, looking completely terrified.

"I'm a little surprised at this place, considering her old man was working for a vet, but she might have her own money." He looked Eddie up and down. "You got your press credentials with you?"

Eddie reached into his suit pocket and jerked out his wallet. "Yeah. They're right here." He dropped his wallet on the walkway, picked it up and took out his press card, dropped the press card, and then picked it up and wiped it off on his pant leg. His face was bright red by the time he held it up for Jack's perusal.

"*Edward* Wentz? You want me to use *Edward* when I introduce you?"

"My mom thinks it sounds more professional."

"Okay, *Edward*. Nice picture." Jack stifled a smile, remembering how nervous he had been in his first few interviews.

He rang the bell, which echoed deep inside the house.

A woman answered immediately. She was tall and reed-slim, with a plain face and intelligent, arresting green eyes. Her dark hair was sun-streaked, and her arms were tanned and bare in her summer dress.

Jack noted her fingernails were chewed to the quick. If pressed, he would guess she was in her early forties, but he was not all that good at guessing women's ages. Most of the time he knew better than to try.

"Good afternoon." The woman offered a smile. "Are you the

men from the newspaper?"

Jack took off his fedora and extended his hand. "Hello, Mrs. Keppler. Yes, Jack Curran from *The Eyes of LA*. This is my associate, Edward Wentz. Thank you for seeing us. As I told you on the phone, we only need a few minutes of your time."

She held the door open. "Come in. Please."

There was no foyer.

A step into Wanda Keppler's house dropped you right into a cavernous, high-ceiled room. Sunshine poured down from skylights and in from the floor-to-ceiling windows. An ocean of light flowed off the white walls.

The rear of the room was entirely glass, with sliders leading out to a patio covered by a latticed roof. The view stretched for miles, past a yard carpeted with dichondra, and into the foothills, culverts, and orange groves in the distance.

The furniture was as unadorned and modern as the structure. Two bright blue molded chairs and a twelve-foot white sofa rested on a stark white carpet. An orb lamp balanced at the end of a curved aluminum pole, hanging over a slab of white marble that served as the coffee table.

An enormous canvas covered with red, orange, and blue paint splatters hung on the wall behind the sofa.

"How do you like it?" Wanda asked Jack, nodding to the painting. "It's by an artist named Jackson Pollack. My husband, Randall, is, *was* related to his current wife."

"It's powerful." Jack smiled. "It fits great with your home."

"Thank you. I'm not sure if I like it either." Wanda pointed to the sofa. "Edward, would you like to sit here in the living room, or outside?"

"Sure. Ah, pardon?" Eddie blushed and looked at Jack.

"Outside would be great." Jack shot Eddie a *get with it* look.

There wasn't much difference in the view outside, but it was breezy and mild. The humidity from earlier in the week had abated. They took seats around a redwood table. It was clear Wanda had been sitting here reading and waiting for them, as a mug of coffee with a lipstick smudge was arranged alongside a copy of *The Los Angeles Times.*

A clean ashtray sat in the middle of the table.

Jack pulled out his Lucky Strikes and lighter. "Would you like one?" he asked Wanda.

"No, thank you. It was my husband who smoked." She nodded at the ashtray. "These are still all over the house. I can't seem to throw them out." She folded her hands in her lap and looked directly at Jack. "What is this all about, Mr. Curran?"

He bent his head and lit his cigarette. She was direct, not the type to bullshit. But he didn't want to tip his hand going in that her husband's death might be suspicious. He blew out a puff and looked her in the eye.

"I'm doing an investigative piece on the LAPD, Mrs. Keppler. Manpower focus. The city council is asking for a tax hike to pay for more cops, which isn't getting much support. But LA needs more police. Their track record on closing out violent crime cases is going down while crime is going up."

"Why is that?" She blinked. "Are the police too busy chasing after that woman who's killing the muggers? Or maybe they're putting too many cops on the so-called monster that killed that homeless man at the zoo?"

"I don't know. What do you think?"

She squeezed her hands tightly together. "In my opinion, if the newspapers didn't spend all this time on sensational stories, the police wouldn't feel pressure to pull away from boring, ordinary crimes like hit-and-run cases. Before the war, crimes like this would have been pursued."

Like many people Jack knew, Wanda Keppler was offended at the level of crudeness now on display in the press. He didn't like it either, but after covering Nazi atrocities and the Bataan Death March, most journalists had grittier sensibilities.

"I hadn't thought about it in those terms, Mrs. Keppler. But papers do stories people want to read about. And the more sensational, the more the public wants to hear it these days."

"That doesn't make it right," she said.

"No. It doesn't." Jack glanced at Eddie, who seemed frozen

with shock at how the conversation was unfolding.

"Have you personally written any of those stories, Mr. Curran?" She lifted *The LA Times* from the table to reveal a copy of Friday's Special Edition of *The Eyes*. "I bought this a couple of days ago because my neighbor was hysterical. She knocked on my door babbling that we had an infestation of monsters in the Angeles National Forest. The poor woman already takes tranquilizers, because she thinks we're going to be wiped out with an atomic bomb by the Russians. This story your newspaper ran is exactly what I'm talking about. It exploits people's deepest fears to sell more copies."

"I wrote the stories on the vigilante for our paper. It's a legitimate story that all the papers in town are covering." Jack lifted his chin and indicated the copy of *The Eyes*. "The monster killing in Griffith Park is a shocking story, Mrs. Keppler, I'll grant you that. But it's an important one. I wish I had written it, but it was an exclusive by one of my associates."

"You?" Wanda Keppler turned to Eddie.

"No, ma'am. I, I, I mostly do research. I can't do a bylined story yet." He blinked furiously.

"Oh?" She sighed. "Well, I'm sorry if I got you off track here, Mr. Curran. As you can tell, I'm frustrated about the police force's failures on a personal level. You said over the phone that you wanted to talk to me about my husband's death. I'm sure you know why I feel the way I do."

"Yes, ma'am. I do. On your behalf, Edward here spoke with Detective Morrell. They still have no suspects in your husband's case. When asked about what they've done to find one, Morrell stated the police have canvassed the neighborhood, done tire molds, and requested that local body shops report anyone who brings in a car with green markings matching the paint on your husband's car. But they have no leads."

Tears crested in Mrs. Keppler's eyes, and she wiped them away quickly. "They're useless. They didn't identify Randall for *five days*. For five days he lay unclaimed in the morgue like a vagrant. Even though I called the Monterey Park police and the LAPD and reported him missing. Despite the list of actions you say they've taken, I have no faith the police will find who killed my husband."

Jack leaned forward and knit his fingers together. "I'm sure it's been a horrible experience, Mrs. Keppler. Is there anything else you can think of that the police should be doing?"

"What do you mean?"

Jack told himself to be careful. He wanted to suggest an idea that had been percolating in his head since Eddie dug up the obit, but he needed to be subtle. "During your discussions with the police about your husband's death, did they ask if there was anyone he was having difficulty with?"

"No."

"They didn't ask if there was anyone they should speak to in order to rule out the possibility your husband's death wasn't an accident?"

Wanda sat up straighter. "Are you suggesting my husband may have been intentionally killed?"

Bingo, Jack thought. "Yes, ma'am. I am."

Eddie sucked in a breath.

Her eyes filled with tears again. "I knew I would sound insane, but I actually asked the police about that possibility, if there was a chance someone followed Randall and ran over him. Sabotaged his car, even. But the police and the coroner told me there was no evidence it was anything other than an accident."

"But you considered the possibility it might be intentional?" Jack's voice was calm. "Can you tell me why you had that thought, Mrs. Keppler? Did your husband say anything to make you think he was fearful of anyone?"

Before she could answer, a loud, ferocious scream escaped from the hedges to the left of the patio. It was followed by thrashing and crashing. A moment later two enormous cats tumbled out onto the grass, wrapped in a hissing, howling embrace.

One was white with long, matted fur. The other looked more like a possum. Instead of a fur coat, it had a chamois-like hide covered in circular black patterns.

"Stop it, you two!" Wanda got up and walked toward the catfight, clapping her hands together loudly.

Eddie leaned close to Jack and whispered. "Do you think Keppler was murdered?"

"I didn't. Until now," he replied.

The warring cats didn't pay any attention to Wanda until she stood directly over them. The white cat then disentangled itself and barreled off across the yard before disappearing over a concrete retaining wall at the end of the garden. The furless beast hunkered at Wanda's feet.

"Poor King Tut." Wanda picked the thing up and cuddled it against her shoulder as she returned to the patio. "Sorry if Tut here startled you. It was one of my husband's avocations, rescuing cats." She pointed at a wooden building beside the house. "We've got seven of the poor dears sleeping in Randall's workshop. But this is the only one that looks like a freak of nature."

Eddie stared at the cat as if transfixed. It had yellow eyes and a stocky, long body that weighed close to twenty pounds. It had long black whiskers, but no hair.

"What kind of cat is that?" he asked. And then sneezed.

"Mexican hairless is what Randall called it. They're rare. The natural mutation causes the hair loss. Only one or two of the kittens in a litter are born this way. God bless you, Edward. Are you allergic to cats?" Wanda walked closer to the patio.

"Yes."

"King Tut shouldn't bother you then. No hair, no dander."

She sat down with the cat and fixed her gaze on Jack. "Now, I believe you were asking me if I thought my husband feared for his life."

"Yes." Jack gave the cat a steady look.

It stared back, cross-eyed and ready to leap.

"No. He never said that. My husband wasn't afraid of anything, Mr. Curran. That's not to say he didn't have enemies. And I know he hated one of his colleagues, and the feeling was mutual."

"One of the staff at the veterinary clinic?"

"What?" Wanda Keppler frowned.

"At the veterinary clinic," Jack repeated. "Your husband was an assistant there, I understand." He smiled. "I assume that's where your cats are from."

"What are talking about? My husband worked for Dr. Ernest Preminger. Dr. Preminger isn't a vet. Preminger is a research geneticist. And a clinical hypnotist. Where did you get the idea Randall worked for a vet?"

Jack glanced at Eddie.

"That's what the detectives in the Hollywood Division said," Eddie replied in an uneasy voice.

Wanda let the cat down onto the patio and watched him slink off. "I never told them that. Now that I think of it, they never even asked what kind of business Randall did. They only wanted the address and phone number. I only got two calls from Detective Morrell in total." She sighed. "I guess this is the kind of inattention to detail characteristic of overworked cops. Is this the sort of thing you'll be writing about, Mr. Curran?"

"Yes, it certainly is." Jack looked at Eddie. "Do you have Detective Morrell's phone number with you?"

"Yes, sir." He patted his jacket pocket.

"May Eddie, eh, Edward use your phone, Mrs. Keppler? I'd like to find out how the cops got that bad information. It might be important." There were a lot of reasons why people might lie to or mislead cops, but why would anyone lie about the kind of work Preminger's staff did, Jack wondered?

"Of course." She pointed to the house. "Use the one in the kitchen." She stood and brushed off nonexistent cat hair from her dress. "Why don't we all go inside? I'll get us a drink."

While Eddie made his call from her kitchen, Jack and Wanda walked into the living room with fresh cups of coffee.

"You're limping," Wanda said. "Did you hurt your leg?"

"It's a long, dull story."

"Are you one of those reporters who only ask questions, never answer them?"

"I answered you." Jack smiled.

"You answered me, but not my question. You're good with words. Handy for a writer." She leaned against the back of the sofa and crossed her slender legs. "My husband was also good at no-information answers. He worked in intelligence during the war, and it was a line of work that suited him well. His people were Dutch. They're pretty stoic."

Another alarm bell rang inside Jack's skull. With every moment he spent with Wanda Keppler, he became increasingly certain Randall Keppler's death was not a simple hit-and-run.

"What exactly did your husband do at Dr. Preminger's clinic, Mrs. Keppler?" Jack took a gulp of coffee.

"Randall said he was assisting in a project involving the analysis of chemical compounds to produce a vaccine. They were doing drug testing on animals. I believe they were also using a few human subjects to assess new techniques of hypnotism."

"Preminger was testing drugs on humans?"

"No. That's illegal, Mr. Curran. Drug testing is tightly controlled by the Food and Drug Administration. Studies on human subjects are only done by huge pharmaceutical companies that follow strict protocols. The testing Randall was involved with was much more theoretical. Preminger is convinced that hypnosis and the introduction of certain drugs can be used to engineer desired behaviors in people."

Jack's mind clawed back his discussion with Lynton Maxwell about the future of combat troops and war. Maxwell had used almost those exact same words to describe the work of a doctor he knew. "What kind of behaviors?"

"That I don't know. As I said, Randall was guarded in what he shared about his work. But I'm guessing that Preminger works for the government. A few weeks before Randall was killed he told me he was helping him with a final proposal."

"Do you know Dr. Preminger well?"

"No. I've never met him."

"He didn't attend your husband's funeral?"

Wanda shook her head. "No. He sent a card. That's all. And Randall's final paycheck. Plus a tidy sum as a parting gesture." She took a deep breath. "Randall was a very educated man. He had a master's in chemistry. But after the war ended, he wanted to retire and enjoy life. I'm his second wife. We only got married five years ago. We got on well, but he was bored at home. He took this job as a lark. Neither of us could have imagined it would end up cutting his life short."

"I am sorry, Mrs. Keppler."

"Me, too." Tears flooded her eyes, and she glanced toward the kitchen.

Jack could tell she was ready for them to leave. "You mentioned Dr. Preminger is a clinical hypnotist. Is that a legitimate medical discipline? Isn't it what magicians do to entertain people? I thought it was a parlor trick."

"It's not fake. According to my husband, many physicians believe it can successfully be used to help people overcome phobias or recover from traumatic memories. There are several hundred thousand American veterans from WWI and WWII, and many were badly compromised by the experience. The theory is that hypnosis, used with counseling and psychiatric therapy, could be of great value to them. The brain is the new frontier, my husband used to say."

"I see," Jack said. But he didn't. He had heard about Sigmund Freud and all of his psychoanalysis mumbo jumbo. In Jack's experience, the veterans who were compromised by their wartime experiences were either going to recover or not. Talking didn't do a damn thing to help you forget what it was like to see the ten guys you had lunch with spilling that lunch out of their guts after being cut down by Nazi machine gun fire.

A huge black cat, twin to the one at the front door, shimmied out from under the couch and stalked off toward the rear of the house.

Jack was glad Eddie was in the kitchen. "You've got seven cats? Do they fight all the time?"

"No." She shook her head. "I think they're too grateful. Even though they act aloof, they know they're fortunate to live here.

They try and give each other respect. Randall brought them home from Preminger's lab. That's part of the reason he hated one of his colleagues. He said Dr. Preminger had demanded the animals they were using in their drug research not be harmed. But my husband believed their colleague did abuse the animals."

"What is that man's name, if I might ask?" Jack reached for his notebook.

Before Wanda could answer, Eddie walked into the living room. "I talked to Detective Morrell. He said a guy named Josef Brandt is the one who answered the phone at the number they had for Mr. Keppler's employer. He's the one who told Morrell that Mr. Keppler worked for a veterinary practice."

Wanda gasped. "That's the man Randall was worried about. My husband hated Brandt. He said he was sadistic."

"Did he give you any examples?"

"No. Sorry, but he wouldn't." She crossed her arms over her chest. "He knows I'm easily upset when it comes to helpless animals."

"Do you know if Josef Brandt knew how your husband felt about him?"

"No. As I said, my husband hid his feelings well. But they had a blow-up, and Randall reported Josef's mistreatment of an animal to Preminger."

"When was that?"

"Early this year. January, I think." She put her hand to her mouth. "Don't you think I should demand that the police reopen the investigation? Get them to check Brandt out, find out why he lied to them?"

"I didn't tell Morrell he had bad information," Eddie piped in. "I thought you might like to do that, Mrs. Keppler."

"I think you should talk to them, Mrs. Keppler," Jack said. "When you give them that information, I'm sure they'll investigate any vehicle that Brandt owns."

"Are you suggesting…" Her voice died.

"I'm not suggesting anything. But it looks like Brandt was covering *something* up." Jack stood and put his hands on his hips.

"May I ask you one more question?"

"Certainly." Wanda's knuckles were white; she was squeezing her hands tightly against her arms.

"Do you know a woman named Alana Maxwell?"

"No. I don't recognize the name." She shook her head. "Who is she?"

"Did you receive two dozen white roses after your husband died?"

Wanda looked surprised. "Yes. But how did you know that?"

"May I ask who sent them?" Jack kept his voice even, trying to disguise the excitement burning in his gut.

"I don't know. There was no card attached. I called the florist to ask who they were from, but they didn't know. I assumed they must have been from one of my friends. Frankly, I'd forgotten all about that until now."

"You've had a lot to handle." Jack waved his hand at Eddie. "If you don't mind, can we take a picture of you for when we run the story?"

"Okay. Or I could give you a photograph of Randall."

"Both would be great. Eddie, grab the camera out of the car."

Eddie hurried out of the front door.

Wanda stood and rubbed her bare arms as if warding off a chill. "Who is Alana Maxwell, Mr. Curran? And why are you asking me about those roses? What the hell is going on?"

"I'm doing a separate piece concerning Miss Maxwell. I can't tell you why I asked you about her now, but I'll fill you in as soon as I clear up a few things. I promise."

"Okay."

"Until then, I'd appreciate it if you don't mention her name to anyone," Jack added. "But call the police about Josef Brandt. They owe you more work on this case than they've given you."

"I will." She met Jack's eyes. "Will you call me before you print anything in the paper about my husband? I'd like to know what you come up with before I read about it."

"I will." He handed her his business card. "Call me if you find out anything from the cops once they approach this Brandt fellow. Okay? And if I can ask you one last favor?"

Wanda looked up from his card. "What?"

"Don't tell the police I came to see you." He glanced down at his banged-up leg. "Last time they found me talking to a citizen they made my limp worse."

"What? They beat you up?"

"Let's say they got my attention."

"Is that another non-answer?"

He smiled. "Yes."

CHAPTER FOURTEEN

I did a terrible job with Mrs. Keppler." Eddie drove the Packard down the hill toward Monterey Park's main business district.

"You did fine. We got what we came for, and more. Don't worry about being nervous. It gets easier."

"If that's what you think, sir." Eddie sounded skeptical. "She was nice. But she has a weird shrine in her kitchen."

"What kind of shrine?"

Eddie shrugged. "I don't know. A gold statue and flowers and fruit. Maybe Hindu?"

"Or Buddhist. Fat guy with a big smile?"

"No. I think it was an elephant."

"Oh yeah?" Jack shook his head. "The rich are different from us, F. Scott Fitzgerald said."

"Yeah, they have more money, Ernest Hemingway added."

Jack laughed and glanced at his watch. "Let's get lunch. You could eat, couldn't you, Edward?"

"You don't have to call me that anymore, Mr. Curran."

"I like it. Except I think it's stuck-up."

"Me too. But don't tell my mom. If you ever talk to her, I mean." Eddie sniffed. "Where do you want to have lunch?"

"First place you see that has a phone booth." Jack's mind was racing, and his stomach was growling. "After I call and get an appointment to get my knee checked out, we'll swing by to meet the mysterious Dr. Preminger and this Josef Brandt character. See what they have to say for themselves about lying to the police about Keppler's employment."

"Do you want me to call Preminger's office and ask for an appointment?"

"No. We'll surprise attack them."

Eddie cleared his throat. "Why do you think Randall Keppler might have been murdered?"

"Something in my gut, Eddie. But we need more information and a lot more facts before he becomes part of our story. Right now he's an unfortunate victim of a hit-and-run driver, nothing else."

The kid made a slow left turn, his eyes focused on the road. "Are you going to add Keppler's death to the roses' story? Imply he's involved with the Thrill Girl case?"

The kid is fast. Too fast, Jack thought. "Imply? Reporters don't imply a goddamned thing, Eddie. They report facts."

"I meant…"

"I know what you meant." Jack took off his hat and rolled his neck around to loosen the kink he had developed. There was a hazy connection forming between the mugging victims and Randall Keppler's death, and it made Jack uneasy, to say the least.

At the center of it all was Alana Maxwell, commiserating with the victims like a weepy member of a Greek chorus, sending them all bundles of roses. Jack shifted in his seat at the thought of the blonde and blew out a lungful of air.

He was mystified by how she had heard about Randall Keppler's death at all. There had been no news articles about it in the LA papers. He took another hit off his cigarette. It was clear what he had to do. Despite her step-brother's warnings and Quentin's misgivings, he had to go see Alana Maxwell.

Today.

He would ask her outright about the roses. Screw playing

cautiously. She didn't seem like the type to go running to a lawyer. She had an aura of confidence rich people often possessed. Maybe she would take his inference that she was involved in the muggings as a challenge, not a threat.

Like she did last night. Jack's jaw clenched at the memory of how she looked in the moonlight, lying on her back and staring up at him.

"How about Q Burger?" Eddie asked.

"What the hell's a Q Burger?"

"It's a square hamburger on a square bun. They're great. My Uncle Teddy always takes, ah, took me there for my birthday. When I was a kid."

Jack grinned. "Did you ask Uncle Teddy why they didn't call them square burgers?"

"No. But I will. They also have the best chocolate milkshakes in town. And there's a phone booth right out front."

Jack threw his cigarette out the window and rubbed his leg. He could use a milkshake. Hell, maybe he should pour it down his pants. It could cool down both areas of his body that were hot and aching. "Sure. Park the boat, kid. Sorry I bit your head off."

"It's okay. You get grouchy when you're hungry."

"That's not true."

"*Who?* Jack Curran. *What?* Grouchy. *Why?* Hungry. I have lots of corroborating witnesses." Eddie grinned and pulled the Packard smoothly up to the curb.

#

Alana opened her eyes. The drapes in her bedroom were drawn, but the sun seeping in at the edges was hot and bright, enough to tell her it was mid-day.

She turned her head. The clock on the bedside table said 1:35.

She rubbed her forehead and attempted to order her thoughts. Was it morning?

No, afternoon. Monday afternoon.

She better start moving. She was supposed to go with Tomas to look at houses in Hancock Park. Alana sat up and stretched, but her vision clouded and the room spun around. Her eyelids began to twitch.

She lay back down and closed her eyes. This headache was worse than usual. Dr. Preminger had warned her about drinking alcohol with the drugs, it was why she had suggested cutting back to Tomas, but she craved drinks as much as the other vices she had been overindulging in.

She needed to get a grip. Maybe Swami Dhani would allow her to come to more sessions. Meditation might help her stop hungering for things to distract her from her worry over Tomas.

Before heading to the bathroom for a shower, she made a detour to order room service.

Her head hurt too badly to open the drapes to see the phone. She switched on the light beside her to find her purse. On the floor, her evening gown and undergarments lay in a pool of black sparkle. Her favorite gold heels were on the dresser, left out since Saturday's dinner at Lynton's.

A white business card lying beside her shoes caught her eye. Alana squinted to read it.

Jack Curran
The Eyes of LA
Phone...Normandy 54366

"Who is Jack Curran?" she asked aloud. The name unsettled her, but no memory of an actual person accompanied it. Another lost night.

The blackouts are getting worse.

Her hand trembled. She dropped the card and pressed her ear as pain stabbed into the left side of her head. For a moment, the room seemed to undulate, and a lime-green glow leaked out from her closet. Bubbles floated down from the ceiling.

There were creatures inside of the fragile orbs.

Alana reached to catch one, but she could not make out what lurked inside. She shook her head and took three deep breaths. The bubbles disappeared. She ran a hand through her hair and walked into the bathroom.

Fifteen minutes later, her wet hair brushed out and her damp body wrapped in a robe, Alana signed for lunch delivery. The bellman rolled in the cart, and she fell on the food like a shipwreck survivor who had been pulled aboard the good ship Lollipop.

She was biting into her second Monte Cristo sandwich when Tomas knocked. "Are you decent?" he called out.

That's a matter of opinion, she thought grimly as she opened the door.

Tomas was dressed in a pale suit and shirt with a white-banded collar. A straw hat and yellow bow tie completed the picture of a young man out and about on a summer day. Even with his impaired left arm and leg, sitting in a wheelchair, he exuded beauty and charm.

"Hello, dear sister. Robinson and I thought we'd come and take you out to lunch before we go on our real estate tour."

"Good morning, Miss Maxwell." The valet nodded as he wheeled Tomas into the room.

"Oh, you should have called, Tomas. I already ate. I'm still eating." She licked her fingers and shut the door with her hip. "Do you want me to order more sandwiches? You two could eat while I dress?"

"No, I had a late breakfast. Robinson?"

"No thank you."

"Not even coffee?" Alana smiled. "I know you're as addicted to the stuff as I am."

He smiled. "Well, if you have enough. Yes, I'd love a cup, Miss Maxwell."

She poured the chauffeur a cup and handed it to him, then grabbed a dish of strawberries and sat down. "How many places are we going to see?"

"Three. I'm concentrating on Hancock Park, although Brentwood sounds appealing too," Tomas replied.

"What size place are you looking for?"

"Two bedrooms. A pool. And quarters for Robinson, if we can coax him into becoming live-in." He held up his hand to stop his valet from replying. "I know you said you don't mind staying the night whenever I need you, but I want you to consider giving up your apartment and bunking with me full time. I think I'll be going out more at night. And entertaining."

Alana tensed. She wanted to tell her brother to slow down, but instead she smiled.

"You won't have to pay rent then, and you can even bring your dog." Tomas stared at Robinson. "Doesn't that sound like a good deal?"

"You have a dog?" Alana reached for the sugar bowl and plunked two cubes in her coffee. She wanted five. "I didn't know you have a dog. Who watches it while you're gone?"

Robinson set his cup on the table. "My landlady takes him in most of the evenings I'm gone, and he has a dog house out in the yard. More her dog than mine now."

"What's his name?" Alana asked.

"Buff." The big man looked uneasy at finding himself the focus of the Maxwells' combined attention. "Short for buffalo. He's got a big old shaggy head. Kind of a mess, but he followed me home one night, and I took to him."

"You could bring Buff. We'll have a place with a yard." Tomas smiled. "And I'll double your salary. I can afford to now."

Robinson looked shocked.

Alana widened her eyes and put her cup down. "Let him think about it for a while, Tomas. Don't pressure him or he's liable to leave us and go to work for people who are less demanding."

"Don't worry about that, ma'am." The valet shook his head. "I'm not going nowhere. And you should know, Miss Maxwell, Mr. Tomas here said that after he moves out the hotel, I'm still to drive you wherever you need to go. You only got to call me."

"I must say I'll miss having the Rolls parked outside. Thank you for your offer. And you too, Tomas, for your generosity with the car."

"You're welcome." Her brother's gaze fell to Alana's bare feet. "And speaking of my generosity, where are those lovely new slippers I bought you? Those Ostrich feathers cost a bundle."

Alana remembered Tomas buying them when they went

shopping for his tux, but after that, nothing. "They're around here somewhere."

"I have your slippers in the trunk," Robinson said. "I'm sorry, I meant to bring them up to you when you got home from the Coconut Grove that night, Miss Maxwell, but I forgot to go back for them. I'll get them now."

"No. That's fine. I'll bring them up myself later." Robinson knows what happened on Saturday night, at least the last part, Alana thought. She could not remember anything after leaving Lynton's house.

"I hate to admit it, but I had too much to drink, and I'm fuzzy about Saturday night. Did you see Mr. Venice come upstairs after his show, Robinson?"

Tomas cackled. "You don't remember if lover boy was there? He must be sadly lacking in the romance department."

"Stop. I already admitted I had a lot to drink." She looked at Robinson. "Did you see Gino?"

"No, ma'am."

"But you saw me after I left his show at the Grove?"

"Yes." Robinson looked steadily at Alana. "I was leaving Mr. Tomas's room, and I saw you leave the lobby. I waited inside for a while, thinking you might want me to drive you. But when you didn't come back inside, I went out to the garden to tell you goodnight."

He seemed willing to leave it there.

"And what did you find in the garden?" Tomas pressed. "Was my sister dancing nude in the fountain?"

"Tomas, shut up!"

Both men recoiled at the anger in her voice.

"I'm sorry." Alana wrapped her arms around herself. "I've got a terrible headache today, and I found a business card from a news reporter on the dresser. I'm worried I may have acted in a manner that will land me in a gossip sheet headlined, *The Rich Misbehaving*." She laughed unconvincingly. "He writes for *The Eyes of LA*. They concentrate on scandals, don't they?"

"No. Actually, they cover hard news on local issues." Tomas frowned. "Small press, but they do good stuff. They've been all over the Thrill Girl murders. But I digress." Tomas leaned forward in his chair. "You found a reporter's business card on your bedroom dresser? My, my, that could be a problem."

Alana glared at Tomas before turning back to Robinson. "The reporter's name is Jack Curran. Do you recognize the name? Did you happen to see him talking to me?"

"Yes, Miss Maxwell. You were having a conversation with him in the hotel garden area Saturday night when I went out to see about you." He swallowed. "Mr. Curran asked me to tell you he takes rain checks if you decide you'd like to have breakfast with him."

"Oh. Yes. Of course. Now I remember." She was lying, but at least it resolved the evening's basic events for her.

She must have run into this Curran person when she went outside for air. Alana flushed as a foggy recollection of a man with big shoulders sitting beside her on a bench outside came into focus. He was intelligent, and great looking, despite a black eye.

Had he said he had hit his head?

"Okay." She smiled brightly. "Thanks, Robinson. For coming to check on me, and for being discreet."

"You're welcome, ma'am."

"What about me?" Tomas asked with a grin.

"I thank you for nothing." She made a face at her brother. "I need a half hour to get myself together. The newspaper is there. Or turn on the radio. Try to find a station playing love songs, Tomas. Suddenly I'm in the mood for a good love song. Maybe Sinatra or Perry Como?"

"Not Gino Venice?"

"Let's stick with old blue eyes," she said before leaving the room.

# # #

The VA hospital doctor was adamant Jack come in as soon as he could, so after the square hamburger lunch and malts, Jack had Eddie drive him over.

After his exam, the doctor went from adamant to stern. "You need to stay and let me drain that cyst, or you'll be back here in the emergency room tonight, where you'll get admitted and be in here for a week. Minimum. We also need blood samples and a tissue biopsy. I'm not convinced you don't already have an infection in the bone."

"I got places to be and people to see, doc." Jack shook his head. "I don't have time to lie around here and let you stick pins in me."

"You don't get that knee drained, you're asking for septicemia, Mr. Curran. You need antibiotics and rest and a brace. This isn't anything to mess with. You could still lose the leg."

Jack shuddered. On one of his final days in Italy, he saw the body of his friend, Donny Stone, after both of Donny's legs had been blown off by a grenade. "I'm not going to lose my leg, doc. I promise I'll keep an eye on it."

The doctor scowled.

"Can't you give me pain medicine?"

"Not without draining the cyst." The doctor squeezed Jack's thigh. "How did you hurt it, a fall?"

"I got kicked by a horse."

The doctor pressed down on his kneecap. "The horse had a good aim. Hit right on top of where those pins fit into the bone."

Jack groaned at the doctor's touch. "Okay. But I have to be out of here by five."

"Hot date?"

"Don't I wish? No, I've got a deadline." He gestured to the door. "Can I speak to my associate? Let him know I'm going to be here awhile?"

The doctor scribbled notes on Jack's chart and walked to the door. "I'll have the nurse send him in before she preps you for the procedure."

"Thanks."

A minute later, Eddie opened the door. "Mr. Curran? You in there?"

"Come on in."

"What's going on?" Eddie looked around the examining room in alarm.

"I've got to have a cyst drained and more tests. I want you to go to the office. Tell Quentin I'll be back in time to finish our lead story by ten tonight."

"Ten? Isn't the shop's cutoff eight?"

"Ten is never a problem. I also want you to hit the clip morgue hard, find out anything you can on Preminger and Brandt. And take the photographs of Wanda Keppler down to art. Have them developed today. Oh, and call the 07 to see if the cops have anything new on Joan Becklund's death."

"You sure you don't want a sidebar on Randall Keppler's accident?"

"Not yet. We don't have anything that ties him to the mugging deaths, except for Alana Maxwell and the flowers. And until I talk to Alana, I'm not going public with it." Jack sighed. "Take the Packard, and I'll get a taxi when I'm done. I'll meet you back at the office by seven. I've got a couple of stops to make first."

"I can come get you."

"No. I need you at the office, *working*. Keep Deville calm, will you?" He pointed to his suit jacket as a tall, leggy nurse came in with a tray of instruments that looked like they were from the Spanish Inquisition. "And before you go, dig out my cigarettes?"

"No smoking in here, Mr. Curran." The pretty nurse smiled at Eddie. "And you'll have to leave now, sir."

"Sure." He backed up and crashed into the supply cart she was pushing. He blushed. "Sorry. Okay, I'll see you at the office, Mr. Curran."

"Be careful with my car." Jack felt the blood drain out of his face as the nurse picked up a six-inch needle.

CHAPTER FIFTEEN

Jack Curran is going to kill me.

Eddie sneezed and pressed a trembling finger against his swollen, tearing eyes. He dropped the keys, sneezed again, and finally managed to unlock the Packard. He slid into the front seat and closed the door. He blew his nose and stared across the street for a moment, then leaned his congested head against the steering wheel.

Jack had told him to go back to the office, but instead, Eddie had driven to the address he had for Ernest Preminger's clinic.

His plan was simple.

He would surprise Jack by doing basic fact gathering while the journalist was at the hospital tending to his leg. Eddie would do a brief interview, allowing Jack to write a sidebar before tonight's deadline.

All Eddie had to do was knock on Preminger's front door and ask to speak to the doctor. He would confirm that Ronald Keppler had worked there until the night he was killed. While he was at it, he would also confirm what kind of business establishment the doctor ran out of the mansion behind the wrought-iron fence, directly across from where the Packard was parked.

He might even ask to speak to Josef Brandt, and what the

doctor's personal feelings were toward Ronald Keppler, and what kind of car Brandt drove. Well, if he could manage to keep his nerves in check.

Except nothing had gone as planned.

To start, Dr. Preminger's office door was locked.

Eddie had been on the verge of leaving when he noticed a chain link fence with an open gate to the left of the main house. He walked through it and around the sprawling house and found himself in a large yard. It was completely and securely fenced. There were two other brick buildings behind the home. Three cars were parked outside. There were no signs of life, but those cars had to belong to someone.

His confidence was disintegrating, but he knew learning to master his nerves a big part of being a reporter. He had pulled out his notebook and copied down all three plate numbers. A closer examination of the buildings made him realize that both had heavy doors with two deadbolts. There was a no-smoking sign and an advisory to wear protective gear on the door of the second building, which also had a huge air conditioning unit and intake fan on the roof. There were no windows.

He was about to take a step toward it when a woman's voice broke the silence. "Stop right there, young man! What are you doing on this property? It's private!"

Eddie had turned to confront a woman standing three feet behind him. She was about his mother's age, angry and she looked it. Her shockingly red hair was piled on her head. She was dressed in a blue suit and high heels, and a hat with three feathers that dangled in front of her right eye, like a drunken quail.

"Hi. Hello." Eddie reached into his pocket and pulled out his wallet. He handed his press credentials to the woman. "Yes. Ah, Edward Wentz. I'm a reporter for *The Eyes of LA*. I was looking for Dr. Preminger. I knocked at the front door, but no one answered."

The woman took his identification and looked down at it. She frowned and handed it back to him. "Why are you giving me your library card?"

"Oh! Sorry. No, here. This is my press card." He jerked it

hastily out of his wallet, reddening with every second that passed. He handed the identification card to the woman, but she waved it away.

"I don't care who you are," she said, her voice rising with every word. "What are you doing on my property?"

Eddie had no ready answer for that. Before he could try and form a sentence that made sense, a man's voice boomed out from the opposite direction.

"What's going on, Deidre? Why is this man here?"

A wiry man with black hair and eyes sunk deep into their sockets walked toward them from the direction of the windowless brick building. He wore a white lab coat and heavy knee-high boots a mountaineer might wear.

"This young man is looking for Ernest. He's trespassing. He's from a newspaper."

Those words stopped the man mid-stride. He lifted his chin and stared at Eddie, his hands closing into fists at his sides. "What newspaper? What is the meaning of this?"

It had all gone downhill from there.

Eddie had tried to remain calm. In a torrent of disconnected words, he had asked if Ronald Keppler had worked there before his death and if Dr. Preminger was home.

The woman had yelled at him for trespassing and threatened to call the cops to have him arrested. The man had grabbed him behind the neck and propelled him toward the gate. "Get out. And don't come back!"

For good measure, he spat on the ground at Eddie's feet.

"Look, I'm sorry." But before Eddie could say anything more, a terrifying, inhuman shriek split the quiet summer air.

Deidre and the man both turned in horror.

A second howl, more ferocious and louder, followed.

Eddie squinted and sneezed, wondering what the heck had made that noise? And where was it?

"Get out and stay out, or I'll shoot you on sight," the man in the lab coat yelled. He pulled a gun out from his belt and ran toward the brick building.

Eddie's jaw dropped.

"You heard him, didn't you?" the woman yelled. She ran in the other direction, toward the house.

Eddie turned and ran as fast as he could down the driveway to Jack's car, and drove off to a side street behind the estate.

As the memory faded, Eddie sneezed again and picked his head up from the steering wheel. He should have followed the man and found out what made that noise. He started the car and drove up a hill, further away from the Preminger compound. He stopped a half mile away, pulled into a stand of trees, and put the Packard in park.

Jack Curran was going to kill him for ruining the interview with Dr. Preminger, and the lab-coated maniac, whom Eddie had a hunch was Josef Brandt himself. He blew his nose and glanced at his watch. It was after three.

There's still time to fix this, he told himself.

Eddie looked out the window. It was a sparsely developed, wild area, but all the roads were paved, and several plots of land had been graded and were ready for building. If he headed to the end of this road, there was a good chance it would wind around to the street behind Preminger's property.

With any luck, he could climb up a hillside and get to a vantage point that would allow him to look down on the buildings he had seen. Get a photo or two to go with the vignette he had observed. He knew the story would sound crazy, but if he had photographs, Jack would take it seriously, and maybe he wouldn't be too angry that Eddie had tipped off Dr. Preminger that the press was looking at him.

Eddie started the Packard. Maybe they could do a story on it, and he could get a shared byline.

A huge sneeze cleared his sinuses. He squinted, wondering what had set him off out here. Usually, he was only allergic to cats.

He thought of the noise he heard a few minutes ago. If that had come from a cat, it was a huge one. A chill skittered down his back as a new thought presented itself.

The Griffith Park monster struck near here.

What happened a few minutes ago could not have anything to do with the other news story rocking LA.

Could it?

Eddie blew out a breath, full of his own disbelief. Stick to Thrill Girl's trail, he told himself.

One murderer at a time.

# # #

Jack walked around to the rear of Susan Baldwin's house. His limp was worse now that the doc had worked him over, but the pain he had been living with had lessened. He had three kinds of pills in his pocket, a brace strapped around his knee, and a follow-up appointment for a week out.

Say what you will about the VA, Jack thought as he struggled up the rear steps to Susan's kitchen door, they take care of their men, even when their men resist.

He peered in through the window.

The scene in the kitchen was one of domestic activity frozen in time. A colander full of peeled potatoes stood on the counter, next to a bowl of what looked like raw batter. A tray of baked cookies sat on a cooling rack, several more stacked neatly on a plate.

The table was set for three, with cutlery and wine glasses and daisies in a vase. Susan must have soldiered on and kept to her cooking plans after the drama and upset of Wednesday night. But something had interrupted her brother's planned visit on Friday.

Three long days ago.

Jack tried the knob. It was locked.

"Damn it!" He glanced around, wondering which house belonged to the neighbor who had let Susan use her phone.

He pulled out a business card and wrote, "Susan, contact me. It's important!" on the back, then added his home telephone number and address. After dropping it through the mail slot in the front door, he hobbled out to the curb where his taxi was waiting. "I'll be another couple of minutes."

The cabby pointed at the ticking meter. "It's your money,

mister."

Jack made his way to the house to the left of Susan's and rang the bell. An elderly woman opened the inner door but kept the locked screen between them.

"Yes?"

"Hi. My name is Jack Curran. I'm a friend of Susan Baldwin's. I haven't been able to reach her, and when I stopped by Bullocks, they told me she hasn't been to work for a couple of days."

The woman's face was impassive. "I don't know you."

"I'm sorry." He slid a business card into the edge of the screen. "I'm a reporter for *The Eyes of LA* newspaper. I was here the other night when Susan's dog got killed, and I wanted to talk to her. Do you know where she and her mother are? It's important."

"You're the man who got arrested." The woman clutched the door.

"Yes. I am. But I was released. The police made a mistake."

"You write for that newspaper that published the monster story?"

"Yes."

"They catch it yet?"

"No." He tried to keep the fact that he didn't give a shit about the monster off his face. "I'm sure they will soon."

Jack and the woman stared at each other for a moment before she peered at his card. "You can't come in. My husband's not here."

"I don't need to come in. I only want to know if you have any idea where Susan and her mother might be and if they're okay."

The old woman pursed her lips. "I'm worried about that too. A man from a hospital called for Susan on Friday morning. Said they needed to talk to her about an emergency with her brother, Paul. I went and got her. Susan didn't tell me what was wrong, but thanked me and rushed off. Susan and Ellen took a cab right after, and I haven't seen them since." She sniffed. "I think the boy's retarded. Nice boy, but skinny. He can't walk."

"Thank you. Thank you," Jack said. "Do you know the name of the hospital Paul Baldwin is in? It's in Santa Barbara, right?"

She shook her head. "I don't know where it is, or what it's called."

"Well, I appreciate your help."

"Good night."

"Good night." He limped as fast as he could to the cab, glancing down at his wristwatch. It was after five. Enough dead ends. It was time to get to the heart of things.

"Take me to the Ambassador Hotel," he directed the driver and slid into the seat.

# # #

Jack paid the cabbie and told him to take off.

He had no idea if he was going to catch Alana Maxwell at home. He stopped in the café off the lobby to see if Carol Johnson was working. She had telephoned him earlier at the office to give him hell for leaving the Grove without saying goodbye Saturday night, but he had convinced her it was work and not another woman that had called him away.

Carol was nowhere in sight. Jack sat at the house phone desk and removed his hat.

"Operator."

"Yes, could you connect me to Alana Maxwell's suite?"

"One moment."

After the fifth unanswered ring, the operator picked up. "I'm sorry, there's no answer in that room, sir. Would you like to leave a message?"

He flashed back to the scene at Lynton Maxwell's, picturing the crippled young man. "Yes. Would you please try Tomas Maxwell's suite?"

"One moment."

"Mr. Maxwell's suite," a man answered. "This is Robinson."

Bingo. "Hello. May I speak with Tomas Maxwell please?"

"May I ask who is calling?"

"Jack Curran. I'm a reporter from *The Eyes of LA*. I think we met very late on Saturday night, outside in the garden."

Jack heard the man's surprised intake of breath. "Please hold a moment, sir."

Jack pulled out his cigarettes and lit one up. Thirty seconds passed. He was hungry. He should have ducked into the café before making the call. To his surprise, the next voice he heard was a woman's.

"Mr. Curran?" Her voice was like smoke and honey.

"Yes. Who is this?" He knew it was her, of course, but he asked anyway.

"Alana Maxwell. I understand you owe me something."

"I do?"

"Yes. Breakfast."

He laughed. "That's right. I take it Mr. Robinson gave you my message?"

"He did."

"Well, would you like to collect now? I know it's closer to dinner, but The Pantry's a few blocks away. It's open twenty-four hours a day for breakfast."

"I would love to share a bite with you, Mr. Curran. But may I ask why you're calling to speak to my brother?"

Because I was looking for you, he thought. But he wouldn't admit to that until he had her face-to-face. "Are you screening his calls, Miss Maxwell?"

"Yes. I am. I take my job as his older sister seriously."

"Lucky him."

"I'm not sure he sees it that way." She chuckled. "But why are you calling Tommy?"

"I wanted to talk to him about his car. I'm a real admirer of the '39 Phantoms. When you told me it was his, I decided to call him up and ask to see it up close. I might do an article about them."

There was a pause. "I told you that? When exactly did I do that?"

"At your brother's, eh, your step-brother's house. Saturday." Did she not remember either of the meetings, Jack thought? His ego felt a slap.

"Of course. Well, Tommy's unavailable right now, but I'll be sure to pass on your request. I'll have him call you when he has a chance."

"Great." Jack snuffed out his cigarette. "Are we on for that bite?"

"You mean now?"

"I do. You can come down and meet me in the lobby, or shall I come up?"

There was a long pause. "I'll see you at my place, Mr. Curran. Give me ten minutes. Room 812. Top floor."

He hung up and rubbed his chin. He wished he had time for a shave, shower, and a scotch. At the least, he needed to check in with Eddie. His eyes scanned for a pay phone, which he spotted near the doors leading out to the gardens.

Before he could get up, two arms wrapped around his neck and a woman's mouth whispered an inch from his ear, "Hey, lover. You looking for me?"

He looked around into the pale eyes of Carol Johnson.

"Hey, Carol." Jack barely managed to keep the shock out of his voice. "What are you doing here?"

"I work here, in case you forgot. But I get off at eight. You want to come get dinner and watch the show and then follow me home?"

"I'd love to come later. But I've got to get back to *The Eyes* first, finish up a piece for a ten o'clock deadline." He got up and put his arm around her and walked her toward the café.

"What's wrong with your leg, Jack? You're limping worse than ever."

"Cramp. I've been sitting behind my desk too long today." He stopped at the door to the café and kissed her cheek. "See you later, babe. Have a good shift."

She winked and turned away.

He took three steps in the opposite direction and nearly knocked Alana Maxwell off her feet.

"Whoa." He grabbed her by the arms. "I thought I was coming upstairs to get you?"

"Change of plans." She smiled. "Do you need to change yours, Mr. Curran? That redhead looked hungry. Maybe she needs a bite more than I do."

"She works at a restaurant. I'm sure she can find things to eat without me."

"I'm glad I get priority."

Jack smiled and gave Alana a quick once-over. She was wearing a white mink over a low-cut black cocktail dress, and looked like a million dollars would look if it were a drop dead gorgeous woman.

"Are we going out for breakfast?" he asked. The Pantry wouldn't know what hit them when she walked in.

"Eventually." She dangled car keys in front of his nose. "I've got the Rolls, and I thought I'd give you a ride since you asked nicely. I know a place in Santa Monica that has cool breezes and hot jazz. Do you like music, Mr. Curran?"

"Yes."

"Does that mean you're in?" She raised one eyebrow.

"All the way."

"Good answer."

He followed her, glancing at the pay phone in the lobby. He would have to wait to call Eddie from Santa Monica. The iron, as they say, was hot.

# # #

"I don't chitchat when I drive." Alana turned the ignition key on the twelve-cylinder, 165-horsepower beast and the Rolls engine growled to life. She shifted smoothly into gear.

"Fine. I'll sit tight and look at you while you drive."

"You can't see much of me in this car."

"I've got a good imagination."

She looked at him sideways. "And what do you imagine right now, Mr. Curran?"

"That you're a great driver, Miss Maxwell."

"You're right. Now be quiet and enjoy the ride."

She drove like a madwoman. Briefly, he recalled Eddie's research and the speculation that she may have been driving the car the day of her mother's accident.

He reached for his cigarettes.

The steering wheel and gear shift were located on the right side of the car. Jack was sitting where the driver normally would in an American car, and consequently, he felt as if he were in a dream where he was driving a car without a steering wheel.

The Rolls hit eighty on the Santa Monica freeway. Without uttering any of the protests trapped in his throat, Jack put his cigarettes away and held onto the dashboard as the car took on the winding, treacherous Pacific Coast Highway. He gave himself over to the experience of riding in luxury, even if he was courting imminent death.

They made it to a place called the *Blue Note*. It was Alana's favorite jazz club, she announced as she pulled into the small parking lot. The trip had taken twenty minutes.

It should have taken forty.

"Enjoy the ride?" Alana smiled as she handed the keys to the valet.

"Immensely." He took her arm and led her into the club.

"Your face looks much better, but you're still limping badly, Mr. Curran."

"You think I'm limping badly? Keep watching. I'll get better with practice."

"Practice does improve performance, doesn't it?"

"Yes. For all involved."

She bit her lower lip and smiled.

The *Blue Note* was a typical jazz hangout, dark and smoke-filled, although more expensively furnished than any such place Jack had been to before.

On a tiny stage set at the rear of a room, a piano player was singing his heart out about a blue moon. Couples cuddled, drank, and did things casually in the dark they would never have done out on the strip in Hollywood.

Jack followed Alana to one of a dozen round tables. The place smelled of rum and the ocean, and Jack had a foreboding feeling about his looming deadline.

Alana ordered a bottle of French champagne from a waiter who called her by name. Jack flicked open his lighter for her cigarette and acknowledged to himself the flash of heat he felt when she folded her fingers around his hand. Careful, he thought. Be very careful.

She blew smoke at him. "Now, what did you actually want to talk to Tomas about, Mr. Curran?"

The look in her eyes made him want to tell the truth. Which was another sign of danger. "I wanted to find out where you were."

"Me?"

"Yes. I called your room and didn't get an answer. Then I tried your brother's suite. It was dumb luck that you were actually there."

"I don't believe in that." She sat back in the chair, further away from him.

"Dumb luck?"

She nodded. "Dumb or otherwise, I've never had any of it."

He stared at her in the softly lit room. She was gorgeous, rich, well-connected and living safe and free in the best country on earth. He thought she might be the luckiest woman he had ever met, but she wouldn't thank him for pointing that out. "Some people get by without luck."

"Do you?"

"That's an interesting question." An image from Italy burst into his head. One warm day in June, six years ago, a grenade smacked against his helmet and landed a few inches away from his feet during a vicious, close-quarter firefight. The instant it hit, he knew he did not have time to toss it away before it went off. Nor could he get far enough away to escape from being blown up.

He screamed a warning to his fellow soldiers and waited to die, but luck, in the form of a fellow G.I. who fell on top of the explosive, saved him.

"Are you going to answer me, Mr. Curran?"

"No. I don't believe in luck either." Jack touched the petals of the red rose in the center of the table. "Do you like flowers, Miss Maxwell?"

"Are you changing the subject?"

"Yes."

She raised her silky eyebrows. "I love them. They are one of nature's most perfect gifts. I have them around me all the time."

"Do you send flowers to other people?"

Alana Maxwell blinked and put her cigarette against her lips. "All the time. It makes me happy to send joy to people."

"It makes you happy?"

"Very happy." She blew smoke over his right shoulder. "I imagine them coming to the door and finding a delivery man with a white box and dozens of roses, all for them. I think they must be elated to know a stranger cares about them. It thrills me to my toes if you want to know the truth."

"Ah, that's why you do it. For the thrill?"

"Yes. Nothing wrong with being thrilled, is there?"

He stared at her lush mouth. She was playing a game. What kind, he could only guess. And he had never been any good at guessing. "How do you know Wanda Keppler?"

"Why do you think I know a woman named Wanda Keppler?" Alana rested her chin on her hand.

"Because you sent her two dozen white roses after her husband was killed."

"I did."

He was surprised she was willing to admit it. "Is Wanda a friend of yours?"

"I've never met her."

"Then why the flowers?"

"Her husband was killed by a hit-and-run driver." She shook her head from side to side. "It must have been horrible."

"How did you know about it?"

"Why are you asking me about this?" Alana took a long drag off the cigarette.

"I'm curious. I'm also curious about why you sent her roses. Despite your enjoyment of sending flowers and the sadness of her situation, it's odd to send roses to a stranger."

"Is it?"

"I don't know anyone else who does it." Jack leaned closer. "Do you often do this sort of thing?"

Alana frowned. "Let's back-up a minute. How did you know that I sent Wanda Keppler flowers? Have you been spying on me, Mr. Curran? Following me around? I think there are laws against that kind of behavior." She sat back against the leather banquette. "My step-brother would be upset if I told him I'm being stalked."

Her voice was full of unspoken threat. "I've kept tabs on you because of my job."

"Really? Are you a private dick?" She emphasized the word.

Before Jack could answer, the waiter returned with champagne. He showed Alana the label, opened the bottle with great fanfare and a running commentary about what a good choice she had made, poured them both a glass and stuck the bottle in a bucket of ice.

"Is there anything else, madam?" he asked.

"No. Thank you." Alana met Jack's eyes as she picked up her glass. "Shall we toast private dicks?"

She was sex appeal incarnate, with a side shot of bitch. Jack's patience slipped. "I'm not an investigator. Private or otherwise. I'm a reporter. Following a story."

"You're following a story about the people I send flowers to?"

"Yes, as a matter of fact. That's exactly what I'm writing about."

"What a dull story." She took a sip, her red lipstick tattooing the glass.

"On the contrary. My research shows you sent flowers to Mr. Yung Kim at the Pearl Grocery Store, a homeless woman named Joan Becklund, two young men named Michael and Bobby Taylor, and Susan Baldwin, a shop girl. All people who were rescued from being mugged by a mysterious blonde woman who ruthlessly killed their attackers. And you've also sent flowers to a woman you claim to be a stranger, whose husband was killed by an unknown hit and run driver. Put all that together, and it makes for one hell of a not dull story, Miss Maxwell."

Not a muscle moved in her face. "The blonde woman who murdered those men is called Thrill Girl, isn't she? You've been writing about her. My brother said he thinks you came up with the name. Is that true?"

"Yeah. I named her. She tells the people she rescues that she's 'thrilled' to help people. Which made it seem like an obvious choice."

"It was." Alana rubbed the corner of her mouth. "But what could she possibly have to do with me?"

"Why don't you tell me?" Jack loosened his tie.

Alana laughed a sound like silver bells. "Poor Mr. Curran, I'm afraid you think I'm someone I'm not."

"Well, who are you?"

"Oh, don't I wish I knew." She set her cigarette down in the ashtray and rested her hand on his. "Let me tell you about my dull life. I spend hours a day calling people on the telephone and asking for money for medical research. I spend nights having boring dinners with rich old men asking for more money. I buy snotty society women lunch, and go to their cocktail parties, all to get support for my charity."

"What charity is that?" Jack asked, already knowing the answer.

"The American Paralysis Research Foundation. I am a director of our family trust, which gives grants for paralysis research. It also means I don't have much of a personal life."

"You don't date?" he said, and immediately wished he hadn't.

Her smile seemed to light up the whole room. "Date? I'm not sure I'd call what I do with the men I see, 'dating.' Do you date?"

"Yes." Jack drained the champagne. He felt like he was losing a game he didn't come prepared to play. "So why don't you date, Miss Maxwell? Even with all the fundraising, you must meet interesting people."

"Any energy I have that would be used to build a relationship, I save for my brother Tomas. Because of his illness, he's confined to a very small world, Mr. Curran. I'm his only hope to help him escape one day."

"That's very noble." Jack leaned toward her. "But what do you do for fun?"

She removed her hand from his and picked up the cigarette from the ashtray. It glowed red against her pale skin. "I read *The LA Times* every morning. When I see there's been a new tragedy, I send flowers to strangers. It makes me feel like I'm helping a fellow human being." She smiled again, a sadder version. "As you can see, my life would make a dull story for your readers."

"You're telling me you are a Good Samaritan, but only the kind who sends flowers?"

"As opposed to what other kind?"

"The kind who kills bad guys."

Her blue eyes widened. "The woman who committed those crimes does not lead a dull life. She's nothing like me."

"You're a lot of things, Miss Maxwell, none of which is dull." He let the sarcasm show in his voice, but it did not seem to faze her.

"You are trying to flatter me, I think." Alana licked her index finger and brushed it against his cheek. "Sorry, I flicked ash on you. I wouldn't want to scar that handsome face anymore."

Jack's skin burned from her touch. His gaze rested on her hair, swept off her face and held behind her ears with diamond encrusted combs. The breeze picked up, and he smelled the tang of the ocean again.

Keep at her. Keep digging, he told himself. Don't be a sap.

"How does Wanda Keppler fit in?" he asked gruffly. "You read obituaries too? Send flowers to all the widows?"

"I knew her husband."

He sat back, shocked. "You knew Randall Keppler? How?"

"I had occasion to speak with him from time to time. He was a charming man. Very kind. I was sad to hear about what happened to him."

"Did you meet him at one of your fundraising cocktail parties?"

She shook her head. "No. He worked for the doctor who is treating Tomas."

Several pieces of research clicked together, although the picture they made was still unclear. Jack recalled a comment Alana had made in the garden outside the Ambassador, about taking too much medicine. "Dr. Preminger is treating your brother...and you?"

"That's none of your business, but yes. How do you know Dr. Preminger?"

"I don't."

For the first time, she looked wary. "Then how did you know that was the doctor I was referring to?"

"A couple of nights ago at the Ambassador, you mentioned you were taking medicine to help your brother. And I know Ronald Keppler worked for Preminger."

She stared at him. It was obvious she did not remember their encounter in the hotel garden. "Are you sure you're not a detective?"

He wasn't going to let her sidetrack him again. "Is Dr. Preminger treating your brother with drugs and hypnosis?"

"I still don't understand how you know Mr. Keppler worked for Dr. Preminger." Alana sat up straighter in her chair.

"His wife told me."

"And she told you Dr. Preminger uses hypnosis?"

"Yes. Lynton also mentioned him the other night when I came to his house. Your brother said Preminger is trying to interest the government in a research project. Do you know what that's all about?" Lynton had not revealed the doctor's name, but Jack hoped Alana would confirm it was Preminger.

"Lynton is not my brother."

"Sorry. Step-brother, right?"

"Right." Alana frowned. "I don't know anything about that, but it makes sense that any project Preminger would mention to Lynton would have a military application."

"I gathered the doctor is doing research on genetics. It's hard to understand how that would help the department of defense."

Alana stiffened. "I don't know, or care, about anything Preminger is doing, aside from what he's trying to do for Tomas. I know he's using hypnosis to try and lessen my brother's pain."

"Tomas is in a lot of pain?" He pictured the slim young man he had seen in the wheelchair. "I'm very sorry to hear that. He's fortunate to have you advocate for him."

"I'm the fortunate one to have him, Mr. Curran. We're the only two remaining members of our family." Her eyes flooded with tears and she looked away.

Other than your step-brother, Jack thought. He wondered again what was behind her animosity. "I'm sure Lynton appreciates your efforts to help Tomas."

Alana turned back to Jack. "My step-brother does not appreciate anything I do. But he does enjoy meeting people on the cutting edge of scientific research. I think he once wanted to be a doctor himself." She narrowed her eyes. "If you don't want to bore your readers, you should avoid writing about him."

Jack thought of Maxwell's unconventional musings on war. And vengeance. "He seems like a pretty fascinating guy."

"Fascinating is not how I'd describe him." Alana took the last sip of champagne and set her empty flute on the table. The piano man behind her was now singing about teardrops falling from his eyes.

"Why don't we take a walk, Mr. Curran?" Alana's eyes were bright. "I have a house very near here, on the beach. We can sit and talk about anything but Lynton. I'll tell you more about my flower sending habits, and you can explain how exactly you found out about it."

"Okay." He reached for his wallet, but she put out her hand and stopped him. "I own the *Blue Note*. Drinks are on the house."

She got up, and he wasted no time in following her.

CHAPTER SIXTEEN

They left the club the way they had come, but instead of walking out to the parking lot, Alana took Jack's hand and led him around the right side of the building and down a short flight of wooden stairs.

The Pacific surf crashed fifty yards away, and gulls hung and screamed at the straggle of beachgoers heading toward their cars at the edge of the highway.

Jack looked up at the sky. It was warm, and the sun was declining, but it was breezy and clear. It felt unreal to be walking along the sand's edge with a woman swathed in diamonds and mink.

"Is your leg holding up okay?"

"Yeah, fine," Jack said. There was a white house at the path's edge, a hundred feet ahead.

"We're here." Alana slid her coat off mid-stride and folded it over her arm. "We should have brought more champagne."

"Shall I walk back and get another bottle?"

"No. No going back now." She turned and opened a wooden gate with a key, and they walked a few feet to the weathered clapboard cottage.

She led him inside but did not turn on the lights. They made their way through a kitchen and into a room with a spectacular view of the Pacific. The space was furnished with comfortable sofas, crammed bookcases, and flowers. A huge display of white roses sat on a table by the French doors.

"White roses. Your favorite?" The fragrance mingled with his gutful of champagne, clouding his senses pleasantly.

"Yes, they are. My housekeeper brings them in. She's off tonight." Alana dropped her fur on the couch and opened the patio doors to the summer breeze. She kicked off her high heels and padded across the room to a bar area. "I bet you drink scotch." She grabbed a decanter and two tumblers.

"I do." He settled himself at one end of a long sofa, hoping to keep space between them. He watched as she poured Scotch and turned on the phonograph, unleashing the sultry voice of Ella Fitzgerald.

"Neat? Or water?"

"Neat."

"Faster that way, isn't it?" Alana brought the drinks over and sat right beside him. She handed him his drink and touched the edge of her glass to his before downing two ounces of scotch in a single swallow.

Jack took a sip and set the tumbler on the table in front of them. He had not had much champagne, but he knew the Scotch would go down easily if he sat here much longer. He waved toward the ocean. He was having trouble concentrating with her this close. "Spectacular view."

"It is. The sea is powerful and uncontrollable." She smiled, her lips wet with liquor. "You said you don't believe in luck. Do you believe in *karma*, Mr. Curran?"

"I don't know what that is." He looked at her. "Why don't you explain it to me?"

"*Karma* is a Sanskrit word. In the Buddhist religion, it's the law of moral causation. In other words, karma results from what actions a person takes in this world. Buddhists believe that nothing happens to a person that he or she does not deserve."

"That's pretty black and white. Are you a Buddhist?"

"I'm not a Buddhist; I've been studying it, along with other philosophies, for years. But the concept of *karma* is one of the principals which govern my life. It sounds simple, but I've found simple concepts are often the most meaningful."

He could not stop staring at her. Her body seemed to glow against the blackness of her dress, and her blue eyes caught the light in the room and refracted it back to him.

"What do you think?" She patted the back of the sofa, inviting him to sit back.

"About *karma*?" He stayed where he was. He thought for what seemed like the first time in years about Katherine, his sister, who was long dead. Then a stream of images of the war in Italy, always playing in the back of his mind, filled his brain like a newsreel he couldn't turn off. "I knew a lot of good men who died in the war. I doubt that they did anything to deserve it, except being in the wrong place at the right time to die."

"That's the logic most people use when they first hear about *karma*. They bring up babies who are born with deformities. Loved ones, who have never done a thing to hurt another soul, but suffer a grave illness. I struggle with this issue myself." Her voice trembled. "I thought when I was a young girl that I may have done some things which affected my brother, Tomas."

"You thought your *karma* affected him? That doesn't seem fair. Is that a tenant of your religion?"

"No. Each person earns their own karma." She smiled sadly. "But I do wonder if we are often born into a certain family to be punished, or rewarded, by being a sister to a sibling who will suffer in order to enlighten you."

"That is harsh." His voice was unsteady as he again thought of his sister. "What kind of God would punish one child to enlighten another?"

Tears filled Alana's eyes, but she wiped them away so quickly Jack wasn't sure he had even seen them. "I don't pretend to understand God, Mr. Maxwell. My brother, Tomas, is a blessing. However, I do meditate for the strength to believe nothing I have done has affected him in negative ways." She met his eyes.

"What have you done that would cause God to punish

Tomas?"

She didn't answer for several moments. When she spoke, her voice seemed relieved. "He was a twin. I saw his brother, who died the day they were born. But I never told Tomas about the other boy. Tomas doesn't know he was a twin."

"It wasn't your responsibility to tell him," Jack said. "Didn't your parents explain what happened?"

"No. Never."

"Family secrets." He sighed. "Homemade sin is the deadliest kind, my mother said."

"Is that what it was?" She looked away. "It felt like a test. One I failed."

"I think you're taking the blame from the people who really deserved it. Your parents."

"Maybe." She sighed. "Most people would say I sound crazy if they heard me admit how I feel inside."

He smelled the booze on her breath and felt as if he had thrown a shot back. "I'm not most people."

"I knew that the moment I met you."

The house quieted around them, even the ocean sounds seemed to stop. Jack reached for his glass. He took a swallow and stared out at the water. "I don't think life deals people a fate that is tit for tat. Justice is for the courts, not life. Life is pretty random." He turned to her. "When young people die or suffer, it's a crapshoot. Especially when young, innocent people die. There's no blame involved. Only chance."

"Buddhists believe people live many times. They return to this life over and over again and strive to improve their immortal soul by making amends for past mistakes. Which means that someone whose punishment seems undeserved might actually be atoning for past wrongs."

"Reincarnation, huh?" Jack set the glass down and felt the heat off her body. "I've heard of that."

"But you think it's silly?"

"It's hard to believe." He shrugged.

"I see." She sighed. "Did you go to college?"

"Yes."

"I wish I had done that."

"Go now. A lot more girls are doing that since the war ended. You're young. What are you, twenty-one?"

"I'm well past twenty-one, Mr. Curran." She licked her bottom lip. "And I don't think I could get through classes. I get itchy if I have to sit still too long."

His groin tightened, inflamed by her suddenly draping her legs over his lap. "Itchy?"

"Bored. Anxious. Like I have to do something, or I'll explode." Alana blinked. "Now do you understand why I send flowers to people who have experienced great tragedies?"

"Not really."

"I want to do everything I can to comfort people, to do good if you will, because then I will earn good things in return. I pray for that."

Alana Maxwell's voice was thick with yearning. And guilt. Jack's brain said her anguish could be evidence of her connection to murder. But at that moment his gut did not believe she would hurt anyone. Intentionally.

"What good things do you want that you don't have?" he asked softly.

"I can't tell you that. Things I yearn for I know I can never have. But they're private hopes and dreams."

"I won't tell anyone."

"Right. And what is it you do for a living?" She sat back and folded her arms over her breasts.

"I'm a reporter. But that's only what I do for a living; it's not my life." He put his arm around her shoulders. "Tell me one thing you want."

"I want you to make love to me."

Time seemed to stop. Jack didn't answer because he didn't think he could.

Alana wet her lips and leaned into him, her face an inch from his mouth. There was a tremor in her voice. "But I won't tell you about what I pray for. It's private. I only explained my philosophy about *karma* so you'd understand that I'm not a superficial rich girl, out for a thrill."

Jack swallowed. There was that word again. Was it a taunt? Was this the woman who had killed six men in cold blood? The woman who told Joan Becklund she was thrilled to help her? Was her motive for murdering street thugs a twisted path to earning brownie points with Buddha?

That would be one hell of an unusual defense.

And one hell of a screenplay.

Fear pulled tight around his gut. Jack stared into her eyes. *Ask her if she murdered those men. Right now.* But he didn't ask her anything. He pulled Alana to him and kissed her as if she were his, plunging his tongue into her soft, hot mouth.

Alana responded willingly. More than willingly, she kissed him as if she would devour him. She was naked in his arms moments later, pulling, clawing off his clothes. They tumbled nude onto the floor, her mink cushioning her silky bottom. She cupped her breasts in her hands and licked her bottom lip as she stared up at him. He rested on his knees, ignoring the bite of the brace and the pain of his wound, and grabbed her by the thighs, sliding her up against his throbbing body.

Jack forgot the pain, his professional distance, and the fear that this woman might be a murderer. He pushed into her and murmured her name with each stroke.

Her only reply was to ask for more.

"I'll give you more," he whispered. "And if I deserve this, I must have done very good things in my life."

Alana smiled and dug her nails into his ribs, then rolled on top of his body and rode him with an intensity he had never known from a woman.

# # #

Neither Alana nor Jack spoke on the drive back to Los Angeles. They shared two cigarettes and listened to the radio.

Jack glanced at his watch. It was almost eleven. He had not

called Eddie or Quentin. He could ask her to stop at a telephone booth, but at this point, there wasn't anything he could say to his co-workers to make up for blowing the deadline.

The Rolls pulled up to the curb outside *The Eyes* office. He turned to Alana, noting her lips were swollen from their evening in bed. "Thanks for the lift. I'll call you tomorrow."

"Will you?"

"Yes." He kept his voice cool. "Unless you don't want me to."

"I think you're the kind of man who does what he wants." She raised her eyebrows. "You've got my number."

"I do."

"*You do.*" She put her hand on his thigh and squeezed.

"Are you okay to drive? You look sleepy." He didn't want to get out of the car.

"I'm taking medication, and I get punchy at this time of night. But don't worry about me." She smiled faintly. "I've got a date at midnight. I'll recover by then."

"A date? With who?" He felt like a jerk for asking, but couldn't not.

"You don't know him."

"Well, have a great time." Jack didn't kiss her goodbye. But he wanted to pull her out of the car and into his arms. She smelled like the soap in her bathroom. They had taken a shower together after screwing each other senseless, but the hot water had gotten it all going again.

"How about you?" She smiled up at him. "You going out with that redhead tonight, Jack?"

"No."

"Why? You a one-woman man?"

"Not lately."

"Good answer. I like a man who tells the truth, even if it's hard to hear."

"And I like a woman who knows what she wants."

"Yeah? Even if what she wants is dangerous?"

"To who?"

"To everyone."

They stared at one another. Ask her point blank if she was Thrill Girl, he told himself. But he couldn't. He didn't want to ask her anything he didn't know the answer to. He touched her cheek. "I want to see you again."

"You have more questions?"

He chuckled. "Yeah, that's my life. Always more questions. I'm a reporter, remember?"

"Hard for a woman to forget that. Sure, we'll see each other again."

"Tomorrow?"

A moment passed, and an unreadable look crossed Alana's face. "We'll see."

"Okay. You've got my number, too."

"I do."

"Drive safe," he said.

"No fun in that." She blew him a kiss and sped down the street without glancing backward.

Wearily he put on his hat, lit a cigarette, and walked toward the office. He had no claim on Alana Maxwell, but she had climbed under his skin. She was different than any woman he knew. She projected strength when you didn't know her, but once you got close, she was fragile, as if she were made of glass windows concealing her secrets.

If she were his, he would carefully open them, one by one.

Jack flushed at his ridiculous thought. He was working class. She was a fucking heiress. A fucking heiress at the rotten middle of a mystery he was chasing. He clenched his jaw and twisted his neck back and forth as if he could shake her out of his thoughts. He had to get a grip and go in and write his columns.

Too much was riding on the Thrill Girl story. He could not get distracted by the allure of a woman he did not really know, and surely should not trust. He had to keep digging and accept whatever the facts revealed about her and anyone else.

Jack pitched his cigarette and reached for the front door knob, but Lucy Cherry pulled it open from the other side.

"Where the hell have you been?" she demanded.

"I've been out. And before you start in, I know you had to pick-up the slack for me on page one, but you've been missing in action on deadline night way more than I have. You owe me." He stepped past her into the office.

"Jack?" Quentin's voice was furious. "Thank god you're finally here!" The publisher walked to the middle of the newsroom and pointed at Lucy. "Call the police and tell them Jack and I will be there in fifteen minutes."

"Whoa!" Jack looked from one to the other. "Goddamn it, hang on. If Jimmy Glass and those asshole cops want to jerk me around again because I've been talking to their witnesses, they can kiss my ass. I'm on a story here, and I'm making progress."

"They don't want to talk to you about Thrill Girl." Lucy crossed her arms and looked at Quentin. She was pale and her mouth a tight line of worry.

"What the hell is going on?" Jack looked around the office. "And where is Eddie? Did you let him go home?"

"Where did you go after you left the VA?" Quentin demanded.

"I went to the Ambassador, then to the Blue Note in Santa Monica."

"You've been out bar hopping?" Lucy's voice dripped with scorn.

"I've been interviewing a subject about Thrill Girl." Jack's face reddened. "I couldn't get to a phone without jeopardizing the whole thing. But I figured you, Eddie, and Lucy could put tomorrow's issue to bed. Did you?" He glared at Lucy.

"Yes, Mr. Deville walked the copy down to the print shop an hour ago. We did a follow-up on the monster issue, for your information, with hot new information."

"Oh yeah?" Jack threw his hat on his desk.

"Yeah." A triumphant look flashed across her face. "While you were out interviewing, I got a police source to confirm the bum who got his head ripped off had human bite marks on his arm."

"Human? Holy Christ." Jack looked at Quentin in disbelief. "The cops are going to go ballistic if you print that. Did Eddie call the coroner? He should be able to get confirmation of that from Hatchett." He looked around for the kid. "Where is he?"

"You're jealous my story is bigger than yours," Lucy said.

"Both of you shut up!" Quentin held up his hand like a school teacher. "Whatever the monster turns out to be is the least of our problems right now. Jack, sit down."

Jack leaned against the desk. He was weaker than he should be, both from alcohol and from his time with Alana, but his next thought came through crystal clear.

Something was wrong.

He glanced down at his desk. There was no sign of his car keys, only a stack of messages, the top of which said, *Call Mary Ann Little…urgent!* "Where's Eddie?"

"Eddie never came back to the office today," Deville said. "And he's not at home. His parents called three hours ago because he didn't show up to a family birthday party in Studio City. They haven't heard from him all day. Lucy called and found out that you left the VA at five, and we were hoping he picked you up."

"Eddie left the VA at two, two-thirty, and I haven't seen him since." Jack swallowed hard. "Where is he? And where the hell is my car?"

"Your car is in a ravine in Glendale." Quentin crossed his arms over his chest. "It went over the side of the road and down a sixty-foot embankment a couple of hours ago. The police identified it by the plates and called here looking for you ten minutes ago. They are in the process of recovering it."

"Oh my god," Jack gasped. "Is Eddie…?"

"They don't know who is inside." Quentin shook his keys at Jack. "Come on, I'll drive."

# # #

Jack and Quentin stood shoulder to shoulder on a two-lane road leading into the Angeles National Forest, watching as a police tow truck pulled Jack's battered Packard up the side of the ravine.

When it was ten yards from the top, the cops braced it with more cable to keep it from sliding. The emergency personnel waiting beside the ambulance were waved over, and six men swarmed into the brush, the LAPD lettering on their jackets glimmering in the light from the mass of patrol cars' headlights.

After five minutes, the LA County Sheriff Deputy in charge of the scene motioned for Jack and Quentin.

"Don't answer any questions about what Eddie was working on with you," Quentin said, his head down. "When I told Detective Glass we were printing that tip about the human saliva in the monster victims' wounds, he asked what you knew about a blonde woman sending white roses to Thrill Girl's victims from a shop on Wilshire."

"What?"

"Yes. He wouldn't say how he found out about it, but he's furious you didn't report it to them. I told him we would have a sit-down tomorrow."

The message from Mary Ann Little now made sense to Jack. *She must have told Glass everything.* "How did Glass know about my car, anyway? Wilshire Division doesn't cover Glendale."

"The wrecker is Stu Martin's brother. He called Stu and told him the car was yours." Quentin shuddered and took a hit off his cigarette holder. "Cops have connections everywhere in town. Reminds me of Berlin."

The wind picked up and blew dead leaves across the asphalt.

"When were you in Berlin?" It was the first time Jack had heard Quentin mention being in Europe.

"During the '36 Olympics." He blew out a breath. "I saw the devil with my own eyes. His people proclaimed the perfect German to be a six-foot-tall blonde, but Hitler himself was a short dumpy bastard who looked constipated. No more than five-foot-five. Pasty skin. Dead eyes." He seemed to be far away. "I also got to see Jesse Owens race. He was magnificent."

"What were you doing at the Olympics?"

Quentin turned to Jack. "Working."

"For a news service? I thought you got into journalism *after* the war."

"I've been a reporter of sorts all my life, Jack. Observe, conclude, report." Quentin took another drag on his cigarette.

"Did you work for *The London Times*?"

"No. I worked for the army."

Jack almost asked, *whose army*, but stopped himself. Quentin, like many wealthy men, seemed to simply be whatever he wanted to be at any given point in time. He recalled the Fitzgerald quote he and Eddie had bantered about. The rich did whatever the fuck they wanted with their twenty-four hours a day. Seldom were they as encumbered by law, convention, or expectation as the rest of mankind.

Alana led that life too. "I spent a couple of hours with Lynton Maxwell's step-sister tonight," Jack said.

"And?"

"Hey, no smoking up here! Fire hazard," one of the sheriff deputies interrupted.

"Thank you!" Deville tipped his hat and snuffed out his cigarette with the bare tips of his finger. "Eddie Wentz is going to get a piece of my mind when we find him." Quentin was ignoring the very real possibility Eddie could be dead inside the wreck.

"I don't know why the hell he would have been driving around up here." Jack looked around at the summer-browned landscape, full of brush, cactus and straggly pine trees.

"We don't know that he's the one who crashed the car."

"I told him to go back to the office." Jack's mind churned as he tried to imagine what the kid might have done after leaving the hospital. The answer hit him with the force of a blow.

"The clinic," Jack whispered.

"What clinic?"

"Eddie and I were going to go over to the clinic where Randall Keppler worked." Jack quickly filled Quentin in on what Wanda Keppler had told them about her husband and Dr. Preminger, the doctor's research, and the troubling Josef Brandt.

"You think this Brandt was behind Randall Keppler's death?

That it wasn't a hit and run?"

"I don't know." Jack squeezed his thigh in pain. Instead of a nicotine hit, he gobbled down a codeine table he had in his pocket.

"You said you talked to Alana Maxwell." Quentin kept his voice low. "Did you find out why she sent flowers to this Mrs. Keppler?"

"Yeah." The memory of Alana, warm and naked in his arms, overwhelmed him for a moment.

"Does that information confirm your theory that she could be Thrill Girl?"

Jack was saved from answering that complicated question by the crunching sound of the Packard being hauled the rest of the way up the cliff. It landed with a thud; its roof was crushed, and windshield smashed.

"God, look at that." Dread filled Jack's body.

"Gentlemen!" The deputy waved. "Come over here, please."

"Is there anyone inside?" Quentin demanded as they hurried toward the scene.

"No one is in the car." The cop had a jutting jaw and bloodshot eyes. "We're searching the hillside now, but there's no sign anyone was thrown or fell out. The side windows are intact. A driver could have gone through the windshield, but we didn't see any blood on the glass. It's looking like someone deliberately sent the car off the cliff to get rid of it."

"What?" Quentin and Jack said in unison.

"Why?" Jack demanded. "Why would anyone do that?"

The cop shrugged. "Trying to hide something. Or collect insurance. You insured, Mr. Curran?"

"Yes. But the car's paid for."

"You have a jaded view of life, don't you, deputy?" Quentin interjected.

"Yeah, we do." The cop looked at Jack hard, his eyes traveling down his suit pants to his wing tips. "We've got fresh boot prints at the edge of the ravine where the tire tracks end. We're making casts of them."

Quentin clasped Jack's shoulder. "But as of right now, Officer, there's no evidence anyone was injured in the crash?"

"We'll check the trunk as soon as we can pry it open. There's a substance that looks like blood on the bumper." The deputy motioned to Jack. "We need your permission to open it."

"You got it." Jack held his breath.

Two minutes later the trunk popped open.

There was a spare tire, jack, a blanket and flashlight, and the leather bag full of bulbs and camera gear Eddie had checked out from *The Eyes* to take photos at Wanda Keppler's.

Fifteen minutes later, Quentin and Jack were in the Bentley heading back to the office. The publisher had fended off the deputy's interest in what Jack and Eddie Wentz had been doing today and managed to take the camera bag without having it impounded.

They promised to be in touch if they heard from Eddie, who was now officially a missing person via a report filed by his parents.

Both men had one thought on their minds.

"We need to get that film developed. With any luck, it might tell us what Eddie did *after* he left me at the VA," Jack said.

Quentin nodded. "I'll call Cimino at home and have him meet us at the office. But first, we'll stop and grab something to eat."

"I'm not hungry," Jack said.

"But you'll eat?"

On cue, Jack's stomach rumbled. "No."

Eddie going missing was the first thing in a long time that killed his appetite.

CHAPTER SEVENTEEN

Y ou call me when you're ready to get out, sir." Robinson stood with his hand on the bathroom doorknob.

Tomas's good hand rested on the side of the claw foot tub, supporting his partially functioning right leg. He was definitely feeling stronger, and the neck pains he had lived with his whole life had lessened dramatically.

He had a towel wrapped around his waist. "I don't need help getting out, Robinson. Shut the door and go home, please. It's after midnight, and you've already put in two hours of overtime."

"It's no problem to wait and help you out of the bath, Mr. Maxwell. You don't want to slip or nothing."

"I've told you before if I'm going to kill myself, I won't do it by slipping in the bathroom. Didn't you see that movie, *Knock on Any Door?*"

Robinson loved movies. He went to a double feature every Saturday afternoon he could. "Mr. Humphrey Bogart, right?"

"Right. Bogart played the murderer's lawyer. Wanted to get the man off by proving the punk only killed because he was poverty-stricken, he never had a chance at a decent life."

"I didn't agree with that." Robinson frowned. "Every man has a choice about what he's going to do and not going to do."

"My thoughts exactly. Which is why I'm going to live hard, die young and leave a good-looking corpse, like the killer in that movie says. Not drown in a bathtub. The last thing I want to do is be found as a bloated, prune-skinned mess."

"Miss Maxwell won't like to hear you talking like that, sir."

"I know. Don't tell her, and please shut the door."

Robinson shut the door.

At the click of the bolt, Tomas dropped the towel from his waist. He sighed with pleasure as he slipped into the hot water. It was the perfect temperature for his aching limbs. He rolled onto his right side to recline fully on his back, settling with his head above the water.

The bracing contraption Alana had purchased for him hung on the side of the tub. It allowed him to anchor himself with a collar around his chest so he wouldn't slip under the water while bathing. Once tethered, he could wash his private parts unaided with his good hand. He was grateful for that shred of privacy, especially since Preminger's medications had caused such unusual changes in his body.

He slipped his head through the brace and glanced down at his chest. It was covered with thick, curly golden hair. A finer layer covered his arms and his shoulders. The doctor said the hair growth was a side effect of the hormones he took to maximize the effectiveness of the other drugs pumping through him.

Tomas didn't mind his new, hirsute look. But he was concerned about another side effect of the treatment. There was a growth at the base of his spine. It had grown over the past month and now measured about half an inch.

Tomas rested his hand on the edge of the tub. What would Dr. Preminger's reaction be tomorrow if he bluntly asked the German if he was growing a tail?

He smiled grimly. *What was the old saying? The cure was worse than the disease?*

Tomas had been born handicapped, paralyzed on his left side – that hand disfigured and unusable – and with limb weakness on the right.

But it could have been worse. Much worse.

Tomas blinked. He had not known until he was ten years old that another baby had been born that day, his twin brother, who had died with excruciating internal and physical disfigurements. Tomas's nanny, Gertrude, had told him all about it one night after imbibing of too much of her Schnapps. She had cautioned him never to tell his mother, Lynton, or anyone else that he knew about the tragedy.

She had not needed to beg. Tomas understood, with blinding clarity, that it would cause major trauma to his mother and sister if they discovered he knew the secret they had diligently hidden from him since birth.

Emrick, the child had been christened, confessed Gertrude, crying as she said she prayed for the babe every day.

After learning about his brother, Tomas was relieved in a strange way. He was no longer the unluckiest person he had ever known, for he, at least, had been able to lead a somewhat normal life. But since that day, he had been haunted by nightmares about his brother.

His breathing felt constricted, and he splashed water on his face. The night terrors were vivid and terrifying; he had gone to Lynton when he was only fourteen and told his step-brother what he had learned about Emrick's existence. He demanded to know if the child had been properly buried.

Lynton was shocked that Tomas knew the truth and had reassured his step-brother that his twin had been buried in Tyrol, at the Maxwell family cemetery. "The headstone reads, 'Beloved son and brother,'" he added.

"With his name? You listed Emrick Maxwell on the stone?"

Lynton had dropped his eyes in shame. "No, not his last name. I escorted the poor babe myself, to be sure it was all done right. Five days after you were born. I went alone because your mother and father were too heartbroken to do it."

Lynton had surprised Tomas after this shocking confession by giving him a hug. "Please don't ever tell Alana you know about this. It will kill her."

Tomas had agreed to keep this secret, the only one he had ever kept from his sister.

The water in the tub stilled. For the hundredth time, he wondered if Lynton had lied to him. Lynton lied a lot. Tomas slipped deeper into the warm water. It was past time to reveal this secret to Alana. She deserved to know. But she already hated Lynton, for reasons he didn't really understand.

Another snatch of conversation overheard the day before his mother's death sizzled inside his head. Even now Tomas could not be sure if he had imagined it, or if his mother had actually said to his Aunt Bridget in a hushed voice, "The other poor babe was *der Katzenjunge.*"

Der Katzenjunge meant cat boy. Boys who looked like humans, but who died horrible deaths shortly after mutating into creatures that killed mercilessly and went mad with remorse. Tomas had never allowed himself to believe those words could be applied to his dead baby brother. Cat boys were part of the local mythology of the Austrian people in the village where his family was from, as fanciful as vampires and werewolves, and all the creatures that went bump in the night. Or at least that's what he had always told himself.

The day after he heard this, his mother died. His aunt had left their home shortly after the funeral and died the next year, leaving Tomas with no clear path to finding out the truth of what he might have heard.

He reached under the water and touched the growth on his tailbone, terrified for a moment that the grotesque changes were occurring not because of Preminger's failed drug treatments, but because of a myth he should have believed in.

Because of a genetic curse that had already killed his twin.

Shivering, Tomas closed his eyes as his heart pounded erratically. Suddenly his right leg cramped. He grabbed it and squeezed tight until the pain passed. With a sigh, Tomas reached around and undid the brace. Slowly his body drifted downward until the water covered all but his nose.

Am I brave enough to drown myself?

Tomas stared up at the light in the ceiling. He could not ask for a more loving sister than Alana, but it would have been good to have a brother. He had imagined once that Emrick was alive and watching over him. Last summer, at an outdoor concert at the Hollywood Bowl, he had spotted a tall, graceful man in a tan fedora, sunglasses, and black leather driving gloves in the far aisle of the season ticket holders.

Staring at him.

Tomas had inclined his head and smiled at the man, who seemed achingly familiar, and the man had smiled back. Tomas asked Alana if she recognized the stranger, but he was gone by the time she turned.

"Who did you think it was, Tommy?" she had asked.

He had not answered.

Tomas closed his eyes and let the water fill his ears, blocking all sound. He would tell Alana about the lost child tomorrow. And about the shocking explanation of her twin babies' physical defects that he had heard from their mother's own lips.

He had to.

Because, despite his sister's desperate optimism, he knew he did not have much time left. If he was going to die because he was genetically cursed, he must make his secrets known to the woman who had suffered so because of his afflictions.

Something that felt like relief burbled through Tomas's veins. As he lay in the warm bath, he realized that once Alana discovered there was *never* anything she could have done to change his fate, she would be better off. She would live a satisfying and happy life, her *karma* bountiful from her past generosity and sacrifice.

His sister could finally live free of the guilt she felt because she was healthy and he was not. She would be free, at last, of worry.

Free of him.

# # #

Down the road from Preminger's property, parked at the side of the street under a canopy of an enormous camellia bush, the man in the Cadillac watched a blue sedan turn out of the gated drive.

By his estimation, the house would be empty for a couple of

hours. He and Janus had walked the grounds late last night, but he had decided to wait until tonight to break into the laboratory. Two nights ago he had easily scaled the roof behind the house and measured the vent in the ceiling. It was big enough for him to gain entry.

He let out a breath that sounded like steam escaping from a kettle. Tonight he would confirm what was going on in there. But he must be cautious. If he got caught by the police or Herr Doktor, it could be a nightmare.

He tugged on his black leather glove and grimaced. "Let's go," he said to his trusted driver, and the Cadillac rolled away.

# # #

Jack dropped Quentin off at Hancock Park well after midnight. Despite their hopes, Al Cimino, chief photographer for *The Eyes*, had been unable to process the photos from Eddie's camera. Their lab was out of developer, and none of the supply stores opened until nine a.m. Quentin was furious about the delay, but as they were all exhausted from the day's drama, he ordered everyone home for the night.

At his boss's behest, Jack kept the Bentley and headed for home. He detoured to cruise by the clinic where he and Eddie were to visit and found its heavy gates locked up tight, and no lights on inside the house. He yearned to check if the kid had talked to anyone there, but he knew if he forced himself on the occupants, uninvited and in the middle of the night, he could get slapped into jail again.

Once home, Jack took more pills for his aching leg, chased by a shot of whiskey. He fell onto the narrow bed and into a dead sleep in moments.

A noise woke him an hour later.

He rolled onto his side and off the bed to the floor in one reflexive movement. In the thick darkness, Jack reached for his M1 carbine.

But his gun was not there beside him.

He had not owned a gun since his discharge from the Army.

His pulse pounding, Jack focused on reality. *It's 1951. I'm in*

California, not the Italian countryside.

But he knew there was danger lurking. A rattle and scrape alerted him that someone had turned the knob of his apartment door. Goosebumps ran down Jack's arms as a solid knock landed on the wood.

Jack tried to stand but fell, his leg buckling under his weight. After a moment, he righted himself and limped toward the door. All he had on was a pair of boxers, but it was enough to wear to chew out the son-of-a-bitch who had interrupted his rest.

He pulled the front door open and yelled at the top of his lungs, "What the hell do you want?"

Susan Baldwin, dressed in slacks and a light jacket, stepped back from his wrath. Her face was pale as moonlight. "I'm so sorry, Mr. Curran. I should have called first. But I don't have a phone, and since you wrote down your address on your card, I thought it would be okay if I came over."

"Oh, geez, Susan. No. It's fine. Come in. Come in."

She hesitated, glancing at his bare chest and legs before averting her eyes. "I'm sorry I woke you up."

"And I'm sorry for yelling like that." Jack gestured for her to come inside. "I'll put on the coffee and get dressed."

"Thanks." She was blushing as she moved past him.

He swore under his breath. A neighbor stuck his head out of his front door. "Everything okay?" the man called.

"Fine. Go back to sleep." Jack closed the door. "Jeez, have a seat. Let me get decent."

"It's okay," Susan said. "I've seen men in their underwear before."

Jack wondered if she meant her brother as he hurried to his bedroom and rummaged for clean clothes. He heard cupboards opening and closing in the kitchen, followed by the sound of running water. He pulled on trousers, forgoing the brace, and buttoned himself into a fresh shirt.

"You finding everything okay, Susan?"

"Yes. The coffee is on."

They met in the living room.

"Come sit." Jack switched on a lamp.

"Thanks." Susan sat across from him. Her face was tear-streaked, but her eyes were clear.

Jack offered her a cigarette from his pack and lit one for himself when she demurred. "I'd offer to make you something to eat to go with that coffee, but I don't think there's much in there. I have eggs and bread, though. Would you like a sandwich?"

On cue, his stomach growled. He flashed Susan a smile of apology. "Me, I can always eat."

"No, thank you. I'm not hungry. But I can cook you something."

"No. I'm fine." He took a slow draw on the cigarette. "How you doing?"

"I'm okay."

"I came by a couple of times. I wanted to apologize for last week, about lying to you. And about your dog and all."

"It wasn't entirely your fault."

"Yeah, well I should have been honest."

"People do the best they can, don't they?" Susan looked down, and then back at Jack's face. "You're a reporter, and you wanted your story. I understand that. We all do things we never thought we would sometimes."

Once again, he was struck by how much wiser than her years this young woman was. "What's going on, Susan? Your neighbor told me you and your mom had to go see your brother. Is he doing okay?"

"No. He's not okay. Paul's missing!" Tears welled in her brown eyes, and she sobbed in big choking gasps. She stuck her fist half in her mouth to try and stop them, but it didn't help.

Jack put down his cigarette and handed her a clean handkerchief, and sat next to her. His worry over Eddie returned like a slap in the head when he heard there were now two people missing. "What do you mean? He disappeared from the clinic where he lives?"

She shook her head. "Yes."

"But he couldn't sign himself out, could he? Isn't he crippled?"

Susan flinched. "He's seventeen, and he can't sign himself out. And yes, he's crippled, and he can't drive. He can't even walk by himself! My mom and I went up to the clinic on Saturday, because they called and told us there was an emergency. When we got there, the administrator told us Paul had been taken away by a Dr. Holtberg last Wednesday. We don't know any doctor by that name, and when the clinic called the number the man had given them, they found out it went to a phone booth in Los Angeles."

"What?" Jack put his arm around her shoulders. "Did you call the police? And where is this clinic, in Santa Barbara?"

"Yes. And the staff called the police before my mother, and I got there. They sent out a missing person bulletin to all of the other hospitals in the area, up in Santa Barbara."

"What do you think happened to him?"

"I think he's been kidnapped."

"What? Why would someone kidnap your brother?" Jack asked.

"I can't explain everything to you, Mr. Curran." She hung her head for a moment and then looked him directly in the face. "I'm not trying to be mysterious, but my brother's life is at stake, and I have to be careful. All I can tell you is that I think I know where to find him. I'm going to get him back safe at home and then I'll be in touch. I want you to do a newspaper article on the people who took him. I want them to be exposed for what they're trying to do. Will you do that?"

"Of course." Jack dropped his arm and got up to put out the cigarette. "But you need to give me more details. Who are the people you're talking about? And why would they kidnap Paul?"

"I can't tell you anything else right now." She stood. "But I've got documents and an agreement these people gave my mother. I want you to look into it and prove these charlatans for what they really are. With the help of your newspaper, I hope they'll all end up in jail."

"You're not making sense, Susan. What kind of agreement are you talking about?"

"I can't tell you now. But I will."

"I don't like this. If these people have stooped to kidnap a crippled kid, they're dangerous." He crossed his arms over his chest. "Let me take you to the police station. You can talk to them, and they'll help you. Then we'll go get Paul."

"No!" Susan held up her hand. "*No cops*, Jack. These people aren't scared of the police. They'll kill Paul, and then hide the evidence of what they've done. You're going to have to trust me. Please." Her eyes were huge in the dim light.

"This doesn't feel right, Susan."

"It's the best way." She stared at him. "Think of the story you'll get. I bet you could even sell it to the movies, once it's over."

Jack flushed. "I need to come with you. I'll stay back, but…"

"No!" Her voice broke again. "I can't risk it. I'll be safe. Don't worry about that. I only came here to let you know what's going on. In case…"

"In case what? In case something happens to you? You said you'd be safe. This is crazy. At least let me drive you."

"No, I don't want you to get involved yet."

The sounds of coffee boiling over onto the stove came from the kitchen. "Can you hang around for another few minutes? Let me make you breakfast, Susan, and we can talk this out."

"Thanks, but I've got to go now. I'll call you tomorrow." She kissed his cheek and was out the door before he could take a step to stop her.

Jack limped to the door and out onto the stoop. Susan emerged from the stairwell and ran across the street to a taxi parked at the curb. She climbed into the back seat and moments later it sped off into the dark.

By the time he grabbed his keys and got down to Deville's car, the taxi would be a mile away. "God damn it."

Jack went back to his apartment and slammed the door. He

flipped off the coffee in the kitchen, unbuttoned his shirt, and collapsed on the sofa. His heart raced, and his left calf felt on fire. He should not have taken the pain pills. His brain was sluggish. He knew he had not handled his conversation with Susan well. Eddie would have done a better job getting the facts.

Eddie.

Jack glanced at his wristwatch. The kid had been missing for more than twelve hours. He leaned back and closed his eyes. Five minutes. He would take five minutes and then get dressed and head to the office.

He had to do something to find him. He just didn't know what.

CHAPTER EIGHTEEN

At three a.m., Josef Brandt unlocked the laboratory and walked inside, followed close behind by Ernest Preminger. When Josef flipped on the lights, the generator clanged into operation, its hum grating against his nerves. At the end of the room, he peered into the last of three caged enclosures.

A silent, bulky shape looked up at him and gave a moan, but stayed concealed under the blanket. Brandt heard its breathing, rough and labored. He would need to take the patient's vitals, administer the injections and the transfusion, and clean its bedding.

He frowned. He didn't have the stomach for it right now.

"How is he doing? Any improvement?" Ernest asked.

"*Nein.*" Josef knew what was coming next, and his already foul mood darkened.

"It's a shame. We had such good success at the beginning, with most of the subjects. But there's no getting around it now, Josef. You have ten dead and this one failing..."

"I don't need to be reminded of that," Josef snapped.

"I think you do," his brother-in-law shot back. "You need to accept the facts as they are, not as you wish them to be. Until we can progress with the pharmaceuticals available to us, the toxic effects are going to make it impossible to find success.

Orzechowski warned us about this."

"I know what Gerhard warned us about better than you, *bruder*. He also warned us about losing our will. I haven't lost mine."

Preminger lowered his voice. "Josef, as far as my research is concerned, I'm done. My report is written. It's time for you to accept that, while promising, your efforts and input are no longer leading in a viable direction. The drug protocol you developed has proven time and again to have undesirable effects on the subjects. The Griffith Park incident was only the latest to prove you can't control the viciousness or violence that results from the usage."

"Get out." Josef pointed at the door. "I am the one who has underwritten this research for years. I don't need your permission to continue. And continue I will!"

"With who? We've exhausted our list of subjects with both the genetic and ancestral ties to the Austrian region. It's too dangerous to attempt to recruit anyone new at this point."

"We still have Tomas Maxwell. The injections we gave the others of Maxwell's blood serum were only the first step. You cannot discount what a breakthrough we've had with that approach."

"Josef! We don't know if the transfusion of Maxwell's cells played any part in the other subjects' reactions. And Tomas is now failing. He's not a suitable subject to test anything on or to provide genetic material for others. Unless he dies and we get custody of his body, he has nothing left to give us."

"He's not failing! It's you who are failing. How can you ignore the signs of what Tomas Maxwell may prove to be? Are you that much of a coward?"

Ernest stiffened. "I am a scientist, Josef. You know what I think of your myths. Science facts are what matter. Now, I came down to help you with the transfusion tonight. I think it's time to end that particular experiment before we have another accident."

"I've changed my mind," Josef said. "Go back to your warm bed and leave me in peace."

"Fine." Ernest stomped to the door but turned back to Josef.

"Are you staying here tonight, or going to your own home?"

"My place. I won't sleep under the same roof as a traitor."

Ernest made an exasperated sound and let himself out, pulling the locked door hard behind him.

"Coward," Josef muttered. He turned away and plodded to the stainless steel examining table and pulled out a chair. His experiments were not going as he had hoped, that was true. But he was close, very close to proving what he had known to be true his whole life. That there lived among us a special group of beings. He blinked rapidly. He would be celebrated far and wide for his research. He just had to be steadfast now that the disaster at Griffith Park had set everything back.

He withdrew a flask from his jacket and took a long drink, relishing the sting of brandy in his throat, and put on his glasses. Carefully he withdrew his prized possession from his jacket pocket.

The leather-bound booklet, faded and creased from use, fit the curve of his hand. He carried the book with him everywhere and knew the contents by heart, but he opened to a random page and began to read.

He never tired of the true story of *der Katzenjunge*, creatures with perfect night vision and unparalleled stalking prowess. Beings descended from explorers from the Brentenjochalm region of the Alps, whose travels brought them to mate with women from the rocky coast of Wales; creating a race capable of transmogrification, changing its form from human to creature at will.

Josef had first heard of the creatures as a child in the village near Innsbruck, during the years after the Great War. He had never tired of his mother's whispered tales, and the nights when she would wrap her arms around him in bed and speak of the untamable, wily, secretive beings who only wanted to be left alone by the inferior beasts called men.

Seine Mutter had warned him that the magical creatures were dying out because men, jealous of their power, now hunted and killed them. She confided to Josef that her younger brother, Milton, who had not been seen since 1916, had been *der*

Katzenjunge.

"But my brother's kind has nine lives," she told Josef. "If they die before they turn twenty, they can be reborn. I'm sure I'll see Milton again, and he will be very proud of you if you help save those like him."

A grunt of pleasure escaped his body as Josef relived the memories of those sacred nights, the musky smell of his mother, the warmth of the blankets and her plump body.

Sighing, he turned the pages. He did not care what Ernest and Deidre said. He had been left more funds from his mother's estate than Deirdre. He could afford to continue his research, with or without their permission.

And if Ernest refused to continue to procure the necessary drugs he was using on the test subjects, Josef would find another medical doctor who would. There were still contacts in Austria, those that had worked with him at *Mauthausen-Gusen.* One had been employed by the pharmaceutical giant Kiel after the war. A man named Fredrick, who had understood what Vice-Admiral Heye's mission was, how the drugs they had used in the D-IX program had helped build super soldiers, capable of fighting ferociously without fear, traveling without rest.

Perhaps he should try and find Fredrick now, Josef thought. Tell him what he had witnessed with Tomas Maxwell. All he needed was more time.

Above Josef's head, the vent creaked, as it often did when he first turned the compressor on, and then creaked a second time.

He looked up.

A drop of cold liquid dripped down his neck.

He leaned to the right and turned back to his pages. The condensation was yet another reminder of how Deidre dishonored his efforts, banishing him to work in what was little more than a shed behind the house she shared with her big-shot husband.

He could have become a doctor if he had not needed to stay home and care for his mother – bathe her, feed her, and change her soiled clothes – all the years she was bedridden. Deidre had not helped her own mother; off she went before the war and found

Ernest.

He spat on the floor and wiped his mouth on his sleeve.

A moving shadow on the wall opposite him caught Josef's attention. He narrowed his eyes and looked around the room. Nothing was there. He took another swig from the flask, but before he could enjoy the bite of the liquor, he was grabbed him from behind and slammed face down onto the table.

Josef screamed as his right shoulder felt the bite of a deadly attack.

He reached into his waistband for his gun, but his unseen enemy threw him to the ground and savagely smashed his head once against the cement floor, sending him tumbling into unconsciousness.

# # #

Ernest Preminger was dressing when the front doorbell rang at ten minutes after seven.

Is it Josef with a new problem? He frowned. His half-wit brother-in-law was resisting all efforts to shut down his farce of a research project.

It was time, long past time, for both of them to admit that Josef's scientific objective – to create a being with the physical stamina and endurance of a superman – was a failure.

His attempts to use hormones, drugs and blood transfusions on specially targeted subjects had seemed promising at first, as the first three subjects had initially gained strength and mobility. But the physical side effects and unexpected emotional complications had proven crippling, and fatal.

The last group was the worst of the lot, for their reactions had become increasingly hard to control. With each of them, as their body developed wider systemic infections and mutation, their personalities became more and more threatening. They had to put two of them down, like dogs.

Preminger sighed. Josef had been of use to him once, but no longer. He squinted out the Venetian blinds at the driveway, expecting to see Josef's car parked there. But it was another visitor.

Alana Maxwell leaned against the door of her Rolls Royce, smoking a cigarette. She was dressed in a pale blue cocktail dress and mink stole, and her legs shimmered in silk hose and high heels.

The expression on her face was grim.

There was no sign of her chauffeur.

Preminger's pulse jumped as several possible complications came to mind. With a blink, he stopped the flood of panicked thoughts and pulled on his tweed sports coat.

Deal with the infection at the first sign of pain. Don't wait for it to fester. That's what his father had always said. A dentist in Berlin, his father regaled the family with countless tales of good teeth that had needed to be pulled out because of a patient's fear, wishful thinking, and delay.

He glanced at the bed where Deidre lay snoring, the smell of last night's alcohol sour in the room. She would be useless for hours. Quickly he made his way through the house and opened the front door.

"Good morning. Is everything alright, my dear?"

Alana tossed her cigarette onto the driveway and ground it out with the toe of her shoe. She walked toward him. "No. No, Dr. Preminger. Not a goddamned thing is alright." Her eyes were bloodshot, and one pupil was enlarged.

"Are you ill, Alana?"

She winced when he touched her shoulder. "No. But I blacked out again for several hours last night. When I woke up an hour ago, I felt like there was a bullet in my head and it was taking its sweet time to kill me."

"My, my, I'm sorry to hear your side effects have worsened." Ernest breathed a sigh of relief to hear her complaints were of this nature. "Please come in."

Alana took a step, but then stopped as if she heard a noise. She glanced around the quiet, woody street, sniffing the air like a doe might.

Preminger smiled at the memory of her doing that numerous times in the past. She was a woman with a strong will, and her conscious mind had proved a challenge to master during hypnosis.

The trigger device, the tinkling of tiny silver bells, had finally been the thing to break through her resistance and leave her subconscious in his full control.

He took her arm and led her inside. "Please. I'll make us tea, and we'll discuss how we can alleviate your symptoms. You should have come to me earlier, Alana."

He stirred the wind chimes at the front door with his free hand. "Let's go into my office, and I'll take care of everything."

The chimes danced on the breeze, the sound like tiny flutes. Alana blinked and obediently followed him into the house.

He remembered the first time he had put her under, how inviting she had looked – lying supine on his couch, her legs slightly spread. He could have done anything to her.

I should have.

I can still.

Preminger adjusted his testicles with his left hand and refocused his mind. It was serendipitous that he had her to himself this morning. He would now have the entire day to prepare her for the final field trial, and Thrill Girl's last drama.

# # #

Hours after Susan Baldwin left his apartment, Jack woke up on his couch, a cramped, stiff mess. His plan to rest had been shattered because he had passed out into codeine-induced sleep. He showered and shaved, and was on his way to pick up Quentin by seven a.m.

He glanced in the rear-view mirror and perused his jaw. He had cut himself shaving. Three times. It was a new razor, and his clumsiness was due to being distracted and worried about Susan Baldwin.

And Eddie.

And Alana Maxwell.

He considered a stop at the Ambassador before he picked up Quentin, but it was too late now. Besides, if he did stop in to see Alana, he might find her with another man, and he wasn't sure he could keep himself from punching the son-of-a-bitch in the face.

As for Alana, he felt pretty much the same level of agitation towards her, though he would never strike a woman. He was convinced she knew more about the muggings than she had told him. And he had plenty of questions that he intended to ask her.

He stopped at the light at Wilshire and Western. Through the windshield, he saw the news box in front of the Good Eats Deli. Three people on the sidewalk were reading open newspapers. A fourth leaned in to buy a copy.

"Is the Griffith Park Monster Human?" the headline screamed.

Jack flicked his cigarette out the window. He had to hand it to Quentin. Despite the shock of Eddie's disappearance, not to mention everything else that had gone wrong yesterday, the publisher had managed to get Lucy's story out on the streets.

He wondered how Sydney Goldblum would react. The producer had probably already placed a call to Lucy to do a script treatment. Allowing himself a sour chuckle at that thought, Jack gunned the big car through the intersection.

Five minutes later, he drove around his boss's circular driveway and parked the Bentley. The grounds of the French chateau-style home were sumptuous. A fountain with a cherub the size of a real boy stood in the courtyard, the water gurgling down over the sides to water dozens of red rose bushes planted around the base.

Jack idly wondered if the neighbors were scandalized by the statue's marble genitals. He opened the door, but before he could get out of the car, two LAPD patrol cars barreled up the driveway as if they had been parked nearby waiting for him.

Jack watched as Jimmy Glass and Stu Martin climbed out of their car. Two detectives he did not recognize got out of the second, along with a fat man in a bad suit and grey fedora.

Jack stepped out gingerly and slammed the car door. "Good morning, Detective Glass. Detective Martin. You boys following me?"

"Should we be?" Martin bellowed. "Heard the Packard went off a cliff yesterday. Where'd you get this piece of shit?"

"This?" Jack leaned against the Bentley and patted it lovingly. "This piece of shit costs more than you make in a year, Detective

Martin. Which I guess makes you worth less than shit?"

"That's enough, Curran." Jimmy Glass motioned toward the fat man and the other two cops. "This is my boss, Lieutenant Donnelly, and Detectives Estrada and Morrell from Hollywood Division. We have questions for you. About a blonde who has been sending flowers to our mugging victims. And a dead guy named Randall Keppler."

Mary Ann had given up his interest in Keppler, but since the flower clerk didn't know Alana's name, Jack knew he still had one up on the cops.

"You got questions?" he said, reaching for his lighter. "Okay. But first, any news on Eddie Wentz?"

"None." Jimmy Glass gestured to the patrol car. "But I'll be called if anyone hears anything. And I'll let you know."

"Thanks." Jack raised his chin and stared at Lieutenant Donnelly. "As for the blonde and the flowers, how can I help you?"

"You're a real mouthy motherfucker, aren't you?" Donnelly walked closer, trailed by the four detectives. The fat man flicked the cigarette out of Jack's mouth. "I'll drag your ass in for questioning, and your faggot boss will have to file a goddamned missing person's report on you, son. It's time you showed us respect."

Jack's hand trembled with anger. He reached for his cigarettes and slowly put another in his mouth. He thought of a sadistic officer he had once seen in action, a lieutenant in Rome who sent four guys to their death one night when he ordered them out to the streets to find him wine.

A few weeks later, in a field in the countryside, Jack had come across the lieutenant's body, its head being devoured by rats. He thought it was justice.

Or what Alana would call *karma*.

"Respect is an earned commodity, I've always found." Jack lit the new cigarette and took a hit. "What questions do you have, Detective Estrada?"

"Why did that punk kid who works with you call the 06 about

that hit-and-run case from a couple of months ago, Ronald Keppler?"

"Eddie Wentz, who is now missing, was following a lead. Mrs. Keppler realized you boys didn't investigate her husband's case very hard. Or very well."

"What the hell are you talking about?" Estrada said. "Morrell and I checked out that story. We did plenty of legwork. There were no leads on the car that got him, which is how most of those cases end up."

"Oh yeah? Did your legwork include checking out the place where Keppler worked? And the co-worker who may have had it in for him?"

"What co-worker?"

"Mrs. Keppler said her husband had several run-ins with a guy named Josef Brandt."

"Keppler worked for a vet. What are you implying; he was killed over dog food?"

"It's not what I'm saying, Detective. It's Mrs. Keppler that's saying it. And what she's also saying is that you guys are fucking incompetent. You would know that if anyone on your squad had actually followed up with the woman."

"We followed up," Morrell shouted.

"Then how come you didn't know Keppler worked for a researcher on human beings, *not* canines. His boss's name is Ernest Preminger." Jack raised his brows. "Josef Brandt lied when you called to check on the dead man."

"I don't give a goddamn about the Keppler stuff, Curran," Donnelly said. "I'm sure the boys from the 06 will follow up with Mrs. Keppler real soon to make sure she's fat and happy. And I don't see what difference it makes if Keppler worked for a vet or a brain surgeon. He's still dead because he didn't practice good road safety. Stop wasting my time and answer the questions Jimmy Glass has for you."

"Ask away." Jack raised his eyebrows and met Jimmy's eyes.

Glass cleared his throat. "Why didn't you report that you found out an unknown woman sent flowers to each of the victims in the mugging case?"

"It's a free country. People can buy flowers for anyone they want, Detective Glass." Jack dropped an inch of ash from his cigarette on the pavement.

"I need to find the woman who sent those bouquets. The girl in the flower shop, Miss Little, said you already tracked her down. Is that true?"

"If it were, she would be a source, detective. As you know, I'm a journalist." Jack dropped the cig on the driveway and ground it out. "And I don't give information on my sources."

"What the fuck is she a source for?" Donnelly demanded.

"Right now, nothing."

"What do you mean nothing? All you're chasing right now is the Thrill Girl story, right?" Glass said.

It was the first time Jack had heard the detective use the nickname, and Glass had nearly choked on it. "Yes, but my next story isn't about her. It's a piece that asks why all the dead perps she offed happened to do time in the main jail a few days before they were killed. Got me to wondering if the killings aren't as random as the cops are saying."

Stu Martin gasped and looked at Glass.

Bingo, Jack thought. The cops do think there's a connection between the Thrill Girl murders and the jail.

"What does some blonde know about that?" Glass's voice had a harsh edge. "Has she told you there's a link? Maybe she is the link. I hear she's a looker. Like the murderer."

Jack smiled. "It ain't a crime to be a good-looking woman, Detective."

"Fuck you, Curran," Donnelly said.

Jimmy Glass stepped between his boss and Jack. "I need to talk to this woman. We'll find her, with or without your help, but if you know where to look, you need to tell me now."

Before Jack could answer, another vehicle came screeching up behind the patrol cars.

Jasper Meeks emerged from his chauffeured car and stepped

into the driveway. "Good morning, Jack. Officers." He nodded briskly at Donnelly. "Unless you have a warrant for Mr. Curran's arrest, you need to leave this property immediately. If you don't, I'll see to it you're all suspended before you leave the premises."

"Who the hell are you?" Estrada demanded.

"Shut up, Estrada." Donnelly gave Jack a look that should have killed him. "Okay, men. Let's get to work." He pointed a fat finger at Jack. "Your ass is mine, war hero. Someday *real* soon."

"You know where to find me." Jack tipped his hat.

"Yes, I do." Donnelly raised his eyebrows. "Counselor. Nice wheels. Make sure your man there keeps to the speed limit."

CHAPTER NINETEEN

Well, *that* went well." Quentin settled into the Bentley and put a fresh Gaulois in his cigarette holder. He waved to Jasper as the attorney's Lincoln veered onto the street ahead of them, heading out of Hancock Park toward downtown.

"Donnelly is a prick." Jack gripped the steering wheel.

"He appears to think equally well of you, Mr. Curran. Lucky for us, Jasper arrived to dissuade him from taking you into custody this morning."

"That's me. *Lucky*." Jack took a left onto Sixth Street, thinking about Alana Maxwell and bad luck. "Did you call Meeks? The cops weren't there for more than three minutes when he showed up."

"Yes. Rosita, my maid, saw you drive in with the sheriff on your tail. She came screaming into my bedroom in a fit of hysteria, and I thought it would be smart to line up some legal muscle. Jasper lives two blocks away. The universe aligned itself on your behalf this morning."

"Thanks for having my back. For the second time. I don't know how I'm going to pay for his fees, but I will."

"You'll have to sell that screenplay you think I don't know you've written."

Jack reached for his cigarettes, shook one out and lit it. "That project is dead. But since you brought it up, yeah, I wrote a screenplay. Since I don't write personal projects in the office, I didn't imagine you would mind."

"I wouldn't mind if you did work on your own projects at your desk. As long as you keep producing sterling copy for *The Eyes*, I'm fine with you following the dreams that brought you to LA."

"Dreams didn't bring me here. You did, with a job offer."

"The urge to report the news may have brought you to LA. But Hollywood's glossy vision of life is what attracts most people to want to write screenplays. I was wondering how long the news business would take to kill your optimistic outlook on life."

"You think I'm optimistic?"

"You're the most positive person I've met who came back alive from the war without brain damage. Hasn't writing about man's inhumanity put a dent in your outlook?"

"I was in the war. I know what men can do, and be driven to do."

"Yet you wrote a screenplay, which I'm sure is hopeful and upbeat. Don't take it as sarcasm when I say I'm impressed."

Jack realized he didn't know how to take anything Quentin said lately. "Don't be. I can't sell it."

"You're giving up? That would surprise me."

"I can take a hint. Hollywood doesn't want positive." Jack gripped the steering wheel harder, needled by his publisher's tone.

"Hollywood is like any other business, Jack. No one hits it out of the park their first time at bat. You know that."

"I don't know what I know anymore." He kept his eyes on the road. "Only thing I'm sure about right now is that we need to find Eddie. And put a lid on the Thrill Girl story. My lid. Until then, Hollywood can pound sand."

The scent of Turkish tobacco filled the car as Deville puffed on his cigarette and let the current topic fade away into the smoke. "I called Eddie's parents. They're worried sick."

"I'll hit the streets as soon as we look at the photos Eddie took. Then I'm going to see this Dr. Preminger." Jack's voice was strained. "I hope to god the kid is okay."

"Eddie is a resourceful young man, and I'm sure everyone finds him adorable. I'm betting he'll end up safe."

"He's green. No telling what he walked into, considering how much Thrill Girl and the monster stories are stirring things up. I'm sure you realize we're making enemies in the cop world and elsewhere." He thought about Lynton Maxwell and his lawyers.

"Thrill Girl may be angry with us, but I doubt it. As for Lucy's monster, well, if it's reading *The Eyes*, I may have to rethink our advertising campaigns."

Despite their shared anxieties, both men laughed.

"Are you going to go see Miss Maxwell again? You never did tell me what you learned from her last night." Quentin tapped his cigarette ash into the tray.

"Not much."

"So where are we with Thrill Girl this morning? What do we need to do first?"

"I have to find Susan Baldwin. She came by my place in the middle of the night." Jack filled him in on his strange encounter with the shop girl. "She implied a shady group is scamming cripples and their families, but I have a bad feeling she's biting off more than she can handle by herself."

"Refresh my memory. What's her brother's condition?"

"He's paralyzed. He's never walked. They had him up at a clinic for paraplegics in Santa Barbara."

Quentin frowned. "Isn't Alana Maxwell's brother also a paraplegic?"

The bell that went off in Jack's head was so loud he nearly lost control of the Bentley. He slammed on the brakes, shocked that he had not considered this commonality. "Yes. He is."

"Hmmm. Two women. Two brothers with the same infirmity. Both involved, in ways large and small, with a crime spree. Interesting coincidence?"

"I don't believe in coincidences," Jack said.

"Neither do I. When a reporter tells me there is a coincidence, it usually turns out they haven't dug deep enough."

"Got you." Jack wondered if Alana Maxwell had been contacted by the men Susan had mentioned. Surely no one would try to shake her down.

"You have a busy day ahead of you," Quentin said. "Keep the car. I'll get a taxi home if you can't make it back tonight, but pick me up in the morning. I enjoy being chauffeured and may have to hire a driver on a permanent basis."

"It's a deal." Jack pulled up to the curb in front of the office. "I'll park around back. Hopefully, the pictures will help me retrace Eddie's steps."

"Al said he would be in early to develop the photos." Quentin stepped out onto the sidewalk.

Before Jack could pull away, the front door of their office opened, and the picture editor waved a sheet of proofs in the air. "You better get in here. I can't believe what Eddie got on film!"

Jack left the car at the curb, and the two men rushed inside.

# # #

Preminger hurried inside the suite of offices he kept in a nondescript Santa Monica medical building. He unlocked the lobby door and glanced in both directions, but there did not appear to be another soul around. There was an x-ray lab and a dental practice upstairs, but it was rare for their clients to wander down his hallway.

He had the first floor to himself. He locked the front entrance behind him and strode across the foyer and down the short hallway leading to the back alley. He motioned to Deidre, who sat behind the wheel of Alana Maxwell's Rolls Royce, to drive forward.

She eased the huge car toward him and jerked to a stop. "I don't like this, Ernie. What if Josef dies? We should take him to the hospital."

"We can't do that now. There's no way to explain how he received his wounds. Calm yourself." Ernest opened the rear door. Josef lay on the seat, his neck and shoulder covered in bloody gauze, a huge lump on his forehead. He was moaning despite the dose of morphine Ernest had given him.

"He'll be fine." Ernest lifted him out of the car and carried him into the clinic. Josef's wounds, which he had quickly stitched up on the floor of the lab, were significant. But in his opinion, they weren't fatal.

Unfortunately.

The doctor returned to the car. He took Josef's Luger from the floor of the back seat and slipped it into his pocket. Then he lifted the locked leather box which held the film and photographic evidence of Thrill Girl's escapades; the log notes of the doses of drugs he had administered to her, and his typed, final proposal for the government. He carried it into the clinic's second examining room and locked the door. For a moment he stared at the closed door of room number three.

His session with his star pupil had not gone as planned this morning. She was agitated, and it had taken more drugs than hypnosis to control her. He finally got her to accept that she was all that stood between her brother's possible recovery and his death, but he had dosed her with more ergotamine to be sure.

He had then fully sedated her.

Thank god, for he had discovered Josef and the missing test subject shortly afterward. Preminger froze for a moment, wondering again who had broken into the laboratory and attacked Josef. The doctor wiped a line of sweat from his brow. It didn't matter. That was Josef's problem. And while events were not occurring exactly as he had planned, he still had things in hand.

He was very good at thinking on his feet.

A minute later, Preminger was back outside next to the Rolls. He leaned in through the open window and kissed Deidre on the cheek. "It's time to drive to the hotel where I booked our room. I'll be by to see you later."

She grasped his jacket and reverted to German. "Come with me, Ernie. We can leave for Vienna before anyone discovers what's happened. Josef can stay and recuperate, and then we'll send for him. You said you dreamed of retiring in Vienna. I can go get our passports at home and get our car, and we can be at the airport in two hours."

He should have known that, despite her calculating nature, Deidre was prone to panic when it was most inconvenient. He put his hand on her neck and caressed it gently, feeling the rapid pulse under his fingers.

"You are not under any circumstance to go back home. The lab is a mess. Until I can clean it up and dispose of several objectionable...eh, things, I don't want anyone to go inside. We're close to the end of my work now, Deidre. As for leaving town, I have no intention of slinking back to Europe without locking down the contract for my protocol first. We won't let this silly accident with Josef undo all our hard work."

His words seemed to sober her. "Alright. But when will you come? At lunch?"

"No. But I'll certainly be done by four."

"Please telephone me if anything changes." Color pinked her flaccid cheeks.

"Nothing is going to change, dearest." He squeezed her hand and waved in the direction of the street. "Remember, don't give the car to the valet at the hotel. There's staining in the rear seat, and I don't want anyone snooping around. Park it yourself." He handed her the key. "Room 12. When you get to the hotel, order lunch and take the sedative I gave you. It will help you rest. Now go."

"Will you be all right? That, that creature won't hurt you like it did Josef, will it? Are you sure it's locked up securely in the lab?"

Deidre did not know Josef's patient was on the loose. Or that someone had helped it escape, which could be even more of a problem.

"Yes. Everything is secure and safe. Now go."

Deidre sniffled, but she put the car in gear and drove away.

Preminger watched as she turned onto Santa Monica Blvd. With any luck, she and her idiot brother would be strong enough to help him with the transportation of his subjects Thursday night. After that, Deirdre would no longer be of any use to him. He wouldn't need her money or Josef's help. He would deal with her in a firm but compassionate manner.

Perhaps a midnight swim in the Pacific?

Deidre was a very poor swimmer.

As for Josef. Well, he would see how his brother-in-law took the news of his sister's death. There was no love lost there.

Preminger went into the offices. His wristwatch read 10:25 a.m. He needed to call Tomas Maxwell and tell him to meet him here for his appointment. It was too risky to allow the boy to go to the house.

Although the doctor chuckled sardonically as he imagined how the heir to the Maxwell fortune would react if he caught a glimpse of Josef's experiment in the flesh.

He wondered if the poor sod would understand he was looking at his own destiny.

# # #

Tomas stifled a yawn and glanced at Robinson. It was one o'clock in the afternoon, but he was already exhausted. "Where did Alana go?"

"I don't know, sir. The message from the desk clerk was written at seven this morning. All it said was that she was taking the Rolls to run errands."

"Seven? *A.M.?* Good god." Tomas settled himself in the passenger seat of the Jaguar. It was time for his doctor's appointment with Preminger. "What time did we see her go into the Coconut Grove?"

"One a.m."

They had caught sight of Alana in front of the nightclub on their way into the parking garage. Tomas had spotted her pale hair and white mink coat and made Robinson toot the horn. She waved but did not come over to the car.

"I assumed she was going in to wait for Gino. His show ends about then. But if they went out, where could she have been going at seven this morning? She wouldn't have had a chance to sleep at all."

Robinson said nothing.

"There's the address on that sign, Robinson. 301 E. Sand Dollar. It's that dumpy concrete building behind those trees."

Robinson smoothly pulled the Jaguar into the lot and parked. He helped Tomas into his wheelchair. Inside they found the suite number Preminger had given them over the phone.

The lights were all on, and Dr. Preminger himself waited in the foyer. There was no sign of his nurse, Deidre, or any other attendants.

"Good afternoon, Tomas." The doctor glanced at Robinson and opened a door in the hallway. "Please put Mr. Maxwell in Room 4 for me, boy. And I think you'll be free for the afternoon, until five at least. Drive down the highway. Maybe get smoked fish? I understand there are several establishments that serve colored in this part of town."

Tomas had not challenged Preminger's condescending attitude toward Robinson in the past. But today the overt racial animus was too much. "I'll tell Robinson what to do, if you don't mind, Doctor."

"Of course." Preminger's eyes glinted behind his glasses.

"I'll wait outside in the car, Mr. Maxwell." Robinson squared his shoulders. "Time's no problem for me."

Tomas leveled his gaze at Preminger. "I'm going to be here four hours today? Why?"

"It's been six months. We need to do full skeletal x-rays, several blood tests, a glucose test, possibly even photographic work to document your progress. I thought Josef explained all this at your last visit?"

"He didn't say it would take half the day." Tomas clutched his right leg to stop a spasm. He turned to Robinson. "Consider this afternoon yours. Pick me up at five. I'll be fine until then, and I'll feel much more relaxed if I know you're not sitting outside."

"Yes, sir. I'll be here at five. Would you like me to find Miss Alana and bring her here?"

Preminger interrupted. "I'm on a tight schedule today. But I'll be glad to make an appointment with her for later in the week."

"If Alana wants to see you, I think you better make time today, Dr. Preminger." Tomas shifted in the wheelchair. "If you find her, Robinson, bring her with you. I'll see you at five."

"Let me push you to your room," Robinson replied. "Number three?"

"Room 4! Not room 3!" Dr. Preminger said sharply.

"Yes, sir."

Tomas reached out and tapped Robinson's hand. "Dr. Preminger can push the chair himself. Please, go get lunch."

"I'll be back at five."

"Good enough."

# # #

Robinson walked slowly out to the Jaguar and slipped behind the seat. He had every intention of staying close by. But first, he had to make a phone call. Mr. Lynton insisted to him that he keep him updated with details of everywhere Mr. Tomas was going this week.

After he called the industrialist, he would drive to the Ambassador to see if Alana was anywhere to be found.

He glanced back at the building. He really didn't feel right about leaving. Robinson couldn't say what, but something was not right at this clinic.

# # #

Jack knew that when Jimmy Glass got Quentin Deville's call to come by and discuss 'urgent new evidence' in one of the cases in the news, he decided against his best judgment he better come. The 07 was taking heat from everyone, his Lieutenant, the Captain, even the Mayor.

He glanced at the folder. He had recognized the buildings from his trip to the Preminger clinic last night, and he was coming out of his skin with anxiety that the cops wouldn't cooperate.

"So what's so urgent?" Jimmy asked Quentin. They were seated in the publisher's office. The lead detective glanced at Stu Martin and sent a look that told his partner to keep his anger in check while they listened.

"Before we go any further, I need your assurance that you'll cooperate with my request for confidentiality," Quentin answered.

"Cooperate? Cops don't cooperate *with people like you*. You cooperate with us." Martin pointed his thumbs forcefully at himself.

Jack leaned forward. "What we've found could break the case wide open in the Griffith Park killing, Detective Martin. Use your head for once. We're doing LAPD's work here. Like we did with the Keppler murder."

"Murder? The 06 said that was a hit and run. Fuck you, Curran."

"Gentleman!" The elegant newspaper man locked eyes with Jimmy. He tapped his finger on the file folder lying in front of him. "Detective Glass, after you've seen the photographs inside, Mr. Curran will take you to the location where they were taken. I'm assuming once you've seen them, the need to make that trip will be obvious. But before I show you these, I need your agreement to allow Jack to stay and do some looking around."

"For what?" Jimmy demanded.

Jack met Quentin's eye. He nodded.

"We think our employee, Eddie Wentz, was at that location. And that he may be in serious trouble. We're hoping when you talk to the residents, they'll tell you something about him."

"Did that dip-shit trespass?" Martin bellowed.

"We don't know," Quentin replied. "It's possible he did by mistake."

Glass's face was impassive as he reached for the folder. The publisher's hand remained firmly on top.

"Do I have your agreement, Detective Glass?"

"Yes."

"Jimmy, we don't need to agree to anything these assholes ask," Martin said. "Those cases belong to the 06. Let him kiss their asses."

"It might have something to do with our case, too, Stu. We need to see what they've got." Glass leaned back in his chair. "But if you two think Eddie Wentz is holed up wherever these photos were taken, why haven't you already checked it out?"

"We'd rather have the police with us from the get-go." Jack stared at the folder. "You've got no probable cause to search the place, with or without the photos, but you've got guns." Jack narrowed his eyes at Martin. "Guns are necessary for a search-and-rescue mission."

"That's the first time I've seen you willing to be law-abiding," Glass said after a moment. "Okay, if we decide we need to check out this location, Curran can lead the way. But if we ask him to leave to avoid hindering official police business, I need his agreement he'll vacate and not hang around to get the scoop for his next story." Glass glanced at Jack. "And if I have to ask you twice, Martin's going to slap you in a patrol car, and you'll do three days minimum in jail."

Jack clenched his jaw. "Agreed."

"I'm glad we have come to terms." Quentin pushed the folder toward Glass. "These were taken yesterday from a hillside behind a residence owned by Dr. Ernest Preminger. The same Dr. Preminger who employed the late Ronald Keppler."

Glass opened the folder. He gasped, and his eyes opened wide. Martin craned his neck to look over Glass's shoulder.

"What the fuck is that?" Martin bellowed.

Glass closed the folder and stared at Jack for several moments. "You know, 95% of the time a case is exactly what it looks like. A woman gets murdered; it's the boyfriend or the husband. Robbery at a bank, it's a disgruntled employee. Kid goes missing, it's a runaway mom. But this…" His voice trailed off.

"What do you think this is?" Jack asked.

"I have no idea. But I need that address." Glass took out his notebook and wrote something down. "And we'll go now." He looked at Stu. "We're going to need backup. Call Estrada. It's his geography anyway." He tapped the folder. "You understand, Mr. Deville, that I'll need to show these to my lieutenant."

"I can't let you take them now, detective. Not until we know exactly what we have on our hands. You can imagine how valuable the pictures of that, whatever it is, could be to one of my competitors." Deville folded his hands together. "And while I trust you implicitly, I can't give away a story like this."

"Okay," Glass said. "But I don't want your newspaper printing this in any way, shape, or form before we put a lid on what we've got here, Mr. Deville. If then. It's going to shake people up bad if that, that thing is real."

"Agreed." Quentin escorted the policeman to the door, Jack following two steps behind. "Good luck, Jack," he added. "Call me immediately if you find out anything about Eddie. And be careful with my car."

"Will do."

# # #

Ten minutes later, Quentin wearily opened the folder and examined the photographs Eddie had taken.

They were of a ghoulish creature, naked and certainly human, though its legs were misshapen and covered with what looked like clumps of fur. Shockingly, it had a growth that looked like a short tail, hairless and skinny, growing out of its tailbone. In death, the appendage lay flaccid against the left buttock.

Its arms were covered by bandages from bicep to wrist. The hands were big knuckled; several fingers were topped by curved and deadly-looking fingernails as long as claws.

Its head was the most distressing feature.

Fuzz and wisps of hair grew on every part of it, and the face was marked with bleeding sores, rough dark scabs, and misshapen, liver-colored lips. The canine teeth in the upper jaw – yellowed and covered in darkening blood, giving the creature a distinctly feline look – protruded prominently from the gaping mouth.

The eyes were open. Human irises, set into bluish-tinged sclera tissue, surrounded by multiple ruptured blood vessels. They told a tale of violence and pain.

Quentin shuddered. He was clearly dead, lying on its side on a canvas tarp. A dark-haired man stood next to it. There was a holstered gun at his waist and a gasoline canister at his feet.

The publisher closed the folder and sank back into his chair and closed his eyes. After the war, he had considered going to work for a New York publisher, or even starting a small press himself. Instead, he chose the news business, convinced that bringing breaking stories into the homes of his fellow citizens was the simplest, most effective way to serve the America he loved.

Unfortunately, nothing about this story was simple. Once he saw the photos, a sense of foreboding had filled him. While he had not hesitated to agree with Jack that the police should be shown the pictures, he also realized it was time to reach out to a few ex-mates in the intelligence community. Sniff around, and see if they had heard any rumors that the monstrous genetic experimentation the Nazis had started was getting a foothold in the Atomic Age.

Quentin felt in his gut that the vigilante story could be connected to the American military in some way. Eddie Wentz had stumbled into, and photographed, something that would be trouble for all of them if he was right.

With a sigh he reached for the telephone, dialing a number he had memorized but never before called. The staff of his paper was playing with fire, and it was only a matter of time before one of them got burned. He thought of Eddie and hoped it had not happened already.

CHAPTER TWENTY

Jack parked behind Detective Glass's dusty sedan at the Preminger estate. The gate across the property's driveway featured a new chain and a padlock.

He had not noticed it when he drove by last night.

It was an unorthodox way to secure a fancy house like this one as if it had been locked down in a hurry. A speaker was mounted on the side of the gate to call up to the house, but it was rusty, and the side was bashed-in.

Jack watched as Glass pressed the top of it. The sound of metallic static exhaled into the peaceful residential air. The cop hit the box a second time, but no one answered.

"No one's home. We're going to have to call the lieutenant and get his okay to go to a judge for a warrant." Glass pushed his fedora off his forehead and looked at his partner. The two men turned toward Jack.

"The lieutenant ain't going to like us being out here already." Martin pointed to the Bentley. "And he sure as hell won't like that we got him with us."

Jack got out of the car. He walked up to the pair of detectives and lit a cigarette while taking a closer look at the house behind them. It was classy. White clapboard and fresh green trim. There was a plaque with the address and the words *Preminger Clinic.*

"Get in the car, Curran," Martin ordered.

Jack narrowed his eyes. "Have you noticed there's a light on upstairs, Detectives? And I think I saw a woman looking down at us." He pointed.

The two cops jerked around to stare at the window. There was clearly a light on inside, but there was no sign of a woman.

Martin shrugged. "No one there now, eagle eye."

"I thought you guys were tough. Can't you force the gate? Shoot off the chain, maybe? It doesn't look that strong."

"We're the fucking police, Curran. You think we'd break and enter because you want a look-see?" Martin replied.

"Hang on," Glass said. "I don't like this. You sure you saw someone, Curran?"

He had not seen anyone. The curtains had moved, maybe by a breeze through the open window. But he was desperate to get onto the property to search for any trace of Eddie.

"Yeah, I'm sure. Looked like a blonde. Why doesn't one of you hop the fence to see if the door is open? I'd do it, but my leg is too screwed up."

"We're going to call the lieutenant before we do anything else." Glass stared at Jack. "You go back to your office. It's going to take a while for them to prepare a warrant and get it over here."

"I'll wait."

"No, you won't."

"I'm not leaving until I find out if the people inside know what happened to Eddie!"

Glass sighed. "I know how you feel. If someone was home, I'd go in. But frankly, I'm not sure Donnelly will go along with getting a judge involved when I tell him I got an anonymous tip to come out here. Judges want evidence, and we've got bupkis."

"You saw the photographs. Isn't that evidence enough?"

"I got no photographs." Glass held out his empty hands. "Your boss wouldn't let me take them, remember? So I'm going to have to drag the lieutenant to your office, let him look at them and then go get a warrant if he says okay. And since that thing in the picture wasn't lying by the address plaque, all we got to go on is your say so that Wentz came after he left you at the VA. Donnelly ain't going to like this whole messy scene, but I've got to get his okay on what's next."

"That isn't what we agreed to." Jack moved closer. "You saw those photos. Whatever that was looked like the sort of thing that could have torn that bum apart up at the Observatory, and you know it. Donnelly trusts you, Jimmy. Tell him the guy who gave you a tip has pictures, that he'll give them to you after you search this place."

"Look," Glass said. "I can tell Donnelly I got it on good faith that a suspicious animal was seen on the grounds. He'll trust me that far. But we still need to come up with something more concrete for a judge if no one answers the door."

"We don't have time to wait for that!" Jack threw down his cigarette and stomped on it before registering the pain it caused. "My reporter could be in there. There's no telling what kind of trouble he's in."

"Which is the only reason I was willing to risk a chewing-out from my lieutenant over this whole thing." Glass gestured toward Quentin's car. "But if I'm going to keep my side of the bargain, you have to do the same. Go back to your newspaper. I'll let you know if we find any sign of Eddie Wentz."

Jack glanced up at the window, the hair on his arm raising in alarm. "The light's off now."

Both cops looked up.

"Son of a bitch. It is off." Martin's voice was spooked. "I could jump the fence."

"You ain't jumping nothing." Glass yanked on Martin's sleeve. "Come on. We got to get to a phone and call Donnelly. I'm not using the car radio to explain this mess to him. With dispatch listening in, we'll have every reporter in the state camped outside of this house. Come on, we need to find a phone booth."

Martin ran around the front of the sedan and hopped in. Jimmy Glass held out his hand to shake Jack's. "Take off, Curran. I give you my word I'll call you when I get in there."

"Thanks for your help, Detective." Jack walked to the Bentley and slid into the front seat. He knew the cops wouldn't leave until he did, so he took off. He drove over the hill, and a couple of minutes later found himself in a development of houses facing the Preminger property. If he wasn't mistaken, this was the view from which Eddie had shot those photographs. He stopped the car and got out.

He popped the trunk. There were binoculars and several tools. He spied bolt cutters next to an opened fifth of scotch.

Jack took out the bolt cutters and binoculars and closed the trunk. He raised the field glasses to his eyes and surveyed the clinic grounds. He gasped when he focused on three vehicles parked by the outbuildings.

There was a truck that looked like a converted ambulance and a dark Cadillac sedan with curtained windows. But his mind stopped worrying over the familiar Cadillac when he realized the vehicle parked next to it was Tomas Maxwell's 1939 Phantom III Rolls Royce.

Was Alana Maxwell in that house?

Jack scanned the entire scene, but there was no sign of Robinson. Without another thought, he climbed down the hill and put the bolt cutters to work on the fence.

# # #

Ten minutes later, Jack limped down the steep embankment onto the corner of the Preminger grounds. There was no sign of anyone. He tried the metal doors on both of the buildings, but they were locked up prison tight.

Keeping to the shadows, he made his way past the empty garage and over to the Rolls. It was unlocked. He saw nothing of interest until he glanced through the rear window. There were dark brownish smears on the creamy leather. His heartbeat raced as he opened the door of the Rolls and leaned down.

There were bloodstains all over the floor.

Fresh bloodstains.

"Shit!" A booklet with a worn leather cover was wedged under the passenger seat. He pulled out his handkerchief and retrieved it.

Der Katzenjunge - Munich, 1929 was stamped on the front in gold leaf, along with a sketch he could not make out. Jack opened the flyleaf. The handwriting was in German, which he could not read, but he did recognize the name.

Josef Brandt. Preminger's assistant. The man Ronald Keppler hated. The man who had lied to the cops.

What was he doing in Alana's car?

Jack looked through the pages. He couldn't read German, but the illustrations were out of the Brothers Grimm fairy tales, animals with teeth and nails who looked like monstrous humans from a child's nightmare.

He slid the pamphlet in his pocket and quietly closed the car door. He frowned at the Cadillac, which he had seen in too many locations for it to be coincidental and took a step toward it but stopped at the sound of a tremendous crash inside the house.

Jack flattened himself against the car and studied the grounds around him. He did not see any movement, but then the sound of a woman's scream rang out, then again, louder. And again. And again.

Alana.

He hurried toward the house as a police siren whined in the distance. It was too early for Glass to be coming back, but the sound reminded him he had to get out before the cops returned. He tried the screen door of what appeared to be the kitchen.

It was open.

I should have brought the damn gun Quentin keeps under the seat, he thought. There were no sounds of distress now, but he was certain of what he had heard. Someone was in the house.

He crept inside.

The kitchen was quiet. Crusts of bread lay on a plate near the toaster, along with a dish of butter. The scent of burned coffee filled the room. Jack's gut ached. He could not remember the last time he had eaten.

Moving slowly, he walked down the hallway toward what seemed the logical area for the living and dining areas. A creak in the ceiling above froze him mid-step.

Two more creaks sounded as if someone was carefully walking across the floor in the room upstairs. Jack kept his breathing quiet and looked around. There was an open door a few feet ahead of him. He inched toward it. It looked like an office, dark and empty. He stepped in as a thud echoed overhead.

Moving as silently as possible, he closed the door and looked around. Heavy curtains were pulled across all the windows, but there was enough light to make out the photograph of a bald man in glasses next to a heavily rouged woman displayed prominently on a bookcase. He walked toward it.

Is that Preminger?

Jack frowned. He had seen this man before. At Lynton Maxwell's house, the night he met Alana. His blood rushed as he thought about what it meant that Eddie had disappeared at a house owned by one of the industrialist's friends.

He looked around, listening intently for sounds of anyone approaching. There were stacks of papers, books, and charts everywhere. And several cameras. He picked up one that looked like it shot 35mm movie film.

A door was ajar next to the bookcase, and he peeked inside. It was a makeshift darkroom. Inside was a trolley that held a tray with about a hundred small glass vials in it. Jack lifted one up to the light. It was marked "LSD-25."

What the hell is that?

He read the labels on several, not recognizing the contents name on any of them. *Ghrelin, Pervitin, Eukodal.* He picked up an uncorked one at the end of one row. Its printed tag read, '*cocaine.*' He knew what that drug was, and realized with certainty that Preminger was a grave danger.

A scream, sharp as a knife in the ribs, shattered the silence, followed by two more screams of a type Jack could neither identify nor describe, a guttural bellow that did not sound completely human. Then came an enormous crash as a mirror or glass table fell, followed by the almost musical sound of a thousand tinkling shards breaking on the wooden floor upstairs.

With the memory of the images in Eddie's photographs pulsing in his mind, Jack pocketed several of the vials and glanced around for something he could use for self-defense. Instead, he spied a telephone on the bookshelf above him.

He lifted the receiver and dialed the operator. He whispered the address and asked for the police and an ambulance as soon as possible. "A woman is screaming, and I heard several gunshots at that address."

That lie was the best bait he could think of to get the cops out here. The police operator demanded his name.

"Ernest Preminger."

Jack hung up and moved back to the door. He put his ear to the wood and heard a scuffle, then another crash. Two sets of steps echoed closer as the heavy, measured tread of someone – *something?* - walked down the wood floor of the hallway.

Toward him.

Jack felt a vibration against the heavy door and clenched his hands into fists. Silence. Then a scraping sound of a something sharp against the wood, followed by a moan that sounded like the cries of a wounded animal.

Jack braced himself against the door, knowing if it opened he would be outmanned, but determined to use the element of surprise to survive until the cops showed up.

The door did not open. More silence, this time broken by the cultured voice of a young man.

"Get the car," the man directed. "We'll leave her here and call the police from the house. You shouldn't have reacted that strongly when she rushed us."

"*Bist du verletzt?*" a second man said. His voice was older. Gruffer. Angrier.

Jack knew a bit of spoken German, but he could not identify the words. The next sound he heard was the slamming of the screen door in the kitchen. His kept his ear against the wood, but the hallway was silent.

Jack opened the door and peered into the cool darkness. There was a figure lying in the hallway a few feet from him.

A woman was sprawled on the floor in the faint light.

"Alana!" Jack rushed to her, but the woman was not Alana Maxwell. It was a much older, heavier woman. The woman in the photographs with Preminger. She was bleeding profusely from a gouge on her face and a nearly severed finger on her right hand.

"Ernie," the woman moaned

Jack leaned down and put his hand on her neck. "It's okay. You're going to be okay. I've called the police." He took out his handkerchief and wrapped it tightly around her hand. She had other wounds on her right palm and her left hand and arm.

The woman opened her eyes. Her lip was ripped open at the left corner, and there was a deep gash cut in her right cheek as if she had fallen on the shattered glass. "I tried to stab it, but it turned over the breakfront to get away." She winced trying to move her arm. "Don't let it come back. That terrible claw...." she breathed through bloodied teeth.

The hairs on the back of Jack's neck crawled. "I won't." He darted a glance at the kitchen. He had not heard anyone come back inside.

"Who are you?" he asked gently.

"Deidre. Preminger." Her eyes brimmed with tears. "Ernie is going to be mad at me. He told me not to come home."

"No, he won't be angry." Jack pulled the Oriental rug on the floor up over her legs and torso. She was shivering from shock. There were more gashes from the broken glass all over her scalp, right ear, and neck, and a deeper wound was spilling blood all along the front of her blue silk dressing gown.

"Is Alana Maxwell here?" Jack asked. "Her car is outside."

"No. She left, in a taxi." She licked her battered lips. "Ernie didn't trust her to drive herself."

"Where is your husband now? Is he upstairs?"

"The beach..." Deidre trembled violently and clutched Jack's arm. "I shouldn't have come back. Ernie said it was locked up. But it must have got out..."

Every ounce of the journalist in Jack yearned to ask Deidre what "it" was, but he knew it might kill her to relive her attack.

"Where's Dr. Preminger? What beach?"

"Who are you?" Deidre focused on Jack's face. "Where's Josef?" Her voice went shrill. "How did you get in my house?"

"I'm a friend of your husband." Jack clenched his jaw and patted her in what he hoped was a comforting manner. He heard sirens, louder and closer with every second. "Deidre, where's Eddie Wentz? The kid reporter who was here yesterday."

The woman touched her hand to her bleeding face. "I'm hurt."

"I know. But help is coming. Do you know where Eddie is now?"

She blinked. "He was snooping around…"

"Where is he?"

She struggled for breath. "Josef has a very bad temper. He shot …" With those words, her eyelids fluttered, and she passed out.

Jack wanted to shake her awake, but got up and leaned against the study door, trying to decide if he should stay or not. It was then he saw the bloody gash in the wood. It was about two inches long and a quarter inch deep. What the hell had made it, he didn't know. But he knew he better be gone before the cops arrived.

Jack limped down the hall, through the kitchen, and out the door. He stopped when he saw the Cadillac was gone.

Which meant whoever he had heard attack Deidre Preminger was the same person who had been following him around for a week.

Jack shuddered, wondering just what had dug that gouge in the door. He scanned the yard and the hills beyond. As for Eddie, where was he? The sun above was intense. He shaded his eyes, but there was no sign of movement anywhere.

The sirens were at the front of the house, and the screeching brakes of police vehicles at the front gate sent Jack hurrying across the parking area toward the Rolls. There was no one in the front or back seats. He hit the lock of the trunk and held his breath as it popped open. Inside the space was empty except for a bloodstained notebook.

Jack grabbed it and stumbled up the brushy hillside.

He could not let himself be found here. Glass would slap him in jail for trying to kill Deidre Preminger, and it would be days before they sorted out the facts and let him go. Somehow he had to locate Preminger.

He would make the son-of-a-bitch tell him where Eddie was.

Then he would find Lynton Maxwell and ask him what the hell Preminger was doing out here in the hills of LA. He would confront him about what he had learned, and ask how he could trust the maniac treating his stepbrother and Alana.

Jack slipped under the fence and scrambled up the hill, his leg screaming in agony. Breathing through his mouth, he got to the top and sighted Quentin's car. He stopped and stared in disbelief.

A young man leaned against the bumper of the Bentley as if he were waiting for Jack.

Despite the impossibly hot day, the man was dressed in a turtleneck sweater, wool slacks, and black leather gloves.

His eyes were covered with sunglasses. "Mr. Curran?"

"Who's asking?" Jack braced himself and glanced around. There were two voices in the house a minute ago. Two assailants. *Was this the man from the Cadillac?*

"Please come with me. I have information you need. The police have surely blocked the main road already, and we can't waste time." With that, the man turned and hurried further up the next hill on a path Jack had not previously noticed. He was as quick and graceful as a panther.

"Wait a minute! Who are you?" Jack struggled to follow, his shoes slipping on the dry grass and rocky soil.

The man lengthened the distance between them.

Jack swore and pushed himself into an agonizing trot. The man was twenty yards ahead, standing at the door of a narrow wooden structure – a guest house, judging from the size. Beyond was a larger home, surrounded by overgrown vegetation that spoke of desertion.

Before Jack could call out any more questions, he heard shouting behind him. He squatted lower and turned around, peering down into the Preminger compound. Cops swarmed from all directions. He realized the Bentley, parked at the fence, would be visible once the police made it across the yard to the tree line.

He had five minutes at the most to get the car. Jack turned. The stranger was standing near the guest house, watching Jack, arms crossed over his broad chest. His body was strong and lean under the dark clothes. As Jack walked toward him, the man seemed familiar, though he couldn't place where he might have seen him.

"How do you know who I am?" Jack shouted.

"Edward Wentz is inside," the man replied. "He should be checked by a doctor. He has a bullet wound. Go and bring your car up the path and get him into it. You can take the construction road on the other side of the big house." He gestured north. "It leads back to the freeway." With that, he turned and disappeared inside the house.

"Shit." Jack took a step to follow him and check if Eddie was really inside, but he had no time. Instead, he turned and ran to get the car.

He threw back a quick glance, reminding himself to bring Quentin's gun with him.

CHAPTER TWENTY-ONE

Eddie's mom, Myrna Wentz, set a plate in front of Jack.

"Eat. Then take this aspirin." She banged a bottle onto the table. "You have a bad limp from carrying my boy to the car."

"The limp has nothing to do with Eddie. But thanks for the aspirin." Jack knocked back four and inhaled the scent of roast beef. He picked up his fork and dug in. He had been at Eddie's parents' house in Studio City for over an hour and had met six members of his family.

Eddie's mother was impressive. Round and pretty, with a direct gaze that took in each nuance of a person, she took charge of everything as soon as Jack knocked at her door and told her he had her son in the Bentley. "His leg is injured where he was grazed by a gunshot, but he wants Uncle Ted to tend to him, not a hospital," Jack had announced.

Myrna had hollered for Ted, and the retired doctor and other family members had arrived like an emergency squad, carrying Eddie inside, asking few questions, but issuing a firm order for Jack to sit and eat.

"Are you going to tell me what you and Edward have gotten your selves into?" Myrna sat across from Jack and folded her hands in her lap.

"We're working on a story I can't really talk about it." He was eating too fast and paused to take a breath. "This is delicious, Mrs. Wentz. But I'm going to have to run. I need to get to the office."

"You should go home and take a nap. Rest your leg. Or take one here, on the sofa." She pointed to the living room behind him. "It's comfortable. I sleep there when I can't sleep if you know what I mean. When Eddie is out."

"I wish I could." Jack shoveled in more roast, every bite tasting better than the last. He could hear Eddie's Uncle Ted arguing with the kid's father and his two aunts in the hallway. He was telling them all to calm down and go for a walk.

"Keep your voices down!" Myrna yelled. She clucked her tongue against her teeth. "Ted says Eddie is going to be fine, but his papa and aunties worry. He's the only boy we have, you know, and they want the family name to continue. Too many of our friends don't even have one child left after the war."

Eddie's family was from Poland. The memories of what Jack saw after the war, the internment camps and piles of corpses, leaped up from his subconscious. He set down his fork, and his stomach churned. "Is Ted sure your son will be okay? I'll run him to the hospital myself…"

"No need for that. There's a superficial wound on his leg, but no broken bones. Teddy's a worry wart. If he thought Edward needed to go to the hospital, he would carry him there himself."

"Eddie insisted that I bring him here." The image of the kid lying on the narrow bed inside that dusty guest house flashed into his head. The man in black had disappeared by the time Jack returned with the Bentley.

Eddie had no idea where the man had gone.

"He's stubborn, my son." Mrs. Wentz leaned closer to Jack. "Do you have family here in California?"

"No. My mom passed when I was in Italy. During the war."

"Father?" Her eyes glimmered in the sunny kitchen.

Jack grit his teeth for a moment, the muscles in his jaw aching. "No father."

"I see. So you have no one? Sisters or brothers?" She touched his arm.

"Just a couple of Aunts in Ohio. And Eddie." His eyes stung as he realized, possibly for the first time, that he was like millions in the post-atomic age, an orphan. Jack tried to smile, but his voice cracked. "Don't tell Eddie I said this, but I care about that kid as much as if we were related."

"Eddie has a kind heart. Everyone loves him. Now, if he could only find a nice girl." Her eyes widened, and she looked up at the heavens. "I worry."

"He will find someone, Mrs. Wentz. Your boy's a catch."

She smiled. "Why don't you go tell him goodbye, if you need to leave. It will clear out that mob of worry warts by his bedroom door, and then he can get some rest."

"Thank you again for the meal. I will go say goodbye, but may I use your telephone first?" He needed to call Quentin.

"Of course. Right there." She pointed to the table in the living room, took the plates and discreetly left him to it.

He called Quentin, who was relieved to hear Eddie was safe. The publisher said he would call Glass and tell them Eddie had been on a bender but had turned up. Jack chuckled at the lunacy of that cover story, and he promised he would head back to the office soon and fill him in on everything that had happened.

He hung up and reached into his pocket for his cigarettes, brushing his hand against the vials he had taken from Preminger's. Quentin was going to be shocked about the attack on Deidre Preminger. He wasn't sure himself what to think about what he had heard and seen. He pulled the vials of drugs out. He needed to find out more about them and realized he had a resource down the hall.

Jack walked to the front door and looked out. Uncle Ted was standing on the front steps, watching the family members he had managed to convince to go for a walk.

"May I talk to you for a moment?" Jack asked.

"Of course." Teddy followed him inside, and they sat on the sofa.

Jack handed him the glass vials. "Can you tell me what any of these things are? I'm assuming they are drugs. I need to know what they are used for."

Teddy, a shorter, rounder version of Eddie, pushed his brown glasses up the bridge of his nose and squinted. Carefully he read each of the labels and lined the vials up on the coffee table in front of him. He turned to Jack. "Where did you get these?"

"I lifted them from a room in the house on the property where Eddie ran into trouble. A doctor's office of some kind."

"I won't ask you any more questions, Mr. Curran, because it's not my business, but these are all very powerful compounds." Teddy raised his bushy eyebrows. "Ergotamine is a chemical derivative of ergot, a grain fungus. A chemist named Albert Hoffman discovered that if you synthesize it, it has amazing powers over the human mind."

"Amazing in what way?"

"It causes hallucinations. But it can also give a person great insight into their own emotions. My understanding from my brother, Ezekiel, who studied in Munich with Hoffman in the 1930's, was that the US government was using it in mind-control experiments." He looked carefully at Jack. "Are the people who ran this lab American?"

"No. German."

Teddy paled and sat back, lacing his fingers together. "I see."

Jack wasn't sure what that meant but figured it couldn't be good. "Where's Ezekiel now? Does he live in Studio City too?" He could be a great source of information, Jack realized.

"Ezekiel died at Auschwitz, Mr. Curran."

"I'm sorry." Jack clasped the old man's shoulder.

"It's a loss to the whole world. He had a great mind. A great future." Teddy looked down at the vials and picked them up one by one. "Pervitin is a stimulant, very addictive and dangerous. Eukodal is a morphine-based painkiller, also addictive. I'm not sure about Ghrelin, but I believe it's a hormone. I think it is used to stimulate the appetite of people who have undergone intestinal surgery but fail to thrive."

"Can you give me your opinion on how a person would react

if they were given all these drugs?"

Ted pursued his lips and considered the question. "Badly. They would have trouble sleeping, would have bouts of hunger that felt insatiable, and they would be hooked very quickly on the intense highs. Pervitin is similar to cocaine."

Jack's gut twisted. "Thanks, Ted. I appreciate the information." He put the vials back into his pocket, his mind going in ten different directions. Locating Alana and finding out if she knew the drugs she was taking were dangerous was top priority.

Quentin and the office would have to wait.

"The German army used many of those drugs on their ground troops, toward the end of the war," Teddy added. "They were desperate to make them stronger, require less sleep and fight more violently."

"Really?" Jack recalled Lynton Maxwell's first conversation with him about this same topic.

"Can I get anyone coffee," Mrs. Wentz appeared, a fresh apron over her dress. "Teddy, are you keeping Mr. Curran? He's a busy man, you know. He needs to get back to his office."

The men stood up.

"None for me, thank you," Jack said. "May I have a quick word with Eddie before I go?"

"Of course, of course," Myrna said.

"Thank you, Ted." Jack reached out and shook the doctor's hand. "You've been amazingly helpful."

"I am always happy to provide information. If you need any more, you know where I am, Mr. Curran." He frowned and looked at Jack's leg. "You are limping very badly. Are you injured?"

"Yes. But it happened in 1945. I'm living with it. Some days better than others."

"I see. Well, if I can ever help you with anything, please don't hesitate. Edward speaks very highly of you."

Jack did not trust himself to speak. He didn't know why, but Eddie's relatives' kindness was turning him into a sentimental blob. He followed Ted down the hallway to the kid's room and shut the door behind him.

"Hey, you should be asleep." Jack limped over to Eddie's bed. "I need to get back to the office after I make a couple of stops. You sure you're okay?"

"Yeah. I can come in tomorrow. If Mr. Deville is using the pictures I took, we're going to have to get a special out."

"Stop it. You got shot at already for this story. Now you need to take it easy and rest a few days." Jack sat down beside him. "There have been developments with Thrill Girl, but I don't have time to bring you up to speed right now. I doubt we'll do a Special this week. We need to nail some things down, but we'll use your pictures eventually." Jack leaned closer. "What happened, exactly? When Brandt went after you."

Eddie shrank back against the pillow and took a shaky breath. "I didn't think he would notice me if I drove up behind the house and stood at the back edge of the property. I figured I could use the telephoto lens. I took the pictures and was packing the camera up, but Brandt got the jump on me. He popped up out of the shrubs and started screaming and waving his gun around. I only wish I could have stopped Brandt from burning that man's body, I mean man or...whatever it was. *Monster*." Eddie shivered.

"Come on, kid. There are no such things as monsters. And if you had stayed and fought it out with Brandt, and not managed to drive away, maybe you would be dead." Jack swallowed. "Brandt's a psycho like Mrs. Keppler's husband said. Only getting nicked was lucky."

"I thought you didn't believe in luck?"

"I don't. Usually." He grinned.

"It was terrifying, hearing those bullets," Eddie said. "And to feel one of them hit me..."

The echo of gunfire inside Jack's head was sudden and disorienting. The first firefight he was in, he saw a German soldier get hit by a grenade. His head disappeared in an explosion of red. Jack swallowed. "You did okay, kid."

Eddie pushed his broken glasses, held together with a piece of adhesive tape, against his eyes. "Do you think that person Brandt incinerated was who killed the bum at Griffith Park?"

"We've got no proof of that, so don't speculate." Jack reached for his cigarettes but changed his mind. He looked Eddie directly in the eyes. "The guy who found you. He never said who the hell he was?"

"He didn't tell me anything. When I woke up inside his house, he only told me he had heard gunshots and found me unconscious and bleeding beside your car. I remember stumbling when I was ducking the bullets, and I think I tripped and fell backward. I must have hit my head and passed out."

"Good thing you're so thick-headed."

"I wonder why Brandt didn't follow me and finish the job?" Eddie's voice weakened with this question. "And I am sorry about your car. I will give you money every week until---."

"Stop it, kid. I'm not taking your money." Jack held up his hand. "I'll get paid by the insurance company, then you and I can go pick out a new car. Finish your story about the guy who helped you. Did you get his name?"

"Nope. I asked, but he didn't answer. He must have carried me up to his house. He had an accent of some kind, maybe German. And he told me he saw a man drive off in your Packard a couple of hours after he found me. From his description it was Brandt. I asked him to call the cops, but he said he wasn't getting any more involved than he already had." Eddie stared at Jack. "I got the feeling he's hiding from someone. But when I asked if he would call you at *The Eyes*, he agreed. Did you talk to him?"

"No. But I've been out of the office looking for you." Jack frowned, recalling the surreal moments of chasing after the guy up the hillside. "Did he wear black driving gloves when he was in the house with you? I didn't see a car anywhere." Hard to hide a Cadillac, Jack thought.

"I didn't either. But yeah, he wore them. Well, he wore one – on his left hand." Eddie's eyes were huge behind his thick lenses. "He didn't say much of anything. Gave me a pill, and tea. All I did was sleep. But he's weird, Mr. Curran."

"Weird how?"

"Every time I woke up at night, he was awake. Prowling around, looking out the windows. He had another man with him. I saw him once, a huge guy. He wore gloves on both hands." Eddie shivered. "Did you notice his eyes? How strange they were?"

"No. What do you mean?"

"They shine in the dark. Like a cat's."

Jack chuckled and got up. "Okay, that's the concussion talking, kiddo. Or your imagination is riled up because of what you saw Brandt doing. Rest. I'll come by in the morning, and you and I will go over our game plan for what happens next."

"I know what I saw, Mr. Curran. The guy never had any lights on in the house, either."

"Well, that is weird. But like you said, he might be hiding from someone. He must be a good guy of some kind, though, to help you out."

There was a soft knock at the door, and Mrs. Wentz peered into the room. "Sorry to bother you, Edward, but this came for you yesterday. I thought it might be something you'd want to share with Mr. Curran before he leaves."

She crossed the bedroom and handed him a note, touched her hand to his forehead, and walked back to the door. "The man who brought it said it was important. He left it here because he couldn't reach you at the office."

"Thanks, Mom," he said as she scurried out.

Eddie opened the folded piece of paper and squinted. "It's from my contact at *The LA Times* research department, Bingham. I asked him for information on the Baldwins last week."

"What's it say?"

"Ten years ago, Susan Baldwin's brother, Paul, aged seven, killed an intruder who broke into the house and attacked the family."

"The crippled kid? How the hell did he kill anyone?"

Eddie looked down at the note. "He shot the intruder with his father's pistol. While the man was making a sexual attack on his sister."

"Jesus." Jack felt woozy for a moment, then furious. "I'll ask her about that."

"Susan Baldwin certainly has had a lot of bad luck," Eddie said. "Do you want me to get a copy of the article?"

"Later. You stay put. I need you in fighting form when you come back to work." Jack said goodbye to Eddie and left the room and said his goodbyes to the kid's extended family.

As he walked to the Bentley, Jack thought again about luck, good and bad. Alana didn't believe in either, she said. He was beginning to, especially the bad kind.

Jack started the big car and something he had been chewing on clicked into place. The mysterious guy in the glove had looked familiar, and he suddenly knew who he resembled.

Alana. He had the same skin and hair color, and strong, beautiful features.

Coincidence?

Jack didn't believe in them. He needed to find the heiress and ask her if she had any idea who the guy was.

And what the hell he wanted.

# # #

Jack called Quentin again from his apartment when he stopped in to shower and change. He was heading to the Ambassador and find Alana, but he knew he had to fill his boss in on everything he could not discuss on the phone in Mrs. Wentz's living room.

Quentin picked up on the first ring. He wasn't happy Jack was not coming into the office, and sprayed several questions at him, particularly about Deidre's attacker. "Did you get a look at who did it?" he asked twice.

"No, but she was hurt pretty badly. And there was a hell of a commotion beforehand. A large piece of furniture got knocked over upstairs. I think there were two attackers. I heard them talking, one guy in German."

"German?" Quentin's voice grew more serious. "No sign of an animal, was there?"

Jack thought of the gouge in the door. "The door had a gouge in it, probably from a weapon, a knife or something. But what the hell are you asking? You think some kind of animal walks around a house like a man?"

"You saw Eddie's photographs."

"Come on, Quentin, you know as well as I do that there is a rational explanation for those. It was a human being, with some pretty serious aberrations, but it isn't a freaking monster."

"Jack, we need to keep an open mind about this story. There are things in life that are completely unexpected. I'm surprised I have to remind you about that."

Jack moved the handset from his ear and stared at it for a moment. Had his boss been infected by Eddie's fevered imagination? "Don't tell me you're buying into Lucy's shit. It is way more likely Josef Brandt is performing depraved experiments on the local bum population. He's a sadist with animals, according to Wanda Keppler, and it's obvious he's a psychopath too."

"I agree with you there." Quentin was quiet for a moment. "Come into the office as soon as you can and get some notes down on paper. We're going to have to be very precise in our eventual reporting of what you heard and saw at Preminger's clinic."

Eventual? His boss was definitely more cautious with these stories than Jack had grown accustomed to. "I've got to find Alana Maxwell first. I want to talk to her, and Tomas, about Preminger."

"What do you think Preminger's connection is to Josef Brandt? Preminger is a well-known doctor. But Brandt? What research have we done on him? Why is he working for Preminger?"

"The only connection Eddie dug up is that they're both Austrian. But if Brandt is connected to the murder at Griffith Park, which our photographs certainly imply, it stands to reason Preminger is involved too. Wanda's husband told her Brandt was killing animals at Preminger's clinic."

"It's disgusting. The cops should have found all that out earlier." Quentin sighed.

Jack gnawed his lip. It was time to share a thought he had been nursing for a couple of days. "I'm sure you read about what went on with Nazi doctors and their 'experiments' during the war.

These two seem like the same kind of bastards."

"That's horrifying. You think they're Nazis?"

"I don't know. A few made it out of Europe from what we know." Jack thought of the booklet he had found belonging to Brandt. "How's your German?"

"Serviceable."

"What does *der Katzenjunge* mean?"

Jack heard his boss suck in his breath.

"Where did you hear that?" Quentin's voice was ice.

"Why, what's it mean?"

"Literally? It means a cat boy."

"What the hell is a *cat boy*?"

"I have no earthly idea," his boss replied.

"Great. We've got two nutcases doing freak experiments, and one of them is carrying around a book about cat people." Jack ran his hand through his hair and wished he had a drink. "Boss, this story is crazy and getting worse. I need to get going. I want to get to the Maxwell's as soon as possible."

"Maybe you should come here now," Quentin said. "I am going to call Detective Glass. I want you to tell him what you witnessed at Preminger's today. He's going to be cranky that you disobeyed his orders not to go in without him, but I don't feel comfortable concealing what happened today."

"What? No! I'm through dicking around with the cops."

"We don't have a choice, Jack. If Deidre Preminger dies, it will mean you were a witness to her murder. We will of course still report on it in *The Eyes*, but first, we need to tell…"

"I'll be in touch." Jack slammed down the phone and was out of his apartment ten seconds later.

CHAPTER TWENTY-TWO

Jack parked the Bentley in the space Maxwell's Rolls usually occupied in the Ambassador Hotel parking lot. Alana's gleaming black Jaguar was parked beside him.

He hoped she was upstairs.

And that Quentin had not called Detective Glass. The police weren't going to be easy to deal with once they knew he had broken into Preminger's.

He made his way through the lobby and pressed the hotel elevator button to go up, wondering what was driving his employer's sudden caution. Instead of giddily celebrating the possibility of a Special Edition with the headline, *"Cat Boy Mauls Doctor's Wife,"* the publisher was pressing him to turn the information over to the cops.

Why?

Something was wrong. Quentin lived for lurid headlines and exclusives, as long as they had the facts to back them up. Thrill Girl and the Griffith Park murderer, who or whatever the fuck it turned out to be, were the two biggest stories to hit *The Eyes*. And they seemed to be converging around the person of Dr. Ernest Preminger.

And an heiress who liked to send flowers.

It was no time for Quentin to get cautious. Jack touched his jacket pocket where Eddie Wentz's notebook was concealed. They owed the kid the truth of whatever the hell was going on.

The elevator opened, and Jack stepped in. He pressed the penthouse button. Instead of trying to hand this story to the cops, his boss should be encouraging him to put all the pieces together for a blockbuster that would give the newspaper fame on a national level.

His hand was steady as he pulled out a cigarette and lit it.

He still wanted nothing more than to file the exclusive on Thrill Girl's identity, but the reality of how dangerous this story might be flared like a hot coal in the middle of his brain.

The elevator opened.

Jack headed to Alana's suite.

# # #

There was no answer at Alana's penthouse. After a moment, Jack tried the knob, but it was locked. He rested his head against the door and glanced at his wristwatch.

Deidre said Preminger had sent Alana home in a cab. Was she asleep inside? It was nearly three.

Thanks to the mayhem at Preminger's house, Jimmy Glass would certainly have traced the owner of the Rolls and cops were surely on their way to the Maxwell mansion in San Marino. Or, if they had talked to Lynton, on their way *here* to interview the industrialist's step-sister.

Jack glanced over his shoulder. He had to talk to Alana and Tomas and find Preminger. But he was running out of time.

Jack reached into his wallet and removed a set of lock picks he had been given by a fellow soldier during a house to house search in a town outside of Rome. The private, Sam La Speiza from Brooklyn, had told Jack it was often safer to make a quiet entry than to break a door down. Jack had carried them with him ever since.

On his third try, Jack found one that fit the lock. He checked the elevator locator, which showed the car had returned to the lobby, and slipped into Alana's suite.

If she were asleep inside, he would try not to scare her to death.

If she isn't here, I don't know what I'll do next.

She had to be there.

# # #

"Twenty, nineteen, eighteen, seventeen." Dr. Preminger stopped counting and waved his hand past his patient's eyes. "How are you feeling, my dear?"

"Fine." The young woman was relaxed and completely under his control.

"We've got many tasks ahead of us. Many important tasks."

"I know."

"Are you ready?"

"I am." His patient moved her head up and down, blonde hair brushing her silky shoulders. "I don't understand why he wants to hurt my brother. I thought he was a better man than that…"

"You can't trust any man, my dear." Preminger patted her arm, letting his hand linger on the curve of her breast. "Reporters are scum. He doesn't care a whit what splashing photos of your brother all over the front page of his paper will do to your family."

The woman dug her nails into the armrests of her chair. "I'll stop him."

"I know you will, dear."

"Don't call me that." Her voice was cold as rock in winter. "I'm Thrill Girl." She met his eyes. "Haven't you seen the newspapers?"

"I have. I have indeed." Preminger beamed. "And you are a star." He shined his penlight at the woman's dilated pupils. "Your journalist friend is going to be sorry when your adventures are over."

"He doesn't matter." The woman pursed her red lips.

"No, I know that. The only man who matters in your life is your brother." He blinked, for a moment overcome by the realization that he was a success. Thrill Girl was living proof of his greatest breakthrough. The LSD-25 and hypnotic suggestions had overcome her natural inclination to shun physical violence. She was as focused as a commando now, and as soon as he gave her instructions, just as lethal.

Preminger checked his watch, running through the tasks ahead. He had to check on Deidre at the beach, pick-up the Rolls and drive it back here.

The Doctor turned to Thrill Girl and snapped his fingers three times slowly. "It's time to rest. You're getting very, very sleepy again. Close your eyes and lay your head back. When you hear my voice again, it will be time to wake up and go home."

"When can I see my brother?"

"After this is all over. I promise."

# # #

Jack closed the door of Alana's suite and glanced around. The drapes were drawn against the afternoon sun, but it was stuffy and too warm. A white satin dressing gown was tossed on the sofa, and there was a pair of feathery slippers on the floor. But there were no other signs that the suite was currently occupied.

Jack relaxed a fraction. He noted a desk strewn with papers, a bar, and a sitting area. Across from him stood a partially closed door, the room beyond it bathed in shadows.

The bedroom?

Jack stopped at the threshold. It was dark, but he made out the bed and a tumble of covers and pillows. A glimmer of blonde hair near the headboard caught his eye. He had already taken a step toward the bed when a movement to his left made him flinch.

He moved into a defensive posture, but it was too late. Preoccupied with thoughts of Alana naked in the sheets, Jack was not quick enough to escape the blow.

He fell to his knees and twisted to throw a punch, but he stopped when his assailant came into view.

The black man towering above him gasped. "Mr. Curran?"

"Robinson!" Jack pushed himself up to a sitting position and exhaled in relief.

"What are you doing breaking in here, Mr. Curran?" He held off landing another blow but kept the impressive club he had used clutched in his left hand.

Jack touched his head where a bump was rising. The valet had whacked him hard enough to draw blood, but not hard enough to kill him. "I'm looking for Miss Maxwell." Jack pointed at the club. "You can put that down. I'm not going anywhere."

"She's not here. But that don't explain why you broke into her place."

"I broke in because I thought she was in here and I need to talk to her."

"Why?"

The men stared at each other. Jack could keep Robinson in the dark, or ask for his help. "I need to warn her and her brother about their doctor. Ernest Preminger. He's involved in some very bad shit."

"Like what?"

"Like that 'monster' that attacked the man in the park."

Robinson's eyes got bigger. "The one that ate the bum?"

Despite his throbbing head, Jack smiled. "You heard of more than one monster in LA? And no, it didn't eat him. Just ripped him up. But the story isn't what you've been led to believe."

"What the hell is that thing?"

"I don't know, but I've got evidence that Preminger's associate, Josef Brandt, is behind it. I was at Preminger's house a while ago and found his wife badly injured. Beat up and slashed." He took a breath. "Tomas Maxwell's Rolls was parked there, but there was no sign of him."

"Mr. Tomas isn't there. He was with me till I dropped him off at his doctor's." Robinson looked very agitated. "Did you see Miss Alana at Preminger's house?"

"No. Preminger's wife said the doctor put her in a cab this morning and sent her back here. But since Alana isn't here, that might not have been reliable information."

Robinson slipped the club into his jacket. "I need to make a phone call."

"Can you help me up first?" Jack reached out his hand.

Robinson lifted him to his feet as if he were a child, frowning at the bump he had caused. "You feeling okay?"

"Yes. Thanks." Jack pulled on the brace on his left knee, willing the pain down to a manageable torrent. He was sure now that the chauffeur was ex-military. "Were you in Italy during the war?"

Robinson blinked. "Yes, sir."

"My god, you were a Buffalo Soldier, weren't you?"

"Yes. I was a member of the 370." Pride lit his eyes.

Jack was impressed. The 92nd infantry's 370 was a regimental combat team. The all-black unit had fought fiercely in the Italian and Mediterranean theatre throughout the war. "Did we meet up over there? You seem familiar to me."

"I never had that pleasure, Mr. Curran. But my men mustered outside Padua in '44 at an estate. Huge old place, like something in a movie. Copper roof and olive groves as far as you could see." A soft smile played on Robinson's face for a moment. "Your patrol stopped in, and one of my friends pointed you out in the distance. Crazy, ain't it? We both travel thousands of miles away from a spot, and meet up again in a new place."

"Yeah, it is. I remember that estate," Jack said. "Faded murals a thousand years old along the stone wall of the gardens. The house was gorgeous, despite having been bombed to hell."

"Our Lieutenant said that day he heard you killed a whole herd of the Nazi bastards yourself. Said you were a hero."

"You know what it was like over there. A man did whatever he had to each day to survive." Jack met his eyes. "Guys in my group, the Buffalo men you served with, all of us soldiers, not heroes."

Robinson looked appraisingly at Jack. "The newspaper said different. I read a couple of months ago about you. Said you killed ten guys yourself."

Nausea burned in the pit of Jack's stomach. He had killed several German soldiers, the day before they walked into Padua. Five men. One no more than seventeen years old.

The last man down was a burly, pale soldier who looked like

Jack's cousin Neil. He'd begged Jack not to kill him, telling him in broken English that his wife and children would not survive without him. Jack had hesitated at the longing in the man's voice, but when the Nazi reached for the knife hidden in his boot, Jack shot him in the chest.

His was the last life Jack had taken that day. The last forever.

"Don't believe everything you read in a newspaper," Jack said.

Robinson grinned. "Say what? Isn't that your profession?"

"Yes. So consider me an expert."

"That I will do."

"And we can stop talking about the war, too." Jack pulled out his cigarettes. "I like the past to stay where it is. Gone."

"It is surely gone, Mr. Curran. But one thing I learned is that some men step up. Some don't. You stepped up. No one can take that from you. Not even you."

Their eyes met again.

"You got that right, brother." Jack clapped him on the shoulder. "Look, do you have any idea where Alana could be? Do you think she's at Lynton's?" He offered his pack of Lucky Strikes to Robinson.

The big man declined the smokes. "I doubt she's at Mr. Maxwell's. She doesn't go there unless she has to." He paused, weighing his allegiances. "She's got a place out at the beach. She might be there."

"I know the place. You got a phone number for it?"

"No, sir. But if you want to check it out, I'll follow you. Then I need to get to the clinic where I left Mr. Tomas. It's about ten minutes from the beach house. I'm not supposed to pick him up until five, but after what you said, I think I should go earlier."

"Good plan." Jack coughed. His head and leg hummed in mutual agony. He brushed the lint off his clothes and glanced around the room. The faint scent of sandalwood burned in his senses.

"I need to hit the head and wash my hands, okay?"

"Sure. I need to make a phone call." Robinson walked toward the desk, and Jack ducked into the bathroom. He washed his face and hands and dried them on a plush towel that smelled like Alana. He looked in the mirror and shook his head. He would have more bruises tomorrow.

Hoping Alana stocked aspirin, he opened the medicine chest. His mouth fell open. It held face cream and nail polish, and about thirty bottles of prescription medication. He picked up one, Grehlin, it said. Prescribed by Dr. E. Preminger.

"You ready, Mr. Curran?" Robinson called out, knocking his big knuckles against the door.

Jack pocketed the bottle, closed the medicine cabinet and opened the door. "Yes." He followed the chauffeur to the door. When they passed the bedroom, Jack stopped. "What is that?" He pointed to the bed. "A wig?"

"Yes, sir."

"Alana wears a wig?"

"She does. For fancy parties. Said once to her brother that she's too busy to get her own hair done all the time."

"Huh. I didn't know that."

"If you don't mind me saying, you don't know a lot of things about Miss Maxwell."

A piece of information from a police report Jack had bribed his way into seeing had mentioned a few strands of hair from a blonde wig were found at the scene of Joan Becklund's mugging.

He sighed. "You're right, there, Robinson. Well, let's go." He limped toward the front door.

"You sure you okay to drive?"

"I can drive in my sleep," Jack replied, privately wondering if he would get through the next few hours without passing out.

# # #

Alana wasn't at the house behind the Blue Note.

The two men took the fifteen-minute drive from the beach to the clinic where the chauffeur had dropped Tomas off three hours ago. They raced into the building and were surprised to find Preminger's office doors locked tight.

"Where could they be?" Jack asked.

"I don't know. I left Mr. Tomas inside."

There would be no good reason for Preminger to have left with Tomas Maxwell in tow. Jack tried his picks while Robinson paced the hallway, but there was a deadbolt on the inside that he couldn't budge.

"Goddamn it. I can't find any way into this lock."

"Want me to break down the door?" From the chauffer's tone, it was obvious he did not doubt that he could manage that task.

"No. I'm sure it's alarmed. We don't want to be busted for burglary today." Jack sighed. "When were you supposed to come pick up Tomas?"

"Five."

Jack looked at his watch. They had an hour. "Maybe Preminger took him elsewhere for x-rays, blood work, or something."

"Maybe. But I don't like it."

"Me either." Jack kicked the door and immediately regretted it.

"We should wait, Mr. Curran. Park down the street and watch for Preminger. He has a dark green Ford coupe. I'll recognize it. We'll be right behind him when he drives up."

"I can't wait around here until then." He considered calling the cops and asking them to come blow the place open. But he wasn't sure if Tomas was inside.

Or Alana. And he didn't want them to get to her before he did.

"I'm going to head into town to check out a couple of other sources." Jack pursed his lips. "You want to follow me?"

"I'll stay here in case Mr. Maxwell comes back early."

"You're right. One of us should be here." Jack lit a cigarette. "Tell you what. There's a coffee shop down the street and a telephone booth right beside it. We'll get the number off the phone, and I'll be able to check in with you."

"They don't serve Negroes at that place, Mr. Curran."

"What?" Jack grimaced. "You ever get furious about shit like that, Robinson?"

"Yes."

The two men regarded each other. Jack blew out a lungful in frustration. "I'll get food and bring it out to the car, and then we'll get the phone number of the booth. That work?"

"Okay. Except if I see Mr. Tomas, I might not be there to answer your call, Mr. Curran."

"I know, but if Tomas shows up with Preminger, can you call my office and leave a message?"

"I will."

"And call the police if anything about Preminger seems out of the ordinary, Robinson."

"Yes, sir." The valet stood taller.

"Okay, what do you want to eat?" Jack and Robinson walked quickly to the cars.

"Cheeseburger would do me fine."

"Works?"

"Yes, sir."

"Smart man." Jack followed the Jaguar two blocks to the restaurant.

It felt good to talk to Robinson about something other than what they both feared. But now that he was left alone with his thoughts, Jack admitted to himself that Preminger might not come back.

And that he might have both Tomas and Alana with him.

# # #

Ernest was careful to keep his car under the speed limit. He glanced at the clock in the dash. It was eight minutes to five o'clock. Tomas Maxwell's colored man would be waiting impatiently for him.

The doctor stopped at the red light, a block from the clinic. The events of the last hour and a half had not gone as planned. He had driven to the hotel to check on Deirdre, only to find out she had never checked into her room. Thinking the silly bitch had disobeyed his warning to go home and get a useless garment, he went there to find her.

But the entire Los Feliz neighborhood was cordoned off by the police and fire department. God only knew what the police had found. Ernest hoped it was Deidre's mangled body. That would simplify things.

Although if they had found Josef's remaining test subject, everything would be in jeopardy.

After tomorrow's business was done, he would go to the police and inform them of his personal suspicions regarding Josef's part in Randall Keppler's tragic accident. And his insane experiments, if he needed to explain certain events. The police would surely appreciate his helpfulness.

Preminger nodded. It was a sound plan, particularly with the protection he had already put in place for himself. Right now, he just needed to forget about whatever was going on back at the house.

The light changed to green and Ernest drove into the parking lot. He spotted the Maxwell's Jaguar and felt for the pistol at his waist. It was loaded. He didn't want to kill the chauffeur – that was Thrill Girl's job. But he would do what needed to be done.

The doctor drove closer to the Jaguar, and the chauffeur stepped out when he saw him.

All he had to do now was let himself in through the rear entrance, then unlock the door in the lobby for the chauffeur and jab him with a hypodermic full of tranquilizers.

Ernest's bald head creased with tension. It seemed as if every action was now capable of causing a reaction that could rip his world apart.

But he would do what he had to. He had done far more difficult things during the war, with far less at stake.

He must concentrate on positive thoughts.

His success. More money than he had ever had. And Thrill Girl's glorious end.

CHAPTER TWENTY-THREE

It was nearly five when Jack parked the Bentley in front of Susan Baldwin's house. The day was overcast and sticky with humidity. Jack took his fedora off and threw it on the seat, wondering if another freak summer storm was about to hit.

The locals always bragged that it never rained in California. Except when it did.

He stepped out of the car and looked around. No one was on the street, but he heard a couple of dogs nearby, their growling and yipping reminding him of Snowball. It seemed like months ago that the pooch had met his untimely end.

As he walked to the door, Quentin's point about Susan and Alana both having brothers who were paralyzed from birth defects echoed inside his skull. It led to questions. Nothing but questions.

Could Preminger be the doctor Susan was talking about?

Where the hell was Paul Baldwin?

Jack rang the bell and waited. When no one answered, he banged on the door. "Damn it! Is anyone in there?"

His mind churned as it searched for connections between the Thrill Girl murders, the monster attack, and Preminger and his partner's experiments. The memory of Alana's gorgeous face and the look of fervor in her eyes when she had told him she would do *anything* to help her brother had to be one of the keys.

But how did Susan's brother fit into this mess?

Jack walked around the house and peered in through the window. The food and table settings were cleared away now, which meant someone had returned to the house since his last visit.

He tried to get in.

It was locked.

"Son of a bitch," he muttered. He walked to the middle of the yard, but the sound of a door opening made him turn around.

Ellen Baldwin called out in an unsteady whisper, "Hey, Mr. Reporter. Come in here quick, before anyone sees you!"

She disappeared, and Jack followed as fast as he could. Ellen was nowhere in sight when he walked into the kitchen. "Mrs. Baldwin?"

"I'm in here," she slurred from a room away.

Jack took the short hallway toward the living room. He heard a hissing noise, like air escaping a balloon. Then he heard sobbing.

"Ellen?" Jack stopped in front of the door with the *Danger* sign tacked to it and gently pushed it open. Ellen Baldwin was hunched on the floor beside a single bed. There were three huge green canisters of oxygen in the room.

A person lay beneath a mound of blankets, his face covered by an oxygen tent. There was a machine on a table next to him, its dials and knobs giving the place the look of a hospital room.

Jack stepped closer and looked down at Ellen. "What's happened? Did Paul come home?"

"Look what they did, Mr. Curran. Look what those sick monsters did to my poor, poor boy." She cried harder, clutching at the sheet.

The figure in the bed turned its head toward him, and the tension in Jack's gut churned with mingled revulsion and pity.

Paul Baldwin's face was not that of a teenage boy. The visage staring at him was something out of a B horror movie, with a broad flat nose, bulbous round eyes the color of dull gold, and a chapped mouth that was slack and drooling. A misshapen tooth protruded from his top gum. His skin was covered in open sores and clumps of thick hair. Spiky black whiskers protruded from his eyebrows and nostrils, and stiff whiskers covered his ears, giving them a pointed, devilish shape.

Paul stared into Jack's eyes and tried to speak, but only managed a low moan, followed by choking as he gulped in oxygen. Though his hands and arms were covered with patches of brown hair thick as fur, his fingers were slender and perfect, but his fingernails, particularly the middle and index ones, had aberrantly long curved fingernails that looked thick as rope.

The ruined boy reached out and motioned for Jack to lean closer, but before he could speak, he fell into a wheezing fit.

Ellen gripped the side of the bed. Jack grasped her shoulder. "Ellen. Come out to the other room and talk to me. Leave your son to rest."

She resisted for a long moment before bolting out of the room. On unsteady legs, Jack followed and shut the door behind them.

Ellen collapsed on the sofa in the living room, her body shaking with the force of her sobs. "My boy. My son. Oh my god. Oh my god."

Jack grabbed a glass and a bottle of whiskey from the dining room table and poured the remaining two inches into the glass and brought it to her. "Here, sit up and drink this."

Ellen downed it in a gulp. "It's horrible. What they did to my boy."

"What's happened? How did he come to look this way?"

"It's the drugs. They've been experimenting on him. They did this terrible thing to my boy."

"So he didn't always look," Jack couldn't find the words. "Like that?"

"No. God, no. He was a beautiful baby. His hair was like silk. And he was a happy boy." She trembled and clutched her knees. "I had trouble delivering him, and he was really sick. The doctors said it was spinal issues, genetic defects, they said. They told us he would never walk, but he was bright and content. But then everything got worse after his father was killed by the Japs. We had to move to this crappy place. And then that man..." She closed her eyes against her memories.

Jack remembered the crime report Eddie's contact had uncovered. "A man broke-in to your house a few years ago."

"He raped me, the pervert. Had Susan tied up and was ready to do the same to her, and she was only a twelve-year-old girl. The bastard didn't think a boy in a wheelchair was going to be a problem to him. But Paul shot him. Right in the face. Killed him." She burrowed against the sofa back, gulping for air. "I need more whiskey."

"That was the last of it. Look, I know this is heartbreaking, but you have to tell me who did this to Paul. Who has been giving him drugs? Did a man named Preminger do this, cause him to look like this, be like he is now?"

"I never heard that name, Preminger. It was Dr. Brandt. He is the one who gave Paul shots, he's the one who did that to Paul." Ellen stared down at her hands which clutched the empty glass. "He gave us money for all the medicine, and so we could buy the oxygen tanks for when Paul visited. He said Paul would get better if we took him to a clinic in Santa Barbara. He was part of a special program. Him and two other poor boys." Ellen looked at Jack. "We drove him up there, Susie and me. Last winter. We delivered him to those people!"

Jack squeezed her shoulder. "Where is Susan? I need to talk to her, Ellen. Do you know where she is?"

"No. She left in the middle of the night." She wiped her eyes with her sleeve. "Told me she was going to go see you, then Brandt. She said she would find Paul. But Paul, he came home right after she left. With that man…" She looked at Jack, her eyes empty of hope.

"What man?"

Ellen shivered. "I don't know. He left a number so Susan could telephone him. He said he wanted to help us."

"Do you still have the note?"

She rummaged in the pockets of the housecoat she wore over her faded Capri pants, then pulled out a folded sheet of paper and handed it to him. "I never saw him before. Must be rich, though. He has a chauffeur. And a big Cadillac. With curtains. Looks like a movie star."

Jack ran his hand through his hair. "Susan said she had papers that would prove this Dr. Brandt was a fraud. Do you know where those are?"

"She took them with her. She said she might need them." Ellen's voice fell to a whisper. "Did you see her? I was hoping you would go with her."

"I did see her. But she went off before I could help."

Fresh tears fell ran down her face as she processed the regret, and fear, in Jack's voice. "Do you have a cigarette?"

Jack handed her his pack. He had to get to the office, see if Susan had called. See if Robinson had called.

To find out if anyone had heard from Alana.

He was missing all three of the people he needed to talk to right now. Jack stared down at the note. The numbers were printed block style. It was the Brentwood exchange. Quentin's neighborhood.

Jack reached into his coat for his lighter.

Ellen stuck a cigarette in her mouth and squinted. "Can you light this? My hands are shaking."

Jack took the cigarette from her and set it and his lighter down on the table. "Calm down first. I don't want you to drop it on yourself."

He took out a business card and wrote down his home phone number again and handed it to Ellen. "When Susan comes home, tell her to call me. If it's late, have her try the house. Or tell her to come find me again. I want to help, Ellen. Make sure she calls me."

"Okay."

"Can I help you with Paul? Drive you to a hospital where he can get treatment?"

"Treatment?" Ellen tried to laugh, but it came out as a sob. "What kind of treatment can help him now? No, we can't call anyone. Paul doesn't want that. He only wants to keep breathing until Susie gets home."

"Okay." Gently he patted her shoulder. "I'm going to take off. Make sure you have Susan call me as soon as you hear from her, okay?"

Ellen leaned her head back against the sofa and closed her eyes. She was snoring in seconds.

Jack let himself out and hurried to the Bentley.

# # #

A half-hour later Jack walked into *The Eyes* of LA office. Quentin was in his office along with the photo editor and a man Jack had never seen before.

"Jack!" Quentin motioned to him. "I need to talk to you in ten minutes."

"Will do." He picked up a thick stack of messages and started thumbing through them.

Trixie left one saying he would try back later.

Mary Ann Little phoned three times.

As had Jimmy Glass. The last message was all in caps, "CALL IMMEDIATELY!"

There was a caller who had left a message late yesterday saying he had information about Eddie, and he would call back later that afternoon. That was probably the young man who had helped the kid.

But there was nothing from Robinson.

Or Alana.

Jack reached for his cigarettes, but he didn't have them. His pulse pounded in his ears, and he wondered if this was how it felt before you had a stroke. Jack tossed down the messages and walked to his boss's door. "Goddamn it, Quentin, I need to talk to you. *Now!*"

The room quieted.

"Certainly." The publisher dismissed the men. "Sit down, Jack."

Jack slammed Quentin's door and sat. "Has anyone called you

about Alana? Lynton Maxwell? Or his lawyer?"

"No. What's happened to her?"

"I can't find her. She was at Preminger's this morning, and no one has seen her since."

"That's troubling. Bring me up to speed on everything you've found out since I last talked to you."

He blew out a breath and in short factual statements recounted how he had broken into Alana's penthouse, how he and Robinson searched for her at Preminger's Santa Monica office, and what Paul Baldwin looked like now. "He resembles the dead creature in the photos Eddie took. An unidentified guy in a chauffeured Cadillac brought Paul there from Preminger's lab and left word for Susan to call him."

"Preminger's lab?" Quentin blinked. "Who is this man in the caddy?"

"I don't know." Jack shook his head. "But I also think he's been following me for the last week, whatever the hell that means."

"You've been followed? I wish you would have mentioned that earlier." Quentin slumped against the back of his chair. "I'm truly sorry to hear about the Baldwin boy. But what we need to worry about right now, Jack is the damage you've done to yourself. All hell is breaking loose. Jimmy Glass knows you went back to Preminger's without them."

"He knows? Did you tell him?"

"What?"

Jack stared. "After I called and told you about Deidre Preminger's attack, did you call the cops and tell them what happened?"

Quentin sat up straight. "No. And frankly, I'm disappointed you are asking me such a thing."

"I'm disappointed too."

"About what?"

"That you have gone cold on Thrill Girl. Why?" Jack suddenly felt like he had in the war, in the middle of a firefight. It was often unclear who was shooting at him, or if the man three feet away was friend or foe.

"Gone cold? When did I do that?" Quentin frowned.

"You've suggested twice we should turn this whole thing over to the cops." He leaned forward. "Why are you willing to give up on the biggest story *The Eyes* has ever had?"

"You sound like you've given this a lot of thought." Quentin's chair creaked. "Why don't you tell me why you think I'm doing such a thing?"

"I think you're scared. For the paper. Maybe even for me."

"I am scared for you," Quentin replied. "You're acting recklessly. You're not considering the consequences of taking on these powerful people."

A light went on inside Jack's head. "Is that it? Or are you scared I'm about to discover things about Thrill Girl that you already know?"

"What would I know that you don't? You're not making sense, Jack. And you're crossing the line from inquisitive to accusing." Deville did not add the words, *be careful,* but they were clearly coming next.

"Let me show you something." Jack pulled out the vial he had taken from Preminger's house. "This is called LSD-25. I found it in Ernest Preminger's study, along with a bunch of other drugs. I'm sure he's using these things on Alana Maxwell. According to her chauffeur, Robinson, she's also been a patient of his, for months. And she told me herself she was taking experimental drugs, to help her brother's doctor develop a vaccine."

"What does LSD-25 do to a person?"

"I asked Eddie's Uncle Ted, a doctor, that. He was familiar with LSD-25. It's a powerful hallucinogenic. Dangerous. Creates craving and inappropriate behavior. Even blackouts and memory loss."

"Holy mother." Quentin was clearly shaken. "But why use those drugs on her?"

"To create Thrill Girl." The words exploded from Jack, and he gripped the edge of the desk. "I think he used Alana as a guinea pig to prove his research works."

"Oh my god," Quentin gasped.

"I can't prove it, but I also think he set-up the muggings and took photographs of Thrill Girl in action." He told Quentin about the cameras and darkroom. "Several witnesses mentioned seeing bright lights at the crime scenes, which may have been flashbulbs. And I have one guy who says he saw men at the scene of the crime, watching, while it went down."

"If this is true, then it would be a conspiracy. Do the police know about this witness?"

"I'm pretty sure they do." Jack pointed at the vial on the desk. "But I doubt they know about the drugs. I heard rumors at the end of the war that our people were testing stuff like this. And Eddie's uncle said the Nazis gave it to their own men to keep them fighting to the death when it was clear they were going to lose. If I'm right about Preminger, his research continued that philosophy."

"But why?"

"Money! I'll bet Preminger has a protocol written up on how to dose and manipulate troops. And turn them into killers. Just like he did with Thrill Girl."

Deville gasped. "Do you realize how preposterous this sounds? Even if it's true, why would he dare use Alana Maxwell for a test subject?"

"Think about it. If Preminger used Alana to demonstrate that his drug protocol could turn a random woman into a fearless killer, it's because he knew Lynton wouldn't reveal his plot to the police and risk Alana's being nailed for the murders. The photographs are insurance Preminger needs to control Maxwell."

"The scandal would ruin his company," Quentin said. "Just the suggestion that he had been involved with that kind of experimentation."

"Exactly. And since Maxwell sent Alana and Tomas to Preminger for treatment, well, it might even look like he was backing *Herr Doktor's* work. "

Quentin sucked on his cigarette holder, despite the fact it held no cigarette. "Do you have proof Maxwell knows about what

Preminger has done?"

"No." Jack shook his head. "That's the thing I don't know for sure."

"What about Josef Brandt?" Quentin's voice was hollow.

"Brandt was obviously working on something equally sinister. He's been performing despicable experiments on disabled men like Paul Baldwin in the hopes of enhancing human strength with drugs. His toxic concoctions resulted in appearances that look like Lucy's so-called monster." Jack took a breath. "I would bet Brandt was responsible for the murder of Ronald Keppler because he feared Keppler knew what he was doing."

"Which would explain why Brandt lied to the police about what Keppler did at the clinic."

"Yes. And I think the pictures Eddie took were of the person that killed the bum at Griffith Park."

Both men sat back in silence.

"Brandt is Dr. Frankenstein," Quentin said. "Do you know where he is now?"

Jack ground out his cigarette, but before he could answer, violent knocking on the outer door made both men turn in their seats.

Lucy burst into the office, her voice a shade lower than a scream. "The cops are here, Mr. Deville. A horde of them. They've got a warrant for Jack's arrest."

Jack looked past Lucy. Outside, the newsroom was crawling with blue uniforms. "What do they want me for this time?"

Jimmy Glass walked up behind Lucy, his head shiny under the artificial lights. "For the murder of Deidre Preminger." The cop pulled out his gun and motioned for Jack to move away from his boss. "She died two hours ago at LA County hospital. But before she did, she named you as her attacker."

Stu Martin pushed Lucy out of the way and stepped into the office. "And Susan Baldwin's house blew up an hour ago with her mother, brother, and probably her inside. According to dispatch, the neighbor lady told the patrols, '*That newspaper guy, Curran, ran out of there a few minutes ago.*'"

Martin slapped handcuffs on Jack. "You're a one-man crime spree, asshole."

"They're dead?" Jack gasped as his arms were pulled behind his back. He locked eyes with Quentin as the facts roiled through him.

I left my cigarettes. And my lighter. In his mind he pictured a drunken Ellen tottering into Paul's oxygen-rich bedroom and struggling to light up.

Deville got up and put his hand on Jack's shoulder. "Go with the police. I'll call Jasper." He glared at Martin. "Step out of my office. I need a moment."

"Fuck you," Stu said.

Glass motioned for Stu to come with him. "One minute." The cops turned and walked out behind Lucy.

Quentin dropped his voice to a whisper as he leaned close to Jack's ear. "Don't tell anyone about Alana Maxwell, the drugs, or Preminger and Brandt. Or about the Griffith park murder. I need to make some calls."

It was not what Jack had expected Quentin to say. "Okay." He was reeling from the fact his carelessness had caused the death of Susan Baldwin and her family. "Okay."

"We're ready to go," Glass said from the doorway.

Jack did not resist as the detectives walked him out to the street.

CHAPTER TWENTY-THREE

L ate that night, the phone on Quentin's desk rang. He leaned
back wearily and picked up the call.

"We need to talk about something. Off the record,"
Meeks said.

*No hello. No pleasantries. No update about Jack Curran's
arrest.* A shiver of dread skittered between Quentin's shoulder
blades. "Please go ahead."

The attorney cleared his throat. "Your newspaper's coverage
of the vigilante murders and the trouble up at Griffith Park has
tangentially touched on issues sensitive to classified government
projects. A friend of mine reached out to ask me to tell you to back
off those stories – at least for now."

Quentin shifted the phone receiver from his left hand to his
right. "Who is your friend, Jasper?"

"I'm not at liberty to say. But let me assure you this friend is
very connected and serious about this. No one wants to make
trouble for you."

Quentin frowned. "That sounds like a threat."

"Don't be absurd. I'm simply passing on a request; one I
would urge you to consider."

Quentin quickly reviewed what he knew about Jasper Meeks.

It was rumored he had run the Europe desk for Army intelligence during the war, but the attorney had never confirmed that in Quentin's hearing. "I thought you were out of the army now. Do I have my facts wrong?"

"No one gets completely out, do they?" he replied. "Did you? I heard a few whispers you moved to a new organization when OSS was dissolved."

Quentin's eyes widened. His time working for the Office of Strategic Services during the war had taught him two things. The first was that intelligence personnel were the biggest gossips, and most jealous competitors, of any government employees.

The second was that, after the intelligence failure at Pearl Harbor, a hardcore cult inside the Department of Defense would go to any lengths to keep America from being caught by surprise.

"That's flattering talk, but not true. When I left OSS in 1945, I became a civilian. A journalist. And I control what's printed in my paper. While I would like to help you and your friend, those current stories have been picked up nationally. Surely your friend realizes the public's interest in them won't disappear if *The Eyes* stops reporting on them."

"But they are your stories. If you pull back, the rest of the world will lose interest. And when the police solve them, which they will soon, I'm sure they will be grateful you cooperated. I imagine you would get exclusives, at least on Thrill Girl."

"To be written by Jack Curran?"

Jasper's voice dropped. "If he cooperates. Since he works for you, I assume you can control him."

"You've met him. His heart and soul are in this story. He's not going to be spoon-fed lies and swallow them. No matter who serves them up."

"Then it's time you explained that another story will come along that he can make his name with. If he doesn't drop his line of inquiry on Thrill Girl, it could be dangerous."

"Line of inquiry? Is that what we're calling good reporting these days?" Quentin struggled to keep his voice pleasant. "I thought one of the things we've been fighting for the last decade is a free press. Your friend can't actually be threatening to silence a goddamn war hero for writing a factual news story."

"Don't lecture me. You know as well as anyone that sometimes the truth has to be concealed to protect the greater good."

"Greater good, my ass," Quentin replied. "All your friend wants is to protect himself and his masters. I'm guessing here, but maybe the real reason he reached out is that Lynton Maxwell is about to be pulled onto the front page. Is Jack Curran being told to take a dive because he's sniffed-out a secret military-industrial project run amok? Perhaps a project based on the research of Dr. Ernest Preminger?"

Several moments passed. "I have no comment on either of those people."

"You mean you won't answer me."

"I mean don't print Lynton Maxwell or Ernest Preminger's name in connection with anything Jack Curran is working on," Jasper replied.

"Or?"

"Do I have to answer that?"

Quentin cleared his throat. "I'm a realist. If you want Maxwell's name kept out of the vigilante story, even though his step-sister may be involved, fine. But as for Preminger, well, when I tell you I can control Jack, I can, but you're going to have to tell me what the hell is going on."

"That's not possible, Quentin. What you need to do is figure out a way to neutralize Jack Curran, or someone else will."

A sharp pain stabbed Quentin in the side. He reached for his antacids, reeling from Jasper's not subtle threat. Could his star reporter actually be in danger of being killed? "Now see here. Jack's in jail. You're his attorney, as luck would have it. Remind your friend that Curran is no problem while he's locked up. Your friend can pressure the police to close out this case while he's locked up."

"That won't work. The police are dropping all charges against Curran related to the Baldwins in the morning. They found oxygen canisters improperly used at the home. And the coroner said the fatal wounds on Deidre Preminger's body came from an accident involving broken glass and a china cabinet that fell on her. They can't hold him much longer."

"Can't you do anything? Put pressure on the LAPD to keep him another day or two?"

"Lawyers pressure cops to get people *out* of jail," Jasper said drily. "I'd have to call in several favors."

Quentin bit his lip. "I seem to remember calling in a favor once, to help a young lawyer working for you escape a drunk driving manslaughter charge."

The young lawyer was Jasper's son-in-law. Quentin had used a connection in the district attorney's office two years ago to help get the charge dismissed, and save his career.

"I'll do what I can, Quentin."

"That's all I ask. Call me when Jack's going to be released, and I will personally pick him up." And lock him in my attic until this story goes away, he thought.

"I will. But remember what I said. No more stories on Thrill Girl until the police solve these things."

Quentin slammed down the phone. A second later a knock sounded at his office door. Eddie stuck his head in.

"May I have a word with you, Mr. Deville?"

"What the devil are you doing here? Shouldn't you be home resting?" Quentin looked the young reporter over thoroughly. "Jack said your arm was injured."

Eddie glanced down at his sling. "Yeah. But my Uncle Teddy is a doctor, and he said it was fine that I come into work for a couple of hours." He closed the door behind him. "I need to tell you some things about Thrill Girl. George Herbert, that ex-cop Mr. Curran uses as a stringer at the jail, called me at home with some information."

"Which is?"

Eddie fumbled with his good hand to turn the page of his notebook. "George spoke to a dozen different guys being processed back into the jail system over the last couple of days. He asked them if they were approached by anyone for work the last time they got out of the joint. Three guys said yes. One man, Esteban Morales, said his good friends had told him about work they got from a German guy, an older, bald guy named Holtberg," Eddie read from his notes.

Quentin leaned against his desk. His head hurt, and he was finding Eddie more tedious than usual, but this information was ominous. "Can you get to the point, Mr. Wentz?" He reached for his cigarette holder and popped in a *Gaulois*.

"Ah, the point is that this man's friends turned up dead."

Deville touched a match to his cigarette, which flared and burned his finger at Eddie's words. "Damn it," he dropped the match to the floor and stepped on it. "What did you say? Who ended up dead?"

"His two friends who were approached for work by this Holtberg when they got released from jail. Their names were Lu Chen and Roberto Salazar."

"Why is this important?" Quentin demanded.

"They are the two men who tried to mug Susan Baldwin. Thrill Girl killed them."

Quentin frowned. "How is this so-called job offer from a mysterious German connected to Thrill Girl?"

"I'm not sure, but I know Mr. Curran thinks there is one. Another one of the jailed men told George he knew another guy who was approached by Holtberg."

"What happened to him?"

"He was killed by Thrill Girl when he mugged Joan Becklund." Eddie's eyes were bright with excitement. "I think Mr. Curran was right, don't you, sir? About Thrill Girl working with someone. A man named Holtberg is setting these crimes up."

Who is Holtberg, Quentin wondered? *And how is he connected to Preminger?* "Give me your notes." The publisher got up and held out his hand. "Take a taxi home, Eddie. I want you to stay there until Jack is out of jail. Say nothing to anyone. Understand?"

"But this could be a great sidebar. I could call Detective Glass to get his take on it. Then when Mr. Curran calls in…"

Quentin ripped the notebook from Eddie's unwilling hand. Brushing past him, he opened his office door and yelled for Lucy to call for a cab. After the kid was gone, he was left with a foreboding thought.

He now had two reporters who knew more than was good for them.

Or for him.

# # #

"Hey, war hero. Get your shoes. You're out of here."

Jack opened his eyes. It took a minute for the jailer's words to register. "What time is it?"

"Almost midnight. And time for you to move your ass, Curran. Come on, you got a broad waiting for you."

Alana Maxwell's image bloomed in his mind, but the guard wouldn't sound this disinterested if the blonde heiress were waiting outside.

Fifteen minutes later, Jack signed for his wallet, shoelaces, and cufflinks, and headed to the lobby.

A diminutive woman who reminded him of his grandmother was waiting by the elevator. She surprised him by sticking out her hand. "Vida Purchase. Mr. Curran?"

"Yes, ma'am?" He was mystified, and from her expression, it was obvious she knew it. "Nice to meet you, Miss Purchase. Did you, eh, get me out of here?" Jack pressed the button, not wanting to stick around the jail for another minute.

"Yes. I did."

"Oh, do you work for Jasper Meeks?" As a housekeeper, he wondered and then immediately hoped she didn't get his implication.

The door opened with a ding and Vida preceded him in. She sighed. "No. No, I'm not exactly the type of lawyer who would be hired for a firm like his."

"Oh. You're an attorney?"

"Surprised?" She cocked her head. "There are many female attorneys, Mr. Curran. We have been admitted to the bar in California since 1878. Clara S. Foltz was first. She was also the first female district attorney in LA, and I believe she was related to Daniel Boone."

"No, I mean, I know there are women attorneys. I'm surprised to see you instead of Jasper Meeks." He smiled. "Thank you for your help."

"I'm glad I could help, Mr. Curran." Her voice changed to all-business. "As I'm sure you surmised, the four charges they were holding you on – arson, burglary, attempted murder, and first-degree murder—were dropped at nine a.m. today. Which means you should have been released by nine-thirty a.m."

"Nine-thirty?"

"Yes. But it appears Mr. Meeks was going to wait until Thursday to arrange your release. My client and I felt you might not want to waste another night in a jail cell."

"What? Why would Meeks wait until tomorrow?"

"You'll have to ask him, Mr. Curran."

Jack pulled his hat down on his forehead. "So Quentin Deville, didn't hire you to represent me?"

"No. My client did."

"I'm sorry, but who's your client?"

"She's waiting downstairs." Miss Purchase tugged at her short white gloves.

"Who is?"

"My client."

He felt like Eddie likely did whenever he made him do the *who, what, where, and when* drill on a news story. The elevator stopped with a chime as the door opened. It was late, and there was only one person standing in the lobby.

Wanda Keppler.

"Hello, Mr. Curran."

"Mrs. Keppler." Jack stared at the woman. She was dressed in a black cocktail dress and diamonds and looked very seductive, not at all like the housewife he had met earlier.

He stepped out of the elevator on the heels of the lawyer. "I don't understand. You hired Miss Purchase to get me out of jail?"

"I did." She smiled at his baffled expression. "Come, let me give you a lift, and I'll explain." She turned to the attorney. "Thank you again, Vida."

"Anytime, Wanda." Vida Purchase touched Jack's arm lightly. "Nice to meet you. I've enjoyed your reporting on Thrill Girl. Hope you get to the bottom of all that nastiness."

"Ah, yeah, thanks. Me too."

Vida Purchase walked toward the exit while Jack followed Wanda Keppler out of the main door. She came to a stop beside a black Ford coupe. He held the door for her, then walked around the car and got in.

A hundred questions crowded into his brain.

"Your limp is worse," Wanda observed as she put the car into gear.

"I know." He glanced out of the window, but there was no telephone booth in sight. "While I appreciate everything you've done, I need to stop and call my publisher."

"Going to ask him why he didn't bother to get you out of jail?" Wanda's voice was cool, but she clutched the steering wheel as if she were being pursued.

"I have a lot of things to ask him." Jack felt his jacket pocket but remembered he had no cigarettes or lighter.

They were blown up with Ellen Baldwin.

"Would you mind making a stop so I can pick-up cigarettes?" Jack said.

"There's a pack in my purse. Help yourself."

"You said you didn't smoke." He pulled out the pack and pushed the car lighter in.

"I started again." She made a right turn and kept her eyes on the road.

Jack lit up and offered it to her. She refused. He inhaled deeply, savoring the nicotine rush. "What's going on here, Mrs. Keppler?"

"Call me Wanda."

"How did you know I was in jail, Wanda?"

"You made the papers this morning."

"Yeah? Well, the papers certainly didn't announce my attorney would be tardy in springing me out of the slam. How did you find out? And why did you hire Miss Purchase to help me get released?"

"Vida is an old friend. She called as soon as she heard the charges against you had been dropped." Wanda glanced at Jack. "She knew you were extremely helpful the other day. About Randall. She offered to help get you out."

"That doesn't answer my question. You went to a lot of trouble on my behalf. But at the risk of sounding ungrateful, I don't get why."

"It wasn't much trouble." Wanda sighed deeply. "But now you're wondering about my motives. I guess I'm not quite what you thought I was the other day. Right?"

Jack made a noncommittal sound. Wanda Keppler was a quick study. He glanced out the window. She was heading toward Westwood, a tony residential area surrounding UCLA, not toward his apartment in Hollywood. "Where are we going?"

"A friend of mine wants to see you. We'll be there in about ten minutes. When we get there, I'll let you in on a few things that should illuminate the situation."

"I'm not any good at sitting quietly, Wanda. No matter what the payoff."

"Do it for me."

"I like you. But I can't agree with being kidnapped." He took another drag, the tip of the Lucky Strike glowing bright red.

Wanda slammed on the brakes, and the Ford swerved and hit the curb before coming to an abrupt stop. "I'm not kidnapping you. You're free to go. But my friend has information that may be of interest to you. It concerns the Thrill Girl story."

Jack made a grab for the dashboard to keep from bashing his head. He scowled and flicked the cigarette out the window. "What kind of information?"

"You're the reporter; it's up to you to judge what kind of information it is."

"I'm not interested in playing games, Wanda."

"I'm not playing games, Jack. I don't do that."

"No? What exactly is it that you do? When I met you, I understood you to be a mourning housewife who likes art and cats."

"When you met me, that's what I was." She clutched the steering wheel tighter.

Bells began ringing inside Jack's skull as several random facts fused. "What did you do during the war, Wanda? You said you met Randall in 1946. I think he might have been in intelligence. And maybe you were, too. I'd be a chump not to wonder if his death might be a whole hell of a lot bigger than an unsolved hit-and-run."

Wanda took a deep breath. "It might be. During the war, I worked for American intelligence. In Berlin. Randall worked for the British. But we were both retired when we married." She looked down at her hands. "Yesterday I made inquiries of an old friend, and it appears Randall may have gone back to work a couple of years ago. But he never told me about it."

"Who was he working for? Other than Preminger."

"The Americans. Army intelligence. I think he took the job with Dr. Preminger and Josef Brandt to keep an eye on one, or both of them, for the government."

"Son of a bitch." Jack squinted. Like a broken movie reel, his brain unspooled a list of things he had to do. Call Quentin. And Eddie. And see if Robinson had found Tomas or Alana.

He needed more pain pills. *And a big fucking drink.*

Jack exhaled. "Is there alcohol where we're going?"

"I'm sure we can get some."

He motioned toward the road. "Okay."

Ten minutes later, Wanda turned into a driveway. A hundred yards up the sloping hill stood a limestone mansion, glowing white in the moonlight. A discreet sign beside the front steps had a single word painted on it.

Nepenthe.

"Nepenthe?" Jack rolled down the window.

Wanda turned off the ignition. "Do you know that word?"

"Yeah. From Homer's Odyssey. It's the potion they gave to Helen of Troy to lessen her sorrow. Opium, I think."

"You're a scholar as well as a gentleman." Wanda motioned to the house. "Nepenthe was actually wormwood, which has the power to make the person ingesting it forget. Sometimes that's the only way to conquer sorrow."

"You sound like you speak from experience."

Wanda gave him a sad smile. "Let's go in. I'll get my own door, Jack. Save your leg."

He followed her to the front of the house. Wanda knocked and a moment later a young man dressed in saffron Buddhist robes, his face and head shaved bald, opened the door.

"*Swaghaat*, missus. Gentleman." The dark-skinned servant held out his hand. "Swami Dhani is waiting in the solarium. I'll bring tea."

"Thank you." Wanda walked down the hallway and turned sharply to the left. She was obviously familiar with the solarium.

Jack followed. He recalled Eddie's comment about the shrine in Wanda's kitchen. Then he thought of Alana Maxwell's discussion of karma.

Jack wondered, *hoped* if Wanda's friend might be Alana. But when he entered the solarium, it wasn't the mysterious blonde who was waiting for them. The man was a stranger, sitting at a table, flanked by two empty chairs. He was dressed all in white.

"Good evening, Wanda. Mr. Curran." He bowed his head. "Welcome to Nepenthe. I'm Dhani."

"Good evening, Swami." Wanda bowed her head and sat beside him, motioning for Jack to take the chair opposite her. "Now we both need to take a deep breath and start talking, Swami. Mr. Curran has been patient, but I'm sure he's about to explode with questions."

"I am sure that is true. Mr. Curran, may we serve you tea or perhaps another beverage?"

"Do you have whiskey?" He sat heavily in the rattan chair.

"Yes. I don't imbibe, but I keep it for guests." The servant who had greeted them at the door returned bearing a tray with tea, cakes, and fruit. Dhani sent him for whiskey while Wanda poured tea for herself and the holy man.

"Let me get directly to my reason for asking Wanda to bring you here tonight, Mr. Curran. She and I are very worried about a dear friend of Nepenthe. Alana Maxwell. We were hoping you might know where we can find her."

Jack was glad he was sitting when he heard this shocking question. He turned and met Wanda's eyes. "When I saw you a few days ago, you said you didn't know Alana Maxwell. Why did you lie to me?"

"I didn't lie." Wanda sat up straighter. "I've met the woman you called Alana Maxwell by another name a couple of times, here at the temple. I didn't know her real name until Swami told me tonight. *Kamini Namita* is the name we call her here."

"Here?"

"Kamini and I both study with Swami Dhani."

"I see." But he did not see anything. Anxiety ate at all his nerve endings – he was running out of time to gain control over the events surrounding this story. He glanced at his watch. It was nearly midnight. "Is there a telephone I can use?"

"No. I'm sorry, that is one modern convenience that I find counterproductive to any kind of peaceful contemplation, Mr. Curran," Dhani replied.

"Okay. Well, to answer your question, I don't know where Alana Maxwell is. I've been in jail since last night, and she was missing when I was arrested."

"I'm sorry to hear that." Dhani leaned forward. "Can I tell you a few things that may help you find her?"

"I can give you five minutes. But then I've got to get back to my office." Jack sat back as the servant arrived with a bottle of Jack Daniels.

The attendant broke the seal, poured a double, and handed it to Jack.

Jack drank half of it and met the expectant stare of his host. "If you two are worried about Alana Maxwell, I suggest you call her brother, Lynton Maxwell, in San Marino."

"Actually, Mr. Maxwell was here earlier looking for her." The swami blinked. "It appears he's misplaced both of his siblings. His young brother Tomas is also missing. He thought I might know where he was."

Jack stilled. He had assumed Robinson had collected Tomas and all was well. "Shit." He slammed the glass down and stood up. "I need to get out of here."

The swami and Wanda exchanged looks.

"Please," Swami pleaded. "If you can give us just a few more minutes. Kamini has confided many things to me, Mr. Curran. One of which is that she has allowed herself to be used as a subject in medical experimentation. For the past few months, the physician treating her brother has been injecting her with drugs. Based on her reaction to them, he was going to refine those drugs for use in treating Mr. Tomas Maxwell's paralysis. But in my opinion, something else is going on."

Jack sat down, gingerly stretching out his left leg. The Swami was confirming his theory. He had to listen to what else he knew. "Did you tell Lynton Maxwell that?"

"No. I did not. Kamini told me they have a difficult relationship. I can't really go into why, but…"

"I know about her brother's twin dying. And that she blames herself for not telling Tomas."

The Swami drew back. "I see. You and Alana must be very close for her to have shared that."

Jack glanced at Wanda, who was watching him closely. He turned back to the holy man. "What do you think is going on with Alana and Preminger?"

"I think this doctor has taken control of Kamini's mind. She hasn't been the same since she started this treatment. She misses class. She told me she sleeps but doesn't dream." The swami's voice rose, his native cadence sharpening as his words came out faster. "And she told me two nights ago she was going to confront this man, a doctor called Preminger, because she thinks he has been secretly hypnotizing her!"

Jack twitched. "And she didn't confront him? Why not?"

"The drugs she's taking are causing blackouts. They've given her insatiable appetites for food and liquor and cigarettes. They've induced her to behave indiscriminately in her sexual behavior. She didn't seem to know what to do."

Heat flooded his face, but Jack said nothing.

"Kamini knows Preminger may be using her. But she doesn't want to stop her brother's therapy." He leaned closer. "A couple of mornings she found bloodstains on her clothes and wounds on her hands. The last time I spoke with her, she said that these things happened on the same days as the Thrill Girl attacks."

Jack longed to sling back the rest of his drink, but he needed to stay sober. "Did she say she was involved in those crimes? Did she admit that to you?"

No one said anything for several moments. When the Swami spoke again, his tone was grave. "No. But it is clear she is worried that it is true. We must find her, Mr. Curran."

Jack turned to Wanda. "Who else have you reached out to about this? Did you call Randall's old friends?"

Wanda glanced quickly at Swami. "I made a call, but I didn't give anyone information about Alana. I kept it to how Preminger may be involved in Randall's death."

Be thankful for small favors, he thought. "Why do you think I can find her?"

"It's more that I hope you can, Jack. You made the connection between her and me without much to go on." Wanda folded her hands in her lap. "I'll help in any way I can."

He stood again. "I need to get to my office."

Wanda and Dhani both got to their feet.

"I'll take you," Wanda said.

"Will you look for Kimani, Mr. Curran? Will you tell her to please contact me and let me know if she is okay?" Swami pressed his palms together. "I fear for her."

"I'll do what I can." He followed Wanda down the hallway. He was furious she hadn't told him everything she knew about what was going on. But Dhani's worry for Alana was the real thing. He was terrified.

Jack's felt no elation over being right about Preminger. His only thought was to find Alana before her mad puppet master pulled her strings one last time.

CHAPTER TWENTY-FIVE

The man who used the alias Dr. Holtberg, Ernest Preminger, stepped quickly into the alleyway. He took a flashlight from his pants pocket and flipped it on and off in three bursts, pointing it at the motionless woman standing in the doorway across from him.

After the third flash, she stepped forward. Impeccably dressed in black and white silk, her smart hat was set at an angle on her blonde hair.

Her eyes were bright, her mouth a cruel line of red.

"Thrill Girl, two men are on the street out there. Your brother's in the car, and they're trying to rob him. You must stop them," Preminger whispered.

He handed her a gun. With a gasp, she bared her teeth and strode past him.

He followed and watched in fascination as the petty criminals he had cajoled over a cheap lunch to show up for a non-existent job on a dark street in LA confronted Thrill Girl. Like the others, these two jailbirds believed they were being hired for movie work. They did not know they were to be part of the performance, and that it would be their last role.

Thrill Girl lunged at them, kicking and beating the startled men into submission in less than two minutes.

Preminger cringed when she fired the gun for a kill shot, but only because of the noise. He nodded happily when she reached for the knife Josef had planted at her feet and dispatched her victims. He watched dispassionately as the second man writhed silently on the ground. With a wave of his hand, he gave the signal for Josef to take the photos.

"Remember, just from the back. Don't show her face," he shouted.

Josef, still in pain and woozy from the knife attack in his lab, dropped the camera before he could frame the shot. The camera bulb exploded dramatically.

Thrill Girl froze, silhouetted by the pale quarter moon, the knife raised above her head.

Preminger charged up the sidewalk. "Josef, you idiot! You better have more bulbs. I need at least one photograph of her tonight."

"The extras are in the car," Josef replied. He was bent over in pain. "Give me just a moment."

"Never mind. Pick up the guns! We have to leave, now!" When things started to go wrong, they often stayed wrong, Ernest knew from experience. Any more delay after the gunshots could lead to discovery. The staging area was on a remote side street, but anyone could come by at any time.

Ernest grabbed the camera and Josef limped toward the car, balancing the discarded guns, the light pole, and the camera.

On the sidewalk, Thrill Girl blinked and stumbled forward, then fell to her knees and started moaning. Alarm spread down Preminger's spine. The flashbulb must have brought her out of her trance.

Do I have time to get the knife?

If I shoot her, I'll need to take her body. But I don't have time for any of these complications.

"Hurry!" Preminger shouted at Josef. "Put all of this gear in the trunk. Then get in the car and wait for me."

"I can't carry everything!" Josef dropped the canvas bag of

guns, and one of them fell out and discharged with a horrifying explosion, slamming a bullet into the wall inches from Preminger's head.

"I'll kill you myself if you don't do it first." Preminger shook his fist at Josef. "Get a hold of yourself. You're about to ruin everything. Go to the car!" The doctor picked up the smoking gun. This was a turn of events he would not let go to waste. He would finish off his incompetent brother-in-law tonight and let Thrill Girl take the rap for that too.

He turned toward the woman to see if she had passed out or returned to her trance, but to his horror, she was gone. Beyond the empty pavement where her victims lay lifeless in a sea of blood, she was nowhere to be seen.

Preminger sprinted toward the Jaguar parked under the streetlight. His pulse pounded in his ears. He pulled open the passenger door and looked inside, praying the blonde was there. But there were only the two male passengers, both now as good as dead from the drugs he had administered. He considered shooting them to be sure the job was done, but it was too dangerous to draw any more attention to his location.

Ernest scanned the street the last time for any sign of her, filling his lungs to call her by her given name, but stopped. She had been trained to return to the office immediately after performing her required tasks, so he would deal with her there. But he had to hurry, as there were sirens now, coming from two directions. Several of them.

And they were getting louder by the second.

He picked up the bloody knife Thrill Girl had dropped and broke into a full run. When he arrived at the car, the trunk was still open, and Josef was sprawled in the front seat. Preminger deposited the gun and camera and slammed the trunk. He ran around to the driver's side and got in.

Josef turned to him, his face a mask of pain. Blood was thick on the shoulder of his coat, oozing from the wounds he had suffered in the lab. "Your girl has flown the coop. I guess I am not the only failure in this family." He bent his head to cough, his spit bloody.

Ernest took the knife from his right coat pocket and drove it into Josef's chest. His brother-in-law grabbed for the blade, his eyes full of betrayal as he fell dead onto the floorboards.

A wave of euphoria broke over Ernest. At last, after years of having to deal with Deidre and Josef, he was free of both of them on the same night. He looked down. The left arm of his suit coat was smeared with blood but other than that, he was undamaged.

He dropped the knife on top of Josef's body and drove the car down the street, heading for the clinic at the beach. He would dispose of his clothes and dump Josef and the weapons with Alana Maxwell's fingerprints and hair samples in one of the examining rooms. There was more than enough evidence to convict her of murder, should he need to press that threat.

Ernest glanced at the slice of moon above. These were the first moments of a new life, richer in every way. He had won, and he was leaving everyone who had failed behind.

# # #

Wanda dropped Jack off in front of *The Eyes* at 2 a.m.

"Thanks." Jack yanked the door handle.

"You're welcome. Call me if you think I can help."

Jack slammed the door and walked away. Wanda gunned the Ford and rolled away as he let himself into the office.

A single light was burning on his desk. Jack pushed his hat up and stopped short. Eddie was hunched over on his desk, the kid's face buried in his arm, his glasses askew on the floor. Jack looked around the shadowy room. Quentin's office was closed and dark.

A spike of fear ripped in his gut, and he crossed the room to get to the kid. He grasped Eddie's shoulder.

The kid jerked away. "Mr. Curran! Gosh, I'm glad you're here."

"What the hell are you doing here this late?" Jack leaned down and retrieved Eddie's glasses. "You should be home resting, for Christ's sake."

"I'm feeling fine. Honest. Oh, thanks." Eddie pushed his glasses onto his face. "I came in after dinner to meet with Detectives Glass and Martin. They wanted to ask me questions about what happened out at Dr. Preminger's house. About the photographs."

Jack stared at the closed door. "Was Deville here when you talked to the cops?"

"No. It was only me. I don't know where Mr. Deville is."

"What did you tell Glass?"

Eddie summarized that he told the cops of his initial interactions with Deidre and Josef Brandt and how Brandt had shot at him. "And I also told them about the man in the guest house on the property next to Preminger's – the one who helped me. They said they were going out there to find him."

"Good luck with that." Jack thought of the muscular blond man in the dark clothes. He would not be found unless he wanted to be. He glanced over his shoulder, making sure the room behind him was empty. "What did Glass say? Does he agree that Brandt and his test subject might be connected to Lucy's Griffith Park Monster?"

Eddie nodded vigorously. "Detective Martin let that slip. You got that right, Mr. Curran."

Jack punched his arm gently. "Good job paying attention. Now if you'll let me sit at my desk, I need to track our boss down and make a couple of other calls."

"Of course." Eddie picked-up the stack of messages to the center of the blotter. "Oh, Wanda Keppler called earlier. And the woman from the flower shop. And another woman who wouldn't leave her name called around noon. She said she would call again tonight." Eddie looked at the clock. "I guess she changed her mind."

"Did you recognize the voice?"

"No. She sounded kind of…" Eddie tugged at his coat lapel, "Kind of out of it."

"Yeah?" Jack wondered if it was Alana. He was worried about her, Robinson and Tomas Maxwell. He reached for the phone to try the Ambassador, but it rang with an incoming call before he touched it.

"*Eyes of LA*. Curran."

"Hey. This is Georgie. You need to hit the streets now, buddy boy. Something big is going down with your girl. Corner of Vine Street and Hope."

Jack met Eddie's eyes, which were huge. He had heard Georgie's words. "What's happening?"

"Word is she killed a couple of guys. Two dead on the street, maybe more in a car parked at the site. The cops have her cornered in a building on Highland."

"I owe you, Georgie." Jack slammed down the receiver. "Call me a cab, Eddie. Offer them a ten spot extra if they can get here in five minutes."

"I have my mother's car," he said.

"Outside?"

"Yes." Eddie pulled out a set of keys attached to a rabbit's foot key ring. "Let's go. I'll drive."

Jack snatched the keys from his hand. "You take a cab home. I'll bring your mom's car back to your house when I'm done."

"But…"

"No buts. If Thrill Girl is captured and identified tonight, we're going to be living in this place for the next few days churning out copy. You need to go home and rest."

Jack tossed a fiver on the desk to pay for Eddie's cab and stalked out of the door. He heard the telephone ring, but he did not stop to see who was calling.

#

Jack parked Eddie's mother's Oldsmobile in the alley, one street over from the roadblocks. Sirens blared like air raid warnings during the Blitz. A helicopter flew above the scene on Highland Avenue, the *whap whap whap* sound of its blades pulling him back in time. Out of reflex, he cringed, remembering the sound of the huge birds of war the Germans used in Italy.

Pushing the war memory away, he tugged his hat low over his brow and walked as fast as he could toward the scene. The police were sure to have dozens of patrols out for crowd control, but he had to try and find out if Alana was there.

He rounded the corner and came face to face with Detective

Jimmy Glass.

"I thought you were in jail!" Glass said in surprise.

"What the hell are you doing here, Curran?" Stu Martin shouted, stepping around from the shadows and pushing Jack against the building.

"Let him go!" Glass shifted his attention to Jack. "You're leaving. *Now*. Lt. Donnelly is on his way, and if he sees you here, you'll be stuck in jail again so fast your head will spin."

"For what?"

"For being a fucking nuisance." Martin didn't release his hold on Jack.

"I've got a right to be here," Jack said.

"You got no right to butt into police business."

"Goddamn it, Stu, I said to let the son of a bitch go!" Glass slapped his hand against his partner's shoulder. "Now!"

Stu released Jack. Both men stared at Glass in shock. Neither had heard the detective swear before.

Glass glared at Jack. "No press is allowed on the scene. And we're making no statements. Get going."

"You know there's no way to keep a lid on this story, Detective," Jack argued. "I got a tip fifteen minutes ago that Thrill Girl has shown her pretty face, and all of LA is going to want to know every detail. I'm going to tell them about her, with or without your help."

"Then tell them from over there." Glass pointed to the other end of the street where several cops were setting up a blockade. "Stu, escort him off this block."

"How many did she get this time, Jimmy?" Jack struggled as Stu pulled him by the arm. He looked around the cop and saw two men on the sidewalk. He also caught the profile of a car parked a half-a-block up the street. All four of its doors were open.

It was a Jaguar.

"Did you get her?" Jack screamed.

"We will," Stu said. "Soon as we go into that building, that'll be one dead dame."

Dread crept through Jack. The black Jag looked like the car Robinson used to chauffeur Tomas Maxwell when the Rolls was unavailable.

"Don't kill her," Jack said to Glass, his voice a plea. "I can help. I can talk to her. Maybe get her to come outside."

Glass grabbed his shirt and pulled him closer. "Are you fucking telling me you know her. You know who Thrill Girl is?"

"I might. I'll tell you who it is if you promise me you won't shoot her."

"We're not killing anyone," Glass snarled. "And I'm not promising you squat. Get out of here. Now!"

Jack stood his ground. "Who's in the Jag? Is it Tomas Maxwell? Is he okay?"

Several shots from a big caliber handgun exploded into the night. Glass slammed Jack to the ground. The detective crouched beside him and pulled a.45 out of his jacket. "If you take a step to follow me, I'll shoot your good leg." The bald cop cocked the gun and then ran toward the gunfire.

Martin charged after Glass. Jack stumbled to his feet and took a step to follow but was grabbed from behind by two patrolmen.

"Get the hell out of here, buddy," the bigger cop hollered.

Jack trotted toward the alleyway, dragging his left leg every other step, heading for Eddie's car. He pulled his hand through his hair, mulling what he could do next. He had lost his hat and suddenly felt disoriented and about a hundred years old; as if he had spent the last week on the front lines at Maginot.

Stumbling around the corner, he saw the Olds. The first thing he needed to do was get to a phone. He would call Lynton Maxwell. The industrialist had the connections he didn't. He could push back on the cops, slow them down if he told them it was his sister doing the shooting. Jack pulled out his keys.

"What are you doing here, Jack?" Quentin Deville walked around from the other side of the car.

Fury filled Jack. "Surprised to see me, boss? Thought I'd still be rotting in jail?"

"I left you in jail for a reason. A good reason."

It was true. "Yeah? You ever been in jail?"

"No."

"Well, if you had, you'd know there isn't a good reason to be left in one." Jack leaned against the car and with shaking hands pulled out a new pack of cigarettes. "You're not going to keep me off this story if that's why you're here."

"Why would I do that? You made Thrill Girl. I came to get you and take you back to the office. We have to decide how we're going to handle what happens next. I think we'll put out a special tomorrow night. The public will be dying for information."

"Do you know what's happened over there?" Jack lit a cigarette. He didn't offer one to his boss.

Quentin folded his arms over his white dinner jacket. "I know a few things. I got a phone call saying Thrill Girl killed two men tonight. The cops think she's holed up in a vacant store one street over. She's surrounded, and they are going to try and talk her out."

"Who did she kill?"

"A couple of drifters who tried to mug someone."

"What do you know about the Jaguar parked down the street?" He blew smoke right in Quentin's face. "Who is inside?"

Quentin blinked. "I understand there's a Negro in a chauffeur's uniform in the car. Unconscious. And another man who is ill."

Jack pressed his hand to his eyes for a moment, thinking of Robinson. "Do the cops know who Thrill Girl is?"

"They haven't said."

"Do you know?" Jack met Quentin's stare.

"I think you were right. It looks like it's Alana Maxwell." The publisher looked past Jack, into the darkness. "Her brother, Tomas, was the other man in the Jaguar with the chauffeur." He snapped his gaze back to the reporter. "The police rushed them both to the hospital, but they didn't give either of them a chance to survive."

"There is no way in hell Alana would attack her brother or Robinson." Jack glared at his boss. "That's the chauffeur's name."

"Tomas Maxwell wasn't attacked. He's dying from an illness.

As for Mr. Robinson, well, you don't know what she's capable of doing, Jack. Especially if what you told me in the office yesterday is true and she's been drugged. She may not know what she's doing at all."

Jack took a step toward Quentin. He wanted to throttle him. "I need to get to a phone and call Lynton Maxwell. These monkeys will kill her if someone with clout doesn't call them off."

"Maxwell's here." Quentin pointed toward the next street over. "Along with the Mayor and the Chief of Police. Those three men won't let anyone kill her."

"How the fuck do you know all this?" Jack's patience burst like an infected appendix. "I'm the goddamned lead reporter at *The Eyes of LA*. How is it you're the one with the golden sources?"

"I have contacts, too."

"With the cops? Since when?"

"Not LAPD. With federal intelligence agents. They have an interest in this case."

"The F.B.I. is interested in Thrill Girl? Why?"

"Not the F.B.I."

All the air went out of Jack's lungs. Quentin had kept secrets about Thrill Girl from him. So much for trust. Or loyalty. "Who are you, man? *What* the hell are you? Some kind of spy?"

"You know who I am. I'm a newspaper guy, like you."

"But you haven't always been a newspaper guy, have you?"

Quentin raised his eyebrows. "None of us are now what we were before."

"Don't give me that philosophical bullshit." Jack put his hand on Quentin's arm. "Have you known things about this case that you haven't shared with me from day one?"

"No. But I did learn a few facts the past couple of days I have kept to myself."

"Why?"

Quentin blinked. "We'll talk about this later."

"I can't believe this." He dropped his hand. "You betrayed me."

"I did not. Now get in that car. If we're going to push a Special Edition on the street in the next twenty-four hours, we need to leave now, Jack."

"I'm not leaving Alana out there. I'm staying."

"Don't be a bigger fool than you have been." Quentin's voice was raw. "You've let your emotions get the best of you with this story. I told you the cops won't kill her. The only thing you can do to help Alana Maxwell now is to be ready to write what you know about her being used badly by others. About the drugs and the experiments. It could be the only way to keep her from hanging, despite her brother's clout."

Jack flicked his cigarette away and punched the side of the Olds. "God damn it."

"You need two hands to type. Now stop feeling sorry for yourself and follow me to the office." Quentin slammed the door of the Bentley and fired up the big engine.

At that moment, four patrol cars rolled up the street and blocked the alley access. Uniformed patrols poured out of the cars onto the sidewalk. Two of them gestured toward Eddie's car. "That yours? Drive it out of here now, or your ass is in jail!"

Two other cops converged on Quentin. His boss put the Bentley into gear and motioned for Jack to follow.

Jack struggled to slide behind the wheel. His left pant leg stuck to the leather seat. He looked down at the dark, seeping stain running from thigh to ankle. His wound was bleeding from when Glass slammed him into the sidewalk. He pressed his palm against it and winced. Gulping air, he fought off dizziness and started the car as the cops pounded on the hood with their batons.

"Move it, shithead!"

"Hang on. I'm leaving." He drove slowly between the blockades and took a right at the corner. He was ten feet behind Deville. He followed him for two blocks before taking a sharp turn a block from the office.

He was nearly blind from pain. *I need morphine. If I go home and eat a vial of pills, I can recover enough to grab a cab back down here.*

He would find Jimmy Glass and make a deal, tell the cop everything he knew about Preminger and Josef and their repulsive experiments. He would give him the drug vials, break open the whole lurid story and make the Detective a hero.

But it was getting late, and he had a very short window of time to help Alana. And a shorter one to write the exclusive story about what happened tonight.

But not for *The Eyes*. He would write the story freelance and sell it to the highest bidder. And he would do a screenplay for Goldblum.

To hell with Quentin Deville. Whoever he is. He pressed the gas pedal down and held on.

CHAPTER TWENTY-SIX

Ten minutes later Jack parked in front of his apartment and dragged himself through the alley and up the stairs. He was losing blood with every step. It soaked his shoe, as a buzz saw of pain worked itself up and down his spine.

He was hot and clammy, and he wondered if the infection was spreading. He tried the knob on his front door, but it was locked. He fumbled with his keys and looked both ways before slipping inside.

He left the lights off.

For a moment Jack leaned against the door and fought to stay conscious. Inside the kitchen, he grabbed the pain medication. He ran water in the sink and rubbed his face raw, before opening the last beer in the icebox. He crushed three pills into the bowl of a spoon and then chugged the beer.

Almost instantly his stomach contracted, but after he inhaled several times, the pain began to ebb.

Drugged but lucid. He thought of Alana, who was surely anything but that.

He moved into the bathroom and turned on the shower, stripped off his clothes and got in. He sucked in his breath from shock as the scalding water hit him full force. The nerves in his hands were turning numb, but he peeled the bandage off his knee and rubbed soap all over the stitched up wound. The steam helped clear his mind as he formulated his opening for the news story.

Ernest Preminger had manipulated everyone.

His wife, Deidre.

Susan and Ellen Baldwin.

The future of Maxwell Industries, if Lynton believed Preminger had discovered a way to engineer a more lethal soldier.

And Alana Maxwell, because of her willingness to do anything for her brother.

Jack stepped from the shower. His leg was swollen from hip to knee, bruised green and black and blue, the discoloration clear in the dank light from the window.

He staggered to the counter and pulled out the ointment and bandages the VA had sent home with him but was too exhausted to attempt to dress it. He wrapped a towel around himself and took two steps toward the bedroom. He just needed to lay down for a couple of minutes.

As he got to the door of the bedroom, he heard a noise that didn't belong in an empty apartment.

Breathing.

There was someone in the room.

His Army training kicked-in and he froze. Gooseflesh rose on his damp skin. Jack thought of the mysterious Cadillac trailing him numerous times the last few days. And of the two men he had heard attack Deidre Preminger.

Silently he grabbed the carved walking stick leaning against the doorframe. The heft of it, the feel of the handle he had carved during the war helped him focus the last bit of strength. *If I'm going to die tonight, I'm going to get a good look at who kills me.*

Jack gritted his teeth, rushed into the bedroom, and hit the light switch.

# # #

"What do you mean, they didn't get her?" Quentin glanced at his wristwatch. It was a quarter to four in the morning. He had waited at the office for Jack for the last hour. The only reason he answered the phone was that he thought it might be his star reporter.

Instead, it was Jasper Meeks.

"They did not find Alana Maxwell in the building they had staked out," the attorney said. "They are going building by building looking for her. I need to know where Jack Curran is. I know he was bailed out of jail by Vida Purchase. Did you hire her? Is he with you?"

"Vida Purchase? No. I didn't. And no, he isn't."

"But you've seen him?"

Quentin hesitated. "He showed up at the scene of Thrill Girl's mayhem earlier, right behind the cops, as I expected him to. But he left when I did."

"Where is he now?"

"I don't know."

"Curran's done, Quentin. No matter what you say, he's a threat. My contacts are very worried."

"What are they going to do?" Quentin clutched the phone.

Jasper's voice dropped. "All options are open. But you know how this works. He knows too much. To my people, Jack Curran will be dangerous forever, even if they manage to control the story."

"Listen to me." Quentin's voice shook. "You tell whoever's in charge of this operation that I still have connections in the government. If Curran is taken out, I'll go public with things no one wants out there."

"I'll protect him, for now." Jasper sucked his breath in. "But you do nothing. Understand? Nothing. I'll be in touch in the morning with the official story about what happened to Thrill Girl out on the street tonight. I don't know if I can guarantee an exclusive, but you'll get the information at the same time as the AP."

"The Associated Press boys are your conduit of misinformation these days?"

"Quentin, for god's sake! Are you going to be a complete

jackass about this?"

"Yes. I guess I am. Fuck you, Jasper." The publisher slammed down the phone but stopped short of pulling it out of the wall as he wanted to do. He set it on his desk and considered what to do next.

Quentin looked at his watch. He had to find Jack before someone killed him.

# # #

Jack watched as Alana opened her eyes and stared at the ceiling. She was sprawled in the middle of his bed, wearing only a white silk slip and torn nylon stockings. Her dress and high heels were heaped in a swirl of black and white on the floor.

She moaned and shut her eyes.

"Jesus! Alana!" Jack looked quickly around the room, his heart thumping. "Are you here alone?"

She opened her eyes, squinting against the harsh light from the overhead bulbs. "Jack?"

He flipped off the light, dropped the club and limped across the room to sit beside her. "How did you get in here?"

"I had your card. I gave it to the cabbie, and he took me here. But you weren't here." Her heavy blonde hair fell across her face. "I know I'm not making sense. I keep falling asleep, and when I'm awake, I see things. Lights. And colors. And myself, only from across the room." She threw her arms around his neck. "I'm so frightened. I think I'm going mad."

Jack held her. "Tell me what happened. The last thing you remember."

"I went to see Dr. Preminger."

"When?"

"In the morning."

"Today?"

"I don't know." She hung her head. "I couldn't take it anymore; the side effects of the drugs were getting worse." Her breath caught in her throat and she met his eyes. "I think he's trying to kill me."

"How?"

"Drugs. I think he might be poisoning me. He gave me a pill when I went to his house, and I blacked out. I'm sorry, but that's all I remember." She pushed away from him and clutched her hands to her chest, crying harder with each breath.

"Okay. It's okay." Jack struggled to form a coherent thought. If Alana was here, who the hell did the cops have cornered downtown? "I think we better get you to the police. You can tell them everything…"

"The police?" Her voice was horrified. "I can't go to them. Please, Jack. Just hold me for a minute." She put her arms around his neck. "I was trying to do the right thing, and now everything is ruined. It's all my fault."

"Slow down, kid. You're not making sense." He rubbed her back, worrying about the platoon of cops a few blocks away. When they didn't find her at the crime scene, they might come here. "Did you leave my apartment at all since you got here?" He had no way to prove she had been here this evening instead of downtown, but looking at her he found it unimaginable that she had been in the middle of a shoot-out with the LAPD in the last couple of hours.

Had the cops, and Quentin, lied about having Thrill Girl cornered?

"I don't think so. I don't know." Her words were slurred.

"Alana, you have got to clear your head. How long have you been here?"

"I don't know. I keep waking up and blacking out." Her face twitched. "I need to call Tomas. Do you have a phone? He'll be worried. Robinson can come and get us. Maybe we should go to Lynton's."

Jack's chest tightened. "Robinson can't come right now."

"What's wrong? What's happened?" she wailed. "I need to talk to Tommy!"

Jack got up clutching the towel and pulled clothes out of his closet. "Stay there. I'll be right back." When he returned five minutes later, she was curled in a ball in the middle of the bed.

She grimaced when he flipped on the light and picked her clothes up off the floor. They were torn and dirty. He stared at a stain that looked like blood.

"Get dressed." Jack handed her the clothes.

Alana sat up with difficulty. She held her dress as if she had no idea what it was. "Will you take me to Tommy?"

"I *will* take you to see Tomas. He's not at the Ambassador, though. He's in the hospital." Jack helped her stand.

"What?" She grabbed her throat. Every fingernail on her right hand was broken, and she had a gash on her arm. "What's happened to him? Is Robinson with him?"

"Yes."

"Is Tomas all right?"

He has to be, Jack thought. *If he's not, it'll be the end of her.*

"Yeah," he said. But he saw, even in the state she was in, that she feared he was lying.

#

The man in the black gloves peered through the window. Crouched on the hospital fire escape, he watched while a nurse checked a tube leading out of Tomas Maxwell's arm. After a moment she pulled up his covers, muted the lights, and headed for the hallway.

As soon as the room was empty, he opened the window and stepped inside.

The door leading out to the corridor was open. He walked silently across the room and listened. In the hallway, a doctor was telling someone that Tomas's condition was very grave and that his brother, Lynton Maxwell, had requested that no one disturb the patient.

The man pushed the door almost closed, leaving it cracked a few inches so he could hear if anyone approached.

He crossed the room and sat on the edge of the bed, his heart swelling with despair at the sight of Tomas as his lifelong journey to reunite with him came to an end.

The young man thought of Dr. Roga, who had taken him in when he was six days old, and told him all about Tomas Maxwell when he was old enough to understand. "You were brought to me as a babe by those who thought I may be able to heal you, to make you strong and fit. Tomas is being cared for by his family and other doctors, as I care for you. You two will meet one day," the great man had promised. "You will both be strong and confident men who will go on together in life, and make peace with the past."

Roga's words had replayed inside his head thousands of times, helping him endure the multiple surgeries to repair his legs and reconstruct his left shoulder and clavicle. They had kept him sane during the excruciating amputation of the growth on his tailbone, which had to wait to be completed when he was sixteen.

The last procedures, to correct his defective hand, had occurred three years ago. A cleft split his palm into two curved and hideous appendages, with freakish retractable fingernails, unknown but for a few cases in human history.

The surgeons Dr. Roga brought him to were going to give him the look and function of a normal human appendage, by grafting bone to create a middle and index finger, and remove the mutated fingernails. During the agonizing procedures, the young man had held onto one thought – that soon he would be fit and normal.

And when he turned twenty-one he would travel to America and find Tomas, and they would celebrate their triumphs over the physical abnormalities they were born with and forgive those that had kept them apart.

But the operations on his left hand had failed. He had nearly died of sepsis, and Dr. Roga admitted that the young man had to face the fact that he would eventually lose his hand because of nerve damage and atrophy.

He stared down at the black glove. He would never be normal. He looked back at Tomas Maxwell, rage filling him. This man had never been well and was now near death. The two lies, the two dreams he had relied on his entire life, merged into one burning betrayal.

"I am sorry, Tomas," the young man whispered as tears fell from his blue eyes. He removed the leather glove from his misshapen paw of a hand, moaning with pain as it unfurled. After a moment he gently touched it to Tomas's head.

Tomas opened his eyes, and his ravaged features contorted with fear.

"Don't be afraid," the man said gently. "It's me, Emrick. Your brother. I'm here at last."

# # #

Lydia Lopez did the necessary reconnaissance of the hospital emergency ward and found that Tomas Maxwell, guarded by one LAPD uniform, had been taken up to the third floor.

She returned to where Jack was waiting in the utility room and handed him a stack of white clothes. "He's in a private room, arranged for by his brother."

Jack peered out the small window in the door. "Do you know if Lynton Maxwell is still at the hospital?"

"No, I don't think so." Lydia leaned close to Jack. "Do you know a cop named Jim Kennedy? About thirty. Red hair?"

"No."

"Good. That's who is guarding Tomas's room. If you don't know him, he doesn't know you." She handed him the clothes. "Put on this lab coat, and have your friend wear the nurse's dress and you two will blend in with the staff going in and out of there."

"I'll go get her. Thank you, Lydia. I owe you." He hugged her, overwhelmed that she had so willingly agreed to help him.

"No, you don't. Joey and I owe you." She squeezed his arm. "Just don't get caught."

Jack hurried down the stairs and out into the parking lot. He had left Alana in the Oldsmobile a few minutes ago with a quart of coffee and a ham sandwich. He knocked on the window and held up the nurse's uniform for her to change into.

"Come on, we need to hurry." He saw she had not touched the food, but she had drained the coffee.

In the back seat, Alana slipped on the dress. "Is it okay?" she asked nervously.

Her distinctive blonde mane was pinned up under the cap. There was nothing they could do to disguise her beauty, but she made a convincing nurse.

"You look fine. Let's go." He pulled on the lab coat Lydia had given him.

Five minutes later, they were outside Tomas's room. The cop

at the door was too busy checking out Alana's legs to give Jack as much as a glance. Lydia opened the door and waved them in and shut the door.

From across the room, Jack saw Tomas. The young man was the color of a corpse. Tubes and wires ran from him to various glass bottles and machines. Lydia whispered to Jack that he was dying from liver failure and had been sedated.

"He is aware of his surroundings," Lydia said to Alana. "It's good you could come now."

"Is he going to die?" Alana seemed in shock, staring expressionlessly across the room.

Lydia squeezed her hand. "Your brother needs you. Go to him." She turned to Jack. "I'll be outside. Make it quick." She tiptoed out of the room.

Alana moaned, and her knees buckled, but Jack cupped his hand around her elbow and led her to the bedside. For a moment she just stared. "Tommy?"

"I'll wait by the door," Jack said. "If anyone comes in, stay cool, okay?"

She looked at him blankly. "I don't understand what's happening."

"I'm talking about the cops. If they bust in here, don't do anything to make them shoot us. Can you do that?"

"Okay." Suddenly she began to rock back and forth, her sobs loud in the quiet room. "Is this my brother, my baby brother?"

He squeezed her arm. "I understand how hard this is…"

"No you don't! He's dying! Tommy's dying! And when he does, I'll have no one." She buried her face in her hands and moaned.

"Yes. Yes, I do, Alana. I had a sister who died in a mental institution, in an accident. She was only fifteen years old." His mind replayed the agonizing visit to identify her mangled body after the building collapsed around her. How his mother had cried alone in her bedroom the entire day of the funeral, and every day he was home on leave from the war.

He had never seen his mother alive again. "I know what

Tomas means to you." Emotion gentled his voice. "Talk to him. Tell him you're here, Alana. Don't let him suffer alone. It's the only good thing you can do."

Alana rubbed her red eyes and clutched the metal sides of the hospital bed. "Okay. I know. Okay."

Jack turned away as his gut twisted. He had never told anyone except for his ex-wife about his sister's death. He was still filled with remorse over not saving her from that dilapidated state facility, or from her illness, before disaster struck.

He looked out into the corridor and then rested his head against the wall. His mind jumped to the list of a hundred inconsistencies that was the Thrill Girl story.

The biggest question was where Alana had spent the last twenty-four hours. If she had been unconscious in his bedroom the whole time he had been looking for her, she couldn't possibly be responsible for those dead men on the street tonight.

But if she had left the apartment, killed those men downtown, and returned after escaping the police stakeout...

He glanced over at the woman standing at her brother's deathbed. He knew what he wanted the truth about her to be, but he did not know the facts. As he watched her, he tried to take the full measure of the woman, to read inside her heart and know if Alana Maxwell, even under the influence of hypnotic suggestion and dangerous drugs, was capable of the violence and mayhem Thrill Girl had committed.

He squinted in the dank light, but all he saw was a woman with a broken heart.

# # #

Alana took her brother's hand and leaned across the hospital bed. "Tommy. I'm here. I'm going to speak to the doctors in a few minutes. Find out what we need to do to help you get better."

The young man's lips trembled, but no words escaped.

Alana wet the cloth on the tray beside him with cool water from the pitcher and pressed it against his chapped lips. "Don't try and talk."

"Emrick..."

It was so softly spoken, Alana did not know if she imagined the word or not. "What?" She knew that name, Emrick. But how, and why, would Tomas know it? And why would he say it?

Tomas stared at her. His voice was barely audible. "I saw him, Alana. *Emrick*. He's alive." His eyes were bloodshot, the pupils fully dilated. They shined oddly in the dim light of the hospital room.

"Emrick? He was *here*?" She trembled.

"A few minutes ago." Tomas nodded at the window. "He came in there, and left the same way, like a ghost. He told me not to worry. That Dr. Roga would help me."

Goosebumps crawled up her arms as she realized Tomas was hallucinating. She put her hand gently on his forehead. "Dr. Roga? I don't know him, but he's my new hero if he can help you."

"Emrick will help me."

She glanced at Jack, who was staring in the opposite direction, lost in his own thoughts, then looked back to Tomas. "What did he say?"

"Many things." Tomas blinked. "You knew I was a twin, but you never told me…" He spoke louder. "Why?"

"Who told you this?" Alana drew back in shock.

"Aunt Bridget. She told me about the other baby. I didn't think you knew, Alana. But he said you did." Tears leaked down his ruined face. "Why didn't you tell me?"

At that moment, Alana realized Tomas was not hallucinating about everything. "Oh, Tomas. I'm so sorry, but Emrick died when you were both tiny babies. He was terribly disfigured. His poor hand was shriveled, and his legs were bent and not functional. He didn't breathe right, and the doctor said he was in terrible pain and was unable to eat…" She started to sob. "He died a few days after you two were born. I didn't tell you about him because he had such a short, tragic life."

"No. You're wrong, Alana. Emrick didn't die. He told me what happened. Father had Lynton take him from the nursery, and leave him with a family. Leave him to die with strangers."

"Oh, Tomas, no."

Tomas made a gurgling noise but kept talking. "But Dr. Roga saved him. Our brother is a healthy, normal man, Alana. Not aberrant like me. Not helpless. He's magnificent. I wish Lynton had taken both of us away that night."

Alana gripped the side of the bed as the room spun in circles. *This was not true. This did not happen.* Tomas was suffering from hallucinations about Emrick, just as she had for so many months. It was the drugs, it had to be the drugs. She inhaled raggedly and put her head down on the bed covers. "Please, please, believe me, Tommy, this is fever talking. Emrick died. I'm so sorry I didn't tell you the truth, but he died. You should have come to me after Bridget told you."

Tomas gasped. His hand squeezed hers, nearly crushing her fingers. "I didn't know then that you knew about this! Don't lie to me now, sister. I don't have any time left."

She tried to pull away, seeing for the first time her brother's disfigured, claw-like nail on his index finger. His body convulsed, and the nail cut into the skin of her arm. His eyes rolled back in his head, and Alana cried out in horror.

Jack ran across the room and caught her before she fell.

At that moment, Lydia Lopez rushed back into the room. The nurse carried a covered tray. "Jack, you two need to leave right now! There are about twenty police in the lobby downstairs. Hurry!" She set the tray down and grabbed a hypodermic needle, stuck into a vial of medication. "Officer Kennedy went to get coffee. If he tries to stop us, I'm going to stick him with this. It'll knock him out, but I won't be able to hold off the others."

"My god, Lydia. No. You're not risking yourself any more than you already have." Jack kept one hand on Alana's back and took the needle from Lydia with his other. "Which way should we go?"

"Go to the right. The stairs are at the end of the hallway. Take them all the way to the basement. Then leave out of the door marked deliveries. Hurry!"

"Alana, look at me." Jack squeezed her arm.

She turned. Her hand was bleeding, but she didn't let go of Tomas. Her brother's eyes were closed, and his mouth slack. He was not breathing.

"We have to go now. Let go of Tomas." Jack ordered.

"I'm not leaving my brother!"

"Look at him. He's gone." Jack stared at her. "You have to come with me. Now. I'll protect you until we sort out this whole mess. Trust me."

"I don't care what happens to me." She was shaking with grief as she patted her brother's waxen face. "Tomas, please open your eyes."

Jack looked down at the syringe and without warning stuck it into Alana's arm.

She went still instantly. He hoisted the unconscious woman over his shoulder and followed Lydia to the door. He was ready to deck the guard, who was standing by the nursing station at the far end of the corridor, a telephone receiver pressed against his ear.

Jack and Lydia rushed to the other end of the corridor. As they opened the stairwell door, police poured out of the elevator ten feet away and ran toward Tomas's room.

Lydia pushed Jack through the door and locked it behind them. She ripped the front of her nurse's uniform. "Go. I don't think they saw us, but if they come this way, I'll tell them three men dressed as ambulance drivers roughed me up and went upstairs to use the fire escape. Go!"

"Thank you, Lydia."

She hugged his arm. "Get yourself out of here safely! That will be my thanks."

Despite his bum leg, Jack maneuvered all twenty steps of the first flight, despite Alana being a dead weight on his shoulder. At the landing, his left knee gave out, and he crashed against the railing and shifted her to the other shoulder.

He was sweating profusely. But he kept one thought in mind, he had to get Alana out of the hospital. Jack clenched his jaw and started down the next flight, wondering if a heart attack would kill him before a cop did.

CHAPTER TWENTY-SEVEN

The front exit of the hospital was crawling with police. When a truck painted with the call letters of K.T.L.A. television rolled up to the emergency room doors, Jack gunned the Wentz Oldsmobile over the curb. He turned the wrong way up a one-way street before taking a right onto Van Nuys Blvd. and heading to his Hollywood apartment.

Alana was in the back, snoring like a horse. He shook out one of his cigarettes and pressed in the car lighter.

He decided the only possible choice among three terrible ones was to take Alana to Lynton's estate in San Marino. There was no proof the industrialist was working with Preminger, and he was banking on the hope that the affection he had seen the man display toward his step-sister was real enough that he would help her with the cops.

Alana was without any blood relatives now and had no one else to turn to. Jack knew how that felt.

He flinched when the car lighter popped out of its hole. He turned on the radio to drown out his thoughts as Frank Sinatra crooned "Night and Day." Cole Porter, who had written the song, understood how a dame could get under a man's skin.

He glanced in the mirror and saw there was no change in

Alana's condition, which meant he was going to have to leave her in the car while he got the pain medication, or carry her up to his apartment.

Sheer will was no longer enough to keep his failing body moving, but he would try. Gingerly he touched his left leg. It pulsed with heat. For the first time he wondered if it might kill him, and chuckled ruefully. An infection would do what the Germans hadn't been able to.

Jack turned the corner and into the alley behind his apartment building, as an urgent voice replaced Sinatra on the radio.

"We interrupt this program to advise all residents of Los Angeles that the LAPD has issued an alert. There is a manhunt on tonight for Alana Maxwell. Miss Maxwell is wanted for questioning about the vigilante murders that have taken place in the greater Los Angeles area over the last few weeks. She is considered armed and dangerous. Citizens are urged to immediately call the authorities if they see her. We are going live now to City Hall, where a press conference is being held by Police Chief Crotche and Lieutenant Ralph Donnelly."

Jack parked the car as a description of Alana crackled through the speakers. *"Miss Maxwell is five feet six inches tall and approximately one hundred and ten pounds. She has platinum blonde hair and blue eyes and was last seen dressed in a black and white silk suit and a black hat..."*

Alana mumbled in her sleep and Jack flinched. He flipped the radio off and stared out of the windshield. There was a car he did not recognize parked about thirty yards away. It looked like a Cadillac.

A curtain covered the back window.

He checked the rear-view mirror. He had nothing but his fists to use as a weapon. Jack considered driving straight to San Marino. But he had to be sharp, and there were going to be cops on the streets. Maybe even roadblocks on the freeway. The police were likely to be in a shoot-first-and-ask-questions-later mood considering that Thrill Girl had fired on them tonight.

He glanced at Alana. *Should I call Lynton to pick her up here? And bring an attorney?*

A moment later he stepped out of the car, keeping his eyes on the Caddy. There was no way he could leave Alana in the car. Bracing himself, he pulled Alana into his arms and positioned her over his shoulder and headed for the stairwell. The alley was as dark and quiet as a graveyard. He couldn't feel his leg half the time, and if not for the railing, he would have fallen. The left side of his body was numb in several spots, and pins and needles crawled up his right hip and groin.

The whine of a car traveling at high speed filled the air. Jack stopped midway on the stairs, Alana warm against his neck, and braced himself for the worst.

A 1940 Pontiac coupe barreled into view and stopped at the bottom of the stairs with a squeal of rubber. Jack squinted but didn't recognize the car. The passenger door opened and out jumped Eddie Wentz.

"Mr. Curran! I'm glad I found you." The young man started up the stairway.

"You're up late, Eddie. Or way too early," Jack wheezed.

Eddie stopped. His voice was two notches higher than usual, and his eyes darted from Jack's face to Alana. "The whole city is awake! Did you hear about Thrill Girl? She got away from the cops. Mr. Deville called me at home to see if I knew where you were."

"I'm here, and I'm glad you came. Who's in the car with you?"

"Uncle Teddy."

Jack glanced at the other end of the alley. An empty space yawned against the brick building where it had been parked. The Cadillac had soundlessly slipped away.

"Bring him upstairs, will you?"

"Sure thing." Eddie gestured to the car, and Jack heard the car ignition stop and the door open.

Eddie climbed to the step below Jack. "Ah, can I help you, Mr. Curran? You look like you're about to drop her."

"Yeah. This is Alana Maxwell; in case you were wondering."

"I figured it might be. But I didn't want to jump to any

conclusions."

"Good man, Eddie."

Jack gratefully transferred the blonde to Eddie's shoulder.

The kid blushed bright red when she nestled into him. "Man is she beautiful." He dropped his voice. "Is she Thrill Girl?"

"That's the million-dollar question, kid." He reached for his cigarettes, but – as if he had been struck from behind – everything went black.

# # #

A half-hour later, Jack woke up in his bed without his trousers.

A fresh bandage wrapped his left thigh. The adhesive was tight, and it pulled at the hair on his calf when he stretched his toes. The leg brace from the VA was laced snugly over the top.

Eddie and his uncle stood beside the bed.

"What the hell happened?" Jack asked.

"You fainted. We brought you in, and I saw to your wound." Teddy nodded at Alana, who was sitting still as a mannequin across the room. "She came around while you were out. She's pretty groggy, but clearly suffering from the after-effects of being drugged."

"What do you mean?"

Teddy raised his eyebrows. "She was hallucinating. Saw bugs and flying things. Has she taken the stuff you showed me? The LSD?"

"Yeah." Jack stared at the heiress. A blanket was wrapped around her shoulders, and there was a mug of coffee in her hand. Her face was pale and ravaged, and she stared blankly at the wall. "I gave her a sedative to knock her out."

"That likely triggered another hallucinatory experience," Teddy said. "From what I understand of LSD, flashbacks can continue for months after a dose."

Jack clenched his fists and turned to Alana. "How you doing, kid?"

"Did you knock me out?" Her eyes were dilated and blank.

"Yeah. I had to get you out of the hospital."

"Tomas was at the hospital," she replied. "Did you see how he looked?"

Eddie and his uncle exchanged glances.

Jack took a deep breath. "Yes. I saw him, Alana. He was very ill."

"He looked like a monster." Tears welled in her eyes. "And he was mad at me. I let him down."

"Don't think about that right now. We'll get to the bottom of what happened to your brother." Jack said the words, but after what Quentin told him about the feds being secretly involved in the case, he didn't have faith that what he said was true.

The room went quiet. Alana put her left hand on her throat. "I don't care about the cops. He died, didn't he? Tommy…"

"Yes," Jack tried to get up but couldn't move yet. "I'm sorry."

Her top lip twitched. She leaned back against the wall and sat motionlessly.

"You know the police are looking for her, don't you?" Teddy asked Jack softly.

"Yes, I know." He swallowed. "Thanks for lending a hand with my leg, doc. How's it looking?"

"You need to go to the hospital. Now. You've got septicemia – blood poisoning." Teddy pointed to a faint red line radiating above the leg brace on Jack's thigh. "I gave you the penicillin I had in my bag, but you'll need more soon. You'll lose your leg if you play around with this, Mr. Curran. And you could lose your life."

Eddie cocked his head toward Alana. "My uncle can drive her wherever she needs to go, and I can take you to the hospital in Mom's car."

Jack looked at his watch. It was a quarter to four in the morning. He gritted his teeth and sat up, slowly moving both feet to the floor. His forehead broke into a sweat. "I need to take her myself. I have to explain things to Lynton Maxwell in person. Why don't you and your uncle head home? I'll bring your mom's car to you after I drop her off, and we can go to the hospital then."

Teddy stepped closer to the bed. "You're in no shape to drive,

Mr. Curran. I only put that brace on as a stop-gap measure of support. As a doctor, I must insist you follow my advice."

"I appreciate your concern, doc. And I'll get this treated as soon as I get her squared away. We've got things to do now that can't wait."

"Do you want me to call Mr. Deville?" Eddie asked.

"No. Don't do that." Jack's voice was sharp. "And if he calls you, don't tell him anything about seeing me, or her. I'll get in touch with him after Alana is safe."

"I can go with you." Eddie pushed his glasses nervously. "You don't want to pass out behind the wheel."

"I'm better off alone." He softened his tone. "But could you get the bottle of pills on the kitchen counter? And I'll take some of that coffee." He tried to stand up and wavered but stayed on his feet when Teddy grabbed his right arm.

"When is the last time you ate?" the doctor demanded.

"I don't remember."

"There are sandwiches in the car," Teddy said. "Eddie's mother packed them in case we were out all night looking for you. I'll get them. If you're taking codeine, you need food in your stomach."

"Thank you," Jack said.

"I have something else you should take." Teddy reached into his coat and flashed a Remington Derringer pistol. It was a two-shot variety. Jack had seen many like it on dead Germans during the war.

"I thought you might need this." He handed it to Jack.

"Uncle Teddy, where did you get a gun?" Eddie was shocked.

"It's your Aunt Sadie's." He winked. "You know I don't like guns."

Jack pursed his mouth. Teddy Wentz, the mild-mannered doctor, was not exactly what he had seemed. That was true of nearly everyone he had run into in the last few weeks.

"Thank you." Jack slid the gun into the top of the brace. He looked at Alana. "How are you doing?"

She nodded.

"We'll leave in a few minutes. You need anything? You look fine in that nurse's dress, but I can loan you a shirt to put on over it."

"I'm sorry, where did you say we're going?" She blinked rapidly.

"Lynton's. You need an attorney, and I'm sure your step-brother will be able to call and get you the best."

"Why do I need an attorney?" Alana asked.

The three men exchanged looks.

"I'll get the pain pills," Eddie said and followed his uncle out of the room.

# # #

The horizon had wisps of pinks and blue as the car sped along the residential streets of Pasadena, heading toward Lynton Maxwell's San Marino estate.

Alana sat silently beside Jack.

For the past few minutes, he had patiently explained why the cops were looking for her. "What it comes down to is that circumstantially at least, the cops think you are involved in the vigilante murders."

"Involved?" Her voice was calm. "The police think I'm Thrill Girl?"

He glanced sideways at her. "Yeah. According to my boss, they do."

"What do you think?"

"I can't see you as a murderess." His voice went cold. "But I've been wrong about people before."

"Me, too," she said.

Neither one of them spoke for several moments. Jack didn't push her further. Would she have been able to give him a truthful answer about her part in the killings if he had? He didn't think so.

Alana touched him suddenly, resting her hand on his right thigh. "I'm sorry about your sister. It must have been horrible, losing her like that."

Jack swallowed. He wasn't sorry he had told Alana the tragic story of his sister's death, but he did regret dredging up the guilt that burned inside. "It's still horrible."

"Some of the things in life that happen to you never go away, even if you do good things to try and atone."

Jack thought of his mother's ravaged face and realized he had never seen her smile after that day. Katherine's death killed his mother's ability to feel joy about anything. "That's true. And yet, the living have to keep at it."

"Do they?"

"Isn't that what your religion is based on?" Before she could answer him, Jack swerved hard to the right.

"What's wrong?" Her voice was panicked.

"There was a roadblock." He spotted a patrol car pulled off the road and three officers standing to the side. The car fishtailed as he steered over the curb onto a side street to avoid the cops parked at Orange Grove. They cruised down a long alley and emerged near the Rose Bowl.

They were both silent as Jack headed up the private road toward Lynton's estate. With the guard shack in sight, he pulled off into a thickly overgrown patch, put the car in park and killed the lights. They were twenty yards from the gate.

"We'll wait here a few minutes and see if anyone drives up. I'm hoping Lynton's there, but I want to see what's going on." If her step-brother wasn't home, there was a good chance the cops would be with him when he returned from the mess downtown.

The heiress turned to him, her voice shaky. "No matter what happens next, I want to thank you. For taking me to see Tomas. And for being so kind to me the other night."

"You mean at the beach?" He squeezed her hand. "I'm not sure what I was could be called kind."

"You made me feel good. In all ways. And safe. I never told anyone else about keeping Tommy's twin brother a secret." She kissed his cheek, her hand gripping his shoulder.

He didn't pull her to him, but he wanted to.

"Thank you also for listening when I explained about

Buddhism and karma," Alana whispered. "You didn't make fun of me. That's rare."

"For you to talk about Buddhism, or for anyone to listen?

"Both."

"You don't need to thank me. I learned a few things from you." The tension between them flamed. "The pleasure was mine."

"I telephoned you that night, you know," she continued. "After I dropped you at the office. I wanted you to come to my place. But no one answered at your office."

He bit down so hard on his bottom lip he tasted blood. "Why did you call?"

"I needed to know if you meant it when you said you wanted to see me again."

"I meant it. Even though you had another date." He tried to keep it light but failed.

"I did have a date. But I canceled it when I couldn't stop thinking about you." Her eyelashes fluttered like a butterfly on a breeze. "I wanted to make love with you again. I felt like if I didn't, I might die."

Jack pulled her to him. He kissed her passionately, and she kissed him back. After several moments, Alana leaned away from Jack. Even in the darkness, Jack saw grief on her face.

"When this mess is straightened out, I'll be here," he said. "Maybe we can go away for a while. Get in a car and head out Route 66. Would you like to do that?"

She didn't reply for several moments, then she turned to him. The suffering, tender woman he had just kissed was replaced by a stranger. "Why, Mr. Curran? Are you hoping to pump me for information so you can write a follow-up story on me? A world exclusive interview with a Thrill Girl, maybe?"

"No," Jack said. "I want to get to know you more. For myself. Not for a newspaper column."

She pursued her lips, her blue eyes glimmering. "I'm sorry, Jack. You don't deserve that kind of crack. After all you've done…"

"It's okay." He took her hand and kissed her fingers. "This has been the worst day of your life. You're allowed to lash out." He leaned into her for another kiss, but she stopped him.

"No. Let's not pretend, even for a few minutes, that this thing between us can go anywhere. Even if I'm not guilty of what the cops say I did, my choices caused the death of the person I loved most in life." Alana wrapped her arms tightly around her chest. "I let him down. I let Tommy die."

"You didn't. You did everything you could to give him a better life," Jack said. "It's Preminger and that psycho Brandt who are responsible for what happened to your brother."

She shook her head back and forth and withdrew, folding her hands in her lap. "We had one night. That was lucky. I won't forget it, or you."

"I thought you didn't believe in luck."

"I don't."

He touched her chin with his finger. "It must have been *karma*. We both did good things to earn it."

"You think so?"

"I do." He looked outside. It was getting lighter by the minute. He would walk her up to the house if there was no guard to open the gate for the car. "You have to stay strong. Lynton will help you with the police, and I'll do all I can to make sure the facts about how you were manipulated and used by Preminger get into the public view. No one in their right mind will hold you responsible for what's happened when they know the truth."

"The truth?" She shook her head. "Don't say anymore. You're not the type of man who lies to a woman, or to himself. And you're a journalist. They deal in facts, right? And the fact is I'm wanted for several murders that I probably committed. Drugged or not, I still killed people."

"Alana!"

"Please, let's just go up to the house. I'm so tired."

Jack accepted he would not be able to convince her of anything right now. He put the car into gear and slowly rolled up to the guard shack.

A man stepped out of the shadows and gestured for them to stop. Jack rolled down the window. "Good evening. Can you call up to the house and tell Mr. Maxwell his sister is here."

"Your name, sir?" The guard had a thick accent.

"Where's the kid who was here the other night?" Jack turned to Alana. "Do you know this guy?"

Alana leaned over and stared out the window. "Is Mr. Maxwell on the premises? I'm his sister."

"I need your name, sir?" The guard ignored Alana. His eyes were almost hidden by a hat pulled low on his brow.

"Curran. Jack Curran. Tell Maxwell I'd like him to come to the door himself when we get to the house."

The man peered through the windshield into the front seat. "Is it only the two of you?"

"She's had a long night, buddy," Jack said. "Make the damn call."

The guard stepped away from the car, revealing a bulky shape on the ground at the side of the shack.

"Hey, what's going on here?" Jack demanded.

The guard made a sudden gesture toward the opposite side of the road.

Beside him, Alana tensed as Jack moved his hand to the gear shift to throw the car into reverse, but he was a fraction of a second too late. Alana screamed as the passenger door opened and she was pulled out of the car onto the ground. A huge beast of a man smacked his hand over her mouth while she kicked her feet.

Jack lunged across the seat for her just as the guard pulled the driver's side door open. The sound of bone against metal rang out as the guard slammed a weapon against the side of Jack's skull.

The newsman fell motionless against the dashboard. The last thing he heard was Alana's muffled scream against her captor's gloved hand.

CHAPTER TWENTY-EIGHT

"How did Lynton Maxwell decide to send Tomas Maxwell to Ernest Preminger for treatment?" The man in dark clothes, his blond hair gleaming in the soft semi-dark before dawn, spoke sternly to Alana.

She trembled and stared down at Jack, who lay motionless on the ground beside her. "He needs medical help. We have to call for an ambulance."

"Answer my question."

Alana met his blue eyes. "How do you know my brother?"

"I'm asking questions, not you."

"Preminger was recommended to Lynton by professional associates. We were told he had much success with paralysis patients, utilizing new techniques and drugs."

"Are they business partners? Preminger and your step-brother?"

"What? No. I mean, I don't think so."

"What is your relationship with *Herr Doktor?*" The man stepped closer.

Alana took a step backward. She wanted to scream that she would kill Preminger with her bare hands if she saw him, but she had to keep her wits. She glanced down at Jack's still body, then back at the young man.

"I volunteered to help in his research. Preminger was working on developing a treatment that would cure my brother's..." She pushed her hair off her face. "I hoped, with my help, that the doctor would develop a cure that would allow my brother to walk."

The man who had dragged her out of the car stood behind her questioner. He leaned forward and whispered in German to the man with the glove.

"Did Maxwell know Preminger was using you in his research?" He grimaced at the last word.

"No. I didn't tell him."

"That's not what I asked."

"I don't know what Lynton knows, or doesn't know." Alana's vision began to blur, and she blinked. In the trees around her, tiny lightning bugs danced in green and red circles. "Why don't you ask him yourself?"

"I intend to." His tone was dangerous. "Did you know Josef Brandt was conducting hideous experiments on human beings?"

"No. Of course not, I only found that out earlier tonight."

"Only then?" the man pressed. "As Tomas's devoted sister, are you saying you didn't investigate Preminger and Brandt's background? You didn't know they worked with the Nazis during the war?"

"What?" She wrung her hands together and sank to her knees. "I don't know what you're talking about. How would Nazis get into this country? Are you saying Preminger is a war criminal?"

"Yes, that's what I'm saying. I'm also saying Lynton Maxwell's company is funding his research."

"I can't make sense of what you're talking about. I'm ill, and I lost my brother earlier tonight. Please, let me go. I need to get help for this man." She rested the back of her hand on Jack's face. It was cold as stone.

The huge man took a threatening step closer, but his boss shook his head slightly, and he stopped.

"Is Lynton at home?" the blonde man asked.

Alana looked in the direction of the house. "I don't know. I think so."

The two men spoke rapidly in German.

Alana blinked. She once knew the language, but now she was unable to understand their words. At the edge of her vision she saw a large black cat slink into the bushes behind the trees. Tearing her eyes away, she pointed at her captor. "Who are you?"

"You know who I am." His eyes glittered in the darkness.

Goosebumps rose on Alana's neck and arms, and in a moment of searing clarity, she did know. The blonde man who wore only one black leather glove, the blue-eyed tormentor staring at her with hatred and contempt, was more than familiar. Strong, direct, blindingly handsome; a man who demanded respect, not empathy or pity.

He was the image of what she had prayed for her entire life. A healthy Tomas, standing on his own two feet, ready to take on the world.

"Emrick?" she gasped. "Oh my god, Tomas told me you came to see him at the hospital, but he was delirious, and I didn't believe him. I didn't know you…" Her voice broke.

"You didn't know I was alive?" Emrick folded his arms across his broad chest. "But you knew I once existed."

"Yes. No." Her hand twitched, but she did not reach out to him. "I saw you a few hours after your birth. I peeked into mother's room because I was thrilled to hear there were two baby boys. But the scene that day was anything but joyful. It was tragic, mother was out of her mind with pain and the doctor's words to my father were grim…" Alana's arms shook but she reached out to him. "My god, you're my brother."

"I was Tomas's brother. But you're no sister to me," he said.

The man guarding Emrick put a massive hand on Emrick's shoulder. He stared at Alana, ready to do whatever her brother asked him to.

"You hate me." Alana dropped her arms to her sides. "I understand that. But I was a child, only five when you were born.

What could I have done?" She struggled to her feet. "I was too afraid to confront anyone about what happened to you. But I thought of you always. And I did everything I could to help Tomas. For his whole life, he knew he could depend on me."

"Then why did he die like he did?"

"He, he was sick. His whole life." She took another step. "But he was getting better. When Lynton recommended..."

"You trusted *Lynton*? You trusted a man who took a newborn baby from its mother's breast, and left it to die with strangers?"

Sobs clogged her throat. The memory of the days after her mother gave birth swelled inside her. The grim silence. The hushed conversations. She was sent to the nursery for days on end and told nothing by nanny or her parents. "You must believe me. I loved you on the day you were born, but it was years before I knew the truth. That Lynton had taken you away..."

"Don't lie to me," Emrick shouted. "Doing what you were told, staying silent as a child is one thing. But years later, remembering what Lynton did, you never asked him to explain about the second child? You never asked about me? And then you trusted him to make medical recommendations for Tomas? He's dead now because of that. You didn't love Tomas, or me, for even a second."

Alana turned to run but tripped and fell to her knees, jarring Jack's body.

He moaned and pushed himself up on his arms, and immediately reached for her. "What's going on?" he asked. "What's wrong, Alana?"

"Are you okay?" she replied. She touched his face, but he turned away and stared at the men who had cold-cocked him at the gate.

"I know you," Jack said. "You're the man who helped Eddie. Who are you?"

"Emrick Maxwell," Alana said in a strangled whisper. "Tommy's twin."

"What?" Jack turned to her in shock. "You told me he died."

"She hoped I had," Emrick said. "But the truth is strong. You can hide it, but you can't kill it with a lie."

"I was telling you the truth as I knew it." Alana balled her hands into fists and met Jack's incredulous stare. "He doesn't believe me. And now he's out for revenge."

Jack tried to stand and faltered. The men opposite him did not help him. "What did you do to the guard? Kill him?" he asked them.

The men ignored Jack. They discussed their plans until finally Emrick gestured to Alana. "Get up. I need you to go up to the house." He took a step. "You're not to tell anyone there that you saw me, understand?"

"What are you going to do? I hate Lynton as much as you do, but I won't stand by and let you kill him. Tomas wouldn't want that," Alana said.

"You have no idea what Tomas would want," Emrick replied. "Forget all about me, like you did before."

She struggled to her feet and motioned to Jack. "What about him? He needs a doctor."

"If you want your friend to survive this night, keep your mouth shut." Emrick gestured to his bodyguard. "Take the reporter back to the car. Make sure he stays there."

"Now wait a minute," Jack said.

The huge man grabbed Jack by one arm, wrenched it behind him, and dragged him into the brush.

Alana's sight dimmed as the sky above her swirled into red and pink and purple clouds. She wondered if she was going to faint and grabbed Emrick's arm to steady herself. He flinched and shook it off.

"I won't say anything about you. But please promise you won't harm Jack," she pleaded.

The young stranger's eyes stilled. Alana thought she saw a flash of pity there. Not for her, but for what, she had no idea.

"You are in no position to ask for favors," he replied. "Start walking."

With a last, desperate glance at the empty area where Jack had been, Alana headed up the road.

# # #

The miserable hulk, smelling of gasoline and lunchmeat, had used a metal chain to anchor Jack by his left arm to the car handle in the back seat of the Cadillac. It was all Jack could do not to vomit. When the thug finally backed out of the car and disappeared into the woods, Jack exhaled and considered his options.

He had to free himself and find Alana. Jack peered out the car window, his eyes focused on the stand of trees she and her newly found brother had disappeared into. There was no movement, no glitter of reflected light, no hint the dawn was due to break in an hour.

His eyes raced around the car's interior. There was a box-like compartment in front of him. He fiddled with the lid and it popped up, revealing a flask, a small zipped bag, and bandages. Frowning, he cracked open the flask with one hand and took a gulp. The whiskey burned his throat and he shuddered.

He put the flask back in the box and opened the zippered pouch. Inside were damp clean cloths and a black leather glove identical to the one Emrick Maxwell wore.

In the dim light, Jack peered at it closely. It was soft and supple, but oddly, the three middle fingers were stitched together. He pressed his fingers against the section and pulled out a cylinder of wood. Finger-sized, it was stuck in the compartment where the middle fingers should have been.

"What the hell?" He stuck the glove in his pocket and peered into the darkness. There was still no sign of any movement. He no longer felt pain in his leg but the muscles in his back burned with every movement. He felt suddenly as he had during the war, listening for the enemy, ignoring the discomfort of his body as he made plans to do whatever was needed to stay alive.

He had to get out of the car and up to the house. Jack unzipped his fly and reached into the leg brace. The gun, tiny as a toy, was lodged against his calf. He drew it out and zipped his pants back up. He hoped it was loaded and that Teddy Wentz would not have given it to him if its only purpose was to intimidate.

He checked the chamber. It held two.41 caliber bullets. He

knew from experience they would move slow and work well only in close quarters. But one would give him a chance to get out of the plush jail he was trapped in.

Staring at the chain that bound him, Jack considered the angle of impact and wondered what the odds were that the burning lead might ricochet off the metal and kill him instantly.

He would bet they were high.

Jack placed the narrow barrel up against the chain, angled toward the floor, and pulled the trigger.

# # #

Alana stepped up the stairs of Lynton's home. She slipped on the second one from the top but caught herself before she fell. She looked back, giving a weak wave before turning away and walking to the front door.

"Alana! My god, what's happened? How did you get here?" Lynton rushed out.

She slumped against him. The industrialist peered into the haze. "Who is out there?" he shouted. When no one replied he ushered her inside.

"My god, Alana! Where have you been for the last two days?" Lynton stared at her in bewilderment.

Alana said nothing.

"Are you okay?" Lynton put his hand on her shoulder, but she shrugged it off.

She moved away from him but stopped short when she saw the man standing between her and the living room. It was Jasper Meeks; an attorney she had met at several social occasions for the foundation.

He looked stunned at the sight of her.

Behind him were two other men she didn't know. They struck her as cops out of uniform, burly and unfriendly.

"Do you know about Tommy?" Alana wrapped her arms around her torso, shivering, and turned to confront her step-brother.

"Yes. I was at the hospital for hours tonight, but he passed after I left." Lynton's voice broke. "I'm sorry, Alana."

Her lips felt as if they were bleeding. "Sorry? You're sorry? For what, for sending him to that monster?"

"Who are you talking about?"

"Preminger. He and his horrible partner, Brandt, killed Tommy! Did you see him, Lynton? Did you see what they did to him?" With clenched fists, she advanced on him.

He grabbed her by the wrists. "What are you talking about? Tomas died from natural causes. In the last two days his kidneys failed and he developed a massive skin infection. The police told me Robinson was driving him to the emergency room, but they were involved in an accident of some kind, and it made everything worse."

"What about Robinson? Is he okay?"

"I don't know. He's in the hospital. But no one *killed* Tommy! His organs were failing and his lungs filled with fluid. This setback was all a result of his paralysis. That's what killed him, Alana."

"Liar!" she screamed and tried to wrest away from him.

"Don't yell at her, Lynton. Can't you see she's under the influence of something?" Meeks placed a hand on the small of Alana's back. "Come with me, dear. Lynton is as devastated about Tomas as you are. And he's been mad with worry over you. Can you tell us where you've been for the last day and a half?"

"No."

"The police are looking for you," Lynton said. "You need to tell us what's been going on. I went and spoke to your Indian guru and he said terrible things were going on in your life. You should have told me, Alana. And you need to tell me now. Jasper can help us."

"I can't remember anything." She pulled on her hair. "I can't remember anything except that Tommy is dead!"

"You can't remember?" Lynton stared at the nurses' uniform. "What are you wearing?"

"I don't know." Her mind emptied and she felt as if she might fall over from the weight of her head.

"I think you better get her into bed," the attorney said. "She's in no shape to say anything useful. I'll handle the police when they show up. We still have time to handle everything."

"Okay." Gently Lynton took Alana by the arm. "Come with me. You need to rest."

"No!" Alana saw one of the men in the hall move toward her. "My god, what is going on? That man has a gun."

"Go back outside and walk the perimeter," Jasper shouted at the two men. "You should have found Miss Maxwell when she was *outside*."

"I told you we thought we saw a blonde woman near the house an hour ago," the red-haired man replied. "You didn't believe us."

"I didn't believe you because you didn't produce her," Jasper shot back.

Alana ran out of energy at that moment and nearly fell, but Lynton caught her. "Dear God, Jasper, call a doctor. I'm going to take her to her room."

"Preminger is due any minute," he replied in a low voice. "He can help."

"Jesus, no. Didn't you hear what she said? She'll get hysterical if she sees him. She's blaming him for Tommy's ..." He sighed and stared at Alana, whose eyes were closed. "Losing Tommy... I don't know what's going to happen to her now."

"We'll help her, Lynton," Meeks said. "But all hell is going to break loose soon. The police and the newspapers are going to be clamoring about the rumors connecting her to the vigilante story, especially after what happened downtown tonight."

"Screw the newspapers," Lynton raged. "And the police. I warned the chief that I would not allow her to be publicly implicated in that mess. And I'll sue any paper into the ground if they mention her name in connection with that maniac blonde. There's not any plausible reason she was involved with that bloody mess with Robinson and Tomas tonight."

"They were found in her car. And a woman fitting her description was seen by multiple witnesses," the lawyer said. "There was also a gun at the scene the police are checking fingerprints on." He shook his head. "There is a lot of circumstantial evidence to tie her to the crimes."

"Alana would never hurt Robinson." Lynton picked her up in his arms, clutching her limp body against him. "You need to find out what really happened. The cops are looking for a scapegoat, but she's not it. Do you understand me?"

"Yes." Meeks looked at his watch. "Dr. Preminger and General Conrad are due here any minute. I'll bring them in through the patio when they arrive and then head back downtown and meet with the police chief. Are you sure you still need to hold this meeting about his project tonight?"

"Yes. I'm going to DC in two days to make recommendations to the Secretary of Defense." Lynton looked down at Alana. "Let me go get her settled."

"Of course."

Lynton tenderly carried Alana, pale and still in his arms, down the hallway.

CHAPTER TWENTY-NINE

J ack crept closer to the open French doors at the rear of Lynton Maxwell's home. Inside he heard men's voices. He ducked into the plantings against the stucco wall and chanced a look through the windows, stunned to see Jasper Meeks speaking with Lynton Maxwell. There were two others present. The man in an army uniform looked like the general Jack had met on his first visit to this house.

Was his name Conrad?

The third guest, standing under the Maxwell family painting, he recognized from photographs. It was Ernest Preminger.

Jack turned and stared into the morning shadows behind him. Emrick and his henchman were out there somewhere. From the tree line he had watched them circle around to the front of the house five minutes before, but now he had no idea where they were.

Jack flattened himself against the wall. Alana was in the house somewhere. Silently he cursed his decision to bring her to her step-brother's house. If Maxwell and Preminger were inside, it meant the industrialist could be colluding with the quack that had drugged and hypnotized Alana. Her step-brother may even be complicit in Brandt's experiments on Tomas Maxwell.

He should have taken her directly to the cops. He could have put Jimmy Glass in touch with the Swami and Wanda Keppler, who would confirm the fact that Alana had confided in them about being drugged by Preminger.

His shoe hit a half-buried rock and pain exploded in Jack's bad leg. He nearly lost his balance but clenched his teeth, and the spasm passed. He had misjudged Maxwell. The man had seemed honorable and empathetic when he spoke about the horror of war, but all the while he may have been allowing his own family to be exploited for profit.

Jack slipped the derringer out of his coat pocket. He had one shot left.

He risked another look into the house. Meeks shook hands with the General and then walked out of the room. The voices of the three remaining men rose in pitch and volume. Jack settled into the shadows and watched as Lynton crossed to the bar and poured himself a scotch. He needed to get into the house and find Alana, but he had to first discover what was going on.

Lynton addressed Preminger and the General. "I appreciate you both coming out here in the middle of the night. This is the only time I could see you, so why don't you both take a seat?"

They settled across from him.

"I'm sure you're anxious for Dr. Preminger to share his final results," General Conrad said. "But first…"

Lynton held up his hand. "Let me ask the questions." He stared at Preminger. "Before we discuss your research, I want to know what the hell drugs you've been prescribing to my sister. She's strung out like a heroin-addict and can't remember as much as her name tonight."

"What?" Conrad's eyes widened and he too turned to the portly doctor. "Have you been acting as Alana Maxwell's physician?"

Preminger put his cigarette in the ashtray beside him as the kerosene lamp on the table flickered. "Ah, you mean, for her headaches?" he replied. "Yes, I have been treating Mr. Maxwell's sister for chronic migraines."

"How have you had time for private patients?" The General did not sound pleased.

"Answer my question. What drugs did you give her?" Lynton pressed.

Preminger took a deep breath. "Why don't I give you both a complete overview of my work these last few months, both as it regards my research into protocols for developing more efficient fighting forces, and my work with paralysis patients. Then I will be glad to answer any peripheral questions about Alana. Or poor, dear Tomas." Preminger blinked. "I was sorry to be notified by the hospital earlier that your brother lost his fight and passed tonight, Mr. Maxwell. Please accept my condolences."

"What?" the General said. "Tomas died? My condolences, Maxwell. Do you want to postpone this meeting?"

"No." Lynton took another drink. "Continue."

From his vantage point outside on the patio, Jack thought the industrialist seemed oddly calm. But dangerous. He gripped the whiskey tumbler like a weapon.

Jack scanned the back acreage again for any sign that Emrick Maxwell and his man were in the area, but he saw nothing moving. He tuned back into the conversation in the den.

"...the focus of my life's work has been research into reversing severe paralysis in the limbs," Preminger was saying. "I felt I had a good prospect with your brother, and I made time for this, at your request. Both before and during the war, I ran tests on hundreds of volunteers to learn more about the regenerative capabilities of the human body, as well as the mind. I learned that in concert, certain drugs and stimulation could overcome extreme injury. But what neither of you knows is that I also utilized your sister, Alana, as a test subject. I told her it was to help design a vaccine to cure Tomas of his paralysis, but in fact, it was to advance my secret research for the department of defense."

Lynton gasped. "What?"

"Alana did not want you to know she has been participating in research with a much bigger scope." Preminger wiped his face with his handkerchief and stuffed it back into his jacket.

"Participating in research? What are you talking about?" Conrad bellowed. "Who gave you permission to test your theories on live subjects?"

"No one. I made that decision myself, and for a good reason."

"Are you mad?" Conrad got up and loomed over Preminger. "I understood your work was theoretical, based on data from the pharmaceutical companies, along with statistics from the unethical research carried out by the Nazis during the war."

"I admit I misled you about that aspect," Preminger replied. "In my tests now, I administered a combination of barbiturates, vitamins, hormones, and an experimental hallucinogen called LSD-25 to Alana, along with a program of action-suggestion during periods of hypnosis. She proved to be a stellar subject, both for what she could and could not do under the influence. Studying her capability to follow my direction allowed me to complete the last of my work, which, when implemented, will guarantee American military dominance into the next century." Preminger smiled. "I know we all share that goal."

Outside, Jack clenched his fist around his gun. The shock and dismay on Conrad and Maxwell's faces didn't match the fury in his gut. It was gratifying to know his speculation about Preminger's work was accurate, but all he wanted to do was to throttle the man who had abused Alana, Paul Baldwin, and Tomas, and God knew how many other people.

"But why in god's name did you use my sister for this?" Lynton walked toward Preminger.

"Why?" The doctor folded his arms across his fat chest. "To be blunt, I needed a civilian participant whose discretion could be guaranteed. The most problematic issues with human guinea pigs not under the control of the military are that they often leak information to unfortunate sources. With Alana, I was confident that you would take steps to protect her from, eh, the repercussions of the study."

"What kind of repercussions?" Conrad demanded.

Lynton interrupted. "What did you make her do?"

"Nothing. I assure you that no one can make anyone do anything against their will, Mr. Maxwell. I have proven that many times with my use of hypnosis. With your sister, I simply amplified instincts which were already present. Having said that, however, there will be criminal inquiries into the collateral damage of certain activities connected to this stage of my experiments." He took a deep breath. "But I am sure a man of your stature can quash them. Will quash them. After all, no one of any importance was harmed."

"Harmed? Who was harmed?" Lynton demanded. "I have no idea what you're talking about."

"This is outrageous." The General stood next to Lynton, both men staring at Preminger. "Spit it out. What have you done? If you've broken any laws, I'll have you brought up on charges."

"No, you won't." Preminger's voice was calm. "As for what I've done, I have proven I can remove the fear of dying from any person and replace it with the discipline to face down their enemy. I've shown through the weakest human vessel, a woman, that I can create a warrior who will never waver. I have engineered a template we can use to build a super fighter that will make the United States army unbeatable."

Jack stepped out of the shadows, gripping the gun. If he went into the house, he might not have the chance to get off a shot at all, but he had to do something.

"Unbeatable?" the General bellowed. "Are you mad?"

Preminger lumbered to his feet, grasping his hands together behind him. "General Conrad. Mr. Maxwell. During the last war, I had the opportunity to test many combinations of new drugs on three groups of soldiers. Drugs that were designed by the brilliant pharmacologist Gerhard Orzechowski, who under the direction of the Third Reich's Vice-Admiral, Hellmuth Heye, discovered that compound extractions which included cocaine, painkillers and an amazing substance called Pervitin, created soldiers who could beat any army in the world. The drugs kept them alert and gave them unheard of levels of energy and strength. They required less sleep and nourishment and fought with a level of ferocity that approached the mythic.

"While the results of that work were promising, it took until now to get to the point where it works."

"What works?" Lynton demanded.

"I created a perfect soldier. One who kills more efficiently than any man who took the field of battle before." He smiled broadly. "My prototype has more than proven my theories."

"Prototype?" Conrad said. "What prototype?"

"You read the papers," Preminger said, his eyes bright. "I created a killing machine called Thrill Girl. She acts without fear or mercy, all by my design."

"You created a murderess to prove your theories?" Conrad's voice was furious. "This is preposterous."

"It's true," the doctor sputtered. He was suddenly aware that his words were not being received with the proper congratulatory response. "And I have the film and photographs of Thrill Girl in action to prove it. They're included in my final report, which I gave to General Conrad on the drive over here. I'm sure the DOD will share them with you. Once they've agreed to a contract and paid me for my work."

Lynton grabbed Preminger. "You sick bastard. You were supposed to help my family! Now Tomas is dead, and you think you can convince me to keep quiet about what you've done by turning some woman into a freak?"

"Thrill Girl isn't *some woman*. When Alana..." Preminger said, but before he could finish, Lynton punched him in the face and sent him crashing into the wall.

General Conrad pulled a revolver from his jacket and pointed it at Lynton. "Stop it. Step back and leave him alone, Lynton. We need to get to the bottom of this!"

Lynton glared at the gun but stepped away from Preminger. "What about Tomas? What did you do to him to turn him into what I saw at the hospital tonight? He looked like a monster, for Christ's sake."

Preminger crawled to his feet and steadied himself against the fireplace. "I understand you are shocked. But if you'll look at my proposal, you'll understand everything I did regarding Alana, Mr. Maxwell. As for Tomas, I had nothing to do with his decline. I learned in the last few days that my associate, Josef Brandt, was experimenting on Tomas, giving your brother unauthorized injections. But I have no idea what you're talking about when you say Brandt turned Tomas into a monster…"

"Not a monster," a male voice yelled from the hallway, silencing Preminger. "A *der Katzenjunge*. Have you heard of one of those, *Herr Doktor?*"

All three men turned in surprise to face the man who spoke.

Emrick Maxwell stepped into the den, followed by Janus, who held a rifle pointed directly at Preminger.

"Put the gun down, General," Emrick ordered.

"Who the hell are you?" he replied.

"Put it down!"

The general put the gun on the table.

Emrick stared at Preminger. "You're lying. You deliberately allowed Brandt to experiment on Tomas Maxwell. And other paralysis victims."

"I did not!" Preminger wiped his brow and cut his gaze to Lynton, who seemed frozen in disbelief at the young man's sudden appearance.

"Yes, you did." Emrick pointed his leather-clad right hand to the General. "Why don't you tell them about the other men you and Brandt poisoned over the years with your vile drugs? Soldiers that you brutalized during the war. And then other men you preyed on."

"What's this man talking about, Preminger?" Conrad demanded.

"And do not leave out what you personally did to Paul Baldwin," Emrick shouted. He and Janus moved closer.

"Who is Paul Baldwin?" Lynton and Conrad asked together.

Preminger's face twitched as if he had received a mild electrical shock. "Paul Baldwin was among a group of young men of Austrian descent born with genetic inconsistencies which caused paralysis. He served a key part of our experiments. I was going to explain to him before we were ambushed by this, this man." He glared at Emrick. "I don't know who you are, sir, but I'm sure the authorities will be interested in finding out how you know about a secret project."

"I'm sure they would be much more interested in talking to you, *Doktor*. Why don't you explain about your dead wife, and how Josef Brandt's corpse is now stored in an office you own."

"What?" Preminger flailed his arms and turned to Lynton and Conrad. "This man is obviously a murderer. It's true my wife was killed two days ago. And if he says Josef is dead, well, he must have killed him too!"

"Stop lying, Preminger!" a woman screamed.

Jack gripped the edge of the doorway, trying to see who had arrived. The woman materialized like a ghost from the dark hallway, dressed in white silk, a close-fitting hat with a red feather perched on her blonde hair. She held a large caliber pistol in front of her, which she kept pointed at Preminger.

Alana. "No," Jack gasped, stepping into the room.

"What are you doing here?" Lynton demanded in shock.

Preminger took Jack's appearance as a chance to run, but Janus tripped him, and Preminger collapsed on the floor.

"You killed my brother, and now you're a dead man," the blonde cried out. Standing in the doorway, she leveled the gun and fired two rounds.

The first smashed into Preminger's shoulder.

The second careened off course and blew up the oil lamp on the table, which immediately burst into flames.

# # #

Jack hurled himself to the ground as a third gunshot ruptured the night.

"Alana, no!" Lynton Maxwell screamed.

Jack crouched lower, struggling to see inside the room. The house was filling with smoke from the smoldering carpet and sofa. The woman ran directly past him, clutching the gun.

He struggled to his feet and chased after her. "Alana."

She turned, her eyes as empty as those of a corpse.

"Don't shoot. It's me, Jack." He held up his hands.

"You didn't help my brother at all. I'll kill you too, you bastard." She fired point blank at Jack. But the chamber was empty.

Another shot split the night, and the woman fell hard against Jack, knocking them both onto the slate patio. Her hat tumbled away, and she lay motionless beside him.

Jack got up on his knee and pulled her close, his heart racing. He had always been clearheaded under fire, but he had never had a woman he was half in love with shot in front of him.

His fingers trembled as he searched her face. "Alana. Alana, no. Please, stay with me."

The flames in the house were crackling aggressively behind him, but he stared only at the woman in his arms. She was bleeding profusely from the mouth, and the bodice of her silk dress was turning crimson from the bullet which had entered her back and come out through her chest.

Her red lips were slack; her brown eyes empty of light.

Jack touched her hair and gasped when it came off in his hand.

What the hell?

It was a wig. A blonde wig that covered the woman's softly curled brown hair.

Jack drew back in shock. Alana did not have brown eyes. Or brown hair.

"Alana!" Lynton came up behind him and shoved Jack aside, pulling the dead woman close. "Alana, oh my god. Don't die. Please don't die."

Jack gripped Lynton by the shoulder. "That's not Alana. It's Thrill Girl. Her name is Susan Baldwin." He felt as if he had been shot himself, weak with sorrow for the young woman Lynton clutched to his chest.

Both men stared at the dead girl's face.

"We need to go get Alana out of the house." Jack struggled to stand upright. "Now. Where is she?"

"Follow me," Lynton said, gently lying Thrill Girl's body on the ground.

CHAPTER THIRTY

E mrick crouched against the sofa as smoke thickened above where he and Janus lay. They heard Preminger groaning by the fireplace. But he couldn't stop to finish him off now. He had a more important target.

"Preminger! Where are you?" Conrad yelled. "Everyone get outside, now!"

Emrick motioned for Janus to head for the front of the house, and the two of them crawled down the hallway until they could stand and run out the door.

Lynton's bodyguards lay bound and unconscious on the driveway where they had left them.

"Emrick!" Janus waved the rifle he carried. "Come this way."

"No, we need to go around the back. I want Lynton." The air was acrid with ash billowing on the dry California breeze. Emrick struggled to breathe as he and Janus circled to the back of the house.

In the distance, the sounds of sirens grew.

Emrick stopped Janus at the edge of the patio, pulling him into the stand of Italian cypress. He heard the flames rustling near the open door as the fire devoured everything in its path.

Janus pointed. Emrick saw Conrad drag Preminger out of the

house and onto the patio. It was clear the general had not noticed Jack Curran kneeling a few yards away on the grass next to Lynton Maxwell, the men flanking either side of a woman's body.

"That's the girl who killed those men that night in Hollywood," Janus said.

"Yes. Susan Baldwin," Emrick replied. "Paul Baldwin's sister." Emrick flashed on the memory of her merciless quickness and the frenzy of her moves as he watched her from the roof of the warehouse as she ruthlessly killed the two men who attacked her last week.

He now understood why Preminger photographed her, egging her on from the sidelines as she cut the two men to pieces. The doctor had flashed a light at her before and after the murders. Three quick bursts into her eyes froze her into a trance as Preminger and Brandt scurried like rats and removed the weapons from the scene.

Moments later, as Emrick watched her, Susan came to and looked around, unaware it was she who had killed the men lying at her feet, their lifeblood splattered on her high-heels.

Janus raised the rifle, aiming at Lynton's skull, but Emrick grabbed his arm. "Wait," he whispered. "I want to be closer."

Suddenly, a second woman ran out of the burning house and into the middle of the patio. She carried a huge silver pistol clutched in both outstretched arms.

"Alana," Emrick murmured. "Don't shoot her."

Janus lowered the rifle. "We should leave now."

"No," Emrick said. "Not until I finish this."

# # #

Jack gasped as Alana raced out of the French doors onto the patio, pointing a gun at Preminger.

"You bastard! You killed my brother." Steadily Alana closed on the wounded doctor leaning against the patio wall.

Preminger had lost his glasses, and his shoulder and arm were covered in blood from the shot Susan had fired at him. General Conrad stepped in front of Preminger, his voice calm and commanding when he spoke. "Drop the gun, Miss Maxwell."

"He killed Tommy!" Alana's voice was agonized. "He's going to pay for that right now."

"You won't shoot me," Preminger said, moving slowly behind the general. "You don't have it in you. Susan Baldwin was Thrill Girl because she fought to the death to save her family. She loved her brother more than you loved yours, Miss Maxwell."

"I will kill you or die trying." Alana bared her teeth and stretched her arms out stiff.

The last pieces of the Thrill Girl puzzle clicked into place inside Jack's head. He tensed, his eyes on Alana, remembering that Trixie had told him he had seen a dark-haired woman the night Susan Baldwin was attacked, and that he had not seen a blonde woman at all.

Preminger had not been able to turn Alana Maxwell into a killer, but he had succeeded with Susan, destroying her entire family in the process. Jack fired his last bullet in the air. "Stop it. Everyone stand still."

Alana swerved toward him and met his eyes.

"You're not a murderer, Alana. Drop the gun," he ordered.

"I don't care if I die," she shouted. "But I'm going to get rid of this monster!"

"You've got another brother to think of," Jack pleaded. "You've got the future to do good things for others. What kind of karma are you creating if you murder, even if you murder someone who deserves it? Tomas wouldn't want you to do this. Come here, please."

She froze. With a low moan, Alana dropped the gun and ran to him.

Jack kept the derringer pointed at the three men in the middle of the patio and hugged her trembling body against his chest.

Lynton took a step toward her. "Alana, I'll take care of everything. Please, come here…"

"Get away from me!" she shrieked.

"Don't come any closer," Jack warned.

"That's a two-shot Remington," the General said to Jack.

"And you've only got one bullet left."

"One bullet is all it takes to kill a man, even a general. Stay where you are." Jack held the empty gun on Conrad and inched backward, Alana molded against his side.

"Think this through, Curran." The general folded his arms over his chest. "You're not involved in this mess. Why not take off? You don't want to be around when the police arrive, which will be very soon, judging from the sound of those sirens."

"You would shoot me in the back before I took two steps," Jack said.

"I could." The general yanked a revolver hidden behind his back, smiling like a magician with a card up his sleeve. "But I'll give you a break, war hero. Preminger is an immoral bastard, but he's done important research. Thousands of soldiers will be saved because of what he proved. I need to get him out of here before the police get here. We'll deal with him. Just drop the gun and leave the girl."

"No one is going to work with that Nazi, or forgive what he did with his experiments," Jack said. "And your career will be dead too, once it comes out what Preminger and Brandt did with your backing. No one will believe you didn't know what was going on." He pointed the pistol directly at the General's face. "I didn't fight for people like you. You're a traitor to everything America stands for."

The sirens blared louder, and Jack heard several cars crunching up the rock drive toward the house. "We need to go, Alana. Just walk with me, okay?" He spoke softly against the side of her head.

Alana looked up and spotted Susan's body on the lawn a few feet away. "Oh my god, who is that?"

"It's Thrill Girl," he whispered.

"But I'm Thrill Girl," she moaned. "I killed all those people."

Jack realized she was fading back into the drug-induced confusion of earlier. "No, you didn't. Just keep holding onto me. We're going to walk away from here. Okay?" Jack kept his eye, and his gun, on Conrad and Preminger.

At that moment, Emrick and his burly bodyguard strode across the patio, emerging from the bushes behind Preminger.

"Lynton!" Emrick yelled.

The industrialist turned. Ash fell over all of them like grey snow.

Lynton waved his hand back and forth as if he could clear it away. "Who are you?" he said.

"Don't you recognize me? I'm the babe you left for dead all those years ago." Emrick grabbed the rifle from Janus and pointed it at his step-brother.

"Emrick?" Lynton's voice was incredulous.

"Hold it right there." General Conrad ordered.

Preminger bolted from behind Conrad and tried to grab the pistol. The General fired point-blank at Preminger's forehead, then turned and fired a second time at Emrick, hitting him in the left side.

Roaring in pain, Emrick dropped the rifle and ran at the general. Janus lunged and retrieved the rifle with a banshee yell, as Emrick tackled Conrad to the ground. The general dropped his revolver, and it went off, the bullet fracturing off the slate, a piece of it catching Lynton in the shoulder.

The industrialist fell moaning onto the flagstones.

Alana screamed as Jack dragged her off the patio. He turned and headed for the side of the house, but she broke away from him.

"Stop it, stop it!" she cried as she ran to Emrick and Conrad grappling and punching one another. Jack followed, dragging his leg. He was struggling to keep track of the danger, but all he could think of was the blonde woman running toward it.

Janus pointed the rifle at the pair on the ground, yelling to Emrick that he couldn't get a clean shot. Emrick punched Conrad in the face, and both men fell on their sides. Alana jumped on the General's back, but Janus pulled her off by her hair, shoving her aside like a rag doll as he viciously kicked Conrad a kick in the ribs.

Emrick grabbed the general's revolver. He turned and pointed the weapon at Alana, who froze, and then pointed it at Lynton.

Alana barreled into Emrick, knocking him down as he fired.

The bullet came across the lawn and struck Jack in the hip.

Moaning, he fell to his knees. "Alana, come back," he called. But she stayed where she was.

Janus leaned down and dragged Emrick to his feet and howled at her. "Don't follow us."

She grabbed Janus by the arm, but he shook her off. "Get away!" he roared.

"Alana," Jack yelled.

With his one free hand, Janus pivoted and pointed the rifle at where Lynton lay crumpled on the patio. Emrick hung onto his friend's strong shoulder, bent over at the waist, blood dripping from his wound.

Suddenly Alana ran to where Lynton had collapsed and shielded him with her arms outstretched. "Tell him not to shoot, Emrick. It wasn't Lynton's decision to take you away from our family. It was our father. He was ashamed of your defects, and he was sick and weak from his own illness. But you're strong now, stronger than he ever was. Strong enough not to kill!"

"Step out of my way," Janus ordered. He pulled the trigger back.

"Emrick, please, for Tommy's sake, no more killing." Tears ran down Alana's face as she stood her ground.

"Don't shoot," Emrick said to Janus.

Janus lowered the gun.

Jack watched as Alana's only remaining relative walked to her. Suddenly Emrick lunged, a black glove closed around her throat. "Lynton Maxwell stole my life!" He gestured to the unconscious Lynton. "He stole my brother, my family. He stole you from me. He wanted me to die."

"He didn't." Alana put her hands on Emrick's glove, struggling to speak. "He took care of us after mother died. Lynton protected me. He helped Tomas. You have me now, Emrick. Don't let hate and revenge end what's left of our family."

Jack lay on the ground and remembered Lynton Maxwell's

words about revenge.

How it was the strongest human motivator. *Maybe tonight Alana will prove him wrong.*

Emrick dropped his hand from Alana's throat and clutched his injured side. Their identical blue eyes met. "You look like our mother," Emrick said, his voice raw. "How did she allow them to just throw me away? How could she give up on me?"

"Father lied. She didn't know you had survived past your birth, Emrick. She loved you and mourned you every day."

Sirens blared at the entrance of Lynton's mansion, and Jack heard men shouting. A window blew out from the upstairs, showering everyone on the patio below with glass.

"Emrick, we need to leave now!" Janus walked to them and pushed Alana away.

"No. Let me come with you," she pleaded. "Wherever you're going. Please."

"No!" Janus pushed her again, and she almost fell, but Emrick steadied her.

"Stop it!" Emrick ordered Janus.

Jack saw the huge man's face cloud with rage.

"Help me with him," he ordered Alana.

She draped Emrick's arm over her shoulder, and the three headed toward the house.

"There's a shortcut through the kitchen, on the other side of the house. We can exit to the garage from there," Alana shouted. "We'll take one of Lynton's cars down the back way."

"Alana, wait!" Jack tried to get up, but his shattered leg was useless. He clenched his teeth as the heat from the fire scorched his face.

Alana turned. "Don't try to follow us, Jack," she screamed. "Thank you, thank you for everything!" She touched her hand to her lips and threw him a kiss, the next instant disappearing into the burning house.

She won't be safe with him, Jack thought. Emrick had carried a grudge against her for his entire life. Alana was foolish, in the thrall of karma and redemption. But she should not trust him.

Panting, Jack crawled to the edge of the patio. He was heading to Lynton when suddenly he was grabbed roughly from behind. He turned to throw a punch and found himself face to face with Quentin Deville.

"Good god, once a war hero, always a war hero?" Quentin stared at Jack's pants in horror. He pointed. "Is your leg even attached to your body anymore?"

"What are you doing here?"

"Rescuing you, it appears." He surveilled the scene around them. "Can you walk at all? My car's on the other side of the property in the trees. It's about a hundred yards away."

"I'll try." He fought off a wave of dizziness.

Quentin pulled Jack to his feet. A wall of smoke now cloaked the mansion from view.

"But first we need to go after Alana," Jack whispered. "She went inside...."

"I saw her leave you here and run off with those two men." Quentin pressed hard on his arm. "She made her choice, Jack. If the police find us here, neither of us will be able to talk our way out of this mess." Quentin surveyed the general's motionless body, Preminger's corpse, and Susan Baldwin. "Are they all dead?"

"I think so."

"What about Lynton Maxwell?"

Jack looked across the flagstone to where Lynton lay against the outer wall of the patio. "He's still alive."

"The police will be here any moment. They'll help him." Quentin pulled Jack against him and glanced nervously at the fire. "We need to go right now. Try and stay conscious. I don't know if I can carry you all the way."

Jack began to shake. His body was shutting down, going into shock. "Jesus Christ, Quentin. Preminger did more terrible things that we thought. And Thrill Girl isn't Alana. She was Susan Baldwin."

Quentin kept them moving, half-carrying, half- dragging Jack along. "Don't talk. We'll hash it all out over drinks tomorrow."

"How did you find me?" he whispered.

"Like a great reporter I know, I followed my nose. I figured you found Alana, and that you would bring her to the only man who could protect her. Keep moving your good leg, Jack. You can do this."

Jack looked up. It was morning now. Streaks of orange and pink against an aqua sky cast the limbs of the lemon trees at the edge of Lynton Maxwell's estate into relief. His mind returned to the war in Italy. To other mornings that had looked as glorious as this one, to other battlefields that had smelled of death and smoke.

He clung to Quentin, and they made their way across the wide expanse of lawn. "What will happen to her?"

"Alana? If she lives through this, Meeks and the feds will protect her. They won't let the real story get out," Quentin said. "Meeks admitted a couple of days ago that some in the government were complicit in Preminger's research."

The rhythmic, powerful smack of a police helicopter's blades above made Jack cringe. "If we get out of here, we need to tell the public the truth about Thrill Girl. I'll write that final column…"

"A hero to the end," the publisher replied. "First you've got to stay alive. I'm going to carry you the rest of the way." Quentin hauled Jack over his shoulder and stumbled down the hillside. They fell again, but Jack felt nothing. He tumbled onto his back, the inferno that was consuming Maxwell's house lit the landscape for miles.

"Alana," Jack shouted with his last remnant of strength.

At that moment, the back of the house blew out. The roof crashed onto the ground around them as the patio disappeared into a wall of smoke and haze.

His last coherent thought was that if Alana and her brother had not made it out of the house, they were dead.

EPILOGUE

June 1953
Two years later

Jack stared at the front page of *The Los Angeles Times'* entertainment section for a long moment before folding it in half and tossing it onto the table next to him.

He made a strangled sound in his throat and leaned back against the lounge chair.

The much anticipated new movie, *The Griffith Park Monster*, had premiered at Grumman's Chinese Theatre the night before. There was a picture of his ex-coworker, Lucy Cherry, the film's screenwriter, standing beside producer Sydney Goldblum and the movie's stars.

According to Miss Cherry, her script was based on the "true" story of a poor local girl named Susan Baldwin who had gone on a shooting spree in Hollywood after suffering a mental breakdown over the death of her brother, who had died of polio.

In the movie, a veterinarian, hired by the police to help find a rabid bobcat terrorizing the citizens living the golden life near Griffith Park, befriends poor Susan. With his help and affection, Susan overcomes her murderous depression. She agrees to stop killing male muggers and make a full confession to the police. But that very evening the star-crossed lovers decide to take a romantic moonlit walk at the observatory where they are killed by the bobcat, which has just given birth.

To offspring that may stalk the city still...

"What a load of crap," Jack muttered. "But good for you, sweetheart." He almost meant it.

He crossed his arms over his chest and considered that plot twist. Sydney Goldblum must be planning to put out a sequel if the movie did well. Jack could see the title in lights, *Son of the Griffith Park Monster*.

Jack closed his eyes, welcoming the burn of the sun on his face. The prospect of the movie had infuriated him when he first read of it, but he no longer cared how badly they mangled the story.

Or misrepresented the truth. It didn't change it.

Goldblum had paid Quentin $50,000 for the rights to use Jack's columns, and original notes for his Thrill Girl stories published in *The Eyes of LA*. Quentin had given Jack half of the money.

Deville had visited him in the rehab hospital a month after the fire, handing him a check and telling Jack that he was closing the newspaper and moving on. He was not going to publish a final story about Thrill Girl.

"Why not?" Jack had growled, his voice forever damaged by smoke inhaled that fateful night at the Maxwell mansion.

"What's the point? We don't know all the facts. Besides, you're in no shape to investigate any further. And from what I've seen printed in the other newspapers, the public is satisfied with the explanation they've been given by the police."

"But it's not the truth," Jack had declared.

"You don't know the truth. And neither do I." Quentin raised his thin eyebrows. "Nor will we. The government isn't going to ever release the full facts of the Thrill Girl case to the public. There are too many people, with more power than our little newspaper ever had that don't want the sordid story told."

"So that's it? You're giving up?" Jack had replied.

"I'm stepping aside, but who knows? The truth has a way of crawling into the light eventually. At the right time. Maybe we'll discuss this again someday," he added quietly.

"Not fucking likely," Jack retorted.

The publisher calmly went on to share the news that Lucy

Cherry was working for the San Fernando Valley Tribune, and had been given an exclusive by the police on the fire that had claimed several lives at Lynton Maxwell's estate.

"Her story reports several illegal aliens, workmen whose names are unknown, were killed. Along with a female cook."

"That's how they covered up finding the bodies of Preminger, Josef Brandt, and General Conrad?" Jack shook his head in despair.

"All I know is what I read in the newspapers." Quentin had shrugged.

Jack squinted in the sunshine and let Quentin's sly words melt out of his brain. He regarded the stack of newsprint beside him, unable to stop his brain from running the past eighteen months of events through his brain. None of the real victims, dead or alive, were featured in The Griffith Park Monster movie. And Lucy Cherry's script made no mention of Alana Maxwell, Tomas, or the mysterious Emrick.

He wondered as he had too many times the last two years if Lucy knew about Alana's long-lost brother, Emrick. The blonde man with a claw-like hand, eyes that could see in pitch dark, and the grace and instincts of a predatory animal. Had she been told about Josef Brandt's obsession with *der Katzenjunge*? About Preminger's history with the Nazis, and his horror-filled research?

Did she realize that human men were monsters greater than anything the public had imagined after the killing at Griffith Park?

Lucy had called him when he was released from rehab and asked to meet, but he had turned her down. Told her he was moving back to Ohio to resume his teaching career.

The cash from Quentin had given him the ability to leave the land of fantasy and seek out the man he was before the war. But that man was nowhere to be found. Jack had not been able to burrow into small-town life in Akron or to return to teaching. After the lights and glitz and drama of the West Coast, it was a bad fit.

As Goldblum told him the night he turned down his offer of writing a treatment about Thrill girl, the world was a different place now than it was before the war, and there was no getting it back.

Jack had been back in California for three months now. His home was a rustic bungalow in Laurel Canyon that wasn't much bigger than his apartment in LA, but it had a pool. He needed it for exercise and swam one hundred laps in it every day.

After which he laid in the sun and did nothing.

As the sun baked down, Jack pictured the small office in the back of the house. In it stood a desk and the 1921 Remington typewriter he had used at *The Eyes of LA*. Beside it was two reams of paper.

Blank paper.

Jack had not written a word since that hellacious night in San Marino. Not the war novel that had been crawling around the folds of his brain for years. Not anything.

The urge to work was present every morning, but by the time he ate and did chores and swam, it was snuffed out by the reality that he did not have anything he wanted to write about.

He read – reams every day. Magazines, non-fiction books, every paper he could get his hands on. Journalism was changing and changing fast.

That thing called television was simulcasting radio shows, and the visual medium was starting to take shape. Moving images captured on film at news events were beginning to change the weight of the news, and the appearance of the story's participants was eliciting rawer emotion than attention to facts.

Jack ran his hands through his damp hair and shifted to his left side, his ribs uncomfortable against the straps on the lounge chair. He worried about the creep of entertainment nudging aside the factual purity of journalism. He feared reporters were going to be compromised by money and fame, and that the American reading public would never be told what they needed to hear about their leaders, their government, their lives.

With a sigh, Jack looked at his wristwatch. It was one o'clock. He wasn't going to work on anything today.

He closed his eyes again. Anxiety was omnipresent, immobilizing not only his limbs but his mind. It was like this every day. Not just when he thought about that night, that terrible night, but all the time. About 3 a.m. every morning he woke up in a sweat. It wasn't nightmares about the war, or even yearning to hold that cool, blue-eyed blonde of his dreams that disrupted his sleep. It was the dull, edgy feeling that he had lost himself.

"Mr. Curran?"

Jack started at the sound of the man's voice and turned toward the house. "Hey, man. Come on out. I'm by the pool."

Eddie Wentz stepped through the open sliding glass door. "I brought lunch." He lifted a bulging paper bag. "Roast beef. With a side of potato salad. Sound good?"

"It does." He sat up and shook Eddie's hand. In last few months, the young reporter had taken to dropping in. Jack enjoyed the visits but was exhausted when he left.

Eddie took the chair on the other side of the table. Despite the eighty degrees weather, he wore a black wool suit and necktie, paired with a heavy suede fedora.

"How's work going? Anything new on the headless woman?" Jack asked. Eddie had landed a job at *The Los Angeles Times* after the shuttering of *The Eyes*. He was doing well on the police beat.

Eddie shuddered and took his hat off. He handed a sandwich to Jack. "Nope. We still don't know who she is. Waiting on fingerprints from the F.B.I. But Detective Glass thinks she's from out of town."

"Why?" Jack bit into his sandwich.

"She's pale. No suntan." Eddie wiped his mouth and pushed his heavy black glasses up his nose. "And no toenail polish. Glass said all the women her age who live in LA paint their toenails in the summer."

"Sounds like good police work, as usual, from Glass."

Eddie nodded and opened the container of potato salad. He passed it to Jack. "He asked about you. If I knew where you went after you got out of the hospital last year."

"Yeah?" Jack kept his voice neutral. "What did you tell him?"

"I told him you moved to Akron."

"Lying to the police?" Jack smiled, but his face felt stiff.

"It wasn't a lie. You did move to Akron. You came back to LA, but like you always told me, don't give gratuitous information to cops." Eddie grinned.

Jack put down the container. He still didn't have much appetite. "That's good advice."

Eddie continued to eat for a few moments before saying in a casual tone, "Glass told me something interesting, by the way."

"Yeah?"

Eddie licked his fingers before wiping them on the paper napkin. "You remember Edward Robinson, Lynton Maxwell's chauffeur?"

Jack pictured the driver. When he woke up in the hospital the day after the fire, he had been more relieved to hear about Robinson's survival than his own. "Yeah."

"He went to see Glass a couple of days ago."

"About what?"

"He wanted to show him something he got in the mail."

Jack met Eddie's eyes. The kid stared at him intently. He knew Eddie was testing the waters, trying to see if Jack was willing to talk. About Thrill Girl.

Jack turned away. He and Eddie had one conversation about that night in San Marino when he was still in the hospital after the fire, but none since. Jack had told him everything he knew about Preminger, Susan, and Alana, and the identity of the man in the black leather glove, but had made it clear he wasn't going to speak about that night again.

Ever.

"Don't you want to know what he got in the mail?" Eddie asked

He did. Jack's lips tightened. "Shoot."

"An envelope. With a second envelope inside. Addressed to you." Eddie's eyes were big. "I guess whoever sent it didn't know where you were living now."

Jack clenched his jaw. "What's it say?"

"I don't know. It's not addressed to me. Read it yourself." Eddie held out an envelope for him to take. Satiny blue, it glimmered in the sunlight, the words *For Jack Curran, Reporter* was typed on the front.

With a jolt, Jack heard a blonde woman whisper inside his head about luck, karma, and what she was going to do to him next. "Who sent it to Robinson?"

"He doesn't know."

Jack snatched the envelope, which was sealed, and peered again at the typed words. He sighed and tossed it onto the table. "It's a fucking prank."

"Glass said the same thing to Robinson, but Robinson isn't convinced. The outer envelope it came in was posted from Italy."

"Italy?"

"I heard rumors Mr. Deville moved to Italy. Florence, I think. Have you heard that?" Eddie's voice was deadly serious.

The kid was digging. Jack exhaled in aggravation. "I heard London. Also Chicago." Only a fool would try and guess where the man with a thousand secrets had headed off to, he thought. "Who knows where he landed? Life goes on until it doesn't."

"It sure does." Eddie finished his sandwich, quiet for a few moments. "My buddy on the business desk wrote last week that Lynton Maxwell is in talks to sell his company." Eddie's eyes got bigger behind his glasses. "And Glass told me that Robinson said Maxwell moved back into his house in San Marino."

"He rebuilt the house?" Jack regretted immediately that he had taken the bait and shown any interest in the Maxwells.

"Yeah. Exactly like it was before the fire. Creepy thing to do, if you ask me. Wouldn't it be full of ghosts? I mean his sister--"

"—*Don't!*" Jack held up his hand abruptly. After a few moments, he brought it back down to his side. He inhaled and closed his eyes again, blotting out the sunshine, the satiny blue note, and Eddie's honest face.

He took a couple of deep breaths and pressed his chest. There had been lingering lung issues since the operation. He had suffered a clot, a close call.

"You okay, Mr. Curran?"

"Yeah, Eddie. I'm good." Jack opened his eyes and pointed toward the living room. "Can you go get my leg?"

"Ah, sure. Yeah. How did you get out here without it?"

"I hopped. Then I swam. *Then I bobbed.*"

Eddie had heard the bad joke several times but had the good grace to chuckle. He stood and dropped his napkin. He reached for it and knocked the table over, sending the lunch bag, sandwiches, and two cups of unopened coffee crashing onto the patio.

Jack started to laugh, a real laugh. He laughed until tears ran down his cheeks.

Eddie turned bright red and joined in. "I'm clumsy as an ox, I know. But you're not supposed to hop around. I heard the doc tell you that in the hospital, for cripes sake. That's how people fall and break a hip. If the wooden leg is uncomfortable, you're supposed to use your crutch."

"I hate crutches. The leg?"

Eddie peered at the sliding glass door. "Where is it?"

"It's in the kitchen. By the door. You're scared of my wooden leg, aren't you? Did you get traumatized by Pinocchio when you were a kid?"

"No!" Eddie's face got redder.

Jack wiped his eyes and swallowed a chuckle. "Give me a hand, buddy. We'll go together." He pushed up off the chaise and leaned on Eddie, and they went inside.

Jack sat on the chair by the sofa. He slipped off his Bermuda shorts and exchanged them for trousers he had tossed on the couch earlier, and slipped on a cotton shirt. Eddie returned from the kitchen and handed him the heavy prosthetic leg. Jack strapped it on.

After the fire, the doctors had operated several times in the hope they could save his leg, but the infection was too deep into the bone, and they amputated it. He was healed now, and able to move around okay, but he didn't like to think about it being gone. Sometimes at night he woke up and tried to stand, but fell in a heap.

The prosthetic was dressed in a black dress sock and leather shoe. "I need to get a sandal for this thing. I'm not this formal anymore," Jack joked.

"You need to wear it more. Every day. Does it hurt? I can take you to the VA anytime you want if you need to get it adjusted."

"It doesn't hurt. But I can't dance worth shit."

They both laughed, and Eddie sat on the sofa. Several moments passed. The younger man watched Jack with an expectant look on his face.

"So what's your take on Robinson's letter? Sent from Italy, huh?" Jack finally asked.

"Yeah." Eddie leaned forward, his arms resting on his knees. "Uncle Teddy went to Positano, near the Mediterranean once, before the war. Said the water is like liquid turquoise. Magic."

Jack adjusted the leg straps and pulled down his pant-leg to cover it. Before he made an effort to stand, he reached into his shirt pocket for cigarettes before he remembered he didn't smoke anymore.

Not since that night.

He stood and stared at the kid he trusted more than any other person he knew. "She's dead, Eddie. Alana Maxwell is dead. You know that, right?"

"That's what Glass told Robinson." Eddie blinked.

"What did the chauffeur say to that?"

"He asked Detective Glass if he was sure. The cop asked him what the hell he meant, was he sure? Robinson said he had never attended a funeral for Alana Maxwell, had never seen her dead body, and that it made him wonder. He asked Glass to swear she was dead."

"What did Glass say to that?" Jack's chest tightened.

Eddie's voice dropped. "He told Robinson to take the word of the coroner about who was dead and who wasn't if he knew what was good for him."

Neither man said anything for several moments.

"Did your Uncle ever ask Millie Hatchett about Alana's body?" Jack asked.

"He did. She told him the same thing that was in the press. That a badly charred woman's body was found at the scene, but as a Los Angeles medical examiner, she couldn't discuss the case with a civilian." Eddie raised his eyebrows. "She never would confirm how many men's bodies were found, either. Uncle Teddy told her that was a bullshit answer."

Jack knew the coroner should have found two women's bodies at the Maxwell house if Alana was dead. Susan Baldwin's and Alana's. But after what Quentin had revealed, it was obvious the scene was scrubbed to meet the needs of military bosses and the official story, not the public's right to know the truth.

"Did Glass keep the outside envelope?" Jack asked.

"No. He gave it back to Robinson. Robinson left the note addressed for you, and Glass gave that to me. Said it would save him a stamp to Akron."

"So the cops aren't going to look into it?"

"Glass said he didn't know what the note to you said and he didn't care. He has no time for wild goose chases about a case that's closed." Eddie fiddled with his tie, which had a spot of ketchup on it. "He also said Thrill Girl was your story." The reporter locked eyes with him. "And Alana Maxwell was your girl."

Jack looked away.

Eddie kept talking. "It's only a hunch, but I bet Detective Glass thinks you have more to write about the case. And that maybe you should."

"I'm not a journalist anymore." Jack pointed at him, bitterness flaming up from his gut. "The Thrill Girl story is done, Eddie. Most of the bad guys were killed, some good people were sacrificed, but that case is a muddy, dead trail of corruption and greed that no one has a chance of explaining now."

"Is that what you fought for during the war? For corrupt men to get away, literally, with murder? For the public to be kept in the dark? I mean, you saw what they did to Paul Baldwin with your own eyes!"

Jack leaned against the chair, the stump of his left thigh pinched uncomfortably against the prosthetic. "No one in the American military will ever again consider implementing a failed Nazi program to juice-up soldiers with drugs and hate and turn them into suicidal killers. And what I fought for was to get rid of Hitler. And we did." He crossed his arms over his chest. "Preminger's dead. His experiments are discredited. And while I agree the public would benefit from knowing what went down, it's not in the cards. If you can't accept that reality, why don't *you* write a piece for *The Times*?"

"I've thought of it," Eddie shot back. "I have."

"Yeah?" Jack dropped his hands to his side. "You want to interview me for an on-the-record quote about this case? Is this what these visits have been about, kid? You softening-up a source?"

"No." Suddenly Eddie had the demeanor of a peer, not the kid reporter Jack had pushed around. "I wouldn't get past my city editor if I pitched a piece about the Thrill Girl story. *The Eyes* owned it. You owned it. I think you're the only one who can tell the real story of Thrill Girl and what happened that night." Eddie did not move his eyes off Jack's face.

"That's what you think, huh? That's a pretty stupid thought. I wouldn't repeat it to anyone if I was you."

"Why?"

"Why? Because the government, our government, and the cops, and the press have already substituted a million lies for the 'real' story. The American public gobbled it all up, and no one cares about it anymore."

"You do," Eddie said. "Robinson does." He narrowed his eyes. "I do."

"Well, you need to god damn let it go!" Jack's turned away in disgust and rested his head in his hands. His chest hurt. He wanted to punch Eddie in the face for saying what he had.

"My mom agrees with me. She said it to me the night after the fire. She said you owe it to all those people whose lives were ruined by Preminger. And to the public, because they trusted you. She trusted you."

Jack's anger deflated with a whoosh at the mention of Myrna Wentz. She was warm and loving. Optimistic. She lived true to her moral standards of right and wrong without malice, despite losing more than half her family to the Nazi monsters. Someone should write a screenplay about her, Jack thought.

He sighed and looked across his sparsely furnished living room and into the dark office. The typewriter was covered. "What does the god damn note say?"

"I'll get it." Eddie returned with it a moment later and handed it to Jack.

He ripped it open. Nine words were typed neatly in the center of the page.

Write the story. Tell the truth. La Verita Publishing.

Jack blew out a breath and handed the paper back to Eddie.

The young reporter read it, his eyebrows rising in surprise. "You think this is from Mr. Deville?"

"I don't know." But if it was, Jack realized with the force of a punch in the gut that he still had an ally out there in the world. An ally with money, clout, and knowledge of what was true. And what was covered-up.

As well as a publishing house.

"Maybe," he said.

The two men stared at each other.

"Let's get out of here for a while. Take a ride." Jack stood up.

"Okay, sure."

"You know where Robinson lives?"

"Robinson?" Eddie grinned. "Yeah. As a matter of fact, I do."

"He got a phone?"

Eddie frowned and pulled out a notebook. "Darn." He flipped a couple of pages. "I don't know. I only got an address from Detective Glass. Robinson lives in Santa Monica."

Jack glanced out the patio door. The sky was the color heaven would be if it was real. Hurt-your-eyes blue, the same as Alana Maxwell's eyes.

"Good day for the beach. Even if we're wearing the wrong shoes," Jack said.

Eddie laughed. "Let me bring the rest of the food inside."

"You still hungry?"

"No. But I will be later."

"Yeah, me too." Jack tucked his shirt in. "I need my other shoe. Then we'll go."

Eddie pushed his glasses back up his nose. "Okay, great, Mr. Curran. That's great."

"It's time you called me Jack, Eddie."

"Oh. Okay, Jack" Eddie beamed.

"I'm going to drive."

"What?"

"Your car's an automatic, right?"

"Yeah, but..."

"I'll drive." Jack limped into his bedroom. He felt a rush of energy. The same as he had his first weeks in the army when every day he woke up with a purpose, a passion for protecting something bigger than himself.

Jack pulled his shoe from the closet and sat down. He was looking forward to seeing Robinson. He wondered if the chauffeur would feel the same, or if he would blame him for what happened that tragic night to the two Maxwell heirs Robinson had cared for all those years.

He wouldn't blame him if he did, Jack thought.

He pulled on his shoe. As he tied the laces, something Emrick Maxwell said that hellacious night rang inside his skull.

The truth is strong. You can hide it, but you can't kill it with a lie.

Susan Baldwin and her entire family were gone. Alana Maxwell was lost to him forever. But Myrna Wentz was right, those women deserved to have the truth known about what they did, and why they did it. Both deserved the world to know about their courage and the sacrifices they made to try and save their brothers. How they fought as hard as any soldier in any war for what was good, decent and right in a world against forces that were not any of those things.

That's why I'll write their book. To honor them.

Thrill Girl, by Jack Curran.

The thought physically rocked him.

Jack placed his hand on his heart and willed it to slow down. The pads of his fingers itched, and he made two fists, flexing his hands like he used to before he started a new column. Alone in a room full of memories and ghosts, he stood and took the first steady step toward the light.

THE END

About the Author

Jack Curran is the pseudonym of a professional fiction writer working in other genres for over twenty-years. This is his first mystery. Residing in the greater Washington DC area, Jack lives with the love of his life and two ancient orange tabby cat sisters, Bella and Lucy.

You can email him at jackcurran.author@yahoo.com or https://www.jackcurran.com/ and on Facebook at www.facebook.com/Thrill Girl

Please leave a review at the retailer where you purchased this book, or at Goodreads or NetGalley if you are a member. Jack knows books belong to readers once authors let them loose, so good, bad or indifferent, Jack's interested in what you thought of the story.

Thank you for your interest in Thrill Girl.

CPSIA information can be obtained
at www.ICGtesting.com
Printed in the USA
BVHW03s1731130618
518945BV00009B/733/P